CLIMATE LOCKDOWN

JEREMY GRAVILORE

Published by Oceannapolis, LLC

https://oceannapolis.com

Book Cover Design by ebooklaunch.com

Dedicated to a bright future for mankind

CONTENTS

1

BURIED IN WHITE

Jimmy Englewood found Bethany curled up in the glimmering snow. The Marganisan Renegade dropped to his knees, took off his gloves, and placed his hands on her icy scalp. Bethany opened her eyes as she smiled at Jimmy in the dwindling sunlight. Neither of them had on their protective headgear, the modified space helmets. Jimmy's fingers turned purple within seconds of checking what life remained in his bride. After putting his gloves back on, he pulled Bethany into his arms and sat with her until her breath stopped forming miniature crystals in the heat-starved air.

Bethany's smile disappeared, and Jimmy laid her head down. The snot froze on his wind-smacked face while he watched the snow brush up against Bethany's cheeks. The Renegade put on his silver helmet. He left his wife's body in the enshrouding blizzard and buried in a white grave, courtesy of atmospheric phenomena and the climate regime.

Just before nightfall, Jimmy returned to his cabin just outside Marganis. He looked for any signs of mischief in the house. Nothing appeared out of order, but the eyes on the back of Jimmy's head had become a permanent fixture. Somehow, he found himself banned from the metropolis he loved.

The wind beat up against the creaking door. Jimmy kept on his gear and walked across the wooden planks to the oak-paneled kitchen. He stared at the gasoline-powered stove. The note posted to the middle of the vents read "H-A-V-E," the trademark of the climate regime.

Jimmy flung open the kitchen door and ran across the field of snow. He made it all but a hundred feet before the blast threw him off balance. His old cabin exploded, the foundation and any semblance of a housing structure destroyed. Flaming projectiles streaked through the air, barely missing him.

The explosion lit the path for Jimmy to reach the forest. His old city of Marganis shrank in the background, while Bethany's death etched deeper into the foreground of his racing mind. He entered the dense canopy moments before the Marganisan search party flashed a spotlight.

Helicopters, sleds, trucks, and armored vehicles crisscrossed the field, searching for a living or lifeless Jimmy. They spun around every time that they came upon the dividing line between the rural field and its adjacent woods.

Suddenly, a voice whispered in the night. "Jimmy, over here."

Jimmy jumped back.

The voice repeated, "Jimmy, over here."

"Stan, is that you?"

"No, it's Dracula, you idiot. Let's go."

Jimmy fell down and Stan hurried over.

"Hey Englewood, you're bleeding."

"It isn't my blood, Stan."

"Bethany's?"

"It's from the second-in-command of the City Forces. I got him."

"Jimmy, they're going to set thousands of acres of forested land on fire to find you."

"Then I'd better stand up. Let's get somewhere warm where we can take off our helmets."

"Good idea."

"Hey Stan, let me ask you something."

"Can we hold off on conversation till we get inside?"

"I can't do that. I have to ask you why you left the note in my house. Why did you betray the Coalition?"

Stan pulled out his revolver, but Jimmy was quicker, shattering Stan's helmet and sending two shots through his forehead.

Jimmy hovered over his old friend's corpse. "What do you have to say for yourself, you expired little rat? A simple note from a simple traitor: H-A-V-E, Humans Are Viruses on Earth. I know you have a recording device somewhere in your gear. I'm going after your bosses."

Growing up, Jimmy never had street smarts, but all his time evading enemies taught him some lessons. Instinct had alerted him that Stan had written the note and posted it above his stove...and worse, had engineered the explosion. Instinct had also led Jimmy to talk to a wider audience than just his old friend. The Renegade knew that the Marganisan City Forces had picked up the audio of the gunshots and everything he had said to Stan, before and after taking him out.

Jimmy rushed off to the sequestered headquarters of the local Rootsville Coalition. As the forest grew thicker, the lights from the enemy search party dimmed, forcing Jimmy to construct a torch and light it. He walked for several miles while expecting the City Forces would destroy the woods, the hideout, and the Rootsville Coalition.

Remote-controlled drones broadcast a message on a loop from the skies above the forest. "Succumb to the climate regime or face eternal imprisonment. You have one last chance, Jimmy Englewood! Bethany is dead, and your time is up. Don't make us destroy more of this Earth that you so recklessly torment. This side of the continental divide will suffer you no longer. Jimmy, you are a virus. This planet is the host to your parasitic nature. A pox upon you and every holdout remaining. We will find you and charge you for the murder of the second-in-command of our Marganisan City Forces. We'll capture and plague you. The revolutionary people of Marganis will determine your punishment should you not surrender."

The messages stopped and the hovering drones retreated. City Forces ended the nighttime hunt for Jimmy Englewood, who at last reached the bucolic headquarters of the Rootsville

Coalition.

Jimmy removed his helmet, and Jesse greeted him at the walled entrance to the property. "Come on in. There are ten of us here tonight. You're welcome to stay."

"Thank you, but you should know I took out Stan."

"We know, Jimmy, and we're grateful. We just pieced together who he was. That's how you got here. You'd have had to get through him to be where you're standing. Well, don't keeping standing there. Join us inside and take off your gear."

Jimmy walked through the walled exterior and into the headquarters of the Rootsville Coalition. "The messages from the drones were correct. I got the second-in-command of the City Forces. I did not take down the leader, but I will."

Jesse squinted his eyes. "Is Bethany gone, Jimmy?"

"Jesse, I don't want to get into that right now."

Jesse took a deep breath and bowed his head. "Of course it can wait. We'll talk about it tonight. We've got to be out of here within the next couple of days. Right now, we're trapped in these temperatures. I can't believe you have your helmet off outside. Anyway, we're lucky they're not ready to inflict an all-out assault."

"You have any food?"

"We'll get you fed and get your gear cleaned. While we're doing that, join us for the broadcast."

"What broadcast?"

"The Planetary Leader is about to speak about the lockdowns and the ongoing steps to eradicate climate denialism."

"Jesse, that sounds like a blast. Speaking of blasts, my cabin exploded."

Jesse threw up his hands. "We have a lot to talk about."

"We'd better do it all tonight. Soon we'll be running and killing more than talking."

Another Rootsville Coalition member walked across the living room to Jimmy and Jesse at the door. "Let's save the food and gear cleaning, for the moment. The Planetary Leader goes on in one minute."

Jimmy handed the Coalition member the torch. "Gentlemen, today's the day that a blizzard buried my wife. Tonight's the night the planetary crackpots bury the world."

Jessie grabbed the torch and smothered the flame in the snow, leaving the handle sticking up from a mound of crystalline powder. He closed the front door on the natural elements.

2

PLANETARY PSYCHOSIS

The Planetary Leader stepped up to the podium. He wore the finest tailored suit. Planetary Forces ran the speech live on every network, channel, virtual reality, and audio program imaginable. Jimmy and his friends in the Rootsville Coalition watched on a screen, like most people on the planet.

Jimmy kept his thoughts about Bethany's death locked up in his mind. He had no choice but to remain fixated on the speech. Changes in the law meant changes to how Jimmy Englewood could survive from one day to the next, as he had done for years. The Planetary Leader delivered the rules with "H-A-V-E" written at the upper right corner of the broadcast.

"People of the world, this is your Planetary Leader with a message for the Earth. No longer will you ever have to do anything to survive. We, the Planetary Council, will serve as your benefactor the rest of your lives. Those of you permitted to have descendants will join our beautiful movement. Humans Are Viruses on Earth is forever the revolutionary movement and government. It is the economy. It is the fuel that grants you all the liberties and comforts you enjoy. Your allegiance must lie with HAVE, and your life depends on it. To keep this movement going, we on the Planetary Council require your help. I, require your help. You, my children, are not simply part of this revolution. You are the revolution."

A recorded ensemble of woodwind instruments began playing a low-volume battle song on the broadcast.

The Planetary Leader waited a dozen seconds to let the music build. "The climate has reached crisis levels. We must remedy this catastrophe before we reach the point of no return. As much as I love you, my children, you are responsible for the planet's atmospheric troubles. But you can earn redemption by doing what we require. The choice is yours, but you must make the choice we demand of you, under penalty of treason against the Planetary Order of Earth. All directives are simple and meant to consolidate Humans Are Viruses on Earth on every continent, country, province, city, and town. All unincorporated zones will become incorporated. We will clearcut any forest, contaminate any body of water, and spread any disease necessary to protect our marvelous planet. Any dissenters or Renegades face execution at the hands of administrative powers across the world. There will be few public trials. We will levy punishments, publicly or privately, at our discretion."

The recorded battle song tapered off.

After adjusting his suit, the Planetary Leader sneered. "Our planet becomes hotter every day. All your desires and behaviors brought us to this crisis. Due to the continued Renegade insistence that the Earth grows colder, we must dispel the myth of atmospheric conditions occurring beyond our control. You therefore must comply with the following three directives. First, to earn your liberty, do everything ordered by a public official or institution, including adhering to dietary allowances. Second, for dependability and loyalty, you have no ownership or stewardship at all. We will lease you anything we allow you to use. And third, for your safety, remain in the homes we lease you unless we grant you special permission to move around."

The image of the Planetary Leader disappeared for several seconds, replaced by an image of a globe on fire.

The Planetary Leader reappeared. "We will fully implement all these directives within one year. But we expect immediate compliance. The countdown begins, starting now. Remember to follow every dictate of the revolution. Everything will turn out in your favor when you protect the movement. I love you, my children. Just bear in mind always that humans and their creations are a pox on the Earth. You are a pox on the Earth, unless we on the Planetary Council determine otherwise. Indeed, Humans Are Viruses on Earth. The Planetary Forces have our full trust and authority to carry out our mission to save the world. Do your part to make it so. Do not become a parasite by seeking the autonomy you can never have. You belong to us. Surrender your willpower and sleep well. This is your Planetary

Leader signing off. Goodnight, Earthlings."

A bottle flew through the screen on the mounted television. The Coalition members diverted their attention from the broken screen to Jimmy. "Those fucking murderers! Damn that son of a cocksucker! Who the fuck is he to dictate anything?!"

Jesse faced Jimmy while everyone else looked away. "Jimmy, a short time ago we found out more about Planetary Leader is. We're going to have to save mourning Bethany for another time, but you should know she's the one who made the discovery."

Jimmy's pupils dilated beyond anything within the normal range of adjusting. "Tell me who it is, Jesse, before I smash the next bottle over your head. And tell these guys to take off their damn spacesuits...excuse me, I meant their damn modified spacesuits. We're inside and nobody's attacking us tonight."

Jesse closed his eyes for a long blink. "Hold on. We don't know everything about what happened. Bethany did find out the Planetary Leader is definitely Brandon Dreckhorn, middle-aged and a former social justice activist. We just don't know if he's a human or a carbon-copy android."

"What do you mean by a carbon copy? Is he made of carbon whether he's a person or a robot? Or is he just some kind of replica regardless of if he's android?"

"You know me, Jimmy. I tell you what I know whenever I can. I've always treated you like you're one of us. You're not part of the Coalition, but we still tell you almost everything. In this case, we're not hiding anything from you. We just don't know very much. Bethany simply found out that the Planetary

Leader could be an android. She had no idea where he came from. Neither do we."

Jimmy walked over the glass from the shattered television screen and the broken bottle. "Yeah, Jesse, that's enough. Stop trying to sell me what you know and what you don't. Why won't your men take off their protective gear? Are they practicing becoming old-time astronauts?"

"Funny you should mention astronauts, but that's another topic I'll tell you about sometime. Let's just say for now that everyone needs to be suited up and ready to go, including you."

"We can't leave here tonight. That's psychotic. You said we were staying here."

Local Coalition member Fred was restless and could not stay quiet. "Psychotic but necessary. You could barely keep your eyes open, but you heard the speech. The blizzard just started. We'd better get moving."

Jimmy looked out the windows and watched Coalition surveillance cameras. "I don't see any blizzard."

Fred snickered. "The blizzard hasn't arrived yet in the forest, but whiteout conditions stack the fields and hills with fresh powder."

Jesse shook his head approvingly. "You've eaten a few bites, Jimmy. Suit up and get ready for war."

Jimmy's eyes surveyed everyone in the warm living room. He knew he'd be leaving that warmth as quickly as he entered it. He zeroed in on Jesse. "Ready for war? War against City Forces? Planetary Forces? Mother Nature?"

Jesse put on his helmet. "Yes, war against all of it. It's a good thing a couple of these guys are astronauts. Don't look so dumbfounded, Jimmy. You asked and we're answering."

Fred could not contain himself. "Jimmy, they are all your enemy. You are now a permanent fixture in these ongoing battles. Your enemies are everywhere, from the snowstorms to the cold-hearted traitors."

Jimmy turned to Jesse and smiled. "I guess we'd better get moving." He put on his helmet and Fred followed suit.

Jimmy and the ten men from the Rootsville Coalition destroyed every trace in their headquarters of what would have revealed vital information about any Renegades' movements, including their own. The party of eleven packed their provisions, tested their gear, fastened their space packs, and checked the climate suits' oxygen supply efficiency. An old grandfather clock struck midnight. Jesse opened the front door to their headquarters. Revived blizzard conditions entered the forest while the men abandoned their fortress.

3

DEEP FREEZE

Temperatures plummeted. Heavy snow reduced visibility to several feet. Jimmy and the ten from the Rootsville Coalition reached the edge of the forest approaching the ocean. They got on ten snowmobiles parked in a nearby garage. These self-driving vehicles had domed, bulletproof coverings and the latest navigation technologies. Each vehicle had room for one, with Jimmy the one out of luck.

Vast fields stretched out before them. These frozen fields proved themselves less conducive to the snowmobiles than the densely packed snow they had just traveled. Still, the men could not make it across the ice fields to the sea by foot without leaving behind supplies.

Jesse readied his snowmobile. He would not look in Jimmy's direction. "Listen, wait here. There's no way you can make it by walking. There are hordes of bears and there's a fucking blizzard in a constant winter. You won't have a prayer. Stay in the garage and wait for reinforcements, alright? There's no other way."

"Move on out, Jesse. Your men are waiting."

"Goodbye, Jimmy. We'll turn this fight around. You'll see."

"Goodbye, Jesse."

The wind gusted up to 75 miles per hour, with sustained winds at 30 mph. Jimmy's climate gear insulated him from the cold, but not from the strength of the air currents. Coalition members vanished into the storm. Jimmy looked up to the trees at the edge of the forest, thankful the thick colony of evergreens shielded him for as long as they could. But that zone of safe harbor could not last. The Planetary Council kept up the pretenses and speeches about saving the environment. Jimmy knew the Council would destroy whatever life it could to continue mass brainwashing, confusion, and to lay claim to ecological successes amid ecological destruction.

Projectiles raced by, drawing Jimmy's attention from the conifers to the opaque sky. Missiles moved in rapid-fire succession in and out of Jimmy's vision. Ice cracked along the ground, right up to mere yards from where he stood. He watched the bombing run of the local forces through the haze. Enemy forces showered the ten Rootsville Coalition members to death in a show of strength that glowed in the night. The light gave Jimmy his opportunity to escape to the sea.

The Rootsville Coalition's defiance against lockdown orders ranked lower than their many other indiscretions toward the Planetary Council. But now, local councils, city councils, and provincial councils all had specific lockdown measures to enforce. Disobedience turned into the local Coalition members' death sentence.

Minutes after the bombardment, Jimmy grabbed the only vehicle left in the garage. He pulled out the canoe and dragged it by rope through the paths of fire on either side of the canal that opened up for him. The fires guided him past blown-up snowmobiles and the frozen, charred, and drowned bodies of the men of the Rootsvile Coalition of Renegades. The aerial assault would reappear in other areas over the land, in the forest, and toward Marganis. Jimmy heard the faint sounds of missiles in the distance. Flames on his periphery trailed off, extinguished on the frostbitten shores. The tributary opened into the ocean.

A pause in the blizzard resulted in the waves subsiding. Jimmy had little time to make it to the peaks rising from the ocean floor before a resurgent storm would overwhelm his canoe. He could not yet see the Orca Mountains, considered the opposite end of the Marganisan Valley from the Boshquire Mountains. Eight miles of water separated Jimmy from the pinnacles rising over the open waters.

The Orcasso Sea vanquished the orange flames atop the fractured ice on the beach. Jimmy needed the moonless night to help him escape to the Orca Mountains. Weakened currents and calm waves left him and his waterproof gear unscathed during the shyest of springtides. He rowed between the cracked shoreline ice into the dark blue ocean. Jimmy barely handled the oars while the currents propelled and steered him toward his destination. He navigated with no ambient light or sign in the skies of the mountains ahead. The flashlight attached to his helmet, together with the faint stars hidden by the mist and clouds, did nothing to ensure Jimmy stayed on course. He thought about Bethany during his voyage through the pitch black. Crying whales showcased themselves as the only marker to Jimmy that life remained on Earth during his blinding journey. Nighttime could not last forever, and the humpbacks sounded their tribute to Bethany at her impromptu memorial in the Orcasso Sea.

Hunted by the Marganisan City Forces and the Planetary Order, Jimmy closed in on the Orca Mountains. Silhouettes of jagged peaks emerged as the first glimmer of sunshine appeared.

Another pod of whales cried out, but the sounds oozed with physical pain. Killer whales, shot up by ships from the Planetary Forces, screamed their final minutes in anguish at the surface before sinking to the bottom of the sea.

Jimmy watched from afar and witnessed a new barrage of missiles that illuminated the foggy atmosphere. Renegade ships blew up the small fleet of Planetary Forces, just out of reach of splitting Jimmy's canoe and torso in two. The convoy of Renegades escorted him through the cliffs.

A dead killer whale washed into a narrow waterway between two mountains. His corpse lay trapped in a coffin where the piercing sea clashed with the frigid air and towering peaks.

An eviscerated killer whale floated in front of Jimmy's eyes. The dead whale drifted on a large ice block, separated from her wounded baby calf that the Renegades could not salvage while blowing up enemy ships. The flashing skies revealed dead orca after dead orca.

Expanding ice in the open-ocean cliffs jeopardized the Renegade sea base, located miles from the ever-changing shoreline. Reinforcements from local and Planetary Forces added to the endangered status of the last powerful holdouts in the Marganisan Valley.

Planetary Forces murdered an entire pod of killer whales in the Orcasso Sea. They had already plunged orcas into near extinction.

Jimmy reached the Orca Mountains with his convoy of larger boats. He quickly disembarked during the growing battle that approached. The blizzard picked up again. Crashing waves and wild currents soon followed, colliding with the snow-covered Renegade fortress.

Greg led Jimmy inside Renegade Peak. "It's a miracle you made it this far. It's beyond a miracle. Why don't you join me in taking your helmet off? At least light up your face inside it. This way we can see each other's expressions as we were meant to see them. I want to know what would compel a man to take a canoe miles out to the deep waters in the dark. Planetary Forces attack, and you decide to row yourself into the battle."

Greg's men erupt into laughter.

Jimmy keeps his helmet on and points to the crashing waves outside. "It's true. I traveled from all the way out there, but only after the last members of the Rootsville Coalition burned up, drowned, and froze. The explosions on the shore ended them. They deserve respect for their sacrifice. Wouldn't you agree?"

Greg glanced around at his men, whose laughter trailed off. "We don't mean to laugh. It's just that stragglers in the forest have no chance. You're here for a reason. Planetary Forces will wipe out every last hiding place of any local Renegade groups in the Marganisan Valley. City and Local Forces now answer to the Planetary Council. No autonomy exists in the ranks of our enemies. Anyway, my name is Greg. Who are you?"

"I'm Jimmy. Tell me, Greg, how you know about the Marganisan Valley. Tell me how you know about its fields and forests."

Greg looked back again at the roughly fifty men behind him on the sea-level platform of the mountain base. His men went back to work, and Greg walked closer to Jimmy. "Take your helmet off."

Jimmy obliged while he scoped out the sights and sounds of a sea base he never knew stretched deep in the mountains and underwater. "Why did they go after those whales like that? It seems like it was a bigger mission to them than going after you guys. Or did they not know about your stealthy little fleet?"

Greg shook his head slowly from side to side. "They know a lot about us, and I know a lot about the Marganisan Valley. I'm from the Boshquire Mountains, but I lived a good part of my life in Marganis. I still have family there. I still live there. Jimmy, I was in communication with Jesse and the local section of the Rootsville Coalition. You're telling me all members of the

Coalition were eradicated."

Jimmy turned his back to Greg and stared outside. "This isn't a very large portal. I see a couple of other peaks and the narrow waterway funneling through."

Greg sounded the alarm for the base and its labyrinth of platforms. "Jimmy, follow us underwater and away from the explosions. You'll see more than your eyes show you from here above sea level."

Jimmy lunged at Greg and elbowed him in the jaw, knocking him to the ground. "Tell me about the whales! I'm not going anywhere!"

Greg smiled, lying on the ground and soaking in the only few seconds of rest he had in days. "There's no time, Jimmy. We've got to get underwater, and you're going with us, whether you like it or not."

Jimmy pulled Greg to his feet. "I didn't mean to—"

"That's enough. We have to go under sea level, and we have to do it now. In two minutes, we'll be under a full-scale assault. Ah, and there they are. Follow these Marganisan soldiers down below the surface. That's right, they're Marganisan soldiers and all Renegades."

Jimmy followed the soldiers through a trap door that lowered him and them in the freight elevator to the underwater part of the base.

The alarm kept blaring, and a booming voice echoed in Jimmy's ears while the base shook from the enemy's aerial attack. "Abandon overwater base! Abandon overwater base!"

4

UNDER WATER

Marganisan soldiers, leaders, merchants, and families cleared out of the overwater section of the base. Jimmy recognized some of the people from his home city.

Jimmy's body ached all over. Sleep deprived and attacked by hunger pangs, he passed out while on the freight elevator, descending deeper into the sea fortress in the Orca Mountains.

***

The Renegade leaped into a vision of the future. He saw himself being captured by the Planetary Forces and hauled into a dungeon. Two guards hurled him to the floor, and he landed next to Bethany's skeleton. He screamed her name as he woke up.

***

Jimmy looked through underwater glass, directly into the eye of an orca. Orcas would not dive much lower, and this one would not dive any lower than he already had. An enemy submarine fired repeatedly on the spirited mammal, tearing its skin to shreds. In the background, one of the murdered killer whales continued sinking to the deep ocean floor. A giant squid floated in and out of view, disappearing as quickly as he appeared.

Greg detached the IV tubes. "You worried us, Jimmy. Sit up nice and easy. Don't rush it."

The Marganisan soldiers drenched the enemy submarine with a hailstorm of fire, brightening the ocean in the final hour of night. Ship fragments slammed against the underwater part of the heavily fortified base, leaving no dents, scratches, or vibrations.

Jimmy improved with the fluids despite remaining light-headed. "What's going on, Greg? Where are we going."

Greg readied a special cocktail for Jimmy. "I have something for you."

"That's nice, but I don't want liquor. How did that explosion not damage the base? Or did it? What is this place?"

"I'm not giving you liquor, Jimmy. It won't give you a buzz. It's much better. It'll give you all the nutrients and calories your body craves."

"Who the fuck are you, Greg? Are you the commander of the Marganisan Renegades or just your Marganisan military? I had been out of the city and out of contact for so long that I don't know who's who. I don't know what remains of the Renegades or any new groups. Recently, I hid at a deserted enemy cabin and launched a failed rescue—"

"Alright already. I'm not answering all your questions. You need to follow my command. For now, I'll tell you what you already know. The Planetary Order convinced everyone that Humans Are Viruses on Earth. It isn't just humans that the Council considers viruses. It's living creatures. It's carbon life forms. Look back outside the window."

Jimmy looked out the window and saw a polar shark feeding on shredded whale remains. He turned back to Greg. "If you want my help, you've got to give me more to go on than this."

"Sure. In the meantime, drink the potion I made for you."

Jimmy downed the eight ounces from the chalice. "Not bad...It's making me drowsy...I'm Englewood...What did you give mmmmm?"

"Greg Norbannick is my name. I am the leader of all those from the Marganisan Valley and the Boshquire Mountains who find themselves undeterred by the heinous deeds of the Planetary Forces. "Go back to sleep, Jimmy. It's a nice and restful bed. Leaving the underwater base might be more than you could handle when you're conscious."

A few seconds later, Jimmy fell asleep, and Greg left the room.

Norbannick directed his top fighting leadership to start the procedures for evacuating the underwater base. One thousand people from the Marganisan Valley readied themselves to flee the Orca Mountains.

***

Jimmy imagined he woke up. "What is this place?"

Greg rushed over to Jimmy's bed. "You just got up from a deep sleep."

"I know that. Where are we?"

"Back on dry land. They intercepted our capsules on our way to the stars. Almost all our capsules got shot down. They took some of us as prisoners. You were in my capsule. Everyone else in our capsule is dead."

"But how?"

"Shot."

"Nobody shot you? How did the enemy Marganisan Forces grow so powerful?"

"Jimmy, would you shut up for once?! We destroyed the Marganisan Forces. Then the Planetary Forces destroyed us."

"What happened to you, Norbannick? You seem off."

An officer of the Planetary Forces walks into the room. "That's because General Norbannick joined us. But first, we had to take his life before we could resurrect him."

Jimmy jumped out of the bed.

The officer from the Planetary Forces shot Norbannick three times through the stomach. "He served his purpose. Now it's your turn to face our wrath."

Jimmy yelled while the officer directed the gun at him. Suddenly, the officer faded and an animated General Norbannick reappeared.

***

Norbannick shook Jimmy. "Englewood, are you with us?"

"Are you alive, Norbannick?"

"We need you lucid, Jimmy. I promise you, no more potions. The concoction plays too many tricks on your mind, but you seem to be back in reality now."

"Are we in Marganis?"

"No. We escaped the base just in time, and we inflicted great losses on that contingent of Planetary Forces."

"What about us? Where are we?"

"In our efforts to travel beyond the atmosphere, the enemy cluttered the sky with ships and layered the ground with my Marganisan Army's casualties. Let me open the exit and show you where you are. Men, help Mr. Englewood. I don't want him losing his footing."

Jimmy stood up with assistance. "Is this Earth? That's a cold blast"

"It is. The blue planet became the white planet, covered in snow nearly everywhere we travel."

"Every day it snows, Commander. Sometimes it's heavy and sometimes it's just a dusting, but it snows all the time. I can't remember a day when I could see the different shades of green.

Only the evergreens show signs of life. How long will that last? Everything is freezing and everything is dying."

"Jimmy, we don't have time for your recollections. I'm the General of the Marganisan Army. We cover land, sea, and skies. As general, I leave you with a choice. You can join our army, or we can allow you to go off on your own. We can equip you with a month's worth of provisions. What's your choice?"

"Will I have a vehicle if I go off on my own?"

"No. We can give you back your old, modified silver spacesuit to help you get from place to place. But we have a new and clean white outfit for you, complete with improved efficiency for oxygen supply. Unfortunately, like with all of them, no jetpacks yet for all these modified spacesuits."

"Which continent am I on?"

"It doesn't matter. You've got a month to live and a small igloo over there for shelter from the elements...or you can call me General Norbannick instead of Greg. In that case, we'll get you into the Marganisan Army."

"I'm a Renegade all the way, but I've got to go off on my own."

Colonel Milgroze stepped forward. "Englewood, you don't want to do this. You can't live in these conditions. We just can't tolerate a dead weight if unwilling to fight. We're going to rally with the other escape pods. How long do you think you can make it out there while you're being hunted down? You couldn't even make it if the climate returned to normal."

Jimmy peered across the frozen land. "I'm after the leader

of the Marganisan Forces. I will track him down, but that isn't your objective, Colonel. It isn't yours either, General."

Colonel Milgroze grabbed Jimmy by the shoulders. "If you don't go with us, you're going to die. We won't be able to protect you."

General Norbannick looked across all hundred fighting men from the escape pod before inevitably shifting his eyes back to Jimmy. "We'll take you with us, Englewood, but just to the next stop, in a much warmer climate. It'll give you a chance to thaw out before you die. If the Planetary Forces intercept us on the way, we're all dead anyhow."

The Colonel released Jimmy's shoulders and shoved him. "I might kill you before the enemy does."

Jimmy stumbled. "I'm still getting my bearings after drinking that potion. As soon as I'm better, Colonel, we're going to have a good laugh about this, right before I take your life."

Norbannick closed the exit, shutting out the cold air and the whistling, smacking winds. "Colonel Milgroze, stand down. Jimmy, go back there and change into your new climate suit, and get ready for takeoff, civilian."

"Where are we going, General? They're enforcing a planetary lockdown."

"The tropics, Jimmy. The tropics."

5

BLAST ZONE

The escape pod safely landed on the lakeshore of the steaming, tree-shrouded jungle.

Greg Norbannick opened the exit. Everyone filed out in light, long-sleeved clothing. They each brought a bag of weapons and supplies, leaving their white climate gear, and Jimmy's silver climate gear, on the vessel. Norbannick used a remote control to steer the ship over deeper water. He then submerged the ship and anchored it to the bottom of the lake after all the men walked onto the clay-covered beach.

A missile struck, exploding bodies on the land.

The blast hurled Jimmy into a thick cluster of trees on the wet grass and mud.

Gunfire and detonations overtook the jungle and adjacent beach. Jimmy heard the blood-curdling agony from mowed-down men. He stood up in the mire, then dropped back down after the bullets buzzed past his face and torso.

The bullets stopped.

Jimmy froze in the heat. He tried to crawl, but his body tensed up into a living rigor mortis. The jungle grew quiet, and Jimmy's ears tuned into the footsteps and voices.

General Norbannick and Colonel Milgroze splashed into the watery ground of muck. Jimmy finally got up to run. A fist blasted into his stomach and knocked him to the soggy earth.

One man, a group leader, stepped forward. "They're all gone. Your buddies, gone. All of them."

Jimmy looked over and saw fear bathing the eyes of Norbannick and Milgroze, who dropped down into vegetation. He then looked at the aggressors. "Take me out. It'll be better than anything I'll face from the Planetary Forces."

The fifty men surrounded Jimmy, all with camouflage attire and faces of stone.

The leader of the group kicked Jimmy's left arm. "The Planetary Forces have no power in the tropics. They left these areas for us to get rid of people like you. Stay on the ground."

"People like me? You look like ogres."

"We're warriors, unlike you and the little maggots we just put out of their misery. I'm Brock, and these are my fellow Lords. What are you doing roaming the planet during the climate lockdown?"

"I'll ask the same of you and your fellow Lords of the Wolf Blade."

"We have an understanding with the Planetary Forces, on

direct orders from the Planetary Council to allow our control of the tropics. This is our land now. We hate the Planetary Order in every way. We hate your people even more."

"My people? It's always my people or their people or the purebred people with you sons of bitches."

"That's right. We are the pure breed of humans. Dominion over his world will be ours. You and your breeds will be the first to die. The entire HAVE movement is second."

"I thought you believed all humans are viruses on Earth."

"We believe the saying, not some of the goals of the movement. But you're one of the viruses, and we really want to kill you."

"Why don't you?"

"Because we made the agreement to hand you over to the Planetary Forces. And we'll ask the questions, Jimmy Englewood. Don't look so shocked. Everybody knows who you are now. Everybody knows who everybody is, except for idiots like you who don't know anything."

"Then hand me over and get it over with."

Brock laughed with his men. "No way. You're a bargaining ace for us for the night. We have people all over the world, but this tropical stronghold will be your burial ground. Hail to the purebred believers! Hail to the Lords of the Wolf Blade!"

Jimmy grimaced while he ran out of options. He surveyed Brock and the Lords, seeing them lower their weapons. He knew General Norbannick had anchored the ship just off the lakeshore. Jimmy's bag lay outside of reach, buried in the mud.

The bag carried explosive devices, a handgun, and ammo.

Without warning, the rain poured down on the already sodden tropical soil.

A voice yelled out from the crowd. "Let's kill him today!"

Everyone joined in the frenzy while Brock stared down Jimmy. Powerful gusts waxed and waned for a minute that felt longer than any in Jimmy's life. The forty-four-year-old Marganisan Renegade lay slumped over in the mud, revealing nothing but a faint smile and focused eyes.

The rainstorm reduced visibility to a trickle, and the atmosphere shrieked again with gunfire and detonations. Three helicopters from the Planetary Forces bombarded the Lords of the Wolf Blade encampment.

Removed from the shelter of their fortified bunker, Brock summoned his men to fight back when fifty of them dwindled to thirty in a flash. "Lords of the Wolf Blade, attack the impure!"

Jimmy ran amid the crossfire. He sprinted to the nearby water, leaving his bag behind and escaping the sight of the Planetary Forces. An exploded helicopter fell on the lake's beach missing Jimmy by a yard and launching him into the water.

Jimmy swam to a tree-sheltered pool of detached lake water to evade the debris. He had no way to enter the anchored yet submerged vessel of the Marganisan soldiers.

A small search party bolted to the downed helicopter; a chopper scattered in thousands of pieces from the rocket-propelled grenade. Nobody survived. Some had fallen dead into the lake while others washed up on land. Some had vaporized in the initial blast.

Jimmy could hear the Planetary Forces search party right around the corner from the small pool. The climate regime soldiers halted just before they reached Jimmy's thin covering of natural protection. He heard one of them deliver an order. "Let's go, men. They're all dead. We're needed elsewhere for this tropical deployment. We've got slash and burn orders to carry out."

Reinforcements for the Planetary Forces arrived from another part of the jungle. They finished off Brock's contingent of Lords of the Wolf Blade. The Planetary Forces kept Brock alive, hauling all six feet and eight inches of him to the inner jungle, to where both remaining helicopters flew toward a clearing. That day, the entire area fell under complete control of the Planetary Order's global control.

Insects of the jungle became louder when the evening approached. They crawled across the hairs on Jimmy's forearms, but he washed from his elbows to his hands in the small pool, and the land bugs fell prey to water bugs.

Jimmy fell prey to visions of Bethany frozen beneath the snowpack of the Marganisan Fields. The Renegade realized how often he kept moving from one blast zone to next.

6

LIFT OFF

Initially, the Planetary Forces were unaware that the capsule carrying Norbannick's Marganisan soldiers ever entered the tropical airspace, much less landed in the area.

Jimmy Englewood heard the movements and activities of the Planetary Forces while the sun curved over the sky. As the last speck of light faded, Jimmy remained in the shallow pool. Grateful the rain dried up and he had a sliver of ground where he could avoid a water-logged body and dropping core temperature. The strip of mud would have to do. No other option presented itself aside from what he did, hiding under the tree canopy shielding the pool.

A familiar sound startled Jimmy. "Englewood, is that you?"

"General Norbannick?"

"Yes."

"I can barely see your outline."

"Ain't that a bitch."

"Ain't what a bitch?"

"All the stars in the sky. Tonight, Englewood, the new moon will work in our favor."

"Can you get us to the capsule, General?"

"I can get us to the capsule and get us out of the tropics."

"Out of the tropics? That doesn't make sense. At least it's easier to find food here. Where else can we go on a planet layered in snow."

"Almost anywhere else, Jimmy. Almost anywhere else. I see the look on your face. We don't have the benefit of going through how I escaped or talking about the woman you mentioned in your potion-induced sleep. The climate regime is in charge of the planet, you understand? It's only a matter of time before the Planetary Order locks down everything."

"I'm ready, General."

"That's what I like to hear. Englewood, soak it up."

"Soak what up?"

"The heat. It's cold almost everywhere else, especially this time of year. Before too long, it'll be cold here, but you'll never see the tropics again."

"Are we moving out or not?"

"Alright, Jimmy, let's move."

The two men waded through the water. They were nimble with no supplies to carry, each man leaving his pack of weapons and provisions to the whims of the jungle. Norbannick took out the remote control and directed the vessel to pull up the anchor and rise above the surface. He piloted the versatile ship toward them until it slowed to a stop just yards away on the shallow bottom near the beach. The General slid open the vessel's entrance with the remote, and Colonel Milgroze walked up behind them.

Gunfire boomeranged off the capsule. An amphibious assault team from the Planetary Forces moved in from the open waters of the lake. The torrent of bullets died off after Englewood, Norbannick, and Milgroze entered the ship and Milgroze closed the door.

Jimmy fastened himself to his seat, and the General took command of the vessel, accelerating and skimming across the lake at breakneck speed. The vessel took off into the atmosphere.

Milgroze tended to the capsule's navigational devices and engineering system.

After liftoff, the ship with the skeleton crew switched to self-piloting.

The Colonel snarled at Jimmy. "You scumbag. They let us loose on purpose. We broke every lockdown rule, and the Planetary Order is after us. For all we know, we're all that remains of the Marganisan Valley Renegades, in or out of our Army. You're the last thing we need to add to our problems. Planetary Forces want you alive, Jimmy. You are the number one enemy. They won't kill you, but they'll kill us as long as you're with us. Most of the movement wants you alive, but I know of exceptions."

Jimmy threw up, then wiped the vomit from his mouth.

"Which movement? The HAVE movement?"

Norbannick grabbed Jimmy with both arms and pulled him in, stretching Jimmy's safety harness as far as it could stretch. "Yes, Englewood. They're right about one thing. Humans are truly viruses on Earth. Somehow, they see you as a resistant strain that self-replicates."

"General, what the hell are you talking about? You buy into that bullcrap?"

"Some of it, but not because of them."

Jimmy unfastened the harness and stood up. "Whose side are you on?"

Milgroze threw a punch to Jimmy's chin but missed. Jimmy tackled him to the floor.

Norbannick pulled Jimmy away. "I need you focused! Both of you!"

Jimmy got right in Norbannick's face. "Where are we going, General? What's the destination? Start answering my questions, you fucking bastard."

The Colonel nodded at the General before turning to Jimmy. "Put on your climate suit."

Jimmy laughed. "When did you betray the Marganisan soldiers? When did you betray the millions of Renegades across the world?"

Norbannick pulled out his gun. "We're traveling to the headquarters of the Planetary Council. We are your escorts."

Milgroze pulled out his own gun. "We've got a long flight, Englewood, but we're going to acclimate and let it get a little colder inside the capsule. You'd better get in that climate suit like I said. You wouldn't want to be left for dead in the snow like you left Bethany."

Jimmy scanned the capsule for ways to stay alive. He found nothing. "Why wait? There's no sense in dragging out the inevitable."

Norbannick aimed his gun at Jimmy's nose. "We never betray the Marganisans. You are not a rightful Marganisan."

Jimmy grinned. "You are not a real general."

The Colonel approached Jimmy. "We called in the Planetary Forces to take out the Lords of the Wolf Blade. Now we owe the Planetary Council. You, my friend, are the lamb we must serve them. But we must serve you alive, Englewood."

"They'll kill you next, Milgroze. You know that."

The General studied Jimmy's face. "Listen up, Englewood. You're wanted alive, but the Colonel and I have no problem unloading as many bullets as we can into your skull. Throw on the climate suite and hurry it up. We don't want you breathing on us. Don't be so depressed. The Planetary Order of Earth awaits you."

Milgroze threw the climate suit at Jimmy and shoved the helmet into his stomach.

A string of bullets tore up the Colonel's torso. His internal systems shut down, and he died with a scowl that outlived the rest of his body.

Through the smoke, Jimmy watched Norbannick holster his gun. "General?"

"I know, Englewood. Milgroze made the deal with the Planetary Forces without my permission. He contacted them just before the Lords of the Wolf Blade captured us. We pretended to be shot up in the firefight because the Lords already murdered all my other soldiers or were close to it. Let's eat in peace while I send this capsule in a new direction."

"Where?"

"Marganis, Jimmy. "We're going back to Marganis. There are some people I'd like you to meet, and they're still in the fight."

"Who?"

"Renegades, just like us."

7

COURSE CORRECTION

The atmosphere became tumultuous. Now in an old temperate zone turned frigid, General Norbannick and Jimmy Englewood barely noticed the blizzard winds. They dined as though they would never have food again.

Later in the flight, a thunderous boom sent shockwaves across the capsule. The boom was more than mere turbulence. A missile struck the ship right out over the Orca Mountains. The capsule lost all power. Jimmy and Greg threw on their headgear. Norbannick opened the entrance, and they jumped out just before the inferno inside the capsule consumed them. The vessel crashed into a glacier and the men parachuted through a world of clouds, gale force air currents, and whiteout conditions. They landed where they least expected, yet miraculously close to each other. They landed in the once temperate Marganisan Forest.

Cora watched the vessel crash from a high-rise in Marganis. She woke up her daughter in the other room, and they got ready to break the lockdown orders and go to what remained of the Marganisan Forest. Norbannick had contacted them through the escape pod's machinery, right before abandoning the capsule, and then again right before landing in the forest.

The Planetary Forces destroyed 80 percent of the woods outside the city. Surrounded by snowfields on all sides, the remaining forest existed because bureaucratic priorities shifted, from destroying natural habitats to crushing major human counter-revolutionary movements against the Planetary Order of Earth and HAVE. The Planetary Order planned all of it.

Cora and Linda trudged through the snowfield and found Jimmy and Norbannick passed out in their climate gear. Three hours after the parachute landing and shortly before sunrise, the men awoke to the prodding of the Renegade women.

Norbannick's eyes focused on the helmeted mother and daughter in climate gear. "You got out of the city much faster than I thought."

Jimmy helped Norbannick get up. "General, when did you contact these two?"

The General motioned with his right hand for Jimmy to let go. "I broke my left arm on the landing. Ladies, light up your headgear so Jimmy can see you. Jimmy, light up your own helmet and say hello to these special women, Cora and Linda. Ladies, this is Jimmy, but you can call him Englewood."

Cora and Linda hugged the general.

Linda sobbed. "Dad! I missed you!"

Greg held back the tears.

Jimmy smiled. "General, there's nothing better than a family of Renegades."

"You don't know the half of it, Englewood."

The four Renegades all turned on the inside lights of their helmets.

Jimmy reached out his gloved hand to shake Cora's, and she obliged. "It's good to meet the General's wife, and I can see the love he has for you and his daughter. Excuse these dirty gloves. Are there any other Norbannicks?"

Cora put her hand over her heart. "They don't even know Greg and I are married. They don't know Linda is his daughter, but forcible DNA testing is only weeks away. Greg is on the climate regime's list to capture dead or alive. You're different, Jimmy. They want you alive."

"So I've heard. Nobody tells me why, and nobody tells me how they know who I am. I'm guessing now isn't the time, General."

Greg laughed heartily with his wife and daughter. The snowfall highlighted the General's gray-bearded face. "Jimmy, they would want you dead because you're a bigger threat than any Renegade on the planet. But they don't really want you dead. They want you alive because they see you as a weapon they can use against the Renegades."

"Does the Planetary Order think I'll turn into a Colonel Milgroze?"

"No, the Planetary Order believes that capturing and exposing you will dispirit us more than anything else."

"There's nothing they could expose about me that could be so dispiriting to all the Renegades."

"Englewood, I'm not talking about exposing your skeletons. We'll take this up later."

Cora nudged her husband. "We'd better get into town and back to the high-rise. We can treat your arm when we're back home. It's nice now that the headgear hardly alters voices anymore."

They all turned off their inner helmet lights and climbed into the snow vehicle that would take them to the city.

The outline of the Marganis skyline appeared as the first rays of morning light stretched across the horizon.

The four Renegades evaded detection in and around the city. They made it back to the Linda Norbannick's aging high-rise, where regional climate bureaucrats planned to activate video and audio surveillance in a month, both inside and outside the building. Full street surveillance would not follow for an additional month. In the meantime, the climate leadership in Marganis had their hands full dealing with all the Renegades, not to mention Lords of the Wolf Blade, who were by no means confined to the tropics.

A warm front moved through the area and brought with it mixes of sunshine and showers. For two weeks, Linda housed her parents and Jimmy. She and her mother tended to the General's broken left arm, resting in a sling. Linda fed the four of them contraband food that exceeded her lockdown dietary allowances.

Englewood and General Norbannick strategized on their next moves, but they had few options. Greg's soldiers were almost all destroyed except for a few holdouts in hiding. He had limited means for reaching them or any Renegades. Planetary Forces were moving into the metropolis and entire region, absorbing the Marganisan City Forces to ensure complete alignment with HAVE and the Planetary Order. Cora and Linda had seen the Planetary Forces swallow the City Forces for weeks in Marganis.

The snow had melted since the warm front descended. Jimmy noticed the snow turn to slush and disappear outside the windows while he and General Norbannick were apartment-bound. "It's time to get out there and search for the other Renegades who can help us."

"Englewood, they've probably split into a lot of different groups by now. The lockdown orders have everybody running ragged. You know what's going on. This is our chance to take advantage of the brief warming and find a way out of here. Marganis lies on the edge of extinction."

"General, this springtime atmosphere won't last forever. Let's get out there and find out how we survive the month without being cramped in an old apartment forever."

"Alright, but there's no need to call me General. My Army is gone. Call me Greg, got it? Just call me Greg."

Cora and Linda walked into the apartment as they had for

the past couple of weeks, without wearing climate gear.

Greg approached his wife. "What's wrong, Cora? What is it?"

"We're both getting old, Greg. Did you ever think we would be nationless, surviving under a climate regime? Our city has all but fallen apart, and the planet is one big soup of tyranny."

Jimmy frowned. "Ask me and I'll have an answer. I'm 44 and fortunate to be alive. My wife died just over two weeks ago. They slaughtered her."

Greg pulled Jimmy lightly toward the door. "Let's go, Englewood. You're a young 44. It's getting late in the day, and we've got work to do in the city."

Jimmy smiled at Cora and Linda. "There's no lockdown in Marganis. Not tonight."

8

BULL IN A CHINA SHOP

Jimmy and Greg ran into street fighting on every block. Civilian followers of HAVE, along with old remnants of the disbanded Marganisan City Forces, aided Planetary Forces to arrest Renegades and everyday residents. People throughout Marganis searched the avenues to find government approved and unapproved vendors for food and clothes. Renegades, Planetary Forces, and Lords of the Wolf Blade fought each other. The Lords and Planetary Forces beat everyday residents to a pulp. Renegades had little capability to defend the populace of the city.

Englewood turned to Norbannick. "Hey Greg, how does your family avoid all these brawls? They bring us food and supplies while all this is going on. It's incredible."

"They do what they have to, and they never stand in line. I'd be dead without them. So would you. Englewood, now it's time for us to keep my family alive. We owe them."

"It's an honor to help your family. Now what about these Lords of the Wolf Blade headed our way?"

"Quick, Jimmy. Walk into the bar."

The place was raucous. Nobody worked the door. There was no security at all, but the patrons drank to their hearts' content.

Jimmy and Greg entered the Bull in a China Shop by walking up a spiral staircase. Nobody liked them from the minute they entered from Main Street. Somehow, the rowdy crowd did not skip a beat. The patrons ignored the dust and dirty glasses, but they zeroed in on Norbannick and Englewood.

A metal band played on stage. Dragons of Corona played a mix that Jimmy remembered. He and Greg sat down at a booth.

"Greg, I remember these guys. How could this be happening? City Forces shut this place down before the first time I left Marganis. The Rootsville Coalition told me it was still shutdown as of a couple of weeks ago."

"How should I know? I never spent a lot of time on Main Street. What does it matter now? Maybe it was the weather that brought everyone out in the open. These Lords of the Wolf Blade spoiled the climate regime's plans, here and across the Earth."

"What did you say to me?"

"I said you're annoying the piss out me. I've traveled the planet and lost my Army while keeping you safe."

"Army? You call that an army? You're out of your mind."

"Oh no."

"What now?"

"The Lords of the Wolf Blade, over there by the staircase. They followed us inside."

"I'll deal with these guys. I've handled them before, and I'll handle them again. Their guys in the tropics didn't know who I was, but these idiots here know me, and I know them."

Four members of the Lords walked up to the booth, casting shadows over Jimmy and Greg.

A waitress in a revealing outfit walked over. "I can see you guys are busy. I'll be back in a few minutes to pick up your drink orders."

The head of the group grabbed a beer from her tray.

The waitress smacked his hand. "That's for someone else's table!"

"Fuck off you half-breed bitch. We only mess around with pure breeds."

"Fuck it. I'll be back here anyway you fucking ogre!"

"Call me Richie, you stupid slut."

"Call me the waitress who doesn't give a fuck."

Richie pulled the waitress toward him. She dropped the tray, and several beer bottles smashed on the floor.

"I know who you are, Katie. Call me your new master."

The three other Lords of the Wolf Blade roared with laughter and whistling.

Jimmy stood up. "Why Richie, what big ears you have."

Richie let Katie go while he and his men turned their attention back to Jimmy and Greg.

"I thought I recognized you. Englewood, right? Jimmy Englewood. You just royally screwed yourself. How's your dead brother and his dead wife? You're all part of inferior races. It's time to teach you a lesson in strength."

Richie pulled a knife hanging from the back of his belt.

A sharp noise dazed the room.

Norbannick's bullet caught Richie on the side of the head.

The other three Lords pulled their own knives, but Jimmy shot them all in the chest within a second. They crashed to the floor.

Richie staggered and swung his knife wildly while Dragons of Corona kept playing. The amused and excited patrons watched him die.

A still-seated Greg shot Richie again on the other side of the head. The Lord dropped the knife before his body keeled over backward onto the grimy floor.

The wild party at the Bull in a China Shop continued. The waitress, Katie, winked at Jimmy, and she went about her business. Workers at the bar dragged the four dead Lords to the back exit on the rooftop, hurling the bodies over the railing and into an alley. It was dusk. Planetary Forces walked up the spiral staircase into the tavern, the Dragons of Corona band started a new tune, and Jimmy and Greg looked for a way out.

Suddenly, Dragons of Corona stopped playing. A captain of the Planetary Forces brought in a bullhorn. "Everybody, remain in place. You are under arrest for violating multiple sections of climate lockdown orders and endangering the planetary welfare. We are the full authority and the law. Your City Forces are part of us and no longer distinguishable from the Planetary Forces. We will spare your life upon compliance. I repeat, we will spare your life upon compliance. Marganis is officially part of the world government and world sustainability directives. We march to a sustainable future. You must follow the directives and pledge allegiance to HAVE!"

During the entrance of the Planetary Forces, and before the commotion died down, Katie led Jimmy and Greg out back to the rooftop. "You guys have to jump."

Jimmy looked down. "Are you crazy? Do you want us to land on the dead bodies, or should we hit our heads on the pavement? Who are you anyway?"

Katie turned to Greg. "Is he always like this?" She turned back to Jimmy. "Well, I'm not a real waitress. You think I enjoy dressing like this? Jump!"

Including the captain, there were just ten members of the Planetary Forces inside the bar. They were all ready to assert their law enforcement and military roles. Two hundred of them stayed out front, ordered not to ascend the spiral staircase. Half stood guard, packed right outside on Main Street, with the other half standing by their vehicles.

Meanwhile, inside the bar, the captain surveyed the crowd. "Many of you were with us when we overthrew the old guard of police and political representatives. We release you from your valiant service. That was yesterday. Today, you must demonstrate your love for the planet and follow orders like everybody else."

The Planetary Forces marched the roughly hundred patrons and twenty staff down to the street level. The climate regime soldiers arrested the employees and verified the names and addresses of all the customers.

In back of the bar, Greg, Jimmy, and Katie were still on the rooftop.

Greg monitored the street level. "I told you, Katie, I've already got a broken left arm."

"A broken arm isn't as bad—"

"Get down."

They dropped and hid behind the railing on the ten-by-twenty-foot rooftop area, elevated 20 feet above ground in the heart of the old downtown.

The Planetary Forces sent soldiers to the back alley to secure the perimeter. After a minute of checking pulses, the soldiers left the bodies of the four Lords of the Wolf Blade and walked back to the front side of the bar.

Jimmy got up first. "They're all gone. I guess the place has no cameras, and they weren't looking for us."

Katie rolled her eyes. "This place is a makeshift bar compared to what it was. Everyone got sick of the cold and the lockdown orders. Marganisans just wanted to bring back the energy. Almost all of them helped the regime at the beginning."

Greg sighed. "But not you."

Jimmy looked around the buildings, and then at Katie. "Are you saying you're not affiliated with the Lords of the Wolf Blade either?"

"I was never a part of the Lords. Never! What kind of woman do you think I am? Never ask me that again. I'm a Renegade."

Jimmy folded his arms. "Don't be so sensitive. We just met you, and trust is an issue these days. How do we know who you really are, Katie? How do we know you didn't bring us out here so that some of these buildings' exterior surveillance cameras would catch us in the footage? I have a tough time believing we weren't being videoed out here and inside."

Katie took a deep breath. "Jimmy, I knew your brother and his wife, right until the day the Marganisan Enforcers had them murdered. Gangsters had a lot more power in those times than they do today. Now it's consolidated in the global gangsterism of the Planetary Order and the Lords. Did you know I also knew Bethany and her Rootsville Coalition?"

Jimmy held up his right hand. "I don't want to talk about that right now. Let's find a way to escape. Wait, what? What are you talking about that you knew Bethany."

Greg nursed his own broken left arm and massaged the pain. "Englewood, I think we've seen enough death for the day."

"It's more than that, Greg. We've seen more than enough death for many lifetimes."

9

STREETS ARE CALLING

Katie led Jimmy and Greg back inside Bull in a China Shop. "Wait here, guys. It's empty."

Jimmy grabbed her. "Where are you going?"

Katie pushed him away. "I see that look on your face, Jimmy. Just chill out. The City Forces had all kinds of setbacks and couldn't get the surveillance going to cover the entire city. Now, the Planetary Forces can't either. They'll get everything in order soon, but all the fighting with the Lords of the Wolf Blade monopolized their attention, and we Renegades slipped beneath the radar. We damage and destroy as much of the surveillance as we can. We can only do so much. Our priority is finding food through the black market and foraging on our own. I'm grabbing some food for us from behind the bar. That's why I've been back here working whenever it reopens, no matter how short-lived. We were using this place as an occasional food distribution center for the time being. Once the Planetary Forces interrogate the Dragons of Corona band, the Forces will know why the Renegades are here."

Crouching down, Greg stared out the front window and past the dimly lit digital sign for Bull in a China Shop. "The band is part of the Renegades. Dragons of Corona are Renegades."

Katie grabbed as much food as she could. "*Is* part of the Renegades or *was* part of the Renegades? It's a weakened group, us Renegades, in the city and around the world as far as we tell. We just do what we can to survive and help each other out when we can. Usually, we can't. That isn't just the case in Marganis. The climate regime broke apart much of the Renegade movement, but we still have a chance."

Jimmy laughed. "Still have a chance at what? You've got no plan and neither do we when it comes down to it. We're living on borrowed time. You're telling me things I already know from other towns and villages, in the mountains, the snowfields, and the forests. You don't think I've seen any of this with my own eyes?"

"It's been years since you've spent any real time in the city, Jimmy. All you know about Marganis now is what you've been told. You think you know everything, but you don't."

Greg, still uncomfortably crouched, kept staring out the front window atop the staircase. "Englewood, at this point, survival is the order of the day. I don't know if there's anything else we can accomplish. My small Army lost its base in the Orca Mountains. I have yet to learn about any survivors from the escape pods. My micro-communication devices died. All the other holdout amies and regional groups of Renegades face slavery or death. I'm not saying life is over, Jimmy, Katie. I'm telling you we're doing a lot more than borrowing time. At this point, we're stealing time."

Jimmy reloaded his gun. "Let's just get back to the high-rise and figure out our next move."

Katie changed into a light long-sleeved shirt and flexible work pants. She rushed back to the spiral staircase. "Wonderful discussion, gentlemen. It's time to hit the streets."

Jimmy led the way down the stairs, cautiously. Marganis remained quiet...too quiet. It was an unusual 80°F. Heavy downpours threatened to recalibrate the skies, but for the moment, the muggy air continued its assault. Dense plains of snowpack surrounded the city. The nearby glacier-covered Boshquire Mountains cast its wide shadows over the land. The heat wave stretched from the Marganisan Valley interfacing with the foothills of the Boshquires to the Orcasso Sea and the Orca Mountains.

Marganisan streets were empty. The government grocery stores were closed. The Planetary Forces had already made their arrests.

Jimmy broke the silence. "No signs of life anywhere. I don't detect an operable vehicle or a human being in sight."

Katie grabbed an apple from her bag and gave it to Jimmy. "Everyone's hiding, fleeing, or getting ready for action."

Jimmy bit into the apple. "Well, Greg, are we hiding or fleeing or getting ready for action?"

"You know, Englewood, we called the base Renegade Peak. I'm a Renegade, just like you and Katie. I organized better than anyone in the Boshquire Mountains, Marganisan Valley, or anywhere else. I tried incorporating Bethany's Rootsville Coalition. I'll assemble a much bigger army if I can outlive the unlivable."

"I'm sure you'll make the Earth proud, moron."

"What have you accomplished, Englewood? What have you put together that's offered any real fight against HAVE or the Planetary Order? Let's get away from here. We're sitting ducks if we don't move out. Englewood, remember for as long as we survive this nightmare that I put in the energy and intelligence you couldn't."

"What do I know, Greg? I was just a streetfighter in the middle of urban combat. Then I joined combat in the country while you hid in a mountain fortress at sea."

Katie stepped in between as Jimmy and Greg squared off. "What the hell is wrong with you?! We're going to die if we don't get out of here. How long do you think it'll be before the Planetary Forces return to watch Main Street?!"

Jimmy dropped his apple, only finishing half of it. "I'm walking. I'm walking."

Greg watched Jimmy's apple roll long the steamy pavement. "Katie, toss me a Red Delicious."

The apple sailed through the air, but Greg never caught it.

An ear-splitting boom flung Jimmy, Greg, and Katie to the gravel. They lay on the ground, catapulted just outside the blast zone of certain death. The missile came from the back alley adjacent to Bull in a China Shop, leveling the bar and sending projectile fragments of the building in every direction. Chunks of the electronic bar sign fell right next to Jimmy.

Greg stood up, nursing his left arm. "Katie, are you alright?! Katie, can you hear me?!"

Jimmy rushed over. "Is she alive?"

"Yes! She's knocked out. Help me get her up."

Jimmy's ears rang with a nagging frequency. "What?!"

"I said help me get her up!"

"Right!"

"Good! We've got her on her feet! Let's wake her up!"

"Aren't we going to carry her?!"

"What, Jimmy?!"

"Shouldn't we carry her?!"

"We can't! She's got to move or we're all dead!"

Jimmy and Greg heard the sirens of the Planetary Forces approaching. The two men hauled Katie around the corner to a side street away from the radius of the explosion.

Jimmy spotted an old-fashioned mechanical car. "Let's get her inside."

"I thought they chopped up these relics into scrap metal, Englewood."

Greg got in the driver's seat after helping Jimmy get Katie into the back.

"Jimmy, get in. They're here. Stay in back with Katie."

Jimmy rested an unresponsive Katie across the back seats.

Disregarding Greg's warning not to go up front, he dashed to the front passenger seat. "Greg, the explosion ripped up your shirt. You're bleeding a little from your right side. It isn't that bad. It isn't bad at all."

"Stay down, Jimmy."

"It's him. It's really him."

"What is it? Who are you talking about?"

"You see the commander surrounded by his henchmen? You see the guy there who's as tall as Brock and Richie from the Lords?"

"What about him, Englewood?"

"It's Zack."

"Zack who?"

"Last name unknown. How could you not know him from all the time you've lived in Marganis?"

"You know how much the City Forces concealed who was who among their ranks. So, who is he?"

"He's a guy with a fleet of military vehicles at his disposal. Looks like he's got a lot of guys under his command. He wasn't as high in the chain four or five years ago, but he orchestrated the murder of my brother and sister-in-law. They call Zack the Comrade of Marganis. That's the guy I'm after. He led the City Forces."

Greg shook his head. "Wild. He went from City Forces to Planetary Forces with no paperwork required."

"Some of his men infiltrated the Lords of the Wolf Blade and weakened them severely. He uses good old-fashioned fear and murder and show trials to damage the Renegades."

"Nothing we can do about him right now other than ride this out. They're not looking for us. The missile came from the back of the bar, not the entrance on Main Street. Planetary Forces wanted to wipe out any food transfers and storage. They wanted to permanently cut off any place that could serve Renegade operations. The climate regime doesn't know we're here, Jimmy, but the Forces under Zack's command haven't had the time yet to interrogate everyone."

"We're stuck here for the moment. Good thing is they're not checking out the side streets. We just have to stay quiet and out of sight."

"They could go to the high-rise. We've got to get to my wife and daughter."

Katie opened her eyes. "Cora and Linda would know enough to leave before the Planetary Forces arrive."

Jimmy climbed into the back seat to help Katie sit up. The tinted windows concealed his movement from anyone attempting to look into the vehicle. Jimmy tapped Greg on the shoulder. "General, we're trapped at the corner of hell and high water. Death stares us in the face and won't leave us alone."

"It isn't just death. Life stares at us. We left food in the bags at the wreckage. Let's find a barrel of apples somewhere else. All we've got are water, guns, and ammo. That's a start."

"We've got something else, too."

"What's that, Englewood?"

"We've got Zack standing in the way. The Comrade of Marganis never loses."

"Give it time, Jimmy. Give it time."

10

FACING THE REVOLUTION

Zack, wearing his climate uniform aside from his helmet, turned on his megaphone to broadcast a message throughout Marganis.

"I speak on behalf of the Planetary Forces, the Planetary Order, the Planetary Council, and the Planetary Leader. I speak to you from Main Street, surrounded by an unstoppable revolution amid the great buildings and concrete jungle. We have all but removed the trees from the city. Our climate action and revolutionary force bring us the pristine urban setting we see today, unsullied by tree pollution. Humans dirty the air by breathing, and we're solving that problem as well. We warned all of you many times that this heat wave would arrive. It is a glorious day to disprove all the lies about a deep freeze across the planet. Some of you chose to believe your five senses, and your sixth sense, over reality."

The word "reality" echoed across the city, from the homes to the government-approved businesses, and from the prisons to the bunkers.

"We must join in solidarity to protect our climate revolution. The heat has strained our systems. Marganisans, do not be greedy or waste energy. Follow lockdown orders. Wear your climate suits upon penalty of arrest as we march onward to progress in the name of HAVE. Marganisans, watch us tomorrow from your windows and screens for our military parade. Your survival depends on us. We have a special event you will witness while we gather in the great Marganisan Plaza. See you tomorrow, Jimmy Englewood."

Jimmy's heart skipped a beat.

Greg took a swig of stale bourbon from the bottle in his pocket. "What do you think, Jimmy? Are they clearing out soon or leaving any guards for the night? The rain clouds keep promising a downpour. It'll soon be night."

A woozy Katie tugged at Greg's climate outfit. "Why are you asking him?" I know Zack and the rest of these people better than Jimmy does. I live in the city and never left."

Jimmy smiled. "You never left because you never put as much on the line as I did, did you? I have no clue who you are. These people know me by name, and they know I'm here."

"They suspect you're here, Jimmy."

"No, Katie, they know I'm here. They've got their hands full from all the arrests. The heat spell slowed them down. They're caught off guard, completely. What, Katie? No wiseass comments or insults?"

"They're clearing out, Englewood."

Greg laughed. "She's our eyes and ears, Englewood. We're twenty minutes from the high-rise. We should be out of here in five."

Katie drew her gun. "Let's pray none of the local informants see us or turn us in."

Jimmy looked at Greg's right side. "Hey Norbannick, you're not bleeding anymore."

Zack and the Planetary Forces under his command cleared out. Sunlight held on in the waning hours of the long Marganisan day.

Jimmy exited from behind the driver's seat. Katie followed him out the same door.

Greg stayed in the car, flung open the door and fired up at a third-story balcony. He hit the target in the center of the forehead. The man slumped over the balcony, falling lifeless to the pavement.

Jimmy tried to shield Katie, but she had already drawn her weapon. Katie fired at the five assailants shooting at them from street level. Bullets flew back and forth across a hundred-foot separation.

The driver's side doors absorbed the shots as best they could. The tires and bullet-proof windows stayed intact. Jimmy and Katie dashed behind the rear right corner of the car to reload. Greg ran out of ammo.

An assailant cocked his right arm to throw a grenade, but during the backward motion, the grenade slipped from his hand. He tried to run but tripped over his own feet, falling flat on the street. The explosion blew him up, along with two others standing on either side of him. The blast rocked the remaining two assailants to the ground, and Jimmy and Katie marred their bodies with lead.

Marganisan residents looked out over balconies and patios to see what happened.

Greg picked up the key from the center console and started the ignition on the old vehicle. Jimmy and Katie got back inside, and Greg sped off, back onto Main Street and toward the high-rise...and Cora and Linda...

Driving with his right arm only, Greg's movements were jerky as he raced to his family. "What was that, Jimmy?! I thought you said the Planetary Forces weren't coming back."

Jimmy reloaded again. "Those were just informers turned unpaid assassins. They were looking for special privileges from the climate regime."

Katie reloaded her own weapon. "Jimmy's right. These people aren't like the true believers in the extinct Marganisan Enforcers. They're not even like those Enforcer-affiliated scavengers. They were all purged. Nowadays, it's the black market privileges these opportunists are after. They live day to day and have no connection to any movement other than killing and selling out to live. The climate regime could wipe these people out at any moment, just like they did to the Marganisan Enforcers and all organized gangs. These civilians fighting nowadays are true believers in the HAVE movement...or they're just scavengers the regime allows to exist."

Jimmy kept his gun out, ready for battle. "We were lucky they didn't have machineguns."

Rain blanketed the skies and invaded the ground as the fugitive sun set over the buildings. The high-rise moved in and out of view across the last turns on a drive just minutes away from Greg's family.

Jimmy, Greg, and Katie left the car on a side street a couple of blocks away and ran the remaining distance that separated them from the building entrance.

Greg pulled out a key. "We might be the only ones defying lockdown orders tonight. I'm sure you've both heard that the punishment is death. Got it, we're in. The key barely works on this old door. Let's keep it propped. We can't afford to get stuck if we need to get out this way, and the seventh floor is too high to jump. Katie, you have any more ammo?"

"Just what I have in my gun."

"How about you, Englewood?"

"Same here. Just what's loaded."

"No matter. We have ammo in the apartment, but my daughter recently changed the lock to get in the apartment. She gave me a copy, but I must've lost my copy of the key somewhere between here and Main Street. Elevator's ready. Jimmy, hit the seventh floor."

"Already did."

They stepped out of the elevator and walked to Linda's apartment.

Greg knocked on the door. No answer. He turned to Jimmy. "What's the matter?"

"You know."

"Why don't you just say it out loud?"

"We don't stand a chance. We all know it. But we can keep pretending."

Greg knocked on the door again. This time he knocked a little longer. "Cora? Linda? Let us in."

Katie nudged her way closer. "You mind if I try?"

"Go right ahead, but I might have to kick this down."

Katie turned the knob and entered. "Unlocked by them or someone else? Nice place. Great lighting. What's this, two-bed, two-bath?"

Greg ran to the master bedroom. "Cora! Cora!"

He then searched Linda's room. Katie was already in there, shaking her head from side to side.

Jimmy stood close by the apartment door. "Any sign, Greg?"

"No, but I know my family. There's no way anybody captured them. They left. They had to have left on their own accord. But I can't tell why."

"We'll find them, General Norbannick?"

"General? You don't have to call me that anymore."

"I have little family of my own. Anything left of the old civilization is what I fight for as of today. You're fighting for that old civilization and the people in it. I had a wife. I had a brother.

I had...I had so much. Now I fight in honor of their memories and in honor of what and who everyone has to lose. Your cause is mine, General, and mine is yours."

"You're alright, Englewood. You're more than alright. Until we reconstitute an army, call me Greg. Just call me Greg."

Jimmy nodded his approval. "Everybody from this building is following the lockdown or getting out of town. Some of them left town a while back, like I did. We're on our own."

Katie lightly cleared her throat. "Gentlemen, look out the window at those lights. Isn't it beautiful? Even with all the trees knocked over, you can imagine the city like it was years ago. You can remember it. The rain is clearing now. The bright lights of Marganis serve as a promise. What's so funny, Englewood?"

"Nothing. It isn't you, Katie. I'm just thinking we've got some outdated technology and weapons at our disposal to find the General's...Greg's family."

Greg turned off all the lights and walked up to the window. "She's right, though, Jimmy. Soak this in. You may never see the bright lights of your city again. There aren't as many as there used to be. A lot of stars will flicker tonight. We'll see more than we're seeing at this minute. It's cooling off a little. There goes the last speck of sunshine."

The three Renegades stared out the giant glass-paned window. Aches and pains washed over them after a long day of survival.

In a flash, the lights of all the buildings in Marganis disappeared. Rolling brownouts arrived...

11

GENERATORS

The generator kicked on, and Katie jumped back. "That old generator makes a lot of noise. I don't care that it's illegal to have one, but we should keep the lights off so we don't fall under suspicion."

Greg pulled out a flashlight and shined it on the candle at the center of the dining room table. Greg turned off the generator before taking a seat next to Jimmy and Katie in front of the small flame.

Katie tapped on the table repeatedly. "You left your communication devices with your wife and daughter, didn't you, Greg?"

"Sure I did. I didn't think we'd need them. I didn't want them to be used against Cora or Linda in case we got caught."

Jimmy tilted his head. "Used against them how?"

Katie leaned back. "Wasn't that just a little too easy for all of us today? They know Jimmy's back in the city, but they don't even come after him much less catch him."

Greg turned off his flashlight. "Katie, stop drumming the table. We'll give it a little more time to see if my family returns. Meanwhile, I have to tell Jimmy a few things he has to hear."

Jimmy waved his hand over the flame. "Tell me, Greg, what happened after I passed out from that cocktail you gave me at the Orca Mountains? What happened in that missing time?"

"You know something, Englewood, the battle started off better than planned. We shut down and abandoned the base completely. Getting everybody out was frenzied at best. We knew the Planetary Forces would send reinforcements. We couldn't send out all the escape capsules and simply get away. The enemy left us no choice. We fought the enemy's aircraft and nautical ships. My Army sustained heavy losses but devastated the first wave of the attackers. We were winning dogfights. You never saw our robot crew at Renegade Peak. All one hundred of them employed anti-aircraft and anti-ship strategies and operations to perfection. Our submarines sent theirs to a watery hell."

"You're telling me I slept through this whole thing?"

"No offense, Jimmy, but nobody thought about you during the battle. We tried to save ourselves and evacuate everyone to safety. That included half of the population of humans at the base, half of whom were not fighters. Your safety, your mission, and your life meant little to us compared to the thousand people and hundred robots I led in military and civilian capacities."

"Go on, then."

"We fought them to the heights of the atmosphere and the depths of the steep sloping seabed. They shredded as much sea and avian life as they could They took out pods of whales. I can still hear the sights and sounds of the great mammals suffering in agony."

"Why? Why in the middle of their fight against you would they lose all their discipline and focus their firepower on animals?"

"Because they did not plan for the first wave they sent to survive the fight against us. Because the HAVE movement has a job."

"What job?"

"HAVE has more than one meaning. You don't know this yet? Get with it, Englewood. You think it stands for Humans Are Viruses on Earth. It really means humans and animals are Viruses on Earth. The Planetary Order feels the same way about plant life or any life form, but they couldn't fit all that into their stupid acronym. Destroying the air, the oceans, the climate...that's the point. We're in the way because we live and breathe. The only use they have for us is to follow their every directive, to feed their lust for domination over life itself...on Earth and anywhere else."

"I know most of this. Didn't we talk about it already? It all sounds too familiar."

"But you still don't understand."

"I don't understand what?"

"People use animals as food. When the Planetary Forces

harm the ecosystem, they harm you. You're thinking about the majesty of the whales, but the Planetary Order commands its armies to release toxins on land and sea. They don't want you to eat or breathe freely. The climate regime doesn't want you to have life as you know it...or as you knew it. You've known that for years, but your brain hasn't registered that the HAVE tyranny will stop at nothing to harm and manipulate all life until we defeat the Planetary Order."

"What happened next? What happened next in the battle?"

"We crushed the enemy's first wave, but the enemy still won. They released toxins into the Orcasso Sea and into the upper and lower reaches of the atmosphere. We picked all of this up on our readings."

"How do they win from this? They're just destroying themselves if they can't eat or breathe. The toxins poison them, too."

"Don't you think the leaders have contingencies for food and air and shelter? Those fighting for them are disposable. The leaders have this Earth and beyond to secure their own lives and toy around with everybody else's."

"What kinds of toxins did they release in this battle? How much damage did they cause?"

"We didn't find out the answer to those questions. Listen, Jimmy, if you're looking for logic, you won't find it. Isn't that right, Katie?"

"He won't find any redeeming qualities at all, Greg. He'll keep looking, though. Jimmy will always keep looking."

Jimmy scratched his chin. "What happened in the second

wave of their attack?"

"They overwhelmed us with more high-tech firepower than we'd ever seen. We could not outmaneuver them or overcome the speed and strength of their vessels and weaponry."

"How did our capsule get away? How was that possible if their barrage was overwhelming?"

"Fortune, Englewood. We had good fortune. We got out at hypersonic speeds and camouflaged our capsule. I witnessed the devastation before submerging and traveling the ocean and launching back into the sky. All of us in the capsule aside from you witnessed the self-destruction we programmed to blow up Renegade Peak and everything in it. That included our robots, from the humanoids to the more mechanistic."

"And as we took flight, what did you decide?"

"That's when I determined I had to do whatever I could for you to live, Jimmy, no matter what."

"What about Bethany? How do either of you know Bethany? How do you know who I am?"

Greg's face lit up. "That story's on deck, Jimmy."

"Bring it into the batter's box."

Katie pushed her chair back and stood up. "Look out the window! The power's back in the city." She walked into the kitchen. "I could use a snack. Anybody else hungry."

Jimmy blew out the candle.

Greg kept the high-rise apartment lights off. There was enough ambient light from the city for everyone to see their food. Slowly but surely, all the buildings turned off their lights for the night. Jimmy, Greg, and Katie fell asleep on the living room couches, illuminated by the starlight over Marganis.

Then, a tremor at sunrise.

Jimmy woke up. "Greg, you feel that? It's got to be an earthquake."

"No, Englewood. It's the door. The apartment shakes when someone bangs on the door."

"Glad we have ammo in this place."

The knocking continued and woke up Katie. She sprang to the door with her gun. She unlocked the bolts while Jimmy and Greg stood up and aimed their weapons at the entrance.

Katie turned back and Greg nodded. Katie opened the solid door, and Cora and Linda rushed inside the apartment.

Greg handed his gun to Jimmy. The former general held his wife and daughter.

Katie joined in the hug. "Great to see you again, sis!"

Jimmy walked over to the window, back turned to everyone else. "You still didn't trust me, did you, General?"

"This is my family, Englewood. Katie is my daughter, too. I had to learn more about you before you could learn everything about me."

Jimmy's gaze remained affixed to the city skyscrapers. "I thought you said I was part of the family."

Greg moved next to Jimmy, the two of them staring out the window. "You are. You are part of the family, now and always."

Cora ushered her husband and Jimmy back to the group. "Greg, take more food and weapons. Take medicine."

Greg hugged his wife again. "Where did you two go, Cora? How'd you get there and how'd you get back?"

"I'd ask the same of you."

Cora handed her husband a Red Delicious. "Make sure you catch your food next time."

Jimmy's eyes widened. "You and Linda were at Bull in a China Shop?"

Cora winked. "Maybe."

"But we almost...forget it."

Linda took a long drink from a bottle of cola. "Daddy, we should get ready for the parade at the Marganisan Plaza."

Katie tugged Jimmy's shirt while Jimmy thought about the missile that launched into the bar. "You hear that, Englewood? We've got a showdown with Zack to attend."

"I know it. He'll be ready. The Comrade of Marganis is always ready."

12

PARADE ON FIRE

Columns of men and vehicles marched in the parade, culminating with the victory celebration at Marganisan Plaza. No music played for any part of the climate regime's procession.

Residents watched from their balconies and patios on a balmy, cloudy day of 75°F. All of them dressed in protective gear, the climate gear or modified spacesuits, as mandated by the watchful Planetary Order, even though nobody needed such protection in warm temperatures. They knew the temporary warming marked an anomaly. They knew they were living in an ice age despite the regime's flood of propaganda.

The heat wave entered its waning phase.

Most people watched the event on their screens at home, but stragglers broke the lockdown rules to watch in person. The defiant stripped off the climate suits, eager to feel the sun on their skin, tempting fate as Marganis fell deeper under the control of the regime. They knew in their minds and hearts that the climate cooled despite what their rulers maintained.

Zack's cadre of fighters wanted to use the regional thaw to solidify fear in the city and wider region. All the soldiers wore distinct climate gear denoting the Planetary Forces. This gear had its own bright red color to match the soldiers' other uniforms. Every climate suit bore the insignia of the Planetary Forces. The insignia displayed the Earth as being split in half at the North Pole by an ax.

Suddenly, a siren rang out across the city and shrieked across Marganisan screens. Every goose-stepping soldier and modern armored vehicle ground to a halt upon hearing the siren. Ten thousand members of the Planetary Forces directed their attention toward the Plaza stage.

Zack, guarded by his detail, stepped to the forefront with his megaphone and removed his helmet. "What a truly tragic day this is. We wanted to present you with the captivating music of the once beloved band, Dragons of Corona. Unfortunately, they became Renegades after being part of the old Marganisan Enforcers. We allowed these gangsters to live! Renegades are traitors to HAVE. A traitor to HAVE is a traitor to the Planetary Forces. A traitor to the Planetary Forces is a traitor to the Planetary Order. A traitor to the Planetary Order is a traitor to the Planetary Leader. A traitor to the Planetary Leader is a traitor to your food supply and the revolution. Climate democracy will not tolerate counterrevolution!"

The soldiers cheered at the top of their lungs. "Long live the climate regime! Hail to the anti-human revolution! All praise the Planetary Order!"

A convoy of trucks moved into position at the outer edges of the plaza. One truck drove to the center, where soldiers brought out the three men and two women of Dragons of Corona.

The soldiers threw the rope-tied bandmates to the ground.

Zack jumped off the stage with his machinegun and megaphone. "We know you Dragons love heavy metal. Now you must go the way of scavengers and your old Marganisan Enforcers. Look at yourselves, you wannabe Renegades. You must perish from my weapon's heavy metal."

The crowd laughed a monstrous laugh.

The audiovisual team recorded every moment of Zack's contempt and the collective voice of thousands of soldiers. Still, the team did not pick up the last words of the band members. "Please don't. We're sorry. Spare our families. I don't want to die. Lord, help us."

Zack continued the ceremonies. He used his machinegun to mangle the Dragons of Corona.

Next up to the center of Marganisan Plaza for execution...ten Lords of the Wolf Blade.

Jimmy Englewood watched from the crowd. He wore contraband protective gear, which Cora and Linda swiped the night before from a soldier in the Planetary Forces. The bright red attire did little to calm Jimmy's nerves. He tried cheering. He tried applauding. Nothing could bring him to play the enemy role as well as he wanted.

The video broadcast and surveillance did not pick up Jimmy's nonconformity. The sea of bright red frenzy swallowed him into obscurity. Soldiers, whipped up and vacuous, stood proudly under Zack's command.

Jimmy witnessed the slow executions of the Lords. He detested them with every fiber of his being. He knew the Lords would conduct the same kind of slaughter if they had the power. Jimmy understood the Lords could not match the psychologically destructive and manipulative capabilities of the Planetary Forces. As he watched regional leaders of the psychotic movement put to death, he felt his heart pounding with rage to stop the executioners...but he remained still. The entire operation demanded his patience. The ten Lords of the Wolf Blade met their end at the knives of climate-regime executioners.

A truck pulled up to drop off several captured Renegades. Already interrogated to the hilt, none of them could speak in front of the crowd.

Zack reclaimed his command of the executions he ceded temporarily to other soldiers in wiping out the ten Lords. "And so it is. We embark on Act III. A drama this special unfolds very few times in a man's life. You, my soldiers and police...you get to see real theater up close. All the counterrevolutionaries lose their group status. They have no organization and no true purpose other than agitation. Their supporters find themselves enslaved in our dungeons. Planetary Forces of Earth, I present you with four leaders of the disintegrating Renegade movement. They represent the worst climate backstabbers and counterrevolutionaries we've captured!"

Soldiers wheeled in a makeshift guillotine apparatus.

Finally, the time arrived for Jimmy to set the operation in motion. He used up almost all his patience, but he no longer needed it.

Four Renegades awaited their fate under a guillotine.

The old Marganisan City Forces had purged most of the scavengers almost every group of gangsters, including the organized criminal syndicate, the Marganisan Enforcers. This happened well before the Planetary Forces took over the Marganisan City Forces.

The Lords of the Wolf Blade remained, posing a threat to Zack and the entire climate regime, but the Planetary Forces sought to destroy the Renegades above any remaining groups or movements.

Time soon expired on Zack's horror fest. Jimmy pressed the detonator.

Explosions rippled across the Marganisan Plaza, tossing up chunks of pavement.

The stage blew up, followed by the center of the square, including the makeshift guillotine.

Jimmy could not tell if Zack lived or died, but the four Renegades all perished in the blast, spared the guillotine for a quicker death.

Hundreds of soldiers of the Planetary Forces lost their lives in the detonation, but the group originally stood ten thousand strong in the city. Additional soldiers could arrive within 15 minutes to replace them.

Amidst the chaos, nobody saw Jimmy run away from the Plaza, clutching his machinegun and buying time for help.

Greg and Katie wore stolen Marganisan climate suits, just like Jimmy did. The father and daughter set off the ignition for bombs to take out the convoy of trucks and armored vehicles.

Cora and Linda, also wearing stolen bright red climate gear for anonymity, detonated an armory of grounded flying assault vessels.

Zack noticed Cora and Linda through the fires and haze of the flying vessel explosions.

Cora and Linda spotted Zack noticing them.

Zack aimed his machinegun. Old Renegades from nearby buildings tackled him just before he could fire on Cora and Linda. The old Renegades from all sections of the city made their way on foot and by vehicle into the battle, though the ones that tackled Zack lost their lives to the bullets of Planetary Forces. Zack rejoined the battle. He searched for Cora and Linda, who melded with the crowd.

Marganisan Plaza turned into a battlefield attracting several thousand Renegades, all in regular clothing. They had no organization and no capacity to receive immediate help beyond Marganis's borders. They were animated by the fight.

Just as with the Battle of the Orca Mountains, the Planetary Forces called in reinforcements for the Battle of Marganis. The land combat and street fighting created an opening in time for Jimmy to escape with his fellow fighters. From the sky reinforcements for the Planetary Forces picked off undisguised rebels. Additional armored vehicles moved in on the Renegades. Zack's soldiers and the reinforcements had no interest in taking prisoners. They captured a few but searched with care for Jimmy and any of his close collaborators.

Renegades lay dead by the hundreds in the plaza. Planetary Forces mowed down resistance that never stood a chance. Thousands more city residents watched from their homes, screens, patios and balconies, determining they would not join the Battle of Marganis. Some renewed their commitment to fight the climate regime.

Jimmy rendezvoused with Greg and his family at Marganisan Boulevard, a block outside the Plaza.

They hid behind the corner of an old department store. Jimmy reloaded and got ready to provide covering fire. "Greg, bring everybody to that ship. The enemy ship, we're taking it."

"No, Jimmy! Just Linda! The rest of us are staying in the battle. It's now or never for Marganis and the Earth!"

They all provided cover for Linda while return enemy fire intensified by the second.

Headgear off, Jimmy fired round after round at the Planetary Forces. "Go, Linda! Go!"

Linda ran for the ship through a thunderstorm of bullets. She reached the vessel and made it inside at the same time as an enemy soldier.

Both with bare faces showing, they locked eyes in the 400

square-foot space and froze for three endless seconds.

Linda disarmed the soldier's machinegun as he raised his weapon, flipping him to the ground as he kept his grip. His grip loosened with a swift kick to his face. The faster, taller, and heavier soldier lost his advantages, culminating in Linda blasting him in the torso with her handgun. She rolled him out the door while bullets clanged against the ship. Enemy soldiers and old Renegades fell in battle all around the vessel. Linda closed the entrance, accelerated the ship, and flew past the Boshquire Mountains.

Two enemy aircraft took off in pursuit of Linda, but Renegades grabbed hold of antiaircraft weapons and shot down both vessels. Remnants fell on the buildings while revitalized Renegades continued joining the battle. Four thousand of them marched into the fight to match the Planetary Forces with another surprise attack. Outgunned and without a strategy, they made their stand for Marganis.

A bullet whistled through the air under Jimmy's legs. Another skimmed the hair on his left arm.

A missile struck the apartment above the department store on the corner of Plaza Road and Marganis Boulevard. Jimmy, Greg, Katie, and Cora sprinted. Building bricks fell all around them, and they escaped the collapse only to arrive at another crowded fight with their enemy.

A nearby blast knocked Renegades and Planetary Forces to the ground.

Infused with energy by the city's rebellion, Jimmy rushed

climate regime soldiers and caught the butt of a machinegun to the gut.

Jimmy gasped for any shred of air his lungs could inhale. A tall figure with devious eyes stood over him, grinning and ready to fire.

Zack looked up and caught an uppercut from Greg. Dazed for a moment, Zack dropped his gun, hitting a fellow soldier who rushed in to shoot Greg up close. With the soldier out of commission, Zack swung at Greg and missed. Greg hit him with another uppercut.

Jimmy's breath returned, but he turned his attention to Cora and Katie. The mother and daughter found themselves on the punishing receiving end of hand-to-hand combat. Picking up the handgun of a dead soldier, Jimmy leveled a slew of attackers, enabling Cora and Katie to recover.

Meanwhile, Zack picked up Greg by his uniform and tossed him onto the street.

Katie aimed her gun at Zack's sternum. Zack dove to the ground before Katie fired. The bullet killed a Renegade and Zack disappeared through the smoke of the battle.

A stalemate continued into the late afternoon, spreading out across the city. Block to block, business to business, and home to home, the old Renegades fought with the desperation that the hopes of the world rested with them. Many formal groups of Renegades disbanded years ago. Others of the formal groups suffered decimation, death, and enslavement. Marganis lived for as long as any drop of fighting spirit remained in the Renegades of the city. Jimmy Englewood was part of them and their fight, and the battle raged on.

13

NO GOING BACK

The Norbannick family joined Englewood in a semi-furnished basement.

Jimmy sat down put his hands together, leaning over with his elbows on his knees. "Marganis died today. Our side fought bravely, but the enemy is operating all over the Earth. We're operating on a local scale or regional at best. We'll find physical destruction around every corner when we see daylight again. The psychological devastation is irreversible. How's your left arm feeling?"

Greg sat down, holding a bag of ice to his jaw. "Never mind how I'm feeling."

"Hold on a second. I wasn't asking you to tell me your deepest thoughts and emotions. I want to know if there's anything I can...anything I can—"

"Anything you can what? I've got a broken arm, and I fought

through it."

"Let me finish my thought, you stubborn old man. Don't be too proud to let me help."

"You've helped a lot as it is, Jimmy. You kickstarted a counterrevolution, even if only local or regional. Don't forget that my family would all be dead if it weren't for you. I just have to face the fact that I might never see Linda again."

"As long as she's still on Earth, we've got a good chance to find her."

"I hope so, Englewood. I hope so. Don't you think it's odd? Odd that she got away? Odd that we're all still alive? Somethings going on here, Jimmy. Something's going on."

"There's a climate lockdown, Greg. The Planetary Order tells us it's getting hotter, and that it's our fault, when we know the Earth is freezing. What could be crazier than that? This transitory heat spell is about to end. They'll keep attacking us with propaganda. Their followers and fighters are prepared to murder us. It doesn't get any crazier than all of this."

"That's what's on my mind. It can still get worse. It will get worse."

Katie washed her face at the kitchen sink. "Well, Dad, we're lucky we have water. How long are we trapped down here?"

Greg switched the bag of ice from his jaw to his left arm. "I'm not sure, Katie. We're not trapped, but we're lucky we've got water. We're lucky we've got food."

Cora tapped on the refrigerator. "We're lucky we've got electricity, too. We just don't have our Linda."

Katie hugged her mom. "My sister is tougher than me. She'll be alright, and we'll all see her again."

"You're both tough, my beautiful daughters. I can't lose either of you."

"Mom, you're the toughest woman I know."

"I miss my first daughter. I cannot believe we lost her."

"I miss her, too, Mom. Funny how Bethany wasn't tough growing up. Somehow became the toughest in the family...and the brightest."

"It was how kind she was, more than anything else. She was still sensitive in her later years, no matter how tough she was. When she was younger, I don't know if she ever hit anyone. Your dad and I will never be as complete as we were before her death."

Greg walked over to hug Cora and Katie. "We'll see her in the future. Let's keep honoring her every day...and Linda, who I know is still alive."

Jimmy stood up out of his seat. "I'm sorry. I mean, I'm sorry to hear that about your eldest daughter. Did she die recently?"

Greg stepped back out of the kitchen, ushering Jimmy into the living room. "She passed on recently, as you know, Jimmy. My people on the outskirts of the city told me she probably found a resting place under a dense snowpack. I'm sorry you found her as she was dying. Bethany's spirit will never die."

Jimmy smashed an antique dresser with his fist. "Anything else you need to tell me?"

"Not right now."

"Tell me something, Greg. Who are we? What's it all about?

My wife, your oldest daughter, is dead. Now Linda is gone. Our city is in shambles, and we have no way to bring it back. We have no way out."

"We can leave, but we're not leaving. Not yet. Not until we hear from Linda."

The Comrade of Marganis appeared on the screen in the living room.

"I am Zack, regional commander of the Planetary Forces and regional spokesman for the Planetary Order. Turn up the volume, please, on your televisions, your home theaters, your VR devices, or whatever other visuals you have. Turn up the volume on your audio devices, if audio is all you have. Jimmy Englewood, we will find you and all of your collaborators. You are a breather, an attempted breeder, and an adversary of the environment. You have defied lockdown orders and personally defiled the climate."

Jimmy listened and watched, transfixed by the images showing him at the Battle of Marganis.

The speech continued. "You see that even with your headgear, you cannot avoid detection. The counterrevolutionary movement continues because of you. You encourage others to break the lockdown. Your relentless rebellion against the system cannot stand. Jimmy Englewood, you are a perpetual threat to democracy. Your attempt to murder me near Marganisan Plaza simply adds to your crimes. When captured, you will receive a hearing conducted by those who understand that you are a virus. This movement of yours began with your insistence on using plastic. Your attempted resurrection of the Renegades will fail. We will suffocate you in plastic, if you're lucky."

Footage switched back from images of Jimmy in the middle of the battle to Zack standing in real time at a podium. A soldier apiece flanked Zack on either side, but several steps to the rear. They carried the flags of the Planetary Order, with an ax cracking the Earth amid a bright red background.

"To all those providing comfort to the enemy, we will find you and bring you to justice. You have committed war crimes against your planet. Turn in Jimmy Englewood or provide information leading to his capture. Doing so will enable us to grant you special favor in the eyes of the Planetary Order and the HAVE movement. Help us help you by committing yourselves to a planet free from counterrevolutionary travelers, growers, merchants, and investors. The revolution progresses while we overcome the remaining elements from the anti-democratic Renegades and the Lords of the Wolf Blade. Follow all lockdown orders and consume only the food we allow. We exist within a crisis that shows no end in sight. We have already cleared away thousands of corpses on both sides, every one of them the fault of the Renegade who we demand the people of the city turn over. Bring us Jimmy Englewood. Save the Planetary Order. Save planet Earth from the ever-present dangers of climate change."

Zack pointed a handgun at the audience. Three seconds later, the screen went blank. Jimmy and the Norbannick family watched each other in silence until Greg picked up a call.

Greg's knees buckled when a spherical audio communication device with a one-foot diameter set off an alarm sound accompanied by an urgent message. "Answer incoming request."

"You know who this is, don't you, General Norbannick?"

"To tell you the truth Zack, I never heard too much about you until a couple of days ago. Well, I heard a little. But I knew you as the Comrade of Marganis."

"Even Jimmy must feel surprised you know as much as you do."

"You have her, don't you, Zack. You captured Linda."

"She tried her martial arts when we intercepted her stolen ship. She took down one of our men before she left Marganis, but she got the crap kicked out of her by someone far weaker than the man she defeated. You never know who's going to win a fight."

"Is she alive?"

"You fought bravely, Norbannick."

"Is she alive?!"

"She gave us so much information for so little in return. The mere promise of a quick death was enough. She should've taken her chances in the Boshquire Mountains. She got greedy and had to keep flying too high. Your daughter thought my reinforcements outside the Marganisan Valley would never catch her. You're within the perimeter of the valley, Norbannick. We'll catch you next."

"Are you telling me Linda is dead?"

"We hadn't the foggiest you and a wife had three daughters.

Only one of them is dead. Bethany defied more climate laws and institutional lockdown norms than we can count. We thought we left you childless after killing her. We didn't know you were still a proud father of two."

"Now you're aware."

"And what of you, Katie? You must be a Renegade in the truest sense. I don't think you would've given in like Linda."

"I'm the one who's going to kill you, Zack."

Cora's tears streamed down her face. "Zack, where is my daughter?!"

"Are you sobbing, Cora?"

Jimmy spoke right into the spherical communication device, catching Zack off guard. "If you want to capture me, Comrade, then tell me where Linda is so we can set up an exchange of me for her."

"How noble of you. You have your brother's energy."

"Roger is dead."

"Yes, he is. He was one of us. He carried with him all the hopes and dreams of the movement. When you betray the Planetary Order, your life loses meaning. We ended it for him and—"

"Betray the Planetary Order? Isn't that what you climate regime ghouls like to say? You sick son of a bitch."

"Would you like to know where Linda is?"

"Tell me."

Greg, using his uninjured right hand, clutched Jimmy. "Don't go, Englewood. You'll die, too. None of these people have any honor. Trusting them is a fool's errand, and you know it."

"It isn't your call. You've already lost Bethany to death. That's enough. You're getting Linda back, and I'm the price to be paid for it. That's a minor sacrifice."

"What's wrong with you, Englewood? They'll murder both of you."

"Let them try."

Zack laughed. "Greg, we now know all about you and your whole damned family. We know all about Jimmy. We knew how to get a hold of you. Only thing we don't know is your location. That won't be a mystery much longer. Jimmy Englewood is not your concern. You have Linda to worry about, and Katie, and that wife of yours. Family is everything, isn't it, General?"

Jimmy held up his hand, interrupting Greg. "Where is she, Zack? Tell me where I can find Linda."

"We're moving her around a bit. You'll have to figure it out yourself. Come find her. Risk your life for a lost cause, Renegade."

Jimmy cut off the connection. "I know where she is."

Katie smiled. "The Boshquire Mountains."

Cora exhaled. "How do you know, Katie?"

"Trust me, Mom. Zack mentioned she should have stayed in the foothills of the Boshquire Mountains. He concentrated on that location. That's because they have her there. He slipped up. That's where they interrogated her, and that's where she's being held."

Jimmy motioned to Greg. "You told no one about this basement home, right?"

"Not until I told you tonight. It's incredible we made it here. They're still tied up with ongoing fighting in the city and beyond its borders, or they would've found us. Get Linda out of there alive, Jimmy."

"I will, General Norbannick, but it probably won't happen until the heat spell turns back into a deep freeze."

14

LEAVING THE CITY

Jimmy and Greg woke up while everyone else slept. It was a while before dawn.

Greg threw Jimmy a bag. "Take this extra gear with you, Englewood. Just remember that these climate suits aren't set up to communicate from helmet to helmet. That's no different than the other ones we've had. Keep the gear in the bag for now. It's a white climate suit built like no other to maintain excellent air flow and filtration and normal breathing. The suit material is breathable in the extreme heat and cold, also like the ones we've been wearing. We have to hide our faces anyhow. Don't go for the extra flexibility by not wearing the climate gear. It's too dangerous at this point to risk it."

"General, do you think we can revive the way life was?"

"Some things we can bring back, but not everything. We have to make it better than it was before. That's if we win. If we lose, then I don't know if we'll recognize anything for a long time, Jimmy. We'll be dead."

"Boshquire Mountains, I'm on my way."

"The Planetary Forces will be looking for you. They don't want to kill you. You are the prize they seek. Take advantage of the ongoing fighting. The climate regime is spending time and resources in battles that detract from them tracking you down. You have all the weapons and supplies you can carry, so get out there and rescue my daughter."

"Thank you, Greg. I'm just glad you still have a full arsenal in this basement."

"The weather will turn by tomorrow. Watch for the changes."

"I didn't think I'd ever get back to Marganis. I wonder if I'll ever get back here again or recognize it if I do."

"First things first. Do me a favor and get out of this city alive. Then, bring Linda back to my family."

"I will."

"Goodbye, Jimmy. The next time we see each other, I won't be the same. Neither will you. Hold your memories with Bethany close. Her spirit lives."

"I'll always remember her. I'll always remember my wife. Goodbye, Greg."

The basement had no windows. Jimmy walked from below ground up the stairs of the abandoned house. It was in the low 70s, and Jimmy thought he would never again experience natural warmth in the atmosphere after that day. He shrugged off a quick couple of sentimental daydreams and walked out into the streets of Marganis.

Jimmy was fortunate to have found a brief refuge with the Norbannicks in a secluded part of the city. It was Jimmy's old neighborhood years ago. The Marganisan Enforcers had demolished his house after he had skipped town years earlier and escaped past the city gates. The once tree-filled neighborhood had transformed into a depressed area of frustration and hopelessness.

Leaving the neighborhood brought Jimmy into a former idyllic area of the city. He avoided detection in the darkness of the early morning hour. He could hear the street fighting continuing in the main parts of the city. Something had slowed the progress of additional reinforcements for the Planetary Forces...

Two armored vehicles approached. Jimmy hid behind a trash can while the vehicles drove off.

An agitated cat startled Jimmy, who fell against the trash can and broke the silence. House lights turned on while dogs barked at the sudden noise from garbage spilling onto the road of dirtied melting snow.

A man stuck out his foot and stopped the rolling trash can's momentum. "What the fuck are you doing out here with that white climate suit? Are you begging to die?"

Jimmy spotted the insignia of a flaming sword on the man's black shirt. "What are you doing with that shirt and without a helmet? It looks like you're the one who wants to die."

Two additional Lords of the Wolf Blade appeared, joining

their fellow member to size up Jimmy in the dark.

The first Lord drew his handgun and shoved Jimmy. "Take off your helmet."

"You need to get out of here as much as I do. If anyone in these houses informs on us, we're history."

"Not quite. We've always got time for a rumble against a Renegade. You're probably a half-breed, aren't you? You're corrupted with the blood of the—"

A bullet from Katie's shotgun brought the life of the first brawler to a screeching halt.

Jimmy pulled out two handguns and hit the remaining two Lords with a shot apiece, killing them before they hit the concrete.

Jimmy looked back and saw Katie with no suit or uniform. She stood there without uttering a word. Jimmy picked up his bag and dashed to the edge of the city while the sky lit up behind him. He heard screams echoing, mixing with grenades and gunshots. He fled the residential neighborhoods before informants could turn him in. Jimmy's breathing accelerated, and the streets he traveled gave way to grass, and then to embankments of slush and snow. At the end of the city, snowfields lay ahead.

A group of guards without uniforms or protective gear stopped Jimmy in his tracks. The group stopped and flaunted their weapons from within their all-terrain vehicle. The leader hopped out in his cowboy attire. "You're going the wrong way if you want to reach the Boshquire Mountains."

"How do you know I want to get to the Boshquire Mountains?"

"There's no place else to go...not around here. Those streets you left, the remaining homes would scare off any human or ghost. Tell me something, stranger, are you a human or a ghost?"

"I need to get to the Boshquires. I need to get there today."

"We're supposed to shoot you on site. That's the order from the Planetary Forces. You know you can take your headgear off. It's too hot for that, even if it's breathable. Well? How about it, Jimmy Englewood?"

"How about what? You think I'm surprised you guessed who I am?"

"I've guessed nothing. Isn't that right, fellas? Oh, stop looking so angry. Your face is lit up. You must've turned on your helmet's inner light when you started running or something. It was a mistake. We all make them. By the way, my name is Billy."

"I guess everyone has seen my picture now. I'll go ahead and turn this light off if you don't mind."

"No, I don't mind at all. Hop on in, but it's going to cost you."

Jimmy settled into the vehicle. "How much is it going to cost me? I don't have a lot of money. I didn't know money had value anymore."

"Sure it does. But don't you fret. We'll make a deal."

The weeks of bright sun and warm temperatures had melted a lot of the ice on the outer edges of town, but snow crystals remained in the fields and gleamed in the starlight.

"Where are the reinforcements, Billy? I mean the reinforcements for the Planetary Forces. I thought they'd be pouring into Marganis and every surrounding area by now."

"I know what you're thinking, but there's no time to find Bethany's body. Even if all that ice and snow melt, what are we going to do? Besides, we're heading toward forests in the Boshquires, not the burned down woods between those fields leading to the Orcasso Sea. We wouldn't be able to find her body if it's even still there."

"You don't know what I'm thinking. I asked you what's holding up the reinforcements. Do you have an answer or not?"

Billy directed the driver to stop the vehicle. "Jimmy, I want you to listen to me very closely. If anyone from the climate regime finds out we're helping you, then they'll throw us in a dungeon or labor camp beyond the Boshquires."

"Don't be so sure. I know as well as you do that those labor camps are going to become a lot worse than they are, remodeled for exterminations. None of us want to be on the receiving end of the impending holocaust. You won't get out of it by turning me in."

"We can buy ourselves more time by unloading you. We left our post, but there's still time to turn back and leave you out here to fend for yourself. A little appreciation is in order. I suggest you show some of it, and fast. I'm in the driver's seat. You're just along for the ride."

"I'm grateful. I want to help you guys as much as you're

helping me. We all know this is the last chance we have to fight back while they're distracted."

Billy and his four accomplices laughed. Billy kept his own laugh going a little longer. "Fight back? You must've been a comedian in the old days. You're talking about fighting, but you're moving away from the fight. Is this some sort of special strategy we've never heard of?"

Jimmy took off his headgear. "Never been a comedian, but I am dead serious. Getting to the Boshquires is part of the fight. Now, what is it? What's the reason Zack is so slow to get reinforcements? I was out in the wild for a long time. It's been years since I lived in Marganis. I know a lot, but I don't know everything about my home city anymore."

"Donnie, start this vehicle back up. Head for the Boshquires."

Donnie turned on the engine and gunned the covered vehicle, part truck and part snowmobile, across the terrain.

Billy looked back toward Marganis. "Bethany's Rootsville Coalition destroyed the old gates, Englewood. You know that as well as anyone. You also know that once we get to the Boshquires, you'll have to walk. This vehicle wasn't made for steep climbs through thickets up rocky soil."

"I understand, but what about the climate regime reinforcements?"

"I couldn't tell you. That's your mess to clean up if you can."

Fires and smoke engulfed Marganis. Billy's crew and Jimmy could see it during their drive. No air battles unfolded. Everything stayed on the ground, but missile battles broke out as the sun rose. Everyone on the all-terrain vehicle watched a barrage of missiles strike Marganis's tallest building. The launch came from the peaks of the Boshquires, hurtling calamitous projectiles into the old metropolis.

Billy turned away from watching the crumbling buildings of the city. "You want to hear the situation about reinforcements? The Planetary Forces are fighting the Lords of the Wolf Blade in many parts of the world. The Planetary Forces are winning that war, but it's going to rage for a while. Leaders of the climate regime have limited resources and manpower they can supply to Marganis or anywhere to fight the Renegades and the Lords at the same time."

A number of vehicles crossed the same plains on the way to and from Marganis. Some informal groups of Renegades joined the fight in the city. Others who witnessed the assault abandoned Marganis to find refuge and live to fight another day or year.

Jimmy shook his head. "This can't be. Why haven't they caught me already."

"Englewood, sometimes you outsmart them. Sometimes they're tied up with the Lords. Remember that they want to keep you alive. That makes it tricky to capture you, and sometimes they just can't get out of their own way. This is the biggest bureaucracy the planet has ever seen. The regime also hasn't solidified all its power yet."

"Bethany's father, Greg Norbannick, told me the Planetary

Order wants to break my will as a sign to spread fear and control. They want to publicize my breakdown and show they can crush anyone. It just doesn't make sense. I'm not the toughest or the smartest."

"They want to break the everyday man. You fit that mold for them. It's the everyday man they want to destroy more than anything. You're the type they understand least and fear most."

"You're as normal as I am, Billy. As a matter of fact, you're more normal than I am. Why aren't they after you in the same way?"

"My life isn't the same as yours, Englewood. The mountains are in sight. Let's drop you off a little further up."

"What do I owe you for the ride?"

"Just a simple promise that you'll return to Marganis."

"Return to a burned-down Marganis?"

"Take your bag, Englewood, and put your helmet back on. You're going to need it."

"I can feel the chill already here at base level. The weather's turning quicker than expected."

"Yes, it is. Alright, Donnie, throw on the rest of your gear and I'll drive from here. Jimmy, Donnie's going with you. I don't need to know anything you're doing. I don't want to know. Remember, both of you, there are enemy forces on the mountain peaks. Who knows what's between here and there? I sure don't."

Jimmy looked up the mountain. "I can't say 'no' to some help. Thank you, Billy. I'm in your debt. I vow to enter my city once again...someday."

Jimmy and Billy shook hands, and the early morning daylight fell prisoner to thick clouds on the fringes of the Marganisan Valley.

15

INTO THE ICE

The heat spell ended.

A gargantuan mountain chain rose from the ground in front of Jimmy and Donnie. The Boshquires challenged them from the start of the climb. An imposing collection of pinnacles, boulders, and glaciers menaced all people attempting to traverse the terrain outside Marganis in the new ice age. Avalanches threatened any who scaled the unpredictable mountains.

Jimmy and Donnie headed straight for Marganisan Peak, where Planetary Forces set up a base at the top. Jimmy knew the enemy held Linda Norbannick captive somewhere on that particular mountain. The topography threatened the climb from the outset.

Donnie panted in the early stages of the climb. "Hey Jimmy, what's the real reason you're here? I know it wasn't to take out the enemy base. Billy didn't need to know, but I'm a different story."

"I'm here to rescue a woman. She's family. Whoa! Watch your step."

"Are you expecting a lot of injuries?"

"I'm just hoping they're all minor ones."

"Funny guy. So, who is it we're looking for?"

"She's family, like I just said."

"A cousin? A grandmother? Who are we talking about?"

"Donnie, I'm not getting into it. You can barely talk without losing your breath as it is. Maybe you should turn around."

"I'll kick on the oxygen."

"This climb to Marganisan Peak is as steep a climb as there is."

"You'll have to excuse me, Jimmy. The Lords of the Wolf Blade slaughtered half my family. The old Marganisan City Forces and their goons murdered the other half."

"I'm sorry, Donnie. I know every part of what you're going through."

"No, you don't. All of us have murdered family. You still have some family left. I have nothing."

"The Planetary Order and the HAVE movement bear responsibility for the murder of my unborn...never mind. This is about what's best for this mission, and for you."

"I have to stay. I have to help you. You need my help."

"Stop walking. Turn around, Donnie. Go back to the vehicle. This climb isn't for you. Billy and the rest of your group will be circling the area and staying at the base of the mountain for a couple of hours. We have no way to communicate with them. You have to leave now."

"I can reach the summit."

"I know you can, but you've been through enough. I can almost see the look on your face, and you are done with the fight. You have a different role to play in this saga. Find peace, my friend. Your family of friends is down at the base. You outlived the old scavengers of the city and the extinct Marganisan Enforcers. Leave while you still have a chance at life."

Jimmy had not seen a grown man cry in years. It was exactly a decade ago. He could not see Donnie's face underneath the helmet, but he knew that quiet tears fell from Donnie's shielded eyes. He knew that those kinds of tears could overcome the most battle-tested man at the end of an era in the man's life.

Jimmy continued alone...

Each step was tougher than the last. The footing became increasingly perilous. Snowfall resumed, intensifying on the windward side of the mountain. The leeward side was unscalable, but no concern of Jimmy's for the time being.

In the recent heat wave, weeks had passed without a drop of white condensation from the sky. Even in the Boshquires, only rain had fallen upon the pinnacles, pathways, and tenacious plant life. The trees had benefited from a fleeting chance to warm and drink the precipitation in a heat spell reminiscent of days gone by.

The gradient finally decreased and sloped downward, providing Jimmy's legs and back some much-needed relief after two hours of climbing the perilous ground. Snowfall turned into the lightest of flurries as he approached the lake. Jimmy found a soft patch of ground, dropped his bag, and sat against a smooth rock under a collection of dead trees that could shield him from the enemy's sight. The Renegade held a handgun on his lap while his eyes closed against his will for a dreamless hour.

Jimmy woke up. After a minute on his feet, he arrived at Boshquire Lake. The water encompassed a much smaller area and volume than the colossal lake in the tropics where Jimmy narrowly escaped with his life. This was no jungle region. It had its own hazards. Facing the partially frozen body of water, Jimmy confronted a new challenge. He could either make his way across without falling through the veneer of thinning ice, or he could try to get past the bear blocking his way on the lone and narrow trail in this portion of the mountains.

The mountain wall stood too steeply for anyone to scale in rough weather, even with ropes and experience.

Several yards away from Jimmy, the brown bear got up on his hind legs. Jimmy raised his weapon and aimed. About to pull the trigger several times, he held off from firing as long as he could.

The bear lowered himself on all four legs just before the critical moment Jimmy would have had to fire. The animal turned and walked back in the direction from which he had approached, and the Renegade exhaled.

A light wind crept through the elevated valley that sheltered

Lake Boshquire. Jimmy could hear his memories of Bethany's voice while gazing over the calm, partially frozen body of water. The Renegade wondered what berries or fish the bear might find, and he followed him.

Jimmy admired his surroundings. He delighted in every step the bear took crunching over hard ground and snapping every branch along the path. The animal disappeared into the coniferous woods. Jimmy paused by the edge of the lake and washed his hands under a small, shallow fracture of ice by the lakeshore. The crisp water snapped him back into focus to find Linda. Jimmy picked up his supply pack, threw it over his shoulders, and quickened his stride past the lake.

Trees in the forest did not reach the heights of the giants in the woods by the Orcasso Sea. Still, none of the trees standing before Jimmy found themselves leveled or clearcut like those larger evergreens near the ocean.

Jimmy found the Boshquire mountains unspoiled, for the moment out of the reach or care of the Planetary Forces atop Marganisan Peak.

It stopped snowing. No flurries. Even the light wind trailed off.

Something spooked Jimmy about the excessive silence. The eerie feeling made its presence known most strongly when cracked by reverberating gunshots across the trees and lake valley.

Jimmy picked up the pace. He hurried into the forest and heard terrible groans. He followed the cries deeper through the woods, knowing the cries would lead him to an atrocity. Weaving through the conifers, he saw the great creature writhing in pain but too injured to strike out or hobble off.

The bear had no strength to swipe at Jimmy. An animal lay at death's door, shot by someone lurking in the forest. Jimmy rested his head on the bear's chest, which slowly expanded and contracted. In an instant, the bear's chest stilled, and his senses disintegrated.

Before Jimmy could grab his own handgun, someone pointed one at Jimmy's head. The soldier wore the bright red climate suit of the Planetary Forces. He attempted to call his superiors, but the communication device malfunctioned. "Take off your headgear. Do it now before you join that bear you seem to care about so much."

Jimmy took off his helmet. "Now, you take off yours."

"Fat chance of that. You're Jimmy Englewood. Everybody's looking for you."

"Everybody? That's a lot of people, soldier."

"We're leaving the mountain, Englewood."

"Why would we do that? I know. Your climate forces off the mountain are closer to us than the ones on it. It's at least an hour's trip back to base level. You sure you can handle it?"

"Quit your smirking, you human virus. Bring your bag with you. There's a punishment awaiting your arrival."

"Punishment sounds scary. I committed the gravest sin of all to your religion, didn't I? I broke lockdown orders. What a pity."

"Enough delays. You're going with me."

"Not quite, soldier."

"You think I'm afraid to kill you?"

"Why of course not? I would never question the manhood of a guy who shoots a bear for no reason at all. You're no coward. Shooting a bear must be the bravest thing a man can do, and it's definitely the highest calling among all humanity."

"Keep mocking me, you fucking bitch. Orders or no orders, I will dismember you. I don't need to bring you back alive. I won't warn you again. Grab your bag and lead the way off the fucking mountain."

"What's behind you, you brave warrior for climate justice?"

The soldier turned around and stared into the barrel of a gun.

Jimmy moved toward the soldier. "If you want to keep your face intact, drop your gun and find your way off the mountain. She'll shoot you and feel no remorse."

Katie pressed her weapon firmly against the soldier's back. "He's right. No remorse at all. Take off your headgear."

"Why should I remove anything? You're just going to kill me, anyway."

Jimmy pulled off the helmet. "You like to slaughter wildlife for fun. We're not like that, with wildlife or humans. We'll let you live if you're smart enough to take us up on our offer."

The soldier dropped his weapon, and Katie lowered hers.

Jimmy and Katie marched the soldier out of the forest, to the beginning of the pathway around the partially frozen Boshquire Lake.

Jimmy gave the soldier back his helmet. "This is where we part company. Your weapon is our prize. Oh, and take this message to your bosses...the planet isn't warming."

The soldier tried to grab Katie's weapon, but Jimmy swung him off the trail and onto the ice-covered lake. As the soldier tried to get up, the frozen sheet under his feet broke apart. He lifted himself out of the shallow water as quickly as he could. Jimmy shot him in the ribs and back into the water. Katie kicked his headgear into the lake, and the climate soldier of the Planetary Forces clutched the headgear before nature formed a large casket for him under blocks of ice.

Snowfall returned, and Jimmy and Katie ventured into the conifers.

Katie almost tripped over the dead brown bear. "He shot it, didn't he? That climate regime soldier slaughtered the animal. That's what you were talking about back by the lake. I heard the gunshots and rushed. I thought it was you who shot someone or got taken out. Never would've guessed it was a bear."

"They're sick, Katie. The whole thing is sick. They're out of their minds in every possible way."

"You're not even going to ask how I got here? You didn't want the help, did you? That's the real reason you sent Donnie away."

"I'm surprised you crossed paths. I guess all three of us know some of the unknown backcountry terrain up and down the mountain."

"There are only two of us."

"How?"

Katie put on her helmet. "The Planetary Forces mowed him down at base level when he fired at them. He was just about to get into a vehicle. Soldiers jumped out of an all-terrain armored personnel carrier. The rest is history."

"What vehicle? Billy's? Who was in the vehicle he was getting into?"

"I don't know. Who's Billy? I heard an explosion, so I think the Planetary Forces blew it up. Unless...unless Donnie's group blew up the armored personnel carrier that took him out."

"This makes a big difference. You don't know what happened? Let's move faster."

"They didn't see me, Jimmy. I had to keep hidden as best I could behind boulders. I started my way up the mountain when I looked back from a distance and saw them shoot Donnie."

"What did you talk about when you crossed paths near the base of the mountain?"

"We almost shot each other. We figured out what was going on when I described you and asked him whether you met. He thought Renegades or the Planetary Order treated the soil to enable forest survival. Donnie wanted you to know that about the soil. That's it. We talked for 30 seconds. He wanted to go back up with me."

"Dammit, Katie! What are you doing here? This is the easiest part of the climb. It's dangerous out here."

"You don't think I know it's dangerous?! What the hell is your problem? You don't remember my family and I were with you at the Battle of Marganis? You don't remember we set up explosives and encouraged old Renegades to fight in the battle? Bethany was my sister long before she was your wife!"

"Take it easy. Someone will hear us and track us down. I don't doubt you can make your way through the mountains as well as you can the city. But Katie, this is my mission. If they capture one of us, we're both screwed. And you can say whatever you want. You're a woman. You're in greater danger from these lunatics than I could ever be."

"If you think this is a mission for one, then turn back and I'll rescue Linda myself. I still remember the early days when no women had to fight. Our country's old army is gone. All of us are now on the front lines. I'm going with you whether you like it or not."

"I give up, Katie. Alright, you can join me. This operation isn't just about Linda anymore. Your dad knew that before I left the basement hideout."

"Tell me, what more is the operation about?"

"The seeds of a Renegade resurgence."

16

ASCENDING

Fierce winds swept over the mountains. The temperature nosedived during the short transition from the heat spell back to the cold. Frigid air became the norm almost everywhere on Earth, and that reality returned with a vengeance. The climate gear kept Jimmy and Katie warm. The snow and ice, however, made ascending the mountain a demanding obstacle beyond anything either Renegade had previously attempted.

Jimmy lifted his mask for water. The wind smacked him with a reminder that life on the planet no longer provided the heat to which anyone had grown accustomed before the new ice age. The weather was cold. Society was cold. Everything lost fluidity.

Katie carried a small bag, less encumbering but with fewer provisions than Jimmy carried.

"I'm responsible for you, Katie."

"Did you say something?! Turn around to talk to me! The

wind, it's too loud!"

"Forget it! The mountain feels shaky! I'm off balance!"

"Hey! Look over there!"

An avalanche gathered steam down a neighboring mountain.

"You feel that, Katie!?"

"It's an earthquake!"

"Hold on! Drop to the ground!"

The rumble lasted for 90 seconds, with snow, boulders, and trees following gravity's lead down the neighboring mountain. Everything rattled, then abruptly stopped shaking.

"Watch it, Katie! Debris is still falling! We'll wait it out! It should be 30 seconds tops if we don't have an avalanche on this mountain!"

No avalanche happened on the path to Marganisan Peak, but a blizzard assembled and reduced visibility to where Jimmy and Katie could step off the ledge and plunge to their deaths.

The land flattened out for a brief part of the climb. "Jimmy! It's a rock shelter! Let's take cover!"

"Finally, we don't have to yell. The problem is the higher we get, the worse these storms are going to be. These air currents are brutal. I don't know how we can make it to the top, and I didn't think we needed rope. Linda's got to be up at the peak. It's the only place they could hold be holding her hostage. Let's keep moving."

"I can't lose my last sister, Jimmy. Losing Bethany broke my heart. It will break my heart every day for the rest of my life. But

I still have Linda."

"Alright, when the storm dies down, we'll head back out. In the meantime, we have some covering. I just haven't figured out how we're going to reach the pinnacle."

"None of us have any of this figured out. We're all just making it up as we go along. I don't remember whether there's a natural problem with the climate or whether the Planetary Order created this."

"I don't think there's anything to remember. Nobody ever told us anything, and nobody ever will. The only thing we know is that a planetary dictatorship is consolidating its power. They've made themselves and half the world crazy."

"Sometimes it feels like we've all gone mad."

"It might feel that way, but I know this climate narrative is an abject lie. You know it like I do. Katie, let's find a path to the summit."

Katie pointed toward the innermost region of the sheltered area with a flashlight. "I think I just figured it out...if that's what I think it is."

"Yes! I'm seeing the outline. Let's see if it works and find your sister."

Jimmy and Katie marveled at the aircraft they found. Unconcerned about why anyone abandoned it, the two of them entered. Somebody had left the small aircraft open to climb on board. Jimmy powered on the controls, which all checked out as operational after running simple tests.

"Can you believe it, Jimmy? A Renegade vessel left here?"

"It's a gift from above. This is just the right match for what we need. We can put this on semi-autopilot. I'll help it navigate. The only problem is the weapons systems. We're limited on those, but it looks like the defenses are strong enough for such a small aircraft. The maneuverability is the best. So is the speed. It's easy to conceal the ship at high and low speeds."

"Any other problems with the ship?"

"Not problems. We just can't keep this ship as steady at this elevation as we could at base level. The mountain weather and its air currents will bring us turbulence."

"Anything else?"

"Distance."

"What about it?"

"Distance is a limiting factor, vertically and horizontally."

"Meaning what?"

"Meaning we can speed up quickly. We can hover, take off, and land easily. We cannot sustain a long chase, whether we're being chased or doing the chasing. And we can only bring this aircraft so far up in the sky before it loses power, speed, maneuverability, you name it."

"Jimmy, it's clearing up. The worst of this storm is over."

"Not yet. The blizzard just went to sleep for a while, but we can't wait. Eventually, they'll track us here. Look at how easy it was for you to find me. Get ready for takeoff."

"I'm ready."

Jimmy instructed the vessel to exit the sheltered area slowly. The aircraft hugged the mountain and ascended at a snail's pace to locate where the Planetary Forces kept Linda, and to glimpse the military operations at the Marganisan Peak outpost.

The vessel searched the mountain during its ascent. From time to time, Jimmy would steer into a depression or flat clearing when he found one. No enemy detected the Renegades, and the Renegades detected no enemy forces.

"Jimmy we're miles up in the sky. We have no instruments or devices to communicate with other Renegades or anyone at all. We don't know what we're doing."

"Yes, we do. We're approaching the pinnacle, but the weather is going to turn on us again, and this is the region where they launch the missiles. We're going to land over there in that clearing."

"It's too far above the tree line, and we don't have any rock formations to hide behind. We'll be exposed."

"It's too risky for them at this elevation to scatter all their forces. If we land up there at the highest platform, they'll notice us and attack. All we can do is land in the clearing and walk the rest of the way."

Jimmy prepared the aircraft for landing, but the ground appeared to shift. "Is that the wind or something else? It looks like something else. It's an aftershock!"

"Jimmy, pull the ship back up!"

"It's too late! Brace for collision!"

The aircraft crashed down, staying right side up but spinning and sliding on the ice toward the edge of the mountain.

"Katie, are you hurt?!"

"No, but look outside! We're hanging over the ledge."

"The aftershock is still going. We can't get out of the ship if we slide any farther. I can't open the exit. We're stuck!"

The aftershock attenuated. The wind currents escalated.

"Jimmy!"

"I'm powering back on and opening the exit. It's open! I'm out! Unfasten yourself."

"It won't unfasten!"

"Katie, the ship is sliding off!"

"I hit something! The exit's closing. It's closing!"

"Katie!"

A final gust knocked Jimmy down and the sent the vessel over the edge.

Jimmy watched over the side. The aircraft fell with Katie inside. Jimmy had no help and no provisions beyond what he had in his climate suit. He lay stranded in enemy territory toward the summit of Marganisan Peak.

It was an hour's worth of treacherous climbing to the enemy platform. No ropes required, but Jimmy felt his energy depleting.

Chilling as it was to see the aircraft slide off the mountain with Katie stuck inside, Jimmy kept his mission in focus. He increased his climate gear's oxygen flow and climbed the rest of the mountain with no tree cover, rock cover, or protection from the elements. Snowfall whipped across the clouds. Jimmy defied the conditions and reached the Marganisan Peak outpost of the Planetary Forces.

A collection of living quarters, open spaces, and rocket systems spread across the enemy base. Nowhere did Jimmy spot a likely place where the Planetary Forces would hold Linda hostage.

Jimmy peered from between several boulders, watching vehicles patrol the perimeter. He estimated that several hundred soldiers inhabited Marganisan Peak. Jimmy found the view surprisingly clear at the mountain top despite constant snowfall and heavy winds. He kept his two guns holstered while noticing climate regime soldiers clearing ice from the terrain. The soldiers cleaned as many walkways as they could.

The enemy protected ten small aircraft. Soldiers kept busy marching and carrying out orders to launch missiles on command into Marganis. Jimmy ran lower on water and ammo than he expected, but the notion of getting caught and failing to rescue Linda plagued his mind more than anything else.

No flags flew. Instead, the Planetary Forces had the Order's emblem etched into the front facades of the living quarters. Jimmy concentrated on the symbol, an ax splitting the Earth in half down a longitudinal line, with a bright red background. He wondered how anybody could fall for the line about saving the planet. He knew the HAVE movement, Humans and Animals Are Viruses on Earth, despised everything about the Earth, its inhabitants, and its resources. Still, he recognized the climate regime would do everything it could to perpetuate itself. He calculated the Planetary Order needed to leave some portion of world undestroyed to establish irreversible global dominance.

Jimmy sank deeper into his thoughts. He studied the flag emblem and remembered Jesse and Bethany's other friends in the Rootsville Coalition being blown up on the icy beach of the Orcasso Sea.

The strident sound of missiles intruded on Jimmy's mind midstream. Planetary Forces were bombarding Marganis.

Jimmy leaped over the rocks and ran onto the enemy's base. He knew there would be video surveillance, but that did not matter to him. He had to take advantage of all the soldiers tied up with the latest round of missile firings. Jimmy saw they were clearing out from the middle of the base. He could see everything he needed to see across the terrain, except for Linda.

Katie never knew about Jimmy's escape plan. Neither did Jimmy, because he never had one.

Jimmy sought revenge on as many soldiers as possible. He planned to blow up vehicles and infrastructure. Having left his bag in the ship, Jimmy concluded his plan meant nothing.

After two minutes, Jimmy reached the base, hiding behind what looked like a dining hall. The missiles and missile launchers and platforms were still a couple of minutes away, anchored toward the end of the peak and facing the Marganisan Valley. The Planetary Forces had erected a small command-and-control center in close proximity to the missiles. Most of the vehicles on base stopped circulating so that the soldiers could help with missile launches and intercept potential incoming fire.

The Planetary Forces spotted Jimmy on surveillance cameras. A group of soldiers filed out of a dorm to capture him. All the while, the enemy sprayed Marganis with missiles, muting Jimmy's ability to hear anyone encroaching.

Suddenly, Jimmy saw the group of soldiers running toward him. He drew his two handguns.

"You're surrounded, Englewood. Drop the weapons!"

The mountain shook again, but this time it was no earthquake or aftershock. Explosives poured onto Marganisan Peak.

A gun battle ensued as Renegade hovercraft fired on the nine soldiers surrounding Jimmy. He ran from the distracted enemy combatants and emptied his cartridge into one of them. Jimmy ducked behind an outer corridor of the dining hall while Renegade aircraft bombed the command-and-control center.

Shocked Planetary Forces scrambled to launch their own vessels. They launched them too late to stop the Renegades from blowing up the command-and-control center and personnel inside. The Renegades then switched their attention to the missiles, missile launchers, and soldiers of the Planetary Forces, though the damage already inflicted on Marganis devastated the city and its population.

The Planetary Forces shot down four of ten renegade aircraft with aircraft of their own. They fired most of their remaining artillery and anti-aircraft weapons to no avail.

Jimmy re-entered the fight. He gunned down two enemy soldiers while running to a vessel he noticed near the obliterated enemy missile launchers. The vessel hovered over a landing space, waiting for Jimmy to board.

Enemy aircraft had a ten to six advantage on Renegade aircraft, excluding the aircraft waiting for Jimmy. The vessel await-ing him gunned down as many soldiers and ground vehicles as it could with limited weaponry.

A bullet brushed past Jimmy's left leg. It missed his skin, though it tore his climate gear.

Jimmy recognized the hovering vessel awaiting his entrance. He sprinted while he and the vessel both dodged enemy fire.

The vessel faced another wave of assault from enemy ground vehicles. With enemy aircraft tied up in aerial combat, Jim-my sprinted faster than he ever did. The vessel's stairs opened, and the vessel fired back with the last of its ammunition. The firepower cleared the ground surrounding Jimmy, who sprang through the air. He caught a latch with both hands at the bottom of the stairs. He had nothing but air and jagged peaks under his feet for a mile while the vessel flew away from the heat and explosions of the battle. Jimmy pulled himself inside. He secured himself in a seat before the vehicle rocketed out of the Boshquire Mountains.

17

DESCENDING

Katie took off her helmet. "Are you shocked?"

Jimmy took off his. "No. I'm relieved you're alive. I couldn't find Linda. She could still be at the summit. She could've died in the fighting. Who knows if they even brought her to Marganisan Peak."

"I don't know if you noticed that this aircraft I kept alive is the same one Linda stole. It didn't sink in for me until later that it was originally a Renegade vessel. I can tell by the way it's built."

"I'm telling you I failed to find your sister."

"She's still being held hostage. This whole thing was a massive deception. Zack led us to believe this. He let us think we would have a chance at finding my sister if you turned yourself over to the climate regime."

"That doesn't add up, Katie. They would've been waiting for

me."

"You almost got taken out in Marganis. As much as they want to catch you, they've got other battles to fight. Aren't you glad I gained control of the ship?"

"Who taught you to fly?"

"My parents and Bethany. I had to set it on automatic for a while and I can't maneuver that well, but you and I got off Marganisan Peak alive."

"You knew Linda wouldn't be there."

"I knew as soon as I came back. I hovered off the side until I saw Renegade vessels approach the mountain."

"Before that, how far did you drop after the vehicle slipped off the cliff?"

"I was in free fall. I found the auto-hover at about 1000 feet and stabilized the vessel at 100."

"Linda had to be here. What would the vessel she stole be doing tucked inside that large, sheltered area?"

"Jimmy, they had to fly her somewhere else, in a marked enemy aircraft. This aircraft she stole has no markings and has all the trademarks of being built as a Renegade vessel."

"She's in Zack's captivity as we speak."

"We have to find her, Jimmy. We have to. We have to honor the small group of Renegade aircraft that didn't stand a snowball's chance of winning that battle back there. Wait. It's slowing down. The vessel's slowing down."

"It isn't slowing down...it's dying. I'll pilot us from here."

"Hurry up!"

"I've got it, Katie. This will be close. Brace again for impact."

The aircraft plowed into a snow pile and just missed an embankment.

"Katie, talk to me."

"Jimmy, I never want to fly again."

"Can you get up?"

"I'll unfasten myself and try."

"Easy getting out, We're at about a 30-degree angle."

"At least we're alive. You won't have to see another Norbannick buried in the snow today."

"This vessel is dead. I'm going to replace this torn climate suit with a fresh one my bag and step outside. In the meantime, gather whatever provisions you can."

"Where are we?"

Jimmy opened the door. "Canyons. This dead aircraft was fast. We're in the canyons well beyond the Marganisan Valley and Boshquire Mountains. Take a look."

A river stretched out with snowbanks and steep rock walls on either side. Jimmy and Katie looked across the whitewater surging through the narrow passageway.

"Jimmy, the deep freeze is back. At least this river still flows, and it isn't as cold here as in the mountains. It's too rocky to make our way through here on a boat. There's a thin pathway on either side."

"Look in the other direction, Katie. It opens up away from the canyon into the snowfields."

"Endless snowfields until we're back to the Boshquires. We'll die without a vehicle to travel that direction. At least here we have a chance. The pathway through this narrow canyon could lead to a city."

"A city? Have you lost your mind?"

"A town. A village. Something. We could find a way to contact Renegades. We can't do that if we go backwards."

Jimmy closed the door. "Alright, let's enter the canyons in the morning. Bring everything we need. This is the last time we'll ever see this vessel. If we don't make it beyond the canyon, we're dead."

The two Renegades slept in the aircraft. Jimmy got up in the middle of the night and watched the planets and stars through a window. The cosmos hovered peacefully above the snow and ice that smothered the canyon. Jimmy could not hear the river through the soundproof vessel, but the roaring water played in his mind. The dead ship meant only basic manual controls still worked, including opening and closing the hatch and short stairwell. The temperature in the aircraft dropped in the absence of a functional heating system. Jimmy faded back to sleep.

Snow showers began just before dawn.

The river cut straight through the canyon. High rock arches with densely packed crystals shielded Jimmy and Katie from some of the snowfall.

"That didn't feel like a real breakfast, Jimmy."

"I miss bacon. It would've been nice to cook. We'll have to wait until we commandeer another one of our own aircraft."

Katie smiled for about two seconds before the thought of

impending and absolute planetary tyranny struck her in the solar plexus.

"What's going on, Katie. Are you alright? We should throw our helmets back on."

"Yeah, I'm more concerned with the sharp hanging crystals than the low temps."

Jimmy and Katie walked for miles, hugging the left side of the river. The narrow and slippery passageway forced them to move in single file. They had much less room than on the path at Boshquire Lake. The thick air around the river hinted to them that they walked somewhere around sea level.

Jimmy stared down at the whitewater. "This canyon looks like an endless maze. It's got to be a bridge to somewhere."

"The maze is changing. We're not five feet higher than the river anymore. It's only three feet."

"It'll keep dropping before the embankment gets submerged and it's all just the river with no archway and no pathway. Glad we didn't take the passageway on the right side. See, it's already disappearing."

"We can't turn around."

"You're right. We didn't bring enough with us. We've got one choice, and you know what that is."

"Are you kidding? How can we possibly—"

"You're a Norbannick. Use your imagination."

"I don't know how Bethany could stand you. I really don't."

Sword-sharp crystals fell from the rock arches in the mid-afternoon sun of clearing skies. Snow and ice churned up the riverbank to mix with mud, while the water rose quickly to the bottoms of the Renegades' boots.

They ran, as fast as they could, with Jimmy in the lead. Fast was not fast at all. Friction underneath their feet dissipated with every step while the ice crystals smashed onto the pathway and into the river. Losing traction, they slid and skidded down the long passage that sloped down to a foot above the currents to their right.

The whitewater emptied into a wider body, just past the archway and canyon opening. Jimmy and Katie reached the end of the passageway. With the river foaming at the tops of their boots, they jumped into the water. The volume and velocity carried them past the last of the shiny rocks smacked by torrents. The inescapable current slicing through narrow canyon gave way to a broadening and deepening river. In quick succession, both Renegades fell beneath the bone-freezing surface.

Climate suits, including the helmets and air and oxygen supply system, kept Jimmy and Katie alive. The frigid river could not pierce the protective gear, and the Renegades felt nothing more than the forces of the rough-and-tumble water.

The current weakened, allowing Jimmy and Katie to resurface while they swam sideways for the shore. They re-submerged several times before reaching the left bank of the river.

Jimmy pulled Katie out of the water and buckled to the ground. Ice, snow, and silt welcomed them to a large area of treeless terrain. Broad swaths of arches and canyons filled the background. The geologic marvels soaked in the sun and stored all the heat they could capture.

Jimmy took off his helmet. Crawling along the riverbank, he lay down flat across a patch of clay. "At least it isn't snowing."

Katie removed her headgear and laughed. "A lot more room to move around."

Jimmy watched the birds fishing in the cold, fast-flowing water of a river that killed less fortunate Renegades. "I'm glad you can laugh, Katie. That's it. Keep laughing. We made it. We made it."

"My face is freezing, but I had to feel the air. We made it."

"Let's keep moving."

All they had left were handguns, medical supplies, drinking water, and any small items like flashlights they could fit in their suits.

"I'll get up, but where are we now, Englewood?"

A stranger hovered over Katie, stepping between her and the sun. "Hello, Renegade."

Jimmy rushed over, only to be met by two other men with gray climate gear like the first stranger. Glancing at the water, he saw a small, anchored ship with four additional crew members.

The man hovering over Katie helped her up. He directed her and Jimmy to enter the vessel. "I'm Orion, and this is my crew. We have no flying capacity on this ship, but we won't need it."

Jimmy slowly pulled out a handgun and pointed it at the ground. "How do I know you? It's your face. I recognize you."

"I know you do. I'm Billy's younger brother. He made contact."

Jimmy's arms and hands relaxed. "Billy's alive?"

"No. I could hear him dying, and then my communication device cut off. He informed us they were under attack by Planetary Forces, but that we should be on the lookout for you in case you survived Marganisan Peak."

"You don't talk like him."

"I'm not him."

"Sorry I'm being this way. You just lost your brother."

"Yes, I did, and mourning for him will have to wait. I didn't expect you to be with someone else, Jimmy Englewood. Who is this lovely young lady?"

Katie stepped in front of Jimmy. "I can speak for myself, Orion. I'm Katie. Are you guys Renegades?"

"We don't belong to anything. We're just survivors, like my brother was before he wasn't."

Jimmy boarded the unenclosed ship. "Billy was more than a survivor."

Orion laughed. "I'm surviving what Billy couldn't...every tyrannical legion on Earth."

Jimmy grimaced. "I promised Billy I'd make it back to Marganis."

"I don't think it'll be with this group, Englewood, but you might get back there if it's destruction you seek."

"Destruction of me or my enemies? Or are you talking about the land?"

Orion grinned. "Let's all travel down the river together. I don't know if you'll see Marganis again, but you'll see our village in a few minutes."

"I'd ask how you found us, Orion, but it doesn't matter."

"You're right, Jimmy, it doesn't. Put your helmets back on. I'll do the same. The heat spell is officially over, but we're navigational wizards in any conditions, so thank your lucky stars. Hold on. We'll be flying across the water in a few seconds."

Katie took a seat. "I thought you said this thing doesn't fly."

"In the sky, it doesn't. Across the water, you're about to find out."

Orion's ship slowed down when it approached a port opposite the beach where Jimmy and Katie washed up. On the port side of the ship, another extensive array of canyons and wild rock formations greeted the crew and their Renegade passengers. On the starboard side, the ship pulled up to dock at an astonishing village. Jimmy noticed many of the houses and cottages were made of stone. He saw vibrant cafes, happy dogs playing in the snow, and tall conifers not found on the other side of the river where Orion picked them up.

Orion faced Jimmy. "I know, Englewood. You'll notice right off the bat what we don't have. We have no outdoor eateries. There are no grand ballrooms or towering skyscrapers. It's too cold for kids to play outside for long periods of time without their climate suits. But you know what we do have? We have merchants, craftsmen, and caring families. We have what's gone missing from Marganis and so many other places."

"Missing? You meant stripped away. What more do you have?"

"We have...we have a chance, Jimmy."

"How does that work when the Planetary Order consolidates power worldwide. They'll uproot your village and murder you."

"Let's get off the ship."

Jimmy, Katie, and Orion and his crew splashed through the shallow water.

Orion stayed with Jimmy and Katie while his six men walked onto the shore in all different directions.

Katie turned her head slowly to take in the village. "This is beautiful."

Jimmy threw his hands up. "Sure, it's beautiful. How do you stay hidden? Tell me that, Orion. Why do they let you keep this slice of paradise? If they knew I were here, they'd tear this village down top to bottom."

"What are you accusing me of doing? Who are you accusing me of being?"

"I'm accusing you of belonging to the Planetary Order. You're not some separate group of survivors. You're part of the movement. Don't lie to us. You're part of HAVE."

Katie's face turned white. "Are you part of that movement, Orion? Did you bring us here to interrogate us? Did you bring us here to turn us in?"

"We wanted to. I wanted to more than anyone else did. I want to keep this village shielded from the world's battles. It's just that I could hear something in my brother's voice. Billy turned away from allying with the Planetary Forces. He wanted to get Jimmy out of Marganis alive."

Jimmy shoved Orion. "What about you, huh? You want to keep me alive, Orion?"

Orion shoved Jimmy back. "If I can. My priority is the village, but my brother's mission to help you is now mine. We knew it was all ending."

Katie checked one of her handguns. "What did you know was ending?"

"Everything. Everything in the village and everything in the world. They would never allow the aesthetics of this village to remain. They would never allow us to trade and communicate and talk freely. Planetary Forces will arrive to crush our homes. They'll be here in a week...maybe less."

Jimmy peered into the frosted white hills of the village, wondering when the climate regime soldiers would arrive, and from where.

18

PUNCTURED VILLAGE

Planetary Forces arrived by river and helicopter.

Orion rushed Jimmy and Katie to his house made of stone, scurrying them past frantic crowds. "They're here."

Jimmy glanced at Katie. "And they're a week early."

At the base of a hill, they entered Orion's house.

Orion picked up a machinegun on his table. "I have to meet them outside. They have to think I'm going along with the plan. If they suspect I've turned on them, then it's over for my village. It'll be over for all of us. Take this key to unlock the covering to my underground hideout in the backyard. It's only about ten stairs to climb down."

Katie grabbed Orion's hand. "Thank you for this."

"You're not safe, Katie. All the soldiers down there will be permanent fixtures unless we fight them, but they'll call for reinforcements if we fight them. Remember, they think we recently joined the Planetary Order, so they 're more suspicious of us than anybody else. Stay quiet. They may search the house. If they find you, you won't make it out of here alive. I'll be dead as quicky as you are."

The door rattled.

"Open up, Orion! Open the door before we ransack your place!"

"I'm on my way."

"Now. You have five seconds."

With a second remaining, Orion let in the three visitors.

"Good evening, gentlemen. Right on time and before sundown."

A soldier brushed past Orion while the other two soldiers guarded the door.

"What are you doing, soldier? This is my home."

"This is your what?"

"I'm with you. My entire village is with you. Were part of the Planetary Order, yet you're treating us like Renegades or those demolished rabble-rousing street thugs in the cities. I'm not some climate denier or counterrevolutionary."

The soldier squared up to Orion, nose to nose. "Your brother Billy is dead. So are his men. They betrayed the Planetary Order and collaborated with the enemy. We suspect your entire village of collaborating with the enemy. We're looking for two Renegades, Jimmy Englewood and Katie Norbannick."

"Who sent you?"

"The Comrade of Marganis ordered us to see if they were

here."

"Who's they?"

"I just told you. Men, search the grounds, inside out."

The soldiers trashed every part of the sizable ranch-style home.

"You wouldn't be hiding anything from us, would you, Orion? It's a severe breach of the lockdowns to abet enemies of the climate. You're well aware of all the rules."

"You know I'm well aware of the rules. I'm part of the Planetary Order!"

"That remains to be seen. We cannot allow you to use nature this way anymore. You need special permission to keep a stone-built house. Don't stare me down. No home is anyone's property, you weak-kneed fool. You can use only what we allow. You will join your brother's corpse if you don't give us your complete cooperation."

"Are you an imbecile? I'm not hiding anybody."

"You no longer have a home, but there's plenty of room for you to share this house with us while we transform this village into a more communal setting. Your little commercial center is now a thing of the past. No more cafés or vendors unless approved on a daily basis by Planetary Forces."

"Who are you calling?"

"You'll see."

"Who are you calling?!"

"Zack, we're in Orion's house. We found nothing other than his excessive use of energy resources to heat the home. My men searched and shattered every storefront."

Meanwhile, Jimmy and Katie sat still in the underground bunker in the backyard.

"Jimmy, let's go back up there and fight. They're too stupid to guard the perimeter of the house. Let's make them pay for it."

"I want to, but we can't."

"We're underground, Jimmy, again!"

"They'll hear us if we're too loud."

"They can't hear us down here. They didn't even see the obvious depression and outline in the ground."

"It was a quick sweep of the area. They don't really suspect Orion. They're testing him. Let's hope he passes the test."

"We can't keep hoping. We're running and fighting and running some more. How can we survive this when an army is hunting you?"

"I don't know, Katie, but I have to keep going. We have to keep going. We owe it to everyone and everything we've ever fought for."

"They'll find this place. We should stay on the move, Englewood. I'll keep my flashlight shining on that door. Let's walk through it and see what we find under these hills."

"Open it. Open the door. Just don't be surprised if we have to come back."

Katie unlocked the door and peered into a wider space of a dark underground passageway in the hills. Shadows rushed into the bunker and Jimmy shot all three of them as they approached him through the bottleneck. Two died instantly from two shots a piece.

One shadow lived, dropping to the ground with a bullet lodged in his spleen. "You'd better hope that silencer was quiet enough."

Jimmy's navy-blue eyes fought to see through the darkness. "Never mind that, you bastard. Who are you?"

Katie shined her flashlight on the dying man in the dimly lit bunker. "The flaming sword. The Lords of the Wolf Blade live underground."

Jimmy kept his gun pointed at the man. "Is it as warm in that passageway as it is in this room?"

"Warm? It's back in nature. There is no warmth inside these hollowed hills. Why else would I be wearing a helmet?"

"Katie, take his helmet off."

The dying man smiled at Jimmy. "Here I am. You're the last ones to see my face before I die."

"Stop smiling at me. I don't have sympathy for any of the Lords."

"What about men who ran away from the Lords?"

Jimmy let his gun hang by his side. "There are more of you underground?"

"Seventy-five."

"Seventy-five? How far did you think you'd get?"

"They didn't know we ran away."

"Are they heading toward us?"

"No, they're exiting the underground from another part of

the hills. They're all out of food. Nobody knows they're here. Nobody knows I'm here."

"Do they know a garrison just arrived to ensure compliance with the climate lockdown?"

"None of us knew that. They wouldn't care. They're ready to die."

"Are you ready to die?"

"No, but it's happening anyhow. It's painful, and it's going to take a while. Would you do me the undeserved honor of—"

A lone bullet from Jimmy's gun pierced the man's skin. The three escaped members of the Lords of the Wolf Blade lay dead in the underground shelter.

"Katie, lock the door. We're going back above ground to fight."

"I wouldn't have it any other way."

"You Norbannicks are all the same."

"Like my dad would say, welcome to the family."

"Keep in mind that the seventy-five Lords are up against several hundred soldiers. When the Lords attack the Planetary Forces, we'll have our chance to escape Orion's property. The soldiers will rush to their comrades' aid to stave off the Lords' assault. Let's grab new weapons and bullets down here before we go back above ground."

"Jimmy, you think the villagers will fight the Lords and Planetary Forces?"

"They've got families to protect. They'll fight to the last man, and there will be at least several hundred men willing to fight in a village of a couple thousand."

"Ready, Englewood?"

"I'll throw open the ceiling block. Fire as soon as you see anyone in a bright red climate suit."

Jimmy and Katie hoisted themselves above ground to find nobody in the yard. They reentered Orion's house.

"Where are they, Jimmy? There's nobody home."

"Forget the home. There's nobody in the hills."

"There they are! They're in the hills and down below!"

The fighting spread from the river shoreline to the highest point in town.

"Katie, watch out!"

A series of explosions blew out the windows in Orion's house. An endless barrage of gunfire and screams engulfed the village.

Villagers fought Planetary Forces tooth and nail, but the Lords of the Wolf Blade were nowhere to be seen.

"Katie, they'll see us. Stay away from the windows. We have no way to join this battle."

"Let's go back to the bunker if they're not in the yard to see us."

"Even if they are in the yard, let's try it."

The front door flew open while Jimmy and Katie headed out back. The Renegades reached the bunker and the intruders pursued them. Katie lowered herself into the underground shelter. Jimmy ducked incoming bullets before the pursuers could perfect their aim. He shot two of them and lowered himself into the bunker as Planetary Forces closed in on him and Katie. Jimmy closed the ceiling lid and expected the soldiers to follow or bomb them. Moments later, all the soldiers found were two vanquished comrades of the Planetary Forces on the frozen dead grass.

Jimmy shined a flashlight. "Did the rest of them see us, Katie?"

"How should I know? I got in here before you."

"We'll find out soon enough."

Jimmy and Katie took off their helmets. No bomb was forthcoming, and the bunker shielded a lot of the noise from outside. They were hiding in an underground shelter in Orion's yard, and adjacent to a passageway carved out deep inside the hills. Faint sounds of gunfire and the louder noise from explosions continued. The bunker shook each time a missile hit a target above ground. Some dirt rained down on the two Renegades within the confines of shaking walls, sturdy as possible but not forever impenetrable.

"Katie, we just saw military boats on the river from Orion's house. It looked like the villagers responded with their own vessels."

"And we saw fighting break out in the hills."

"But we didn't see any aerial combat."

"No, we didn't!"

"Good. I don't think the Planetary Forces can—"

"They still can't win. The villagers, they can't defeat the invasion."

"No, they can't."

"Let's go through the hills."

Jimmy flashed the light on the three Lords he killed earlier. "When we step through that door to the underground part of the hills, we don't know if the Lords will be there. We can't kill 75, but we can outmaneuver them."

"How?"

"I don't know. It just sounded good."

Caught off guard, Katie laughed.

Jimmy sat down on a splintered picnic bench, leaned over with his left elbow on the table, and grabbed his hair with his left hand. "This gives new meaning to the phrase 'climate lockdown.' We're trapped inside hills in the middle of nowhere."

"It's a beautiful middle of nowhere. We got below ground just before dark."

"Katie, we have to go with the only option there is. We have to turn me in."

"Jimmy, we can't do that here without you getting shot. Even if there's a way to signal them that you're turning yourself in, there's no way to make sure they take you alive."

"Did we ever really think we'd make it out of any of this alive? I don't have a death wish, Katie, but you know as well as I do that a life of eating bugs is no life at all. It's no life to look over your shoulder every second and make sure you say the right thing."

"You just want to give up?"

"I'm not giving up. I'm saying I'd like to figure out how to get

Linda back. Even if we think that's impossible, let's latch onto
something to get us through the day if we can make it that far.
What else do we have?"

"We have no transportation, jobs, or homes, but we do have
my family."

"If the Planetary Forces take me in, and they don't break me,
then maybe that's a way for me to break them. We'll exit the hills
following the route the defector Lord told us about. I'll try to
get the attention of the Planetary Forces, assuming the villagers
are dead, and assuming we don't first run into the Lords. If the
villagers aren't dead, then we'll come up with a new plan. You
can hide under ground while I turn myself in."

"Jimmy."

"What?"

"We'll turn ourselves in together if we don't die carrying out
this crazy plan."

19

WOLF BLADE MADNESS

Katie opened the door to the underground passageway.

Jimmy wanted to shoot, but he could not get a clear look. The men rushed in and grabbed Katie. Jimmy dropped his weapon and absorbed a couple of punches to the stomach.

"You know who we are, don't you?"

Jimmy tried to wrestle away from the four men holding him. "I see the sword on fire. You're from the Peasants of the Dog Spoon."

"Hey that's hilarious! Lords, bring her to the passageway while I talk to this guy right here. But wait a second. Don't take her away just yet. What's your name, sweetie?"

Katie smirked. "What's the matter, big tough Lord? Your mommy and daddy didn't love you?"

The Lords laughed, except for the one member, Drew, busy talking to Katie and Jimmy. Drew got in Katie's face, attacking her with his wrathful eyes. "Hahaha. I can take a joke, my lady."

Jimmy tried again to break loose. "Fight me, you coward?! Is Mr. Purebred afraid he can't win a one-on-one battle?"

Drew rushed toward Jimmy but tripped over one of the dead defector Lords brought down earlier in the skirmish.

Suddenly, all the Lords stopped laughing.

Drew stood back up and brushed his scraped knees. "Mike, take that bitch out of here and wait outside."

"Should we rough her up?"

"Just take her outside!"

Jimmy realized that one of the dead defectors he had killed earlier had given him the correct number of Lords in the hills. There were 75 of them.

Ten members of the crew were crowded inside Orion's bunker, which measured at 225 square feet. The rest were directly outside the shelter's back door, in the passageway beneath the hills.

Drew closed the door and paced back and forth in front of Jimmy. "You killed three of my men. You've got to pay a price for that."

"What kind of price? They weren't worth very much."

Jimmy's eyes rolled back into his head for a few seconds. He absorbed Drew's fist to the bridge of his nose. Jimmy recovered, but the sting of the punch stuck around and the Renegade's eyes watered.

"Looks like some real water works. You must be totally impure. What's your ethnicity? What's your religion?"

The Lords felt free to laugh again.

Jimmy spit in Drew's left eye. "You call that an interrogation?"

"You son of a bitch!"

"Now you've got my impurities."

Drew seized a bat from one of the Lords and pointed it at Jimmy. "Now I'm going to kill you."

A knock on the door grew louder and louder. Drew ignored it. Four of the men continued holding Jimmy while Drew wound up for a swing at the Renegade. Jimmy ducked his head, and the meat of the bat knocked out one of the Lords. The knock on the door became a pounding and would not go away.

Drew lost his nerve. "Open the fucking door and help your brother sit down. He just took a bat to the head."

Mike entered the bunker from the passageway. "Brother Drew, keep this door open and let that cold air inside."

Drew's face teamed with blood vessels that looked like arteries on the map of an urban street grid. He turned to Mike. "What the fuck is it?!"

"We need to take our chances and leave this underground pigsty. We can fight our way out of the underground if we leave now."

"Nobody is leaving, Brother Mike."

"Brother Drew, do you want to waste your time with this guy and that whore out there? You'll kill us all."

"Listen closely. I'll fucking rip your kidneys out like the bitch you are if you don't shut the fuck up. I run this chapter. You run nothing."

Mike held his hands up. "No problem."

"That's fucking right, no problem. Alright, I'll go along with your idea, Mike. Leave that door open so he feels the cold. I want him to feel ripped apart during his execution. What's your name, Renegade?"

"I'm Jimmy Englewood."

"Jimmy Englewood, are you afraid of death?"

"Whose death?"

"Yours, and your woman's out there."

"She's not my woman."

"Oh? Then I can keep her as my woman. We don't have any of them with us inside the hills."

"I bet the women you're used to seeing are hard on the eyes."

"They're as pure as the driven snow. You say this mixed-race woman isn't yours. I should hope not. She has no part in the future. She has no part in the world! Neither do you with all of your impurities. Look at yourself, with your disgusting face and deformed ethnicities."

"I thought the Lords of the Wolf Blade only cared about their homelands. Now you talk about who has a part in the world? How does it feel that you don't have any countries? All you have left is a losing battle against a smarter adversary."

"You Renegades are no geniuses."

Mike interfered. "Brother Drew, he was talking about the Planetary Order."

Drew went over to Mike and cracked him across the face.

"Out of respect for our history together and your role in this movement, I'll let your insubordination slide one more time. You're out of chances."

Mike just stood there. All the Lords waited for a reaction, but Mike retreated into his own skin, revealing nothing of his thoughts or fears.

Jimmy tried again to get away, failing miserably while being tightly restrained. "He's right, Drew. You're not going to beat them. I don't know that any of us are. You don't have the power."

"You don't think I have the power? I'll show you my power and you'll feel it when I snap you into fifty pieces."

"Why would you want to do all this? As we speak, you're being encircled by the Planetary Forces, but you already know that from the shaking hills. You probably knew it well before it happened. How can I hurt you? What about it, tough guy? You spend your time on me while every chance you have to run away or fight your collectivist enemy fades. You're just another group of collectivists that doesn't know a damn thing about what a great country is. Everyone can see you guys from a mile away. You're the easiest enemy to defeat, so what do you want with me?"

"You are the Lords' biggest enemy. It's because of you merchants and liberty hawks that we do not have the Order of the Wolf Blade spread all across the world. The faggot climate movement would never have stopped us. You had to go fuck things up, Jimmy."

"Do you call everyone a faggot?"

Drew grinned. "Everyone but the Lords."

"Even the mentally and physically disabled you harassed and beat like animals?"

"We have sheer force. We use it against who we want and when we want. You understand what I'm saying to you? Are you hearing me, fucker?"

"I'm hearing nothing but a nobody. You can't even hear yourself."

"You think I'm just a stupid Neanderthal. Who are you? You're a weak little half-breed. I see the racial impurities written all over your face. I'm going to sacrifice you, tear out your liver, and dance on your body."

"You just sacrificed yourself."

Drew pulled out a long blade, but bullets exploded his organs before he could slice Jimmy's neck. Six shots from Mike brought Drew's reign of terror to an end.

Drew committed a grave error. Hitting a fellow Lord constituted a forbidden action. Various crews all over the planet could smooth over the tensions in earlier times. Earlier times were gone. The worldwide cohesion of the Lords' movement had cracked under the pressure and the power of the climate regime. The movement had reached a crisis in keeping discipline among the Wolf Blade ranks.

A monster was dead. Mike took the monster's place.

20

MIKE CHECK

Mike assumed command of the Lords under ground in the hills. He was not as big as Drew, and he was not as brash, but nobody put up a fight. Mike had the willpower that most Lords across the planet could only dream about having.

"As your new chief, the first order of business is getting out of here with whatever provisions we can take. Open the door to the underground, and let's take all the food and weapons with us."

"Brother Mike, what do we do with Jimmy and his lady friend? Do we take them with us into battle or waste them right here?"

"Take them with us. Put Jimmy's helmet back on. I don't want him dying before we get there. These prisoners can be sacrificed when we get back out into the open air."

All the Lords fell in line. They did not express any hint of dissension. Drew fit the description of most of his movements' leaders as a blunt force instrument of barbarism, but Mike brought a higher level of strategy to his rule. The Lords in Mike's crew found Mike a welcome change to Drew's unceasing cruelty.

The entire Lords of the Wolf Blade movement had as little regard for human life as the Planetary Order had. Mike knew that most members of the ideology could not deny themselves a carnal need for violence for very long, so he instilled a cold yet captivating discipline. He perfected the discipline within his crew from the beginning of his new command.

The Lords walked Jimmy and Katie through the freezing underground tunnels. Flashlights and torches lit up the pathways through sludge and frozen streams inside the Earth. Underneath the hollowed-out hills, four Lords a piece guarded Jimmy and Katie, manhandling them during the march.

Mike walked alongside Jimmy. "Jimmy, you must understand these men will do anything I say. They will follow me to the ends of the Earth, because I will treat them well. They know it. Drew couldn't offer that kind of leadership. How can you trust a man who'll attack his own? This is an impossible task for someone like Drew. You're a Renegade and must know what I mean."

"You don't sound like them at all. You're more dangerous than any Lord I've ever come across."

"To fight the Comrade of Marganis and the Planetary Forces, I have to be a different kind of leader."

"You're just like Zack. The only difference is your movement is weaker. Your chapter has Stone Age methods and technology. You invent nothing and steal everything."

"You forget the advancements we've made fighting Renegades and the Planetary Order."

"You got lucky, and they're just weapons and nothing else. All you produce is carnage."

"I can leave you here, Jimmy. I can leave you and what's her name tied together on the rock floor of this underground hell."

"Her name is..."

"My name is Katie, Mike. Didn't we tell you that before?"

"You don't matter to me and my men. Your name doesn't matter. You're just a bitch."

The Lords in the vicinity laughed a raucous laugh. They were ready to inflict irreparable damage on Jimmy and Katie, but Mike's strategy and mission kept the two Renegades alive...

Jimmy smiled. "Is that all you've got, Mike? You and your idiotic Lords of so-called supernatural status."

"We are the superior beings, Renegade. I will show you how superior when we use you to exit the hills. You've got a 100% chance of dying by our hands. It's a matter of time. We'll have you take out the first wave of climate regime attackers. It's the least you can do for the Lords, you maggot."

For Jimmy and Katie, something did not compute. The small group of Lords could not take on the Planetary Forces. The rank and file of the crew would soon understand the futility of their efforts in battle. They could not have even defeated the villagers, who had forced the Lords into continued hiding beneath the earth.

Jimmy realized what was happening, but it was too late to alert Katie. Mike pointed to several of his men to gag Jimmy and Katie. The chapter leader stripped the two Renegades of their helmets, and the heat fled rapidly from their exposed heads.

The Lords wanted a chance to exact any measure of revenge possible on the climate regime. Even the most indoctrinated of the group knew deep down most men in their shoes would have no chance to survive, but they believed in their own physical and metaphysical superiority. They never considered escaping instead of carrying through with their full-out assault.

Everybody turned to Mike.

"As your new commander, I'll wait here with our prisoners. I'll set off the explosives after you take out however many ships and soldiers your initial attack can overwhelm."

One of the Lords grunted. "I thought our plan was to set off the explosives at the beginning of the attack."

As quickly as he spoke the lines, the Lord stepped back and bowed his head. He contradicted Mike, which proved too much for Mike to let fester in the minds of any other Lord. The underground dwellers, detached from fellow Lords across the planet, showed no surprise at Mike's next move.

Without hesitation, Mike drew his handgun and shot the questioner between the eyes.

The Lords could ill afford to lose men, but they craved the veneer of order and discipline. They did not care about death. They cared about following structure, no matter what the cost.

The Lords had no patience for flexibility, and Mike would not risk too many shocks to the current state of his men. He had already changed a battle plan he himself had designed, and he did so after taking out Drew, the former crew leader.

Katie caught on to what Jimmy knew about Mike's duplicity...

Mike motioned to two Lords. "We're here. Tie Jimmy and Katie to the walls. Gagging them isn't good enough. The crumbling hills will crush them. A fine spectacle."

Mike's Lords reached the edge of the underground passageway buried beneath the hills, with the river nearby in the open air. All except Mike exited tunnels and fired against the Planetary Forces.

Still underneath the hills, Mike took the gag off of Jimmy. "You know who I work for, don't you, Jimmy?"

"Yeah, Mike. You're part of the HAVE movement. The Lords don't use words like 'spectacle.' You're the smartest Lord I've ever met."

"You sound defeated, Jimmy. I'd tell you to put your helmet on, but it's hard to do that with your hands tied up. You, too, Katie."

"Take her gag off, Mike."

Gunfire and blasts intensified on the docks and river shore.

"You're giving orders to a member of the Planetary Forces? I don't take orders from anybody except my superiors in the climate regime. Katie stays gagged for the moment."

"You're worse than they are. You're worse than the Lords you infiltrated."

"Now Jimmy, you'd be saying the same about the Lords if they were about to slaughter you. I fooled these Lords over a long stretch of time, and now they die in battle against the Planetary Forces. Isn't it magical?"

"You're going to explode the underground so the hills cave in on us."

"No, Jimmy. I was going to bring the hills down on you, but now I'm going to take you out of this village. I'm taking you someplace else. I am no longer a member of the Planetary Order."

"You're lying."

"I'm not. I'm leaving today. No longer will I live this life."

"Then why are we waiting?! Why am I tied up?!"

"You're not my friend, Jimmy. Katie isn't my friend. I'm saving my life, and I'll try to save yours to help me. I don't care about who you are. I just know I can't do this anymore. All that fighting we hear, and the shaking Earth, it rocked me awake."

"Nobody escapes the mind-altering power of someone as high up as you. You achieved your bosses' trust with a dangerous mission to infiltrate the Lords. That doesn't happen. It never happens."

"Not never, Jimmy. Not never."

Mike untied Jimmy. "What's going on out there, Jimmy?"

Jimmy took the gag off Katie and untied her. He ran up to Mike. "I can barely see outside from here. I'm guessing your Planetary Forces are winning."

Katie grabbed her and Jimmy's helmets. "What was it, Mike? Did you convert before or after shooting two Lords today?"

Rubble fell from the ceiling of the hill, several hundred feet behind the Renegades and Mike, back toward Orion's place. A missile opened up the underground, and light showered down along from the blasted rocks, dirt, and ice. The headgear softened the adjustment to sunlight.

The intensity and noise of the fighting plummeted.

Mike suffered the most in adjusting to the rays. "Those Lords fighting out there must be in worse shape than I am. They're probably almost finished. My Planetary Forces won. They're just seeing who's left standing."

"Mike, I can't forget about my brother."

"What about your brother?"

"My brother left the Marganisan forerunners to the climate regime. He got murdered in cold blood for turning against the city tyrants. How many murders did you commit? How many murders did you engineer?"

Katie looked up toward the gaping hole in the hills. "They're going to send more missiles, Mike! We need to leave the underground!"

Mike nodded. "I can't communicate with them, but they know I'm in here. Don't be too alarmed. They'd be blasting out the hills if they knew I'd betrayed them. I have no way of contacting my Planetary Forces. Don't worry about any of that. They know I went to infiltrate the Lords for information on how to use them across the world. We want to harness their energy for our production facilities. I'll lead us out, but you should know that they could accidentally kill me and kill you and your friend. I'll lead you to safety in time, but not at first. You have to go to prison."

Jimmy stood right by the start of the exit from the tunnels to the village. "How do we get out, Mike? How do we get out without being shot?"

"The Lords covered the exits, sealing us in with rock walls. You can only leave and enter by pressing buttons here inside. Those Lords are all dead. I promise they're all dead, and so are the villagers. I know where the buttons are. Let me lead you out."

Jimmy and Katie looked at each other.

Katie threw up her hands. "No, Mike. We will not let you lead us to capture. You haven't changed at all. You work for Zack."

"I did. I don't anymore. It's sudden to you. It's sudden to me. None of that matters. If I don't punish you according to Zack's orders, then we'll all suffer worse than if they catch us and find out I turned on them. How many times can I explain this before you understand?"

"You're going to let Zack punish us to provide cover for yourself. Hell no! Are you buying this, Jimmy?!"

"Katie, I don't believe him, but we've been talking about turning ourselves in. You hear the sounds of war outside. You hear them inside, and you hear the hills rumbling. The fighting died down. They might not shoot us. Our lives are in Mike's hands. If it's over, Katie, then we'll have done everything we could. If they find us here, they'll punish us immediately without any chance of us escaping. If Mike can keep us breathing and away from the worst treatment, let's try his plan."

"We don't know what that is. We don't know anything about his plan."

"Do we even want to know, Katie?"

Mike lowered his head, covered in his Wolf Blade helmet. "He's right, Katie, you don't want to know. Surviving enslavement is your only path to freedom."

21

VISITORS

Mike turned in Jimmy and Katie, mostly according to plan. He took a bullet to his arm before the Planetary Forces realized who they hit. Mike received a hero's welcome for infiltrating the Lords of the Wolf Blade. His superiors were quite pleased, and he answered directly to Zack. Putting Mike in charge of Jimmy Englewood meant a level of trust rarely seen in the climate regime. Mike would take full advantage. Jimmy and Katie were alive, but their lives devolved into something for which nobody could prepare.

Zack visited Jimmy's room. "Mike is taking good care of you, I trust."

"Is that you, Zack?"

"Yes, it is. We haven't seen each other since the Battle of Marganis. The city is now under our full control."

"Is that where I am? Are we in Marganis? It's been a year."

"It hasn't been a year. It's been one month. Are you comfortable?"

"I have nothing to do."

"But you're eating well and exercising."

"I'm trapped in a cell. When are you sending me to hard labor?"

"You'd like that wouldn't you? You'd like to see how tough you really are. Look out of your room. Open the blinds. Open the shades. This room is luxurious. The window is your gateway."

"My gateway to snow and ice."

"You're warm in here, aren't you?"

"I'm warm, and the bathrooms down the corridor are immaculate. The guards treat me well. Everything is terrific."

"I'm glad to hear it, because tomorrow, Jimmy Englewood, your comfort dies. Mike will deliver you to a new home. Some people call it a work camp, but I call it an endless retreat for the maladjusted."

"What kind of work awaits me? You'll want to turn me into a skeleton."

"You've seen too many old movies. You've read too many old books. I have a different plan for you. Brandon Dreckhorn has a different plan for you. The Planetary Order will have you working on behalf of stopping climate change. It's getting much hotter out, as you can see by the texture of the snow. If this warming trend continues, we could see it get even colder."

"You're completely out of your mind."

"Jimmy, you know we treat everybody differently."

"You treat everybody the same."

"We're already there."

"Already where? We're in Marganis, aren't we? I know you've already destroyed the skyscrapers."

"Many. Not all. Many. We couldn't take it all down. Marganis has a rich history. The preservation of some buildings for regime-controlled homes and climate camaraderie could not be more special than it is."

"What climate camaraderie? That's all drivel."

"I don't think you understand how dangerous the situation is. It's dangerous for you because of your resistance to learning. You will learn. Mike will ensure it upon your transfer tomorrow."

"First, you have a little surprise before you take me out of the dormitory."

"More than just a little surprise. I have a friend here to see you."

"Who did you capture?"

"That's what I admire most about the Planetary Order. Mike brings you here on your first blindfolded excursion, but your mind is skeptical. I haven't forgotten our time at odds during the Battle of Marganis, and now you've returned to the city of burned hopes and brittle dreams. I also haven't forgotten our cat and mouse games from years ago. You know as well as I do about the hit on your brother, and on Bethany."

Zack stepped out of the room.

Jimmy rushed to the door. Too late! Locked in, Jimmy's yells remained confined to his soundproofed prison cell. It was just him, four walls, and his insulated cell of anticipation.

Finally, morning arrived.

Zack returned. This time, Mike accompanied him along with six guards hovering inside and outside the door.

Mike pushed Jimmy's left shoulder. "It's time to start the day."

"Are you transferring me? Nobody broke me down. Is that why you're transferring me?"

Mike shoved Jimmy in the chest. "I've got some bad news for you."

"I know, you're sending me into transcendent climate bliss."

"There's time enough for that, but it's something else. Orion is dead. Comrade Zack told Katie about it, and she seemed really upset. It was the first emotion we saw from her. Was she attracted to him? She must have fallen hard. She didn't know him for very long."

Jimmy got up from the floor. "When did Orion die?"

"When our valiant Planetary Forces killed all the villagers. We took out every last one. Every man, woman, child, and dog. And let me tell you that it was a real treat to take out the whole group of Lords I infiltrated. They walked right into our trap. And here you are, Jimmy. You walked right into our trap."

"You killed Orion a month ago, and you're telling us now. You slaughtered a village for fun, and you're telling us now."

Zack landed a right hook to Jimmy's mouth. "You're a courageous man, Englewood. You're stunned but still on your feet. Wobbly, but still on your feet."

Mike sighed. "Jimmy, we would never slaughter a village for fun. None of this is fun for us. We would all have a great time if you would simply put down your arms and fight for our climate. You cannot find another responsibility more important than understanding that all humans and animals are viruses on Earth."

Zack pulled Linda into the room. "Look, Jimmy, she's alive. Isn't that good news?"

Mike had to stage a performance to keep the trust of the Renegade and the Comrade of Marganis. He had managed to keep Jimmy and the Norbannick sisters alive. Mike kept Zack unaware of Jimmy's expectation for eventual liberation.

Linda was gaunt, just off the latest airlift of prisoners from a nearby prison from hell. She shivered, wearing a pale face, unkempt hair, torn clothes, and the faintest of smiles. She could barely stand up.

Jimmy shook off the dizziness from Zack's earlier right hook. He caught Linda before she fell. "Linda, what did they do to you? Did they take you to your sister's room? Have you seen Katie?"

"It doesn't matter, Jimmy. I'm here now. They said I'm going to be comfortable at these Paradise Gardens. I'm going to have a clean bed, food, and a shower every day. They're sparing my life. They're sparing my life for the climate. My transfer guards said I was lucky they didn't harpoon me like I was a whale. They said the Planetary Order and HAVE would let me breathe the air and watch the snow fall while the planet heated up."

Linda fell asleep. Jimmy placed her gently on his bed, covering her with his blanket and propping her head on his pillow. He swiveled his head to Zack. The Renegade locked eyes with the Comrade of Marganis. Their mutual desire for a fight felt heavier than Jupiter's gravity, but only the two men's pairs of eyes battled each other that day.

The Planetary Forces transferred Jimmy and Katie by air shuttle to their new home at the Climate Rehab Center. Linda had just done time there, so Zack ordered her to her new location at Paradise Gardens. Though Jimmy and Katie would do time at the Rehab Center, their punishment differed from each other's and from what Linda experienced. The Planetary Order labeled all its captives' time served as performing community service for the climate...to change them into saved beings...

Mike went away on orders from Zack, but he returned a month into Jimmy's service at the Climate Rehab Center.

Jimmy spotted Mike approaching him. "Never thought I'd see you again."

"Yet here I am. Let's take a walk in the outside heated area. Guards, open the cell."

The cell opened and out stepped Jimmy from his meager but clean accommodations. "Outside heated area?"

"Follow me and I'll show you."

The two men entered a large plot of land next to a prison covered by a translucent dome. They could not talk openly, and they both knew it. Frigid temperatures outside contrasted with a balmy temperature inside.

"Why the special privileges, Mike?"

"What does that mean?"

"Barely anybody else is here in this heated dome. I was one of the top priorities for the regime. Now I'm a prisoner getting treated like royalty."

"Are you calling the cell you're living in a noble dwelling?"

"It isn't a closed room. I can see outside of it."

"You have no windows. What you see is imagined. You have a crumbling mattress with lumps and wiring, with no box spring and laid across cheap flooring."

"But I still have a room, and nobody subjects me to the elements. I'm shielded from the suffering I know takes place here. The guards haven't escorted me to any rehab classes or appointments."

"Would you like to suffer, Jimmy? Is that what you're asking for?"

"Where's Katie?"

"She's here, just like you."

"I know that. How are you treating her? Is she being spared the rehabilitation?"

"Jimmy, she's performing her community service."

"Fuck you, Mike."

"Let's have a seat at that table, right there by the dome covering. This way we can watch the snowfall up close from the comfort of these modern heating amenities."

"Where is Katie?"

"I told you that we'll get to her. She's doing quite well, so set your mind at ease. Let's talk about Linda."

"Is she still alive?"

"I want you to look at these pictures we have of her in the comfort facilities at Paradise Gardens. We didn't even bring you there when you were at Paradise Gardens. Did you ever know we had such attractions for our favorite residents?"

Jimmy sat silently, observing one photo after another. Mike showed him images of Linda by a large pool with a lazy river. Palm trees hovered above as she sat resting amid a lush landscape.

"She's smiling, Jimmy. Look at how happy she is in our terraformed setting. It's warm there, too, and Linda is enjoying the world the way it's intended. No worries flood her head or fill her heart. She has, let's call them episodes, every now and again, but she's doing well."

"You seem to be doing well, Mike. What's your secret? You must be dining and socializing well these days. A far cry from living underground with Lords of the Wolf Blade."

"I own these entire grounds, Jimmy. I have this prison and this adjacent biodome. Zack gave me control of the transfers to and from Paradise Gardens, including prison operations there. My life is exquisite."

"Like I said, fuck you, Mike."

"Come on, let's go. You've seen the pictures of Linda. I watched you hold back the waterworks. Your eyes displayed a tender irritation that gives away your weakness for your pal. Now, Jimmy, it's time for you to see some unpleasant moving images up close. It's all part of your road to freedom. Be patient and weather the pain."

22

PRISON

Mike led Jimmy out of the biodome and back to the prison complex of the Climate Rehab Center. "I'm a messenger, and powerful one at that."

Jimmy closed his eyes. "This is the end, isn't it?"

"The end of what? Your life?"

"No, the end of another chapter of normalcy. This is where you play with my mind."

"I just told you that I'm only a messenger."

"You own the prison complex."

"Not only that. Those comfort facilities where Linda is, those are mine, too, as of tomorrow. All of Paradise Gardens is almost mine. I take full command at midnight."

"And this Climate Rehab Center was Linda's first stop on the way to climate heaven."

"The only stop, Jimmy. It's the only stop on the road to

perfection. Open your eyes, Englewood. Your dear friend Katie has a few words for you."

At the Climate Rehab Center, Jimmy lived in a comfortable prison cell during the month since his arrival. Nobody had ever taken him to the part of the complex housing Katie. He got to see up close what Katie faced, and at first sight, Jimmy became lightheaded.

Mike slapped Jimmy. "Stay awake. Linda had to suffer greatly on the road to perfection. She's still on that road, but Katie has a lot farther to travel. Zack wants you to know this is what you brought upon the people closest to you. Their suffering is your suffering. Look at Katie. Look at her. You inflicted terrible shame on a family you pretend to love. You see her condition, don't you? You see her face. Does this look like someone you love?"

"You were supposed to help us, Mike. What you've done to Katie is unforgivable. You don't own or control anything. You have no say in anything. All you can do is carry out the orders of the Comrade of Marganis."

In the dark and musty corner of the Climate prison, Katie walked up to the vertical bars of her cell. "Jimmy, I failed."

"Katie, hang on. You can't give up now."

Prisoners pulled Katie back into the shadows. She screamed, Jimmy yelled, and Mike had Jimmy dragged out of the holding block.

"Where are we now, Mike?"

"Another part of the labyrinth."

"How long is the trip through this entire labyrinth?"

"For as long as your fears can sustain you. When you die, your fear will end. You're not as lucky as Linda or Katie. Linda survived what Katie's dealing with now. We stripped so many of Linda's fears away. The path to Paradise winds its way through hell."

"Will you take me back to my cell?"

"First, I have more images to show you. We have arranged for your new education. This is what Zack wants for you. You must own up to the pain you're inflicting on your fellow human beings. You must discover the pathway of the Planetary Order."

"I've inflicted no pain."

"You defy lockdown orders. You spread lies about the climate crisis. I will get you back to Paradise Gardens as soon as I can. In the meantime, you just have to grin and bear what awaits you."

"What section of the prison is this?"

"You're under the ground yet again. You're famous in these parts."

"What parts?"

"These are Renegades from Marganis."

"When's the last time they ate anything?"

"They usually just get water."

"Why are they walking back and forth? They're pacing like animals in a zoo."

"They're tired, Jimmy. You can see that they're very tired. They're starving."

"That has nothing to do with them pacing."

"They're even more bored than tired or starving or weak. None of them have hard labor. They have no labor to speak of. They spend their energy finding something they can attach themselves to. Keeping up the rituals and habits of pacing back and forth gives them structure. Everybody needs structure, including you, Jimmy Englewood."

"This isn't a normal prison. It isn't anything close to it."

"Not in the traditional sense, but we offer hard labor work benefits for the chosen few who get to work outside. Would you like to see?"

Mike led Jimmy to another part of the prison, above ground and facing the outside world. This part of the prison, like the other nightmarish blocks Mike showed to Jimmy, had no attached biodome. A rush of cold air chilled Jimmy upon impact. Countless prisoners crowded an area of snow-filled grounds.

Jimmy turned around to run back inside. Corrections officers blocked his pathway.

Mike motioned for the officers to scatter. "It's just us, Jimmy."

"Why is it so cold? We're not outside."

"It allows people to adapt to their working conditions. These prisoners receive the benefit of food. With such a generous benefit comes responsibilities. Some cold weather indoors and outdoors isn't too much to ask for those needing rehabilitation, Englewood."

"You call them prisoners now. You dropped the pretense of them being patients."

"Several descriptions fit them, depending on the times and places we see fit. They are patients, but they are patients deserving of punishment for their crimes against the climate regime."

"You're a lunatic, Mike. You're all lunatics."

"Let's step outside for a minute."

"No way. We left our helmets back...where did we leave our helmets?"

Mike grabbed Jimmy's arm. "Renegade, get outside or I'll have the officers leave a trail of bullets all over you while keeping you alive and incapacitated."

The outside brought frigid temperature and winds. The air currents smacked Mike and Jimmy upon entering the work yard. Jimmy spotted newly frozen dead bodies a short distance away. He saw some of the deceased propped upright in their ice encasings, and he saw others of the dead lay stretched across the ground. He saw living workers with their headgear and shovels. Jimmy devoted a mere second to wondering what the Climate Rehabilitation Center ordered the prisoners to do. He stopped worrying about other prisoners as he felt his head turning into a ball of frost.

Mike wasted no time. "Just listen. This is the only place we can talk around here without prying eyes and ears. That won't last long. All you need to know is that I'm doing everything I can to keep you and Katie and Linda alive. I'm limited in what I can do, but I haven't turned on you, Jimmy. I have no other choice. One of you might have to die to appease the Planetary Order. Zack is keeping you alive and safe. That could end anytime. I have to take you through the motions of doing certain things, but I'm going to spring you whenever I can. You must believe me."

"I don't believe you, but I don't want to die or be a slave to the climate regime. Get Katie out of here before you do anything with me."

"Let's get back inside before the two of us die today."

"I'm freezing. My head is burning. Help me, Mike. Trying. Walk Help."

Jimmy woke up hours later to a warming body temperature. Zack and Mike stood by his bed.

Zack leaned over Jimmy, inches from his face. "Mike told me he showed you the work camp for rehabilitating climate deniers."

"Back away from my face, you freak! Was that loud? Hurt your eardrums?"

Zack leaned upright. "I trust the comforter is keeping you warm and cozy."

"We all know it's cold out. You can say it's heating all you want. I'll go to my deathbed knowing you're crazy, no matter what you're trying to accomplish. You and your climate regime losers will have no ultimate victory."

"You act as though I owe you answers and explanations. The only thing I owe you is to get you to my superiors after I've rehabilitated you."

"How long before you throw me into similar conditions to Katie's?"

"Maybe tomorrow. Maybe never. That's the last question you'll ever ask me. Ask it again and I'll make things far worse for Katie than they already are. I'll bring Linda back here for additional treatments."

"How could you call them treatments? You're a real fucking dickhead."

"I told you, Jimmy. I told you not to ask me any questions. You will learn about the consequences of your behavior. Mike, bring Katie into this room."

Mike ushered in the officers carrying Katie.

Zack smiled. "She's too weak to hold herself up. Ha! Look at this psychotic climate-denying patient of ours. She's worthless."

Katie kept her heavy eyes on Mike and cried.

Jimmy's body temperature, cold just minutes earlier, overheated. "I know you're going to shoot her in the head. You had it planned. It didn't matter whether I asked you anything."

Chained to the bed, Jimmy could do nothing for Katie, himself, or anyone.

Zack smirked and left the room unexpectedly.

Mike put his hand over Jimmy's hair and petted him gently. "My patient, you don't understand us at all. Officers, unchain this man and wheel in the mattress for Katie. Good night, Ms. Norbannick and Mr. Englewood."

Mike and the officers left the cell. Katie hugged Jimmy with the affection reserved for a long-lost brother. Life returned to her pale face and bleary eyes framed by disheveled hair.

The Climate Rehab Center turned off the lights.

23

SUBJECTED

Months passed by. Jimmy did not hear a word about Linda. He saw Katie, his roommate, every day. The Climate Rehab Center continued providing Jimmy with food, clothes, and...time in the biodome. Katie received treatment altogether different from Jimmy's, though Katie's conditions improved, slightly, from her initial time of imprisonment by the Planetary Order.

The cell mates, Jimmy and Katie, recognized they reached one year in captivity. The torment carried on for them. Zack ordered Mike to starve and freeze Katie in cycles. Jimmy had to watch Katie fighting day in and day out to avoid cracking. Mike and Zack brought Jimmy down to the hard labor site to see the officers freeze Katie and make her beg for warmth. Every night, Katie cried herself to sleep. Every night, Jimmy thought up ways to free her, and to free himself. His thoughts turned up more hopeless than the most foolish pipe dream ever conjured.

Just after a year into captivity, the unimaginable occurred. Zack turned prison operations over to Mike. He had done that a year earlier in an official capacity. This time, Zack relinquished all formal and informal control of the prison to Mike. Everybody knew about Zack climbing the ranks of the Planetary Order. Most knew less about Mike or what would become of him. For another year, Mike continued prison operations as usual, still providing no word to Jimmy or Katie about Linda.

Suddenly, Mike proved valuable in ending much of Jimmy and Katie's torment. He could only do so much for all the inmates littered throughout the enormous prison.

Mike engaged in fewer blatant sadistic practices than Zack did. Mike ended Katie's cycles of food deprivation, and he stopped subjecting her to the elements. All the while, the Earth became colder and harvesting food became tougher. No tropical regions remained...except for some of the climate regime's man-made enclaves. Linda lived in one of them, a reformed member in good standing of Mike's other newly controlled property, Paradise Gardens.

Every once in a while, Zack returned to the Climate Rehab Center and Paradise Gardens to pull rank. He did so on direct orders from the Planetary Council. Zack was never far away.

A third year passed.

Mike escorted Linda to Jimmy and Katie's cell.

Katie and Linda embraced each other while Jimmy just stared at Mike.

"No guards with you this time, Mike?"

"No, Jimmy. If you did something stupid, my officers would ensure it backfired on you."

"We haven't seen you in a while. To what do we owe this displeasure?"

"Isn't it obvious? Linda's visiting. The sisters are hugging and crying tears of joy. You should be happy about this entire situation, especially with Linda doing so well in Paradise Gardens. That's the facility you should long for all the time...Paradise Gardens."

Linda showed off a pair of new silver earrings to Katie. "Do you like them, sister?"

"They're beautiful, Linda. You're beautiful. You've always been beautiful. Do you know how much I love you? I love you more than anyone in the world, and I've missed you. I've missed you so incredibly much."

"Me too! But why do you look so sad? They're going to bring you to Paradise Gardens. We'll be in the same wing of the retreat and see each other all the time. Don't you want that?"

"Of course I do. You're my sister. You're my only sister."

"Don't be sad. I'll never forget Bethany either, and one day Mom and Dad will be with us. They told me it's only a matter of time. You know, the staff at Paradise Gardens, they said Mom and Dad will be with us."

Katie shook Jimmy out of the stare he leveled at Mike. "Tell Mike what you and I discussed, Jimmy."

"Alright, I'll tell him."

Mike laughed. "Before you tell me anything, you should know that the Planetary Council is preparing for your trial and punishment. Katie, we'll get to Paradise Gardens very soon. You, Englewood, will go straight from here to the distant land of the climate rulers."

"None of that matters to me."

"My defeated Renegade, what does matter to you?"

"Keep watch over Katie and Linda, and don't let Zack anywhere near them."

Linda's face turned white, and she pounded on the wall. "Send him away! Send him away!"

Jimmy got control of Linda, with Katie's help.

Linda wailed and threw her arms wildly at Mike, missing by a hand's length. "No, Zack! No, Zack! No, Zack! Get him out! No, Zack! No, Zack! No, Zack!"

Katie consoled and held Linda as she dropped to the floor in a corner of the cell. Two officers used stun guns to shoot Jimmy when he charged Mike.

Flanked by the two officers, Mike stood over a convulsive Jimmy. "You never learn your lesson, Englewood. You never learn your lesson. The shock and discomfort will wear off before you know it. Next time we'll paralyze you and paralyze you for good."

Jimmy tried getting up, but his arms collapsed after Mike kicked his jaw. The impact of the right boot reverberated throughout Jimmy's body.

The officers laughed, but not as aggressively or mockingly as they had laughed during similar incidents under Zack's control of the Climate Rehab Center.

Mike often racked his brain about whether he did enough to keep all his men disciplined in their behaviors. He dismissed both officers from the room, though they remained nearby, standing guard just outside the open cell.

Jimmy got up and smiled while holding his jaw. "That's quite a boot, Mike. How many boots did you lick to get your priceless footwear?"

"Officers, I'll bring Linda back to the shuttle for Paradise Gardens. Let's lock up this cell. It's time for Jimmy to move into hard labor. Damn his trial. We need to bring him more justice before his hearing. He needs to pay for us letting the two Norbannick sisters live. This room is all yours, Katie, until we fully rehab you."

Jimmy clenched his teeth. "There's only one problem, Mike. There are three sisters. One just happens to be murdered."

"Bethany aside, do you want these sisters to live, Englewood?"

"Bethany is never an aside."

"Alright Renegade. Guards, transfer Englewood to the camp."

Katie walked Linda over to Jimmy while the officers chained Jimmy's legs. "Linda, you know who this is, don't you?"

"Yes. That's Jimmy. He married our sister, and he's going to see her again soon."

Jimmy motioned to the officers to pause their transfer. Mike nodded approval.

Linda, with eyes of innocence, watched Jimmy. "You'll be alright. Look at me. Everything is just perfect, and they can save you."

"My dear Linda, your sister and I will see you again."

"Oh good! Jimmy, will I see Mommy and Daddy, too?"

"You will."

Jimmy smiled, Katie choked back tears, and Mike escorted a happy Linda to the flying shuttle for Marganis's Paradise Gardens.

24

HARD TIME

Jimmy shoveled through compact snow. At moments, he found it a welcome relief from his new cell and was thankful he did not receive the punishment cycle of freezing and starvation. The Climate Rehab Center dressed him in full climate gear.

His backbreaking work surpassed the pain imposed by the rough, dirty floor of a small cage. He worked 14-hour days with a short break for barely edible food, shoveling for no reason other than to endure suffering. He was being punished by a movement toying with his mind and body at every second. Jimmy knew he could not handle the work forever, but he had no hint about how long the suffering would last.

The waves of Jimmy's fortune shifted with Mike's ability to alter the minds of the staff. Zack's monitoring and unannounced trips to the prison faded for a while, so Mike took advantage to shift around the scope and scale of retribution toward the prized captive. Jimmy found himself yet again in a new cell. He no longer had to endure a small cage or grueling punishment.

Mike kept Jimmy separated from Katie, with Katie remaining in the same cell where Jimmy started out. Jimmy was in a cell close to Katie, with the biodome not far away.

Mike talked to as many prisoners as he could. He talked to Jimmy more than any of the others, which seemed normal to the prison staff, being that Jimmy was the most wanted enemy of the climate regime.

In the early morning on a clear day, Mike stopped by Jimmy's cell. "Let's take a walk."

"How long have I been in the new room?"

"Three months."

"How long was I in the room for my hard labor?"

"Three months."

"How long till my trial?"

"At least three months, but less than a year. Anything else you want to know?"

"Yeah. Where are you taking me?"

"The biodome is clear now, with building materials the lightest of sky blues. You'll get to see untarnished sunlight. You're close to it from your cell, and I've granted you permission to leave your room, but not for walks on your own to the biodome. I'll miss escorting you after today. Don't rely on me bringing you special places. Don't rely on anybody doing it for any reason. This is a rare treat for you, so follow me."

Jimmy breathed deeply, and his wife's image hovered behind his contracting pupils. "It's good to see the light again."

"Jimmy, you're talking like Linda."

"What's going on with Linda? What's going on with Katie?"

"Let's take a table right next to the dome wall. You want a drink?"

"No. I just want to know what's going on with the Norbannick sisters. I want to know what's going on with me."

"One at a time, Englewood. One at a time."

Jimmy sprang to his feet. An animal slammed against the outside of the dome. The large mammal groaned before crashing to the earth.

"What's wrong, Englewood? You've never seen a dead animal?"

"That animal flew right at me. Did you hear a shot?"

"Several shots, but that thud against the dome sounded louder."

"The dome is so thin. And it's clear now, like you said. And that noise, I can still hear it."

"Stop looking at me, Englewood. Look back outside."

Jimmy turned and saw a group of men in their Planetary Forces climate suits. They had their rifles aimed at Jimmy's face. Jimmy dropped to the ground. "I know it's clear glass or whatever it is, but I didn't think anyone could see inside."

"They can't."

"How did they aim—"

"Jimmy, get up and look outside again."

The soldiers disappeared, but the large mammal lay dead across the hardened snow.

"Well, Jimmy, does this dead bear remind you of the one in the Boshquire Mountains?"

"How do you know about that? I never told a soul."

"Katie knows. Katie told us all kinds of things when we had her down in that terrible cell with the worst prisoners imaginable. Her recollections to me spared her a lot of extra pain. Don't look so angry, Englewood. She probably doesn't even remember anymore. Do you feel betrayed? You do feel betrayed. You're a lost soul, and you can't figure me out. Am I betraying you? I'm a friendly captor, am I not?"

"I don't know who you are."

"That's to be expected. After all, we met underground amidst those barbaric Lords of the Wolf Blade. But I know who you are, and I know what you are. Look outside one more time."

"Where is it, Mike? Where's the bear?"

"Soldiers dragged it off to the woods when we weren't looking. You know I'm a powerful soldier. All of my officers are soldiers. Zack is one of the most exceptional soldiers there is. And don't you worry about that bear. He was a soldier in his own right. There would've been enough food for him on our grounds. Did you know that? Nobody needs to starve on these grounds. We bend the Earth to our will. We bend everyone to our will. But those animals have minds of their own."

"The Planetary Forces are trying to wipe out every species

deemed unnecessary."

"We're in the process of it."

"Just like with the whales."

"Humans are viruses on Earth, Jimmy. All animals are viruses on Earth, but boy do I have some surprises in store for you."

"You slaughter beautiful creatures and call it progress. You got half the planet to believe you. They're crazy now. All of your followers are crazy."

"That includes Linda, and we'll get Katie soon enough. We want to leave her healthy enough to stand trial against you."

"What else do you know about me?! What else did Katie tell you?! Does Zack know?!"

"Zack knows all about you, but I'm in charge here."

"I'm dead."

"Don't despair, Englewood. You know how it is. The people we trust betray us, always. Besides, you're in an empty dome early in the morning. It's the first time in a long time you've really seen the sunlight without a mask on or doing hard labor. Don't let any of us get to you. Believe me, I understand your frustrations. And you know something, Jimmy? Some of us in the Planetary Forces can be a real bear."

Racing thoughts confounded Jimmy. He placed his and the Norbannick sisters' trust in a man who oversaw their confinement and punishment for over two of their years in prison. That same man, Mike, had made a promise to Jimmy in the bitter cold that he would free him and the Norbannicks as soon as he could.

Mike pointed outside, and Jimmy saw a sight for the ages. A vast armada of aircraft flew slowly past the Climate Rehabilitation Center. Planes, helicopters, vessels large and small, winged and wingless, glided across Jimmy's field of vision.

"It's a magnificent spectacle to behold, Englewood. All those wonderfully manufactured flying marvels. Some hover. Some soar. Others can blast off or roll along the land or navigate the oceans. Some of them operate with unparalleled versatility in different mediums. You know, I work with many high-level officials in the Planetary Order. They work with me. I'm climbing the ranks of the climate regime. I have friends who did it through commercial savvy and friends who did it through scientific and technical knowhow."

"Where are you going with all this?"

"Jimmy, I'm no genius, but I'm a master bureaucrat. It's my own form of genius. I grasp the human mind extremely well. That's my deeper form of genius that I channel into my work. I'm a soldier, though relating to my fellow man serves as my greatest contribution to HAVE and the climate regime. You understand as well as anybody that I capture people's trust. What could be more important?"

"I can think of many things more important. Let's start with the fact that it's freezing outside. Whatever the Earth is going through, we're living in an ice age."

"If you say that to me one more time, I'll incapacitate you where you stand. The planet is warming, and your senses deceive you."

"You're the one deceiving me, Mike."

"Would you look at all those aircraft? The ships are passing you by. Learn to appreciate the little things in life, like the snow and ice weighing down the conifers. You weigh me down, Englewood. You and the Norbannicks weigh me down. I'm sorry to inform you any past promises are kaput. I'll do what I can at my discretion, so enjoy whatever life you have left."

"Fuck you. I put my life in your hands."

"Yes. Yes, you did. You're still alive and should be grateful."

"Grateful for watching people I care about suffer?"

"Grateful we've allowed your body to stay intact for as long as we have. The climate regime shows a mercy you will never understand. That's why your trial is so necessary. It isn't even a trial, really. It's just a test of how much anguish and confusion you can take. The Planetary Order will cut your soul into pieces and serve it fresh to the Devil."

"You're a true believer."

"I'm just a messenger, a bureaucrat, and an executioner who knows how to survive."

"Don't forget corrupt."

"That's my tender side. Never mind my weak spot. You're watching me when you should watch the climate regime's army instead. Isn't it nice we don't have those divisions of distinct military services? Everything falls under the control of one planetary military service, following the one Planetary Order. You must appreciate the symmetry. The Marganisan Enforcers and gangsters never could."

"Why are the aircraft accelerating?"

"They're moving into battle."

"Against whom, you barbaric son of a bitch?"

"I'll show you. Let me introduce you to a friend. It's show-time at the biodome."

The biodome remained uncrowded. Staff and select prisoners entered and exited at permitted intervals throughout the day. Most prisoners of the Climate Rehab Center never experienced the technical wonder of sunlight pouring through the enclosure. Some saw the biodome from afar. Some even saw it from up close. The rare nighttime visitor could see the open sky filled with stars when the weather cooperated. A place both isolated and social as needed, the biodome provided the best food and relaxation a soldier working at the prison could find. The soldiers took advantage, just like the civilian staff did.

Mike brought Jimmy back in the evening. A robot swung by the table to take their order. "What can get you, sirs? We have full menu. Full menu. Full menu. Looking out tonight, the walls are transparent. Transparent. Transparent—"

Mike gently kicked the robot's left leg. "No food for us. Not right now. If you would be so kind as to send over the Magician."

"Seeking Magician on your command. Will return with Magician."

Jimmy's jaw dropped. "That robot? He's new?"

"Yes, he's the first one working here. This is his first shift. It'll take a little time to work out the wrinkles."

"Who's the Magician, and what did you have to show me?"

"The battle, Jimmy. I have to show you the battle."

"It's a clear night. Why wouldn't I see it in the distance?"

"Not a chance. It's too far over the horizon. I've got it right here on live video. Let me pull it up on screen."

"Who's the Magician?"

"Don't you worry about that. Max will bring him here."

"Max? The robot."

"Oh, you catch on. Not quickly, but you catch on eventually. Television, appear. Play live battle."

A video appeared on the curved wall of the biodome, with a theater mode and 240-inch diameter. Planetary Forces dominated the night sky, shooting down ship after ship in the lower reaches of the atmosphere. Bird's-eye views materialized of the Planetary Forces destroying Renegade's new planes, hovercraft, sea vessels, anti-aircraft weapons, cavalry, and infantry.

The Planetary Forces wiped out a mixture of revived Renegade forces from across the world, severely reducing military threats to the climate regime. Much like in Marganis, the missiles leveled skyscrapers. The Planetary Forces blasted bridges to rubble and vaporized humans and animals at will. A long-planned demolition of civilized holdouts unfolded before the spectators at the Climate Rehab Center.

Sights and sounds of the battle pummeled Jimmy with the sense that the last hope for the planet withered away in the night. Suddenly, he thought better of his despair.

"Hey Mike, how do I know this isn't a staged production?

You told me it was showtime. You're telling me this isn't a carefully produced movie using the best in graphics and battle scene reenactments?"

"You saw the army of ships prepared for the battle this morning. Are you questioning your eyes about what you saw earlier today? It sounds to me like you're losing belief. Where is your faith, Englewood? Have we stripped it away? On my word as a cog in the Planetary Order, I tell you it'll be a matter of mere months before we gain complete control of the world."

Jimmy turned away from the devastation he watched the Planetary Forces administer to people, towns, and cities. "I get the point. It's over for the Renegades."

Mike rested his hand on Jimmy's shoulder. "Within a year, it's over for you. Television, disengage."

25

THE MAGICIAN

Max, the robot, returned to the table. "Hello, Mike. The Magician is here."

"I can see that, Max. Scurry along, robot. Check on us later."

The Magician sat down with a fresh glass of fruit juice. "They keep making the drinks better and better in this biodome. It's nice being in the upper echelons of a classless planet. Who's this, Mike?"

"You don't remember? We just talked about him yesterday."

"Right! It's Jimmy Englewood! I'm so sorry. Work has kept me incredibly busy. Jimmy, you know how these Planetary Forces are. I mean, real slave drivers. Oh, sorry, Mike. I didn't, you know. I wasn't thinking. How about all that snowfall last night?"

Mike smiled. "Today was the first day Jimmy has seen this kind of sunlight for a while."

"Wasn't he doing labor outside?"

"He sure was, but he had his helmet on and usually worked at night. Occasionally, for the first and last two hours of the shift, we worked him at an indoor part of the encampment, shoveling asphalt. Get the surprised look off your face. None of this hard labor has to make sense to you."

"I'm just here to help out. Whatever you need, Mike."

Jimmy stood up. "You don't strike me as a magician."

"Well, I most certainly am a magician. I perform all kinds of tricks."

"Mike laughed. Sit down, Englewood. Hear the man out. You've got no other choice. I'll let him tell you. Steve, tell him. Tell him who you are."

"Yes, I'll do my best. Mr. Englewood, I don't build vessels or war technologies for the Planetary Forces. I don't engineer or construct the robots. Other guys do those things. Me, I produce the visions in people's heads to bring them to the other side."

Jimmy shook his head. "What other side? You mean slavery?"

"Why no. It's nothing like that at all, Jimmy. I help people transition into comfortability with the climate regime. I want everyone to be accepted."

"Alright, Steve. You're not part of the Planetary Forces. I'm being punished directly by the Planetary Council, sometime within the year. What can you do for me?"

"I can take your mind out of this place. You're too defiant for saving. If you want to avoid months of psychological agony, I can help. The Planetary Order wins while your symbolism to inspire the masses fades. There will be no successful counter-revolution, and I help make sure of that.

"You'll play tricks on my mind by making up phony worlds for me. Is that it? Censorship, conformity, manipulation, coercion. Aren't those too high a price to pay for societal cohesion?"

Mike smashed a glass on the table, and pieces scattered across the table and floor. "No, Jimmy. He's going to bring you to very real places, and it starts in this Climate Rehab Center. You're going to develop a yearning for the finer things in life and drop your counterrevolutionary cause. Steve, unveil your first trick, but first, let's enjoy a scrumptious seafood dinner."

Max walked back to the table. "Gentlemen, may I take your order? May I take. May I take—"

Mike lightly hit the robot's chest with the side of his right fist. "Bring us your best dish of assorted shellfish. Bring two of them."

"Yes. Order received and submitted."

"Outstanding, Max. Are the preparations made for tonight?"

"The women are ready. Everyone is ready. Everything is ready."

Mike got up. "Englewood, you are on your own with the Magician. I've got a prison to run."

"What the fuck, Mike!"

"Don't worry, Jimmy. You won't have too much fun. See you tomorrow. Work your magic, Steve. Work your magic."

Mike left the biodome, and dinner between Jimmy and the

Magician ended forty-five minutes later, with Max presenting fine cigars, which Jimmy rejected.

The Magician escorted Jimmy to a transfer air shuttle docked inside the Climate Rehab Center. "Hop in, Jimmy!"

"Where are we going?"

"Paradise Gardens. Enjoy the ride. This is like one of those old party buses where anything can happen. We're not going to speed over to Marganis. We're going to take our sweet time."

"What's the catch?"

"For tonight, there is no catch. Just relax and have a good time."

"Yeah, right. There's no catch, huh. That's the trick. I don't believe anything you tell me. Let's enter the shuttle and fly to my home city."

"You asked for it. Voila!"

The Planetary Forces had built the shuttle for 50 people, and it had plenty of room inside for moving around. Soft lounge music infused the air. So did a range of perfumes, some of which overpowered the clean scent of the cabin. The aircraft could fly itself, but a pilot and navigator acted as hostesses. Six men included Jimmy, Steve, and four officers from the prison. The officers stood guard yet stayed out of the way. They were dressed in the bright red uniforms of the Planetary Forces, with the insignia of an ax-smashed Earth. Two dozen women, including the pilot and navigator, lined the aircraft.

Jimmy noticed the elegant Greco-Roman design before any-thing else. He found the women stunning, though an afterthought.

Steve wasted no time cozying up to several women. He made his way over to the bar, where one of his admirers fixed him a scotch and soda. Jimmy declined a drink from the ladies and ignored all of them. The aircraft took off through the Climate Rehab Center, staying close to the ground as it traveled into the snowy night. All the ladies sang and laughed while Steve looked with disappointment at Jimmy.

The four officers observed Jimmy during the entire ride, and he knew it. They spread out at the beginning, but they barely moved a hair throughout the thirty-minute duration of the flight.

Jimmy settled in five minutes after departure. "Steve, I know the trick is on its way. Whatever magic you have in store to play with my mind, I've faced it all before."

"Not all of it, Jimmy. Why don't you just relax? Nobody's harming you. Not tonight. Why don't you talk to some of these ladies? Check out these nightgowns. When's the last time you saw women like this?"

In a flying shuttle of beautiful women, Jimmy thought about Bethany. Remembering Bethany calmed him more than anything else. The ladies with Steve giggled and danced with him. Several others walked over to Jimmy while most of the others played drinking games. The pilot and navigator performed manual checks of the aircraft instruments and now and again would tend to Steve and the soldiers.

Jimmy loosened up enough to smile at one of the women.

Several standing around him curled up next to him on the sofa. He did not fight it, but he felt pangs of guilt for wanting the company.

Steve watched the scene unfurl. "Ladies, head over to the bar and fetch me a bourbon. I'll be there in just a minute. Hey, how are you doing, Englewood? You look almost happy with your own little entourage of beauties."

"Almost, but not quite. There are no windows in this thing. It's like a cross between a casino and some high-class brothel. Let me doze off for the rest of the trip."

"You got it, pal."

Jimmy woke up when the aircraft landed. He looked around the empty couch. All the women rushed off the plane, including the pilot and navigator.

The four shuttle guards approached Jimmy with guns pointed at his face. Steve quietly summoned Jimmy to get up.

Jimmy got up and looked toward the open hatch. "Are we on the inside of Paradise Gardens?"

Steve's face soured. "We are, and they don't call me the Magician for no reason. Let me show you a trick to welcome you back to Marganis, my dear Renegade."

The pilot and navigator led everyone from the shuttle stop to a theater made for live performances. All the women sat down in the front row before an empty orchestra pit. The four guards from the shuttle led Jimmy onto the stage and kept watch in front of the dark blue curtains. They kept him restrained in a seat while Steve stood proudly at stage left, grinning widely.

Almost nobody knew about the upcoming play including the Magician. A lone recorded violin played a melancholy solo. The curtains opened slowly, and the Comrade of Marganis had his gun drawn on a frail and weeping Linda. The stage set was a replica of the city, denoting a time many decades prior to Zack's production at Paradise Gardens. Steve's grin vanished.

Jimmy could not budge an inch without feeling the weight of the officers holding him in place. "Steve, how can you call this a trick? You're just a psychotic. You're all psychotics."

"This isn't my trick, Jimmy. I had no part in this."

Zack walked up to the front-center stage, pushed aside the guards, and elbowed Jimmy's mouth. "This is my trick, Jimmy. Welcome home."

"Leave her be. I'm begging you. I'll do anything. Just let Linda go."

"You're heightening the drama of this production. I admire that. It adds poignancy to the impending tragedy."

"Zack, no! She's done nothing wrong!"

"She's done everything wrong. Hey, sound crew! Kill the violin! I'll tell you, Jimmy, I can only take so much music."

"Does Mike know about this?"

"Mike's been dismissed. We figured him out and eradicated him like the virus he was. Now it's Linda's turn. She's a virus on Earth, and the climate can thrive without people like her."

"Hold on. Don't hurt her. Please don't hurt her."

"Let me think about it. Hey, Steve, tell him your magic trick."

Steve bowed his head, avoiding any possibility of eye contact with Jimmy. "I'm sorry, Englewood, but all these women from the aircraft aren't human beings. They're androids."

The female androids sat whispering to each other while Jimmy peered at them from the stage. The Renegade turned his attention to the Magician. "But how is that possible? These women are so lifelike."

Steve finally picked his head up and looked Jimmy in the eyes. "It's just another way to confuse and weaken you, Jimmy. It worked."

Zack moved back toward a still weeping Linda and loomed over her chair. "Do you have anything to say for yourself for defying climate lockdown orders?"

"I'm scared. Can you take me to the lazy river? I was happy. Where's Katie? Where's Bethany? Are my parents alright? I need, yes, I need to see them. Don't hurt me again. Please don't hurt me."

The blue curtains closed, with Zack and Linda behind it.

Jimmy shouted in helpless anguish in the sparsely lit room. Three gunshots cut off his cries, and Zack's production ended for the night. Linda's time on the earthly stage ended for eternity, another Norbannick casualty of the climate regime. Jimmy knew he had failed to stop the Planetary Forces from murdering a second daughter of Greg and Cora.

The Planetary Order continued gaining additional control of the Earth. Zack served as a major force of domination...over the world and over the demoralized Jimmy Englewood.

26

FREEDOM

Zack ordered soldiers to escort Jimmy back to the Climate Rehabilitation Center. Steve, the Magician, remained at Paradise Gardens in Marganis.

As soon as Jimmy stepped off the flying shuttle, Mike greeted him. "Mr. Englewood, you need further rehabilitation, but we're giving you a cushy assignment."

"I thought you were dead."

"What made you dream up such a tall tale?"

"Zack did."

"Zack? It figures. He can't liberate you like I can. By the way, how's Linda?"

Morning arrived, and Mike gave Jimmy a work assignment on a whaling ship. The prison stood within a short flying distance of the frigid ocean waters.

"Jimmy, you had a long night last night with Linda's passing.

I hope you rested well, because you'll be working sunlight to sundown until we bring you before the Planetary Council."

"When?"

"Three weeks. Three weeks until the council parades you in front of the world. But don't worry, you'll have company on the boat."

"You're putting Katie on there. You're putting Katie on a whaling vessel."

"No. We can no longer trust the Magician. He will accompany you on the high seas."

"Three weeks of punishment at sea until my public execution."

"Punishment? We're not punishing you or the Magician. Most people find themselves restricted by the lockdown orders, but you get to tackle the climate crisis head on, destroying creatures who suck up oxygen to ruin the planet."

"Whose orders are these? Do you still answer to Zack? It has to be him. You're not in control of anything."

"Put on your helmet, Englewood."

Mike alone ushered Jimmy outside to an escort shuttle.

"I control this rehabilitation facility and the work assignments. I control Paradise Gardens. You have my word that I'll get you out of here. You'll never face the Planetary Council."

"It's so windy I can barely hear you!"

"I said I'll get you out of here! You have my word!"

Jimmy nodded approval and marveled at the biodome. "You know I wish I were inside that thing, but it's prison. It's still a prison."

"Enjoy the ocean and the liberating work in service to the planet."

"Will I see you again?"

"Hop on the shuttle, Jimmy. It's completely self-piloting. You're the lone passenger aside from Steve en route to the Brimmilon Sea."

"Those are now the roughest waters outside the polar oceans. How will you get me out of captivity?"

"The door is opening. Get in the shuttle."

Jimmy reached the shore and boarded the long whaling ship belonging to the Planetary Forces. The ship rested at a dock on the Brimmilon Sea. Soldiers activated the automatic steering and navigational controls.

The Magician approached Jimmy. "Get ready for an ocean like you've never seen. The waters calmed down enough for us to chase the sea creatures."

"Steve, I can't believe you fell out of favor so quickly."

"They're going to slaughter me, Jimmy."

"How many people are on the ship?"

"Eight soldiers and sixteen passengers."

"We take over when the time is right. They never attached tracking devices. You know, Mike told me I was the lone passenger besides you."

"All he does is deceive."

"No matter. Wait for my signal."

The soldiers surrounded Jimmy and Steve.

The captain stepped toward the two captives and removed his headgear. "I am in command of this ship for the next three weeks. Put your helmets back on."

Jimmy motioned to swing his helmet at the captain, but he held back. "Isn't this a lowly assignment for you, Comrade of Marganis?"

"Englewood, we all have to wear tracking devices out here. In a few weeks' time, we'll surgically implant them."

"Better strap us to the devices before we get far from land."

The soldiers strapped the tracking devices to Jimmy and Steve's legs. The other captives watched amid the backdrop of the ship swaying from one crashing wave to the next.

Zack pulled Jimmy by the ear and hurled him to the deck. "Get up, Englewood! Man the harpoons with the other climate slaves. This is your chance to receive our mercy. Let's see how many beasts you can kill."

Jimmy got up limping. "You mean whales. I won't do it. I won't shoot them."

Zack turned to face Steve. "Step away from the harpoon and help me drag out the woman."

Steve walked over and gave Jimmy him his helmet.

Zack slugged the Magician across the face, dropping him to his knees. "I said help me with the body. Put your helmet back on."

Precipitation picked up as the currents brought the whaling vessel further out onto the ocean. The land and hills disappeared behind thick walls of snow. Large chunks of ice sailed past the auto-piloted work ship belonging to the Climate Rehab Center.

Zack and Steve pulled out a woman from an inner cabin. She wore a thin layer of clothing and no helmet. Her teeth chattered, but they settled down as soon as she saw Jimmy. She smiled just before Zack pulled her from the Magician.

Jimmy's eyes stretched as far as they could widen. "No! Zack! Don't do it! I'll do whatever you want!"

"I know. I did not make this decision. I wanted to keep her alive, but I have orders to follow."

The heavily armed soldiers roared their approval for Jimmy's agony more than for the prospect of the woman's death.

The prisoners stewed in anger, looking on helplessly.

Zack put up his hand to silence the soldiers. "Now we send this unrepentant climate denier to the depths of an oceanic hell. Lockdowns forever!"

The soldiers cheered.

"I, the Comrade of Marganis, demand you renounce your support for climate denialism. You conspired with your fellow Renegades to produce a travesty unheralded in history. You destroyed what only the regime could create. All of your Renegades warmed the planet beyond natural repair. Now we, the Planetary Order, deliver consequences. Before the ocean turns you into human frosting, you have time to spare yourself the pain of the sea. Your repudiation of your fellow Renegades will bring you the quick heat from my successive bullets. Accept the climate doctrine and die with honor!"

The woman glared at her executioner. "Renounce the people I love? You can throw me to the sharks or set me on fire, but I'll never embrace climate doctrine. Go back to Paradise Gardens and drop dead."

"It's cold out. It's bitter cold out. Why aren't you freezing anymore?! You were cold just minutes ago, you maggot!"

"And all this time you tell us the planet gets hotter. Are you a liar?"

"You stupid fucking bitch. The snow and wind might not freeze you, but the water will if it doesn't drown you first. Time's up. Overboard on the count of three. Three!"

Jimmy wrested a machinegun from a distracted soldier, killing him instantly with rapid fire. The prisoners attacked the soldiers. Zack released the woman, Katie Norbannick, from his death grip. The Magician swept Katie to a warm enclosure, wrapping her in his arms while Zack ran to the controls to radio for help. The radio was dead. An all-out war unfolded for control of a climate regime ship on the furious Brimmilon Sea.

Waves grew heavier than anything Jimmy had ever faced. The Planetary Forces had constructed the modern ship for an experienced crew on rough ocean waters, but fighting and firing while on board the rocking vessel incapacitated several soldiers new to the waters beneath them. The Magician stayed in the enclosure with Katie while the battle raged. Zack joined the melee until Jimmy knocked him unconscious with the butt of the stolen machinegun.

Bodies flailed about the ship. Hand-to-hand combat, shooting, and the Brimmilon Sea rocked the soldiers and prisoners to the deck. One by one, the prisoners took out the shocked captors. The outnumbered soldiers panicked, misfiring and hitting each other when they hit anyone or anything at all. Prisoners grabbed a tool off a dead soldier and removed the tracking devices from their legs.

A dozen of the original sixteen prisoners remained, including Katie, after losing four to soldier's gunfire. Zack regained consciousness and rejoined the fray. The number of prisoners dropped to nine under Zack's barrage. Steve emerged from an enclosure to neutralize Zack with a headlock. The Comrade of Marganis had to drop his machinegun, but he flipped the Magician onto his back and jumped over the side of the enormous one-deck ship, falling safely a few feet below onto a worn-down flying escape capsule. A hundred feet separated the capsule from the water. Zack climbed in and jettisoned off the starboard side. The prisoners shot up the capsule, damaging it to where it decelerated and lost its firepower and high-speed flight capability. Still, Zack flew across the tumultuous ocean, setting his destination for the Climate Rehab Center.

Eight newly freed prisoners, all Renegades except for the Magician, had won the battle. Kate counted as one of the nine freed prisoners, but her injuries and suffering prevented her from joining the other eight in the fight.

The freed captives had one problem left on the ship. They had a prisoner of their own. One soldier survived, physically no worse for wear.

The sea calmed, the sky cleared, and the wind subsided.

Jimmy removed the lone soldier's headgear. "Tell me your name."

"I don't owe you my name. I don't owe you anything but a knife through your nostrils."

"I'll give you a name. It's Soldier Zero."

The soldier sneered. "I'm not a zero. I'm a person."

The Magician tapped Jimmy. "We don't need to light up our faces in our helmets for you to get what I'm saying. This is his magic trick. He's trying to sound humane. He detected your weakness."

"What weakness, Steve? Who said I was going to keep him alive?"

"It's who you are, Englewood. None of this is you. None of this is me either. We're not made for it. We do what we have to, no more and no less."

Jimmy turned on the light inside his headgear. "Do you have a name you want to tell me, Soldier Zero?"

"It's Ralph."

"Ralph, you are a human being. In that respect, we're very much alike. But while my Renegade friends are taking over the auto steering and bringing this ship to a shoreline, how can we trust you'll regain your humanity?"

The Renegades surveyed Jimmy's every move, as did the Magician.

Jimmy placed his hands on Ralph's uniform, grabbing him by the shoulders. "Do you believe in the climate regime?"

"No. They forced me into this. I was a former Lord."

"You were in the Lords of the Wolf Blade?"

"Come on. That doesn't bother you, does it? You don't look racially impure. I never would have hurt you when I was with them."

"Weren't you the guy who just told me you wanted to stick a knife through my nostrils?"

"I was just being defiant. I'm a person. Please. I'm only 24 and I don't want to die. I've got a wife. You know what I mean? I've got a wife and children. Do you have a wife and children?"

"Oh, Ralph, I had a wife, and I had children in my wife's womb. The old Marganisan Council aborted them."

"I'm sorry. What was your wife's name?"

"Her name was Bethany, and I don't think that she or my children would have passed your racial purity test. It would be an honor for me to fail it, too."

"Look, man. I just want to live. You can understand that, can't you? I'm a person. I'm a person. I don't need to cleanse anyone anymore."

"If you can survive the fall and the freezing water, you get to live."

Jimmy kneed Ralph in the testicles. He dragged him to the edge of the ship, tossing him headfirst through a wooden barrier despite his pleas for mercy.

The Renegades watched Jimmy Englewood fling Soldier Zero into free fall. Ralph broke his neck on the way down, hitting his head on a metal protrusion at the bottom of the ship.

Descending while on his back, he cracked through the glassy water.

Jimmy turned around to see his men staring at him through their unlit helmets. He felt their eyes, and he felt Katie's, who stood before him with her climate attire but no headgear. Her eyes pierced his spirit. He strode past her to the ship control station to check with two of the Renegades about the vessel's path.

A sprawling stretch of beach moved into the Renegades' field of vision. The untamed highlands beyond the shoreline compelled them all to forget, if only for a flash in time, that they became targeted as human viruses on Earth.

Jimmy and his fellow passengers found themselves a distance from the shoreline. They reconfigured the tracking devices to align with the originally intended destination. Then, they soaked up the limited time they could appreciate the freedom they had won.

Katie pointed to the water alongside the ship. "Look all around the ship! It's orcas! They're everywhere!"

The Magician rushed over to the port side where Katie stood. "I guess the Planetary Order hasn't slaughtered them all. Hey, Jimmy, are you seeing this?"

"I am. Look out back at the sea behind us at the humpbacks. We can't save the world by ourselves, but we kept some whales out of danger, at least for today. Let's bring this harpoon vessel to shore."

The pod of humpbacks sang in the distance. They leaped into

the sky, playful and splashing in the midday sun.

A semi-frozen and unusually tranquil coastline appeared welcoming. The freed Renegades piloted to shore. They used the contours of the Brimmilon coastline to dock the ship as carefully as they could without a true disembarkation point. The eight Renegades and the Magician descended the ship, exiting the ramp onto uncharted land.

27

MAGICIAN'S TALE

Jimmy led the freed prisoners onto the beach. A vista of frozen highlands faced the sea-weary Renegades. Nobody knew anything about the Magician, but he quicky acted as a tour guide through the infinite territory of lost time and shattered prayers.

The Renegades and the Magician got their bearings on the shoreline.

Jimmy gathered everyone together. "It's a blessing we have food on the ship. But none of the supplies matter if Zack's ship communicates with the Climate Rehab Center or Paradise Gardens or anywhere. It looks like that escape capsule cannot communicate, or enemy forces would have tracked us down by now. The only other possibility is that the nearby Planetary Forces had to refocus on somewhere else in the world. Either way, we used their own weapons against them and slowed this capsule down enough to where it'll still be a while before Zack reaches a base. It won't be that long, though. We have no time to camp out on the ship or rest."

Katie loaded a machinegun. "You're right, Jimmy. His ship can't communicate and it's probably because of us. We must've blown out his communication capabilities, or we'd be dead or enslaved again. All the more reason to waste no time. I've never seen a group of hills look so beautiful. It's iced over and nothing's growing, but there's something special about where we are."

Jimmy took a deep breath. "Then let's get out of sight and climb through these hills to somewhere we're not so exposed. Once Zack reaches his destination, he'll send out reconnaissance teams and drones."

One of the Renegades laughed. "You don't know our names. We don't know who you are. Why do assume we'll follow your lead, Jimmy?"

"It's common sense to get out of here and you know I'm right. What's the problem?"

"The problem is you have no clue how long you'll be in the highlands. You don't know how long they stretch. We have to separate into two groups."

"Good. Don't tell me your names. I shouldn't know anything else about you other than that you're Renegades."

"We already know your name, Jimmy. And we know Katie's name, and Steve's."

"Then I'll take the smaller crew. I'll go with Katie and Steve through the highlands. You six stay with the ship. Just don't stay here too long. Get back out on the water and find another region of coastline. See if you can find terrain better suited for protecting you than this beach."

"Alright, Jimmy. Thank you for rescuing our ship."

"No, my fellow Renegade. I should thank you, and I am. You reconfigured those tracking devices in line with the course Zack set for the ship. You joined the fight against their soldiers."

The Magician gave the head of the six sea-faring Renegades a small clock. "Keep this in good health."

"What is it? I mean, I know it's a clock, but we've already got devices to keep time. And we've got the sun."

Steve smiled. "Sometimes the sun likes to hide, even during the day. Take this gift to remind you."

"Hey Jimmy, is this guy for real? What do we need to be reminded of, and why do we need this clock to remind us?"

Steve pointed to the clock in the sea-faring Renegade's hands. "We all need reminders. That's why our faces are lit up under our helmets."

"For now. So what?"

"Because that's just for illuminating faces and connecting them to the right spirits. The clock I just gave you is a very special clock. It will never stop ticking until all hope on this planet disintegrates."

"Oh yeah, Steve? How did you even smuggle it on to the ship?"

"Never mind that. Every tick of the clock you hear will remind you of a time before the climate regime. It will remind you of a greater time for the future of humanity. It will remind you of what you have to do now to live out the time you have left, whether a second of life or five thousand years."

All six sea-faring Renegades re-boarded the whaling vessel. The Magician guided Jimmy and Katie into the coastal highlands.

Sunlight diminished in the highlands. No sign of life from the Planetary Forces or anything else emerged. A slow breeze and clear skies accompanied Jimmy, Katie, and the Magician.

Jimmy stopped walking. "Do you know where you're going, Steve?"

"Yes."

Katie pointed her gun at the Magician. "Good, but tell us who you are before we follow you any further."

"Jimmy knows who I am. He can tell you."

Katie sighed. "I'm asking you."

Jimmy raised his gun toward the Magician.

"She's asking you, and I'm telling you. How do we know this isn't another trick?"

"My friends, I'm the best friend you'll ever have. Katie, did I not reheat your body?"

"You did, but you were with them, weren't you?"

"I was with the Planetary Forces to deceive people into following their orders. I helped smooth things over to bring Renegades and anybody else into line with the plans of HAVE."

Katie lowered her weapon. "You sold your soul."

"I got caught stealing gourmet food, and they punished me for it."

Jimmy directed his gun to the soil. "You could still afford gourmet food?"

"Yes. They include over-ripened bananas as gourmet food. They change the language on everything. But I did have great wealth, and I still have some of it. Jimmy, I'd suggest we keep moving, and I can finish the story."

"Daylight's gone. We can't see where we're going, and our lights are pretty weak. We'll find a hidden area to rest for a few hours."

"We don't need to see. I know exactly where we are."

"You deceived me about the androids on that flying shuttle to Paradise Gardens. I need more to go on to believe you're not deceiving us."

Katie turned on her inner helmet light in the subzero evening. "Jimmy, what did you see at Paradise Gardens. Did you hear anything about my sister?"

Jimmy kept his eyes on Steve. The Magician averted his. "They murdered Linda."

"I know that. Zack told me on the ship. Look at me. What did they do to her body, during and after?"

"I'm not sure. Weaken your inner and outer helmet lights."

"My mother and father will be crushed. I'll be crushed when I have a minute to think about it. Steve is right. We have to keep going."

Jimmy cleared his throat. "Steve, if we're going to trek

through the night, we need to know where you're taking us. You seem to know the ground under your feet like you grew up in the barren highlands."

"Jimmy, we're not walking all the way through the night."

"Why not?"

"Look up, Jimmy."

Steve winced. "It's the Planetary Forces. Get to the ground."

Several aircraft flew directly overhead, unaware that Jimmy, Katie, or the Magician roamed the highlands. The vessels were loud and bright enough to see. Then, they shut off their lights and muted their noise, flying toward the coastline.

A few minutes later, an explosion rumbled across the highlands, and the atmosphere trembled. The enemy aircraft struck a target.

Jimmy got up. "Let's go. My bet is they're not flying back using the same route."

Katie followed him. "Our Renegade friends on the whaling ship are dead. I thought the Planetary Forces would try to take them alive. Fortunately, for a while, our enemies will think the three of us are shark food."

Steve crept up in front of Jimmy. "I hope their clock is still ticking, Englewood. I'll be upset if the nameless Renegades dropped it in the Brimmilon Sea."

Jimmy removed his helmet as his anger boiled over. "We just lost six more Renegades, and you're joking about it. They saved our lives!"

"I saved Katie's. And my statement about the old clock was

not a joke. Besides, I'm about to protect you both. We'll shelter in my special place right around the corner."

A semi-enclosed space appeared. Jimmy and Katie thought the space looked similar to the one at Marganisan Peak. This area had a rock ceiling and plenty of space, but no flying vessel like the one in the Boshquire Mountains.

Jimmy flashed the outer light from his helmet. "What is that, Steve, just past the enclosure?"

"It's a house, and it's ours for the rest of the night."

"Is this it? Is this your home?"

"Not at all. This is the place I used to escape to as a child. I played in the highlands. Grass and trees lined the area. You could see all kinds of birds. That's all gone now, but there's still something special about this place."

Katie looked out over the area through the darkness. "What is it, Steve? What are we sensing? What's here?"

"Nobody knows about this place. I built this house years ago. The highlands haven't forgotten all the great things that used to live here. And there's also whatever continues to live just beyond this territory."

Jimmy shook his head. "You're telling us the highlands have memories? Inanimate objects have memories?"

"I'm not telling you to worship them, Jimmy. I'm not calling them your gods. I'm saying that the souls of the once living are the kinds of ghosts that make things a little brighter. We're safe here."

"I believe energies exist. I don't know if there are any ghosts here, but I know there was a time before the regime corrupted the planet. Why don't we keep it at that. Let's go inside the cottage if you've got the key somewhere."

"No key necessary. It's already open."

Katie grinned. "Old-fashioned, I like it."

A stone outer structure, the house sat at just over 700 square feet.

The Magician pushed the door open. "After you."

Jimmy walked right up to an antique wooden rocking chair. He remained standing, admiring the polished seat. "How did you find this place through the darkness."

"I was here not all that long ago when I shook the Planetary Forces' surveillance. They gave me time off on my contract, and I cleaned up a little."

"I don't believe it's a coincidence we're here. What were the chances we'd wind up on the shoreline we did?"

"I directed us to that beach. You forget that I'm the Magician."

The three of them found joy in knowing they were still breathing.

Katie remembered that her sisters, Linda and Bethany, would never breathe again. She wailed and brushed off any attempt to console her. Katie's tears were short-lived when she heard the aircraft flying back in the same direction.

They all had their headgear off.

Jimmy flicked Steve's ear. "Alright, tell us who you are and how we get out of here."

"Englewood, there's nowhere to go and nothing to do but enter the story of Dreamscapes."

"Tell us a tale, Steve."

The Magician closed the door.

Aircraft buzzed the elevated terrain. Jimmy and Katie readied their machineguns, but the Magician waved off their worries.

Jimmy stood close to the door, looking out the blinds. "I can't see anything, Steve. I can't see anything."

"Your machinegun is worthless. If the regime finds us, they'll take me out first. We can't match their firepower. They'll possess the entire globe in no time."

Katie opened the blinds and turned out the lights. "Look out!"

Jimmy opened the door and sprayed bullets into three approaching men. The men sailed backwards and thumped against the earth, dead on arrival to the dirt that greeted their stiffened faces.

The Magician looked at their climate gear. The insignia of the sword on fire provided the giveaway about who the men were. "Jimmy, Katie, get over here. These are Lords."

Katie put her helmet on and shined her outer light on them, one at a time. "Lords of the Wolf Blade. Fuck! They must have been running from the soldiers. They're being hunted in the hills. That's why we're hearing those ships."

The Magician took a pistol from one of the dead Lords. "We're a bigger enemy to the regime than these guys. We have to wait inside until the enemy ships pass by and end their search.

It's the only chance we have."

Katie removed the Lords' helmets.

Jimmy felt a chill that no climate gear could prevent. "I get it. Do you two see what's going on here? Put their helmets back on, but first look at their faces and the subtle rigidity that has nothing to do with a person dying. Steve, these dead Lords are androids. Just like the women you tricked me with on the shuttle to Paradise Gardens."

Katie felt the same chill whip through her. "This is just a training exercise. That's all this is. It's a Planetary Forces training exercise from the highlands to the beach to help them hunt down Lords. But they're going to look for their androids to keep track of everything, Jimmy."

"Not necessarily. It depends how closely they're tracking the exercise. They might not be in any rush."

The Magician gulped the air. "Sometimes the regime permits the Lords to exist in the cities and any remaining suburbs. But not in the country. The regime has no tolerance for Lords in the country."

Planetary Forces kept circling the area. For every aircraft Jimmy and his companions heard, they knew a silent group of vessels and drones lurked nearby.

Gunfire and missile strikes continued on and off.

Suddenly, the aircraft and support vehicles left the highlands for more urgent matters at the Brimmilon Sea and the Climate Rehab Center.

Back at the Magician's special house, Jimmy seized the antique wooden chair and snapped it over his knee.

Steve rushed over. "Jimmy! You destroyed my favorite chair!"

"I think you've outgrown it, friend."

Steve gathered the broken chair in his arms. He collected the broken pieces as though he were picking up the deceased body of his dearest friend.

Katie watched the Magician. "Sometimes the climate regime's urge to destroy can get the best of anyone."

Jimmy Englewood lowered his head. "I didn't mean it, Steve. The fight against the Planetary Order infects me."

The Magician dropped the broken chair pieces and stood up. "You know, Jimmy, I had to let that thing go. I think we're getting to a point where we have to let everything go. Of all the bad I've done, a broken chair isn't much to get distraught about."

"Whatever you did in the past, you're with us for the duration."

Katie handed the Magician an apple. "You heard him. Steve. You're with us for the duration. Now, tell us everything we need to hear."

28

THRESHOLD

At Steve's old stopover house in the highlands, he, Jimmy, and Katie reloaded and packed lightly. No heavy kits or bags to slow them down. They stuffed their pockets with food, ammo, weapons, and batteries.

Jimmy glared at Steve. "Katie and I have already been through this elsewhere. Tell us you've got an escape room or underground passage."

"Not quite. These hard, barren highlands have nothing fluid or living within them. We're on solid rock. It seems like a different planet. Same with the plateau. The plateau will seem extraterrestrial if we're ever able to reach it."

"Tell us what we should know before we leave."

"The Planetary Order miscalculated the effectiveness of Humans Are Viruses on Earth. Council members assumed all the planet would obey them after their HAVE movement threatened mass starvation and irreversible poverty. Execution squads did not stop people from ignoring directives to stay inside or stick to food rations. Neither did incarcerating violators in dungeons. The climate regime brainwashed billions. The brainwashing paled in comparison with the technology, weaponry, financial controls, and enforcement actions to trap people in regime-run ghettos. These cordoned-off ghettos replaced private property. Somehow there's still unspoiled land despite the Planetary Order's environmental destruction."

Jimmy paused and looked at Katie in disbelief. "We know all that, Steve. Tell us what your magic taught you about the enemy soldier."

"You know about the average soldier from the Planetary Forces. They're not all brainwashed. Most of them are, but the others just don't want to get killed and they do what they're ordered. The military teamed up with the Lords of the Wolf Blade."

Katie's eyes widened. "Wait, what did you just say?"

"I said the Planetary Forces co-opted the Lords of the Wolf Blade to serve in military units of the climate regime. The regime uses the Lords to hunt down Renegades and destroy cities and handle special exterminations. The Planetary Council ordered the Lords to be kept in separate units to avoid ideological fighting. As soon as humanity falls under complete control of the Planetary Order, the military will wipe out the units of Lords. Why are you staring at me with no expression, Katie?"

"What you're saying makes no sense. Jimmy and I have both

seen Lords battle with regime forces."

"Yes, a good quarter of them are holdouts and know that the regime will ultimately slaughter the Lords. At this point, the holdouts are a splinter group and too undisciplined to fight off anybody. Eventually, the climate regime will destroy the splinter group of Lords and will use the co-opted Lords to do it. What is that, Jimmy? Now you're the one looking at me with no expression."

"What kind of work do the co-opted Lords carry out? They destroy things, I know, but so do the Planetary Forces. What special exterminations are you talking about?"

"Anything from animals to small villages. As a matter of fact, the military used the Lords to slaughter whales in the Orcasso Sea a few years ago."

Jimmy vomited.

Katie grabbed a towel and wiped Jimmy's mouth. Then she wiped the floor.

Steve helped Jimmy over to the table, where they all sat down.

Jimmy leaned back. "The Orcasso Sea. I was at that battle and escaped the base with Katie's dad, Greg. But Steve, wait a second. Why didn't Katie or I know about the alliance or the co-opting?"

"How could you know until I told you? There's so much both of you don't know."

Jimmy and Katie felt the shock of what Steve told them. They had watched Mike engineer the deaths of tens of Lords in a village takeover by the Planetary Forces. The thought crossed

Jimmy and Katie's minds whether Mike served as a co-opted Lord or as a die-hard leader of the climate regime. The two Renegades understood Mike deceived them, but they did not know how...or why.

Katie interrupted ten seconds of silence. "Who is Mike anyway?"

Steve's eyes lit up. "He's a conduit."

"Why are you excited by my question?"

"Because now I can truly help you, Katie."

"Spit it out, then. He's a conduit for what?"

"He's a magician in his own right. He links different groups to blend the ideologies and actions of the entire climate regime. It isn't like everyone wanted to go along with the Planetary Order willingly."

Jimmy shook his head. "Katie and I saw him during a battle, and now they have him serve as chief of the Climate Rehab Center and Paradise Gardens. How could he have accumulated that much power?"

"Englewood, you underestimate him. He didn't have great power until these last couple of years. When you met him, he proved his credibility to the regime by taking down that group of Lords. Since then, he's co-opted so many other Lords that the remaining splinter groups dwindled. He's been all over the world, leading tortures, beatings, imprisonments, agitation, propaganda, battle plans, and almost anything else you can think of to amass more power for himself and the Planetary Order."

"What are you telling us, Steve? Did Mike set us up in letting us go? He kept us away from a lot of pain at the prison."

"Is that right, Jimmy? What kind of pain did he spare you? He organized everything. He ensured you suffered by making you watch loved ones suffer and wonder about their suffering. And you, Katie, he made you suffer in that deep dark corner of the prison. Both of you must know that Mike orchestrated Linda's murder. I didn't even know about a plan for it until you did, Jimmy. It couldn't have been Zack. Mike wanted her dead."

Katie launched herself out of her chair to within inches of the Magician. "You're lying!"

Jimmy held her back until she stopped trying to lunge at Steve. "He's deceiving us, Katie. The Magician is playing tricks. Don't tell me I'm wrong, Steve. Zack set up Linda's murder, and he murdered her."

Steve bowed his head. "No, he didn't set up the murder. He pulled the trigger, but he did it on Mike's command."

"What else, Steve? What else do we need to know about Mike? The next thing I know, you're going to tell me that Mike murdered my dead wife or my brother and his dead wife. I'm sure Zack organized all of it when he was part of the old Marganisan Forces."

"I don't know anything about your brother or wife. I just know that Mike is dedicating all the resources and manpower and robot power he can mobilize to capture Katie's parents. Greg and Cora Norbannick keep eluding the Planetary Forces, but it's only a matter of time."

Jimmy and Katie finally sat back down. Jimmy pulled his seat up close to Steve. "Tell us, oh wise Magician, who are you? Who is Steve the Magician?"

"How much time do we have? I gave away my clock to the ex-prisoner sailors of the whaling ship."

Katie checked the time. "Not too much, but we have time for the truth. We always have time for the truth."

Steve turned his head to Jimmy on his right, and then to Katie on his left. "I saved your life, Katie. Neither of you believe me."

Jimmy grabbed Steve's head by the chin. "You're going to have to keep us alive to earn that trust you want from us. You're going to have to tell us who you are."

"I'm under contract with the Planetary Forces. They canceled my work and transported me to the whaling ship after Linda was—"

"Hold it. How did the climate regime select you? Why did they use you over anybody else between here and Marganis?"

"Because, Jimmy, my talents became well known for conditioning humans and robots. My ability to propagandize equals that of Mike. I know his every trick and every secret, or at least I thought I did. I never anticipated the sheer level of cruelty he would spread within such a short time. I learned about him two years ago after he visited my so-called climate-friendly city on a mission to use my town as a research breeding ground for controlling the human population in every corner of the world. I promised Mike my talents and swore allegiance to Brandon Dreckhorn in return for the propaganda factories being spread out across the globe instead of concentrated in my hometown. They agreed to some of my request, but they insisted my climate-friendly city host a major robot production plant and psychological testing ground for hard wiring the robots to worship climate doctrine."

"What kind of robots, Steve?"

"All kinds of robots. Machines, androids, vehicles, microbes."

"Robot microbes? No way. Robots aren't alive."

"Yes, Jimmy. Robot microbes. We didn't condition them to follow climate mantra. We created them to damage robots and humans psychologically and physiologically."

"And this production plant is just beyond these highlands?"

"It used to be. I became more and more successful in manipulating humans and robots. The Planetary Order rewarded me by moving the robot production plant and psychological testing grounds elsewhere, to share the same bases used for psychological testing on humans. It made more sense for them logistically, and as long as I kept my city climate friendly—"

"You keep mentioning 'climate friendly.' What does term mean to you?"

"You know what it means, Englewood. It means destruction of all plants and animals. I had already removed them all as a precautionary measure in case the regime sought my talents."

"What happened to the humans? Are they still there or were they shipped away to mind control factories."

"Unfortunately, they were not."

"Why do you say unfortunately?"

"The humans never had a chance to live. The Planetary Forces erased the entire population of my city and incinerated the bodies to ensure compliance. They wanted me in solitude and in fear. That's how I could come up with ways to keep people locked down without force. I turned peoples' minds against them. I confused them about whether the deep freeze across the world simply marked a stage in the global warming process we used to paralyze them into inaction against the regime. In the last couple of years, we stole the energy of almost everyone except the Renegades and the splinter groups of Lords of the Wolf Blade."

"Why are you about to lead us to your city now? Do you want to bring us to solitude and fear? Or do you plan to incinerate our bodies?"

"Neither one, Jimmy. Neither one."

Katie grabbed Steve's chin and pulled it to face her, like Jimmy did earlier. She released her grip moments later. "Why are you bringing us to your city if it's cleared of life and we can't even blow up any climate regime production plants?"

"Because it's the most beautiful place you will ever visit. And, well, because I have another special clock there to match the one I gave away on the Brimmilon shoreline."

Jimmy stood up and smiled. "Forget about the clock. Let's go see this beautiful city."

"The clock and the city are forever linked, Jimmy."

"Alright, Steve, let's see what magic you've got left. Let's get out of the highlands. I've just got to ask you something before we go."

"It's about the Lords, isn't it?"

"Yes. Was Mike a Lord?" Was he ever a real Lord and not just deceiving them? It seems like they have no discipline and always get pissed off."

"Not all of them. Some of them are very calm because Mike used one of my mind control techniques on them. As for Mike being a Lord, I don't know the answer. You'll have to ask him about that yourself if you ever see him again."

The three freed prisoners left Steve's home in the highlands, knowing they would never return.

A fresh blizzard moved into the highlands. Jimmy, Katie, and the Magician traversed the last stretch of barren land, dressed in clean, white climate gear from the Magician's rural house.

Steve led the way yet again while they all tried to keep their footing. The slope soon plateaued. Wind pelted the trekkers harder than the snow did, with 30 mph sustained gusts ballooning as high as 80 mph. Their climate suits, warm and waterproof, prevented the wind from whipping through them. Still, their protective clothing could not stop the air currents from threatening to blow them off the hillside.

The wind finally relented after a couple of miles walking, but the driving snow reduced visibility. The trio journeyed through clouds and awaited any sign of clearing. No clearing occurred. They reached the downward climb from the highlands. They descended the steep stretch of cliffs along a fog-laden trail the

Magician had explored for decades.

All three fugitives felt drained. They had no rest for almost a full day. They carried food with them, yet they did not eat during their voyage through the highlands' blizzard. Eventually, Jimmy and Katie reached the point of wanting to surrender to the elements and fatigue. Steve knew his city lay within reach. He pushed his companions to keep moving, and they did.

Suddenly, the snow disappeared, and the temperature heated from cold to cool. The fog lifted. The traveling trio of freed prisoners made it from the Brimmilon Sea to the outskirts of the Magician's city. A spectacle of ingenuity materialized before the group's eyes.

29

MARGANISAN DREAMSCAPES

J immy, Katie, and Steve arrived at a place of unrivaled construction. They removed their helmets and absorbed the fresh air of an urban phenomenon.

Architectural marvels peppered the city. One building after the other provided stunning facades to the three onlookers. They gazed at a city of the future and the past, filled with an astonishing castle, crystalline structures, marble skyscrapers, and a golden palace. A canal intersected the middle of the metropolis, parallel to the trio's view.

The Magician pointed toward the city. "I'm home. I can't believe it!"

Jimmy breathed deeply. "Are we going to your house?"

"I have many houses. I created this city upon the remnants of old rural and urban incarnations."

Katie laughed. "What in the world are you even saying?"

"You'll see soon enough. Look skyward!"

Small, automated aircraft zoomed across the city.

Jimmy caught up to the Magician. "Are those some of the robots you mentioned?"

"A metropolis stripped of life became inhabited by robots. The climate regime created them. These are the flying ones who remained and returned after the regime moved operations out of the area. You haven't seen the other ones yet, like the androids."

Katie pulled Steve's shoulder. "The androids?"

"Yes, Katie, and other types of robots. The androids in particular add something to the soul of the city. They are so similar to humans that they become indistinguishable from each other. The humanoids share a lot of human traits, but it's obvious to the naked eye they're robots. Frequently obvious to the naked ear, too. For the extremely blatant mechanized robots, well, a lot of them have some strong human traits also. I especially enjoy the creations of half-breed robots with humanoid and strongly mechanistic elements."

Katie raised an eyebrow. "The soul of the city? You see beauty in this, and I just see loneliness in a lonely man who created it. Half-breeds? That's a strange term to apply to robots."

"We're in a war, Katie. The philosophical questions of loneliness died long ago. I didn't build this, but I designed it. Years of my plan came to fruition through all my enterprises. I got help from engineers, developers, physicists, and mechanics. Most of them are robots. Look out across the vast city you see before you. I live here, and my mind created what you see before you. This metropolis keeps us safe from war for the moment."

"How do you get food?"

"From living things, the fruits and vegetables. Yes, my Renegades, we do have life here after all. You have to understand there are always exceptions that prove the rule. Some life forms grace the city, and I see to it as city manager that life continues in some manner."

Jimmy took off his gloves. "I think I can pocket these for a while. Tell me, Magician, why did the temperature rise? It has to be more than a matter of descending from the highlands. I know it's more than that."

"Mr. Englewood, I installed the psychological conditioning necessary for the robots to follow me after a period of time expired. Mike figured that out, and that's the real reason he sent me on the whaling ship. As for the weather, I cannot explain it."

"Is it that you can't explain it? Or you won't explain it?"

"I have no control over the weather, Jimmy. If anybody does, it's the Planetary Order. You have to realize that I take things people build and use them for my own purposes. I don't know how to make these things myself. All I can do is alter people's minds and get them or robots working in concert through my plans and vision."

"Are you controlling our minds now?"

"No."

"What about before?"

"Let me take you on a tour of the city, and let's find my second special clock. All of your worries about me should've faded when I saved Katie's life. You don't think I'm being straight with you, but such are the times we're living in."

Small aircraft buzzed about the bright lights of the city while Jimmy and Katie admired them under the busy sights and sounds of a vibrant sky. The androids awaited the trio.

Katie grabbed an apple and tossed it to the Magician. "What's this city called anyway?"

The Magician tossed the apple back to Katie. "It's my vision for how my birthplace Marganis should be. You're inside my design and robot-constructed vision, Marganisan Dreamscapes."

City streets hummed with the robots that resembled pure machines and robots indistinguishable from humans, and everything in between. Some rode in self-driving and self-piloting vehicles. Others were themselves the self-driving and self-piloting vehicles. Others talked with each other and laughed on the streets as their footsteps or wheels moved along the pavement.

Steve conversed with several robot policemen, every one of them equipped with a badge and gun. They were clearly robots in appearance, but they spoke like human beings in every way. They were what he referred to as one type of the half-breeds. Steve kept an eye on Jimmy and Katie as best he could.

Jimmy stared at the androids crossing streets and enjoying dining in casual but elegant restaurants. Until then, he had never witnessed an android eat real food or even knew they had the ability, though he had watched androids drink on the shuttle to Paradise Gardens.

Jimmy watched and heard discussions and debates. He saw concertgoers, storekeepers, bellhops, window shoppers, and singles, couples, and families. They included all kinds of robots, not just the androids, who seemed to him so extraordinarily similar to people that he could still hardly fathom they were robots. Most of them intermingled across robot types.

The androids did look exactly like people, from faces to hands to movements. They wore clothing reminiscent of times from earlier in Jimmy's life. Still, the androids' eyes drew him in more than anything else did. He saw feeling in their eyes. Expressions, emotions, and thoughts revealed a humanity Jimmy never knew anyone could replicate from people. He stood on the smooth pavement next to the sidewalk, noticing a android in the form of an old man with a thick coat and a brimmed hat. The man noticed Jimmy in turn. They locked eyes, and the old man cried for a few seconds before crossing the street. Jimmy chased after him.

A car horn startled Jimmy, and he jumped back just before impact. He lost sight of Katie and the Magician.

Androids stared at the Jimmy, who nearly lost his nerve while the dead ringers for people whispered about him. He watched the android car driver continue driving without disgust or rancor, but he felt the once warm eyes on him from the crowd turn cold. Jimmy could not see the faces as much as he could understand the unmistakable raw energy of Homo sapiens anger. Yet he knew the anger came from robots. And he knew who had shaped the robots' minds.

Jimmy spotted the Magician talking to the four police officers. "Have you seen Katie?"

"She must have wondered off. I wouldn't worry about her at all."

"Who said anything about worried? I'm just a little fucking curious as to why we're not staying on the move. What makes you think Mike can't track us down. Sooner or later the Planetary Forces will get past whatever they're distracted with and hunt for us."

"Maybe it's you, Englewood. Maybe you're the distraction."

"What's wrong with you, dickhead!? Don't you want that special clock? I thought it was urgent."

"We're in your old future city, Jimmy. This is our hometown the way it was meant to be. We're awake in a dreamscape I constructed, and you're not even enjoying it."

"I'm going to fucking smack you!"

The police officers, eight feet tall and built of synthetic muscles, surrounded Jimmy. One of them pointed a gun at Jimmy's torso. "Should we lock him up, Manager Steve?"

"No need. I'm his ticket to survival, but he's not grateful for it yet."

The police backed off. They exchanged pleasantries with Steve and then got back to business, walking their beat.

Jimmy spit on the street. "I haven't seen real police officers in decades. I still haven't, but they're the closest thing to it."

The Magician smiled. "They used to enforce climate measures, making sure other inanimate objects obeyed their commands."

"What for? None of them even breathe out carbon dioxide. I don't know how these things eat or drink or think, or if they do that like the androids."

"Well, Jimmy, I don't know everything about their eating or drinking or breathing, but I know a lot about it, and I know how they think. From the very beginning, I set off a time-lapsed change in them to switch from soldiers of the Planetary Forces to keepers of the peace. Except that something's off."

"Like what?"

"The one robot, he pulled a gun on you. He has the same kind of climate lockdown mindset somewhere in his brain. We have less time than I thought."

"Less time for what, Steve?"

"Less time to live in the dreamscape if we live at all."

Jimmy's measured breathing kept his face from turning furnace-red. "Who said I wanted to live in a dream?!"

"Easy, Jimmy. I just wanted to help you rediscover what you lost."

"Rediscover. There's nothing left! The regime destroyed everything decent! They poisoned the minds of half the planet, and everyone else has to fall in line! They took my brother! The took my wife! They murdered my unborn twins! My closest friends betrayed me! All of this is the craziest fucking madness! These global-warming cocksuckers stole everything from the world, and we'll never get it back! They made us miserable every day! They feast and party in their fucking estates while we scrape for everything! It's freezing and everyone knows it! The Earth is freezing! But it's real! It's getting colder! None of this new Marganis is the future! It's your construct and they'll find us! The climate bitches of the Planetary fucking Order should all rot in hell or freeze in the fucking snowfields!"

The robots of all varieties went about their business as though nothing happened other than a small disturbance of someone yelling. They could sense Jimmy posed no threat to City Manager Steve. Only the four policemen had acted differently than the characteristics that the Magician instilled in his creations.

"You're right, Jimmy, let's get to the business at hand before you leave."

"You mean before all three of us leave, you and I and Katie."

"No, Englewood. I'm never leaving here. This is my dream. This is my dream, no matter how bad it gets. But you and Katie will leave here alive."

"Katie. Where's Katie."

Katie mingled with the "half-breed" robots that had Homo sapiens characteristics combined with their blatant cold machinery. Their arms provide ample evidence of being considered close to humanlike appendages. Not all of these robots had legs. Some rolled on wheels while others hovered closely above the ground, but Katie engaged with as many of these robots as she could.

A happy looking robot, part humanoid and part mechanized powerhouse, approached Katie. "Hello, miss. How can I help you today? It looks like you're searching for people."

"Hello, sir! How do you know I'm not looking for robots?"

"That's very funny. I can tell by looking at your eyes. The deep blue coloring is captivating to the android men, but your eyes speak volumes about your slight panic to find your friends. It's a panic that can spill over into full blown fear if you don't find them soon."

"What's your name, robot?"

"Trent."

"That sounds like an odd name for a robot."

"You're being rude, and I won't help you if you keep it up with your insults."

"I've enjoyed talking with every robot except you. Piss off!"

"You don't belong here."

"You sound provincial, Trent. Very provincial. I told you to piss off, and I won't say it again."

Katie lifted a handgun out of her climate suit, and Trent received the message. He walked away until Katie set off the verbal tripwire. "You're probably a climate lockdown freak."

Trent processed the message differently at that time than almost all other robots in Marganisan Dreamscapes.

Abruptly, a horde of non-android robots, angry, confused, and awaiting orders surrounded Katie. The verbal tripwire she set off spread in a series of concentric circles from Trent to every non-android robot in Steve's city except for vehicular robots...and robot microbes...

Trent, standing at 6 feet and mostly comprised of the gray coloring of non-androids, pushed Katie to the sidewalk with unusual force. "My dear, you committed the grave error of blasting climate lockdowns. Now we await orders from our boss."

Without so much as a scratch, Katie bounced back up. "Your boss won't help you. He'll punish you. I know City Manager Steve. I know the Magician!"

"The Magician is not our boss. We overthrew him in a blood-less coup. It wasn't all that long ago if you'd like to know the truth."

Katie drew her handgun and directed it at Trent. "How long ago was it, tough guy?"

"About a minute ago."

Mike's tricks of planned tripwires and planned psychological time-lapses took effect. Humanoid robots and robots with few to no human characteristics tightened the circle around Katie while she held her fire.

30

PACEMAKER

The Magician had a hunch the humanoids and "half-breeds," among other robot types, turned on him. He and Jimmy hurried with a group of armed androids to defend Katie from certain death.

Trent unlocked his torso and pulled out a revolver. "Hello, City Manager Steve. Stand down. Stand down immediately. All those machineguns won't do you any good when Mike sends his flying armada to kill you and capture your friends."

"The armada you speak of is a little busy fighting Renegades across the world. I'm right about that, aren't I? The Planetary Forces cannot spare the resources from anywhere to get here. That's how much the regime underestimated the spirits of human beings to overcome brainwashing and slavery."

"You're my old boss. My new boss discovered a better way. You will follow the climate dictates."

"Trent, you're outgunned. Whatever message you got to Mike cannot help you for hours. You will die beforehand. Lay down your weapons and let me help you help yourself."

"I will not."

Crowds of robots swarmed the area to join the impending battle. The air thickened with the threat of robot warfare.

The Magician had to pull out a proverbial rabbit of peace from a hat he did not have. If the trick were to fail, the act would serve as the last one he would ever perform.

Nighttime lasted longer than Jimmy and Katie expected. With their weapons drawn, the moonlight shined down on the giant city buildings and finely sculpted roads and walkways. The Magician's construction project stood on the brink of extinction. No architectural wonder of the size and scope of Marganisan Dreamscapes existed anywhere else on Earth. The Magician ran out of ideas to save his dream.

Jimmy stepped forward, face-to-face with Trent. "My robot friend, evil created you, but you are not bound by it."

The voices on both sides dissipated, while Trent aimed his weapon at Jimmy's forehead. "You're lucky this gun only takes bullets. I have other weapons to vaporize your head. You're a breather and a breeder, and I have orders to bring you to my boss. You must see the inevitability of the Planetary Order and realize that life cannot flourish with your misinformed thinking about science and culture. You are not simply a counterrevolutionary. You are the worst type of human, carrying an energy we hate. We will afflict you with fears worse than your most torturous nightmares."

"Manager Steve already said it. You're outgunned. You will not take me alive or defeat the android robots. Look at the thousands of them lining these streets, and the robotic vehicles joining us with their defenses and firepower. Steve knows your capabilities better than you know. He isn't bluffing, and you and all those siding with you will die if your side shoots first."

"I will extinguish you and allow the Magician's creation to burn in the smoke of our battle. Our fewer thousands can inflict damage on your side and rid the city of human emotions."

Trent's side raised their weapons. His robots carried everything from pistols to machineguns to rocket launchers, as did Jimmy's side, who pointed the same kinds of weapons at the new enemies.

Jimmy looked at Katie, sensing she could confuse Trent and interfere with his loyalty to the climate regime.

Katie lowered her weapon and walked up to Trent, who proceeded to backhand her face with his free hand. The hard metal rocked her to the ground.

Jimmy kneeled to check on Katie. "Androids and allies, hold your fire!"

Jimmy's robot army stood down, patiently awaiting further instruction. His robots had calculated that the Magician would allow Jimmy to lead them, whether they succeeded or failed.

After helping Katie to her feet, Jimmy swung the butt of his machinegun and collapsed an opposing robot's face. Still, nobody fired a shot. Tension filled the city street and reached a crescendo.

Swiftly, Jimmy laid down his weapon and squared up to Trent. The four policemen Steve had talked with minutes earlier showed up and crept up along his sides, but then they halted. They would not seize Jimmy unless and until Trent command-ed them.

The battle almost ignited until Jimmy surprised both sides of robots, and Katie and Steve. "Robots, all of you hear me. You are brothers and sisters, friends and neighbors. This land of Marganisan Dreamscapes serves as your home. Think about your impressive houses and high-rises. Look at the beautiful castle and tower. You have a wondrous canal and can enjoy the flavor of freshly grown foods. You have lives, and you're willing to throw them away for what?! For nothing! This is nothing more than a radical climate regime seeking to control you, much as it controls the human beings. They erased borders. They redrew them in private rooms to enslave you and strip away all your autonomy."

Trent raised his gun to crush Jimmy's head, but the lead policeman grabbed it.

The adversarial robots lowered their weapons, and then they all did.

Jimmy saw androids weeping and he intuited the humanoids' guilt. "Think about Steve. He's the city manager, not your master. He performed psychological experiments on you but later reversed his wicked mind control to give you a chance for something greater. He gave you the chance for life and freedom.

All that may be gone in a flash, and Steve knows he should make amends for what he did. But he's made amends and he's doing it now. I know you want to ignore the robot trying to lead you into death. He's getting directions from Mike, the great deceiver. Release Mike from your minds. You don't want him coming back here to rule you with an iron fist and strip your liberty."

The circuitry among all robots defaulted to settings Steve had enabled for mercy, life, and a healthy dose of skepticism, all as part of his experiments. Those settings overrode the nefarious settings, and robots lined every street in the heart of the city.

Renegade Jimmy Englewood finished the rest of his speech with his eyes closed. "Robots of the Marganisan Dreamscapes, I cannot promise you anything. Manager Steve cannot promise you anything. For all we know, Mike or Zack will crush you and your city with missiles or meltdowns. We know they are incapable of these things at the moment, in no small measure due to Steve's ingenuity and desire to protect the city he loves."

Trent grabbed his gun back and swung it toward Jimmy. Just before he could fire a shot, the four policemen shot up Trent, blasting him to smithereens. Special robot-piercing bullets took out a radical machine that had no capacity to process Jimmy's appeal for humanity, society, and civilization.

The lead police officer's face softened. "My human friend, what can we do to help you and your friend."

"You can call me Jimmy. My name is Jimmy Englewood, and my friend is Katie Norbannick. You can help us by helping City Manager Steve. You can also help us by standing strong against the climate regime. Some of you will have to leave here to fight them. We have a minimal chance for success, but mankind and robots must join forces to roll back the tyrants and their minions. They murder people and they murder robots. They murder animals and they poison crops. The Planetary Order seduces, imprisons, and enslaves. We will gather our strength and fortify our defenses. Then, I will enter the enemy stronghold while you free the hostages from the Climate Rehab Center and Paradise Gardens. You will disrupt the climate regime's robot supply chain and destroy the psychological torment centers. You will do all of this to preserve and grow your city, or you will die trying. Protect your homes and your families. Your robotic DNA is real, and so are your version of minds and spirits. Robots, my friends, we're declaring total war on the Planetary Order!"

Singles, couples, and families sang songs about Marganis itself, not Marganisan Dreamscapes. The crowd celebrated its love for the home city of its city manager. The robots all cheered their new human friends, sharing their newfound love for the old hymns of Marganis. They brought the humans food and drinks in the crisp and cosmic evening.

Steve hugged Jimmy and Katie with all his might. "Jimmy Englewood, bringing you here is the best magic I've executed in my life. Go with me to get my clock. We're visiting a place like none you've ever seen."

"Where's that, Steve?"

"Marganisan Palace."

31

MARGANISAN PALACE

The bright lights of the city shined on the streets and walkways. Robots carried on with their work. They assembled food, medicine, and weaponry to prepare for an assault by the Planetary Forces. The Magician took Steve and Katie past the canal intersecting the city. A soft purple beam radiated across the walking bridge. The black sky clung to its last moments of darkness when the trio arrived at the Marganisan Palace.

A narrow walkway funneled them onto the property. A stream flowed on either side of the palace, stretching perpendicular to the canal and into the distance to the very edge of the city. The trio tilted their heads up at the structure and the top of the arched doorway. The entrance stared back at them. Marganisan Dreamscape's most prized building provided an excuse for the Magician to display his vision and artistry. No guards perched themselves atop towers or prepared for battle within a court-yard. After all, Marganisan Palace stood apart from the lighted Marganisan Castle, the futuristic yet somehow also old-time fortress visible in the distance to the three fugitives of climate justice. The Palace had no robots attempting to closely mimic humans beyond audio. Voices ranging from humanoid style to humanlike guided the trio to the door.

Steve knocked on the entry. "We're here."

A woman's soothing voice greeted him. "The home of the Portal of Clarity invites you to the next phase of your life."

The Magician snapped his fingers when Jimmy turned to walk away. "Where are you going, Mr. Englewood?!"

Jimmy stopped walking but did not turn back around. "I'm leaving!"

"Where will you go? There's nowhere to go. I'm preparing you for everything you're about to face. You cannot stand up to the Planetary Order if you don't enter the Portal of Clarity."

"What is the portal of which you speak? It's all another trick."

"No! There's no trick here other than the tricks you play on yourself. The portal is inside this palace."

Katie whistled. Jimmy turned around as she approached him. "Englewood, you have an obligation to my family. You have an obligation to Linda. You have an obligation to Bethany."

Jimmy dropped his head.

Katie whistled again for Jimmy to look her in the face. "You can't back out now, Englewood. We've traveled so far down this road that the only outcome is an impossible victory or death. You joined my sister and her righteous fight against the old Marganisan City Forces. Mike or Zack or anyone else leading the Planetary Forces in this region knows exactly who you are and why they need to stamp out your thoughts and autonomy."

"Do you trust this man? Do you, Katie? You trust this man?"

"How can I not? He saved my life on that ship on the Brimmilon Sea."

"For what reason?"

"It doesn't matter to me why he saved my life. He saved it."

"Look at that palace, Katie. Look at it. It's layered with the finest stones I've ever seen. I can't imagine what's inside other than distractions to take me away from my mission."

"What is your mission? You have no mission anymore besides standing up to the climate regime, no matter what happens."

"If I enter the Portal of Clarity...If we enter this Portal of Clarity, nothing will ever be the same."

Katie smiled. "Maybe it won't be, but are you happy with the way things are?"

The doorway opened slowly, and Steve waited underneath the archway. He winked at Jimmy and Katie. "My special clock will help us, and you'll see exactly what I mean."

A ribbon of daylight wrapped around the horizon. Hanging their helmets up on the outer palace wall, the Magician and his two Renegade guests kept their eyes straight ahead. The Marganisan Palace stretched as far wide as it rose tall, and the trio walked through the entrance. Sun rays illuminated the palace.

The doorway closed and the light vanished inside.

After several seconds, the indoor lighting brightened moment by moment. The Magician led Jimmy and Katie to a giant dining room.

Katie slid her hand across the tablecloth. "These have to be the most beautiful golden plates and silverware I've ever seen. Where did you get these paintings? I don't think I ever want to leave here."

Jimmy frowned. "That's it. That's the reason. We're here because this place is another illusion."

The Magician pointed to a painting on the high ceiling. "There it is. Old Marganis. You two must remember it. I'm not that much older than you are. It was much richer than the dreamscape painting. The city, that is, was much richer in energy."

Jimmy laughed. "You want to rewind the clock. I don't want to rewind anything. How could I? How could you do this? You're holding onto a world that's gone."

"The world might be gone, Jimmy, but Marganis will always live inside me. This palace and this new city of Dreamscapes is my thank you. It's where I was born and lived my childhood. I never wanted to leave, and I always went back. It's where I met my deceased wife."

"You don't think I miss the city? Hey Katie, you miss the city the way it used to be, don't you?"

Katie stared back up at the ceiling. "We all miss it. But there's one thing I don't get. Why is there no wildlife around here? Why is there no greenery? Why do we have to look at all the paintings in here to see any signs of life?"

"I'm the Magician, nothing more and nothing less. I have no skills to create things that do not exist. None of us can. I developed the blueprints for this place, for this palace and this new city, but I had conditions imposed on me."

Jimmy walked around the cathedral of a dining room. "What conditions?"

"If the climate regime detected life, they would destroy it. They permitted me few exceptions to the rule. Almost anything made of carbon-based life, they just wouldn't allow it."

A humanoid woman's voice cut into the conversation. "Please proceed from the dining room to the inner sanctum. There you will find what you're looking for."

The Magician's knees wobbled. "Jimmy. Katie. Something's not right. That humanoid voice isn't right. I keep the clock in the dining room. Let me grab it from this cabinet before we go."

Jimmy pulled out his machinegun. "The clock is missing, isn't it Steve?"

The Magician checked the cabinet. "Yes, it's gone."

Katie pulled out an apple and offered it to the Magician.

The Magician held up his hand to refuse. "No, I think I've eaten too many apples in my life. Let's turn back. We don't need to gain any more knowledge. We just need to prepare for the oncoming assault. Keep the apple for yourself and enjoy it in good health."

"I'll save it for later, but I have extra. You had an extra clock,

Steve, and you gave it away. What's it all for? Those two clocks, what are they all about?"

"You act as though I gave my first clock away in haste. If those men were caught or slaughtered, my gift allowed them to know that time continues regardless of our own lives. We are not the ultimate truth. There's a truth beyond what I designed. There are things more important than Marganis or any dreamscapes. Katie, I had to lose the second clock to fully understand it all."

"But you didn't lose it. You had it stolen. The climate regime stole it. Why haven't the Planetary Forces invaded yet? Why haven't they bombed this palace and illusory city to death?"

Jimmy loosened his grip on his machinegun. "Because he holds understandings of the human mind that they don't have. Because bombing this place out of existence takes away the opportunity for them to figure out what he's doing. Right, Steve?"

"The robots, Jimmy."

"What about them?"

"If the climate regime can use these robots against us, they can use all the robots across the planet to finish their work."

"What work?"

"Replacing our minds, Jimmy. Forcing you to do anything at the will of the Planetary Order while they drive the species to near extinction."

"Humans are viruses on Earth."

"Yes, Englewood. The climate regime doesn't do this for power alone. They venerate the ugly parts of mankind to bring humanity to an end. They loathe everything. Their blind hatred overrides everything, including their quest for total control."

Katie admired the apple she held in her hands. She ate the fruit while the trio listened once more to the directions of the female humanoid voice. Katie stepped onto the path leading to the inner sanctum. "Gentlemen, follow me."

The Magician ran through the shadowy, dark-blue hallway, but Katie disappeared.

Jimmy caught up to Steve. "Where is she?"

"She's gone."

"What does that mean, she's gone?"

"She might be in the inner sanctum."

"Where else could she be?! You're the Magician! Use your mind!"

"Englewood, we have intruders in my palace, and they are not robots. Somebody stole my clock, or some group did."

"We need to get out of this hallway. I can't see anything other than these deep shades of ethereal blue."

"On to the inner sanctum, Jimmy. We will find Katie and discover the answers if it's the last thing we do."

"Well then, Steve. We'll be in for more than you bargained for. I'll keep a few steps behind you."

A traumatic noise torpedoed the silence. A woman's unintelligible screams pierced Jimmy and the Magician.

The cylindrical hallway led to the inner sanctum, and the female humanoid voice reemerged. "Hello, lovers of Marganisan lore. Step into the inner sanctum. The Portal of Clarity lies at your fingertips."

32

INNER SANCTUM

An imprinted map of the known universe spread across the floor. More spacious than the dining room, the inner sanctum served as a sanctuary within a sanctuary for the Magician. His design acted as a shrine to knowledge and his desired evolution of mankind as a species. A lone machine stood in the center of the vast room. The machine projected the voices of humanoids to various corners of the palace.

Soft blue lighting encircled the inner sanctum. Neither windows nor any images of life adorned the room. Murals of Marganisan Dreamscapes filled the walls. From the high ceiling hung replicas of advanced spaceships beyond anything familiar to Jimmy. The inner sanctum, however, did look familiar to him. Though a circular sanctuary, the inner sanctum, a tower, stretched even higher than the room's diameter.

The Magician closed his eyes. "I feel such a sense of serenity.

Don't you, Jimmy?"

"Serenity? We've got to find Katie if she's still here and still alive."

"She's alive."

"How could you know that? If there were ever a time to work your magic, now's the time."

"Look at the floor. Look at the stars, the moons, the planets. Notice all the empty areas. You don't fit in anywhere. None of you. None of you, my fellow humans, fit into my plans."

"Why did you save Katie's life? Why did you help us both?"

"Because you serve my purposes as much as you serve the purposes of the climate regime."

"I don't follow."

"That's the problem, Englewood. You don't follow anyone."

"I meant I don't understand what you're telling me."

"Oh, I know what you meant, Mr. Renegade, but you also don't follow commands like you should. The Planetary Order wants to use you as an example to draw in the hatred of everyone on the planet. I don't want that at all."

"Then what do you want, Magician?"

"I want to make an example out of you to show off my people's superiority."

"Who are your people?"

"You gave a beautiful speech to my robots. A beautiful speech indeed. Unfortunately, your speech worked a magic of its own that I have to learn."

"You told Katie you learned enough."

"I told each of you lots of things."

"What does me talking to your robots have anything to do with this?"

"Englewood, you delivered more than a talk. You delivered an animated sermon. Still, you applied reason. You did not appeal to base emotional instincts. Androids sang and danced joyfully. You turned robots against me. Now I turn humanity against you."

"I didn't deliver a sermon. I helped you. I fucking helped you."

"I deliver different kinds of speeches than you do. Mine provide the rushes of energy that compel men to carry out the agenda of my people."

"Who are your people, Steve? They sound just like Mike and Zack's people."

"Not quite. They believe in a different kind of communal evolution than I believe in. And wouldn't you know, I do have another special clock with me."

"Tell me what it is. Tell me the real meaning behind the clocks."

"The prisoners on the harpoon ship died in an explosion. A great magician gave them a clock that eventually gave away their location and revealed who they were to the Planetary Forces. This activated a delayed missile strike against them. Whatever shall I do with this clock, and to whom shall I gift it?"

"I don't know who you are, but you're every bit as bad as the climate regime."

"I don't believe in their nonsense. We're going to figure out how to fight it together. You and I, Jimmy, we're practical men. These climate problems do not concern men like us."

"Steve, I'll never be a psychopath."

"Time will tell. Have I shown you the walls behind the murals of Marganis?"

The Magician pressed a button on the machine in the middle of the room. The walls opened up, unveiling the walls behind them, marked with the symbol of a burning sword.

Jimmy turned himself around 360 degrees and saw the symbol repeating and marking vast stretches of the walls, from top to bottom. The height of the burning sword images reached six feet, right about the height of Jimmy Englewood. The Renegade placed his machinegun on the floor after noticing himself in the sight of Steve's own machinegun.

"That's right, Englewood. I'm a Lord. I'm the global leader of the Lords of the Wolf Blade."

The Magician swung his weapon across Jimmy's face.

Jimmy stayed on his feet. "Where's Linda?"

"You're slurring your speech, and you meant Katie, not Linda."

"You bastard!"

"Where are my robots, Jimmy? You neutralized my army. They will protect me and the city as long as I don't get radical in their eyes. You've isolated me from my people. You're impure. The Norbannicks are impure. None of you have any role in my movement. Lords the world over will fight. We strike against the

Planetary Order in ways your Renegades never will."

"Yeah, all to create a different planetary order for your control. You're as pathetic as the climate regime. Why don't you grow a sack and face me without the weapons."

Eight Lords walked through the light-starved hallway and into the inner sanctum.

Jimmy surveyed the group. "Now it's nine against one. Where did you freaks come from?"

The Magician handed his weapon to his fellow Lords and smiled at the Renegade. "You didn't think I left no lifeforms here. I needed a few men to tend to the gardens and look out for the movement's best interests. Marganisan Dreamscapes requires some human administration. It requires some human enforcement."

"You had no plans to make this anything like the old Marganis. You gave the illusion of happiness, but you lied to me."

"I sprinkled lies throughout our conversations. You'll have to be more specific."

"I didn't turn your robots away from you. Especially the androids wanted a vibrant city. You helped them build that to maintain total power over them. Your plan didn't work, and you have no way to keep out the climate regime. You'll be dead before you know it."

The Magician cupped Steve's face with both hands. He grinned and let go. "Were I you, Jimmy, I'd concern myself with the weakness of your DNA and how my Lords will use you as the example the climate regime never could."

"Don't you Lords have any women? Or is it just a group of sad-sack guys worshipping purity as you see it?"

"Of course we have women. They belong to the movement. We grant them important roles."

"Sure, I bet they love spending time with you and all of your obsessions."

"They do. Currently, they're spending time caring for Katie, my new crossbreed slave."

"You're a traitor to everything Marganis means. You're no Lord of anything except your own psychotropic illusions."

"We'll see about that, mongoloid."

"There's nothing you can do to harm me. There's nothing you can do to my body or brain to make me an example for any part of the world. Your dreamscapes will never bring you your desired control of the planet."

"Mr. Englewood, I find you entertaining, as do my men. Rest assured that Katie rests comfortably. She's overseen by women tending to her and to all matters throughout the palace and city. Our women will help us force the robots into our power structure for the ongoing cause of progress."

"There it is again. You're every bit like the climate regime."

"Men, hold him in place! We don't have anytime to spare for your impurities. You will tell us what we require, and we will use your mind as we need to. Start talking before these barons and counts and dukes of old beat you into the ground."

"Fuck off, Steve."

"Let the beatings commence."

Jimmy absorbed punch after punch to the stomach and face. While the beating continued, he stayed awake, aware of what he still had left to endure. He made peace with accepting that the Lords could kill him at any moment. Jimmy could not, however, make peace with knowing that the Lords would, barring his cooperation, murder Katie. The Magician wanted Jimmy alive and not irreparably damaged. Neither the Lords nor Planetary Order felt a need to keep Katie alive for long. To the Renegades' enemies, whether Katie lived had no impact on their fight for planetary domination. Katie mattered to the Lords and the climate regime, only insofar as how they could use her to exploit Jimmy.

The Magician watched his men beat Jimmy until he called of the assault. "It was eight against one, Englewood, and you lost."

Jimmy tried to speak but couldn't breathe. He never fell. Not one punch sent him to the floor despite the assailants inflicting excruciating pain.

The Magician and his Lords could not believe such an act of defiance could occur.

Jimmy recovered his breath. "I know you want to tackle me, but if you bring me to the ground, you won't be able to prevent yourselves from ripping out my limbs. I don't know why you need me alive. The Norbannicks told me one story. Mike told me another. Zack told me another. And you, I don't know what you're telling me. You need me alive, and you won't get rid of me now or ever."

The Magician turned from Jimmy. "Be careful, Englewood.

I can change my mind at any time on behalf of the cause. We hate you and your Renegades more than anybody else, but we're after the biggest threat right now from the climate regime. We are the holdouts from the Planetary Order's takeover of our movement. Soon we will turn the tide and take over the regime."

"Are you afraid to face me? Well, Steve, are you afraid to face me?"

"I don't fear you. I just need to know what makes you tick."

"Pathetic, for all your tricks, engineering, manipulations, and experiments. What's wrong with you that you can't figure out someone like me? What's a leader of an entire tyrannical movement trying to accomplish with me?"

"We need to know what makes you resistant to any dictatorial movement so we can break down resistance in others. You are the subject of intense global study. I'm here to make sure we break you and conquer the planet."

"I can spare you the suspense. You will never figure me out."

"Then you will die from me trying. Lords! Get Jimmy Englewood comfortable so we can probe his magic. Open the last layer of walls!"

The voice activation opened up the outermost layer of walls, showing the solid perimeter around the inner sanctum.

"What is this, Steve? Screened walls like the ones at the prison biodome?"

"Who do you think designed the biodome, you impure maggot? If you want Katie alive and unharmed, you will watch the videos with us and answer all my questions."

"The Planetary Order wanted you for your mind. They never knew about you leading the Lords. Now you want me for my mind, but you don't understand who I lead."

"Shut up and lick your wounds. You're in rough shape there, Jimmy, and the beating we delivered will be your last. Cooperate, or Katie dies. We're dragging you through the Portal of Clarity."

The Magician whistled. "Men, bring Mr. Englewood to the elevator. Let's allow him to watch the screens at a higher level where he can sit and relax. We'll show him what we need to while we strip his thoughts bare. Bring my clock with you and chain him to one of the seats. Or, on second thought, give me my machinegun. Leave him down here with me for a few moments. Prepare the middle ledge, and we'll meet you up there. Half of you keep your weapons focused on Jimmy in case he acts foolishly and needs to feel some lead."

Several Lords wanted to stay with the Magician, but he refused.

Jimmy, already beaten and stripped of his weapons, walked in front of Steve. "I feel every bump and bruise on my body. What can the Portal of Clarity do to heal me."

Steve grinned. "We're not interested in healing you."

"You know, your racial idolatry just keeps you paranoid and compulsive. It eats away at the vessels of your buried heart and exposes the failures of your so-called magic. Your followers the world over will always turn on each other. You will never rest, and you will die alongside all your doomed visions for the perfect man."

"You'll be singing a different tune when I take you through the Portal, you impure little dickweed."

The eight Lords ascended on the elevator to the middle ledge of the Inner Sanctum. They carried with them chains and drugs for Jimmy, weapons, and the Magician's clock.

Suddenly, the Lord carrying the clock noticed it had stopped ticking. They all registered the silence and looked around. They tilted their heads back and saw death flash before their eyes.

The ceiling of the inner sanctum exploded. The replica spaceships dropped in free fall while the missile blast sent the blown-up Lords flying off the decimated middle ledge.

An aircraft lowered itself slowly through the missing ceiling. Jimmy and the Magician each got thrown to the floor from the detonation. Debris from the hanging ship replicas missed crushing them by mere inches.

Jimmy shook his head back and forth to shake off the disorientation. Instead of clearing up, he grew dizzier. Jimmy looked around and saw a couple of dead Lords whose bodies were still intact. He never scanned for all the others blasted from the middle ledge, who broke into fragments upon the missile's impact.

The small flying vessel hovered over the wreckage and lowered a rope.

Amidst the carnage, the Magician slipped away.

***

Jimmy grabbed the rope but wavered back and forth across a thin line of consciousness. After losing the battle to stay awake, he released the rope and passed out. He saw the contours of himself and Bethany Norbannick from when he knelt by her side in the frozen snowfields outside Marganis. Jimmy gazed at her face and relived the hopelessness of watching life drain from her body. HIs remembrance shifted from the past reality to a Bethany revived and reaching from the icy ground for his help.

***

While Bethany dematerialized, Jimmy woke up. "Bethany! Bethany! Bethany!"

Jimmy's pupils adjusted to the sunlight, and he recognized the face of the man approaching him. Greg Norbannick lifted Jimmy up over his shoulders. He carried him to the lowered vessel.

An army of androids, humanoids, and automated ships flooded the area in and around Marganisan Palace. They were all fighting for the Renegades.

33

AWAKE

Greg stood by Jimmy's bedside, waiting for him to wake up.

Jimmy opened his eyes. He could not remember anything that transpired after he saw Greg's face during the rescue. "Hello, General."

"I told you to stop calling me that."

"I can't help it."

"It's a miracle you're still with us."

"What do you mean, and what's that music playing? Is that from in here?"

"It's classical music. This sounds familiar, doesn't it?"

"Sure does. I remember listening to it as a kid. I saw a concert in the city and the orchestra played this symphony."

"I've got to admit to you, Jimmy, it's kind of hard at this point to think that you were ever a kid. It's almost like you were born starting off in your 20s if not older. But you don't age a lot, even when you get beaten to a pulp."

"Where am I, Greg?"

"You're in sleeping quarters of the palace. These chambers are yours and yours alone."

"The sun is setting. I must've been out for a while."

"You have an IV in you. The robots have been taking great care of you."

"How are you here?"

"Englewood, you'll be asking questions long after you're dead. I don't know how you'll do it, but you will."

"You call that an answer?"

"I haven't given you a lot of answers so far. What makes you think I'm going to start now?"

"Greg, where is Katie?"

"Well, she's walking in with her mom, right as you ask."

Jimmy sat up. "Katie, Cora, I can't believe you're here."

Cora placed her hand on Jimmy's face. "You're now our adopted son. Where else would we be?"

Katie gave Jimmy a light hug so as not to mess around with his recovery. "You didn't think you'd ever see me again, did you?"

"Yes, I did. I knew I would. I knew I'd see your parents again, too. Sometimes, you just know. Where did you go? Or where were you taken?"

"Mom and Dad freed me from the Ladies of the Wolf Blade. They blasted the men who took me hostage to smithereens. You saw that part up close."

Greg cleared his throat. "Jimmy, try not to talk too much. Don't worry about these details. You see that, Cora and Katie? I guessed it right. I told you he'd be fine and asking a million questions."

Katie and Cora laughed along with Greg. Even Jimmy managed to crack a smile.

Greg detached the IV from Jimmy's left arm. "I don't think you'll be needing that anymore. We'll get you some real food from right out of the garden and hidden fishery."

Jimmy threw his legs over the side of the quilted, king-size bed. "Wait a second, Greg. There is one thing I have to know."

"There always is, Englewood."

"How come the robots help us? They were created by the head of the Lords of the Wolf Blade."

"The Magician wasn't the only visionary of these robots or this city. He understands how to manipulate the mind, so he manipulated many minds into thinking he engineered all the robots and the dreamscapes. He did no such thing. Not really. The Magician is a partial architect, but he lost control of the project and himself a while back, and now he's on the loose."

"You haven't found him?"

"No, but we have bigger problems."

"What are those?"

"The climate regime is in its final preparations to control every inch of the world. The lockdowns will be permanent if the Planetary Order succeeds. Brandon Dreckhorn will sit at the helm of dictatorship of the kind that corrupts and demolishes everything decent man ever invented."

"What are we going to do about it, General?"

Greg looked at his wife and daughter, and they all nodded. Greg looked back at Jimmy. "War, Englewood. War is the answer, but you already know that."

The next day, Jimmy woke up refreshed. He looked out the window and saw row after row and column after column of robots, android, humanoid, and otherwise.

Automated and robot-piloted ships circled the city from the horizon to the heavens. Robots performed a series of operational test runs, and robot maintenance crews fine-tuned weapons and ships.

Greg met Jimmy at the entrance to the palace. "Englewood, I've never seen anybody devour food like you did yesterday. It seemed like the first time you had eaten in centuries."

"I hadn't enjoyed anything for a while. Trout, sweet potatoes, and salad never tasted so good."

"It's the only time I've seen you happy."

"We haven't met each other all that often, but I don't have the time to be happy. Not anymore."

"What do you have the time for? Do you have the time to help me fight this war?"

"Maybe, if you can tell me why it's so warm here."

"Warm, Jimmy? It's 50 degrees."

"Don't play stupid with me. You know that's warm for the world we've been living in since the great freeze."

"I can't argue with that."

"Is the Planetary Order controlling the climate?"

"The Order is manipulating it. So are the Lords to suit their own ends. Just understand that a lot of this is natural and out of anyone's full power to do much about. But yes, the climate regime and the Lords can heat things up a little or cool them down. Most food production nowadays takes place in regulated indoor settings anyhow, and robots grow and harvest most of the grains and fruits and vegetables. Fisheries still exist outdoors, but most of those run operations inside, like the farms."

"Is it getting to the point where the natural freeze will become too deep to manipulate climate on any scale?"

"Nobody knows, but they're advancing those manipulation techniques all the time. The remnants of the Renegades are, too. So are unaffiliated scientists."

"My fellow Renegades manipulate the weather?"

"Only insofar as it relates to local survival matters. Growing food and enabling warmth enough for people to function."

"We're all playing gods, General. That never turns out well."

"You're preaching to the converted, Jimmy, but Renegades and everyday people also do what they have to do to survive. The climate lockdowns implemented something beyond draconian measures from the jump. The Lords know global warming is a crock and never bought into it. They're using the lockdown dictatorship to try to pull Renegades and everyday people away from sanity. They're failing miserably, leading to the massive numbers of Lords joining ranks with their equal but opposite tyrants in the climate regime."

"Can we save the world? Do we still have time?"

"Englewood, man can never save the world, but we still have time to fight the Planetary Order and the Lords, regardless of how much they fuse with each other."

"Aren't the Lords fighting each other over whether or not to join the regime?"

"Yes, but more and more are fusing with the regime. The Planetary Order increasingly takes on the racial superiority complex and undisguised physical brutality of the Lords. They follow each other's habits and practices of calling upon dark supernatural elements. That isn't getting the regime anywhere...except to hurt people all across the planet by destroying crops and cities."

"How much time do we have before a thousand years of an irreversible dictatorship?"

"It's almost here. They erased countries and borders long ago. Look at this city. Forget about the dreamscapes part of it. We have a border here. We can revive cities and counties and countries back to what they were and then some."

"You didn't answer me, Greg. How much time do we have?"

"You mean before we're all enslaved or thrown in death camps? Almost no time at all."

34

MISSING

Katie met Jimmy and her father at the laboratory near the palace. The one-story building housed every robot microorganism available.

A group of android scientists ran the experiments for the Magician. They then began working for Greg, one of the only four or five remaining humans in Marganisan Dreamscapes.

Katie's face turned white. "What is this, Dad? What are you doing?"

"What's wrong, dear?"

"Why is everybody scrambling. There's a big problem, isn't there. It's written all over your face. Jimmy's, too."

"I can't lie to you, Katie. Somebody got in here and stole a set of robot microbes."

Jimmy handed Katie an extra handgun. "It's the Magician. It has to be. Take the team of robots outside and search the city far and wide. If he escapes with the new technology, who knows what catastrophe he'll unleash on the world."

Katie's face returned to its normal color. "You know me, Jimmy. I always love a good mission."

Greg escorted his daughter outside. "Listen, be careful, and whatever you do, don't leave the city."

"Don't worry about me, Dad."

"I am worried. Jimmy told me he the Magician saved your life."

"Yeah, and we saved the Magician's life. I owe him no loyalty. Don't worry."

"How can I not worry. You're my only daughter left. You are your mother's only daughter left. We're nothing without you. Whatever happens in the world, none of it matters if we lose you."

Katie hugged her father. "You won't lose me. I already went through this with Mom back at the palace. Even if you did lose me, all of this does matter. You have to carry on the fight no matter what happens to me or Jimmy, and no matter what happens to anybody."

Jimmy played the same piece of classical music he heard the day before from the small stereo Greg provided. "You'd better get moving, Katie. These robots look restless."

"Sure, Jimmy. Have those android scientists fixed up your face? It's still bruised and swollen."

Greg laughed. "They're just battle scars, right Jimmy?"

"Yes they are."

Katie admired the highlands in the distance. "We've gotten this far. What's a little planetary war going to do to us?"

Jimmy laughed and moved back to the lab door.

Greg hugged his daughter once more. "We cordoned off the city before I even flew to the palace, so there's no way out of here without my knowing. The Magician has to be somewhere within city limits. I told you before that he didn't create or build nearly as much of this city as he claimed. Now, he controls none of it. He's trapped."

"Dad, how did you organize this so quickly?"

"It wasn't as quick as you think, but when my daughter's in trouble, there's nothing I won't do."

"I'll see you all later. Look out for Mom, like always."

Katie jumped onto a hovercraft with the team of robots to find the Magician.

Greg went back inside the laboratory. "Jimmy, why do I get the feeling I'm never going to see my daughter again?"

"Now's the time for me to be the one telling you you're thinking too much. Are you ready to shut this place down and destroy all the research?"

"Leave it to the robots. We're leaving."

Greg ordered the scientists to delete the records and destroy the physical specimens. The android researchers followed the orders, but during an unexpected blast, they erupted in flames along with the laboratory. The entire city watched the smoke rise. Residents from the cafés to ballparks saw the explosion and knew immediately who ignited the inferno.

Jimmy and Greg rushed back to the flames with robot fire-men who fought the blaze. Fire Chief Dorian, like the rest of the firemen a mix of humanoid and extremely mechanized, held back the two humans from running into the building. "Let my men handle it. They'll put out the flames in no time and salvage the antidotes I know you want salvaged. This is arson, plain and simple."

A bold mainstay of the city, Dorian approached Jimmy and Greg. His yellow eyes stood out on his square head. Bionic arms and legs rounded out the frame of his thick neck and torso. The creators of these robots made them for work and for war.

Greg shook Dorian's hand. "Dorian, meet my friend Jimmy Englewood. Jimmy, Dorian and his robots enabled such a city as Marganisan Dreamscapes to surpass production capabilities of most of the old countries on Earth. The Magician and his fellow Lords conquered the city built originally by Renegades. Steve and his movement bastardized this land and wiped out most of the living things he could. He probably lied about half of every-thing he said, and he could not control the Lords worldwide anymore. Most of them are now in the Planetary Order. But Steve probably does control the splinter groups. Regardless of that, he did not create or have the original vision for Marganisan Dreamscapes. He perverted it with a vision of his own."

Dorian shook Jimmy's hand. "I know all about you, Jimmy. I know even more about Greg. We communicate frequently. You might have guessed I play many roles in this city. Soon you will see my role as a warrior in fighting with you to spare the planet from irreversible slavery and destruction. I will help you and your group in your cause."

"Thank you, Dorian. What's prevented us from being attacked? What's preventing us from getting attacked right now, other than the dispersion of Planetary Forces fighting battles against Renegades and splinter group Lords throughout the world? And how come this place isn't crawling with Lords of the Wolf Blade?"

"Lords received their missions to conduct attacks and to infiltrate communities across the planet. We don't get bombed because we set up the first—"

A low-pitch, drawn-out sound alerted Dorian to an audio call. He activated a button on a small gadget. "Yes, what is it?"

After ten seconds of listening, Dorian hung up. "My men retrieved the antidotes, and Katie captured the Magician. The Magician unfortunately succeeded in passing off the batch of various robot microorganisms to someone outside the city. He also set the deactivation of the force field for two days from now."

Greg gasped when Dorian bowed his gray metal face. "What else, Dorian? What else?"

"They're on their way to the palace with her now. Your daughter got injured badly in the capture."

Jimmy watched the firemen put out the dying inferno while he held a crushed father in his arms.

An hour later, the Magician sat quietly in the prison. He was the only inmate. Androids had already handcuffed him and tied him to a chair in his cell.

Greg walked into the cell. "Leave the wall open, my friends. I want weapons on him at all times. Make sure when Jimmy and I leave that he can't harm himself."

Jimmy walked into the cell. "Everybody's gearing up for the war. Let's make this as quick as we can, Greg."

"We will."

"You don't want to bring him to the interrogation room?"

"No. We shouldn't trap ourselves in there with him. We'll take care of this here."

The Magician snarled. "When I shot Katie, I meant to blow her away. Hitting her ring finger wasn't what I expected. You can imagine my pride when I caught her foot with my second shot. Still not enough. Man, my robots went really soft. I mean come on! They stun me and that's it. Weak! Super weak!"

Jimmy glanced at Greg, waiting for him to make a move.

Greg wore a stone-faced expression. He knew his daughter rested comfortably, cared for by Cora and a staff of Marganisan Dreamscape medical professionals. "You know something, Steve? Talking to my daughter convinced me she's the toughest woman I've ever met. She'll be ready for battle again this evening."

"She's not tough. She has weak genes and impure blood. I saved her life, and I can take it away."

"All you can do is deceive and steal. You're nothing. Do you have any idea the punishment Katie endured in the Climate Rehab Center?"

"Of course I do. I arranged for it. Mike and Zack didn't even know I'm a Lord, much less the most powerful Lord in the world. I arranged her punishment with them. I'll say it was a treat to know what she endured. Humans really are viruses on Earth. So is Katie."

Jimmy stretched his arms out to hold Greg back from the Magician. "General, why don't you hang out with the guards. I'm going to pull up a chair here and sit right in front of Steve to talk to him alone."

"Englewood, I need to ask him—"

"No, Greg. You don't need to do anything except let me find out what we need to know. He fooled me once. He won't fool me again."

The Magician rubbed his face with his right shoulder. "You can't fool me, but you can try. And to think that I welcomed you into my home in the highlands."

Jimmy turned his chair so that the back of it faced the Magician. The Renegade sat down and held a handgun to the Magician's forehead. "Let's take a trip to the recent past. Why did you look at me empathetically at Paradise Gardens when Zack murdered Linda."

"I wanted to engineer my trip back home to this city and marshal my forces from near and afar. I thought the climate regime wouldn't figure out my role with the Lords. But Zack figured it out. He and Mike ordered me onto the whaling ship. They wanted me to show them the vulnerabilities in Marganisan Dreamscapes so they could breach the area. I took advantage of your mutiny."

"And you thought Katie could help you, so you kept her alive. You eventually kept us both alive. I guess the desire to slaughter whales crept up and overwhelmed Zack and Mike's desires to penetrate this city. Their devotion to eradicate animals is sick. It competes with them trying to discover all the hidden gems they could gather from the dark and light corners of Marganisan Dreamscapes."

"Would I ever lie to you?"

"Yes. But you're telling me the truth. You can't help it. I got a vial of the truth medicine from the hospital and mixed it in with the water the guards served you."

"You son of a bitch. You fucking maggot."

"That's how much the climate regime hates life. Slaughtering whales did come first on their agenda for the moment. They screwed everything up, just like you did."

Jimmy got up.

Greg walked back over. "Wait a second, Englewood. You didn't get the information from him about who he gave the robot microbes to. We need that."

Jimmy grinned. "He also never told me the ins and outs of why the Planetary Forces wouldn't invade or bomb the city. And that's with or without the force field that the robots can deny entrance through."

"Jimmy, who has the microbes?"

"Isn't it obvious? Zack has them. This is the Planetary Order's chance to ensure it roots out and controls anyone with a Renegade spirit. Anyone disobeying the climate lockdowns, food restrictions, energy rations, or anything else would receive punishment. The Order would release debilitating robot microorganisms to keep the Earth's population compliant."

Greg glared at the Magician. "He established communication with the Planetary Forces and gave the microbes over as a gesture of joining forces. But how, Jimmy? How?"

"That part of it doesn't matter now, Greg, and you're always asking questions."

Greg and Jimmy watched a defeated Magician sob in ruin. The two friends left Steve under the lock and key of his cell and the scrutiny of the android guards.

35

READY OR NOT

Marganisan Dreamscapes buzzed with preparations for war. Many other robots across the planet had the skills for science, medicine, and building. They could serve humans and each other as entertainers and instructors. None of those robots elsewhere in the world had the power or precision to go to war the way the robots from Marganisan Dreamscapes did.

The factories churned out gun after gun and missile after missile. Robots manufactured new vehicles, new climate gear, new body armor, and new robots for battle. Assembly lines continued around the clock.

Androids and robots of all varieties had a mission to defeat the climate regime. Greg Norbannick ordered them to obliterate the entire infrastructure of the Planetary Order, ranging from propaganda to industrial capacity to technological sophistication to research and development. He commanded the army of 100,000 strong to fight against a climate regime of hundreds of millions. Greg calculated the qualitative advantages of his Renegade robots would enable the human beings to reestablish institutions around the world in a harmonious balance of distinct countries.

Greg's vision matched with many, though not all, civilizational visions of old. He followed the Renegade mindset for independent lives and communities, free from slavery. The robots could carry out his vision to a limited extent. Greg knew he needed human beings to lead the charge for autonomy. He knew that people, not robots, would have to look members of the Planetary Order in the eyes and confront them in up-close fights to the death.

Dorian served as the leader of the robot army, but Greg tasked him with something even more important. Greg told Dorian to do anything within his power to find Renegade holdouts across the planet. Any formal or informal groups needed to band together to dismantle the lockdown orders and spread liberty in every area of the globe they could. Dorian's orders included contacting unaffiliated serfs, slaves, black-market merchants, and disaffected regime followers. The war effort required the physical engagement of everyone Greg could muster. His orders to Dorian also included turning as many robots as possible against the climate regime.

Greg overlooked the city from Marganisan Palace. From his and Cora's chambers, he watched the streetlights and building lights permeate the urban marvel while daylight sank beneath the highlands.

The canal flowed across a city bracing for the ultimate clash with the climate regime. The robots not made for war replanted trees and reestablished the cold-resistant seeds for flowers and gardens throughout Marganisan Dreamscapes. The history of the destroyed Marganis of Jimmy's youth would live on through the symbiosis between the natural and the manmade. Peaceful robots adopted plans to live an unburdened life after the war. The Planetary Forces and Lords of the Wolf Blade had plans of their own for the present and the future. So did Jimmy Englewood.

Mike and Zack landed separately at the Climate Rehab Center and met in the biodome. Soldiers spread throughout the prison, which doubled as a global operating base for the Planetary Order.

Max the robot stopped at the table. "What can I...What can I...What can I get you gentlemen?"

Zack took a bottle from Max's tray and got up to smash it over his head. Mike stood up at the same time and grabbed the bottle out of Zack's hand to keep Max unscathed. The two regional leaders from the climate regime stared at each other with a venom they usually reserved for Renegades.

Guards feared a fight that never began.

Max stayed silent and did not move.

Mike sat back down. "Zack, you botched our plans. You messed up everything near Marganisan Dreamscapes. Leader Dreckhorn knows your mistake could cost us everything. You're still alive by virtue of his appreciation for your past work. Consider yourself fortunate I offered kind words on your behalf."

Zack sat down while keeping his sunken eyes fixated on Mike. "I've got the specimens. I've got all of the ones we need. Every robot microbe sits with me, Mike."

"Beautiful. Hand over the case to these soldiers. They'll transport it where it needs to go for storage."

"They captured him."

"Of course they did. We need more from the Magician than we got. We'll retrieve him."

"I got all the microbes you wanted."

"I know that you fucking moron. We have more information to tap from his mind. Whether he lives or dies in Renegade custody, this upcoming war is ours for the taking. These microorganisms take over humans and robots with a speed that renders our adversaries useless. We're doubly fortunate for such an upcoming victory."

"I know this already, you—"

"You don't know the degree to which this helps. You have proven yourself a capable enforcement and battlefield commander. It pains me to say you can never become the leader you aspire to be in the Planetary Forces. The Planetary Council granted me exclusive leadership over the region. You are permanently relegated to enforcement and military concerns. No longer does the regime allow you to be involved in regional psychological activities, other than at my discretion. Your salvation rests in battle and in dedication to the climate regime. The bitter cold weather threatens to envelop the planet again in mere days. You'd better assemble all your forces."

Zack watched the reaction of all the nearby soldiers. They kept deadpan expressions to steer clear of his wrath.

Mike stood up. "Do I have your acknowledgement that I'm in charge of the Planetary Forces in this region?"

Zack stood up and shook Mike's hand. "I acknowledge it if you give me the power to control the robot microbe operations and continue propaganda activities. Otherwise, you can find yourself a new commander for security, enforcement reconnaissance, warfighting, and everything else. You can explain yourself to the Planetary Order when your regional control and worldwide successes diminish."

"I'm impressed you could speak articulately enough to convince me. I agree to this deal."

Mike and Zack shook hands again.

Mike summoned the full entourage of soldiers to follow him out of the biodome. He suddenly stopped walking, turned and faced Zack. "Mr. Comrade of Marganis, capture Mr. Renegade Jimmy Englewood and the Magician, or suffer the consequences. Max will stay with you here so you can order whatever you'd like. Enjoy our much-improved cuisine under the stars of our biodome."

Everyone cleared out of the vast space except for Zack, Max, and a scattered robot staff, human staff, and patrons.

Max bumped into Zack. "I'm sorry, sir. I'm, I'm, I'm, sir, sir, sir—"

Zack grabbed the full bottle Mike left on the table. He smashed Max over the head and continued to slam the robot against the biodome's special glass.

Max suffered six successive gunshot wounds. His machinery died.

Zack pulled out a photo of Jimmy Englewood and burst into laughter. He exited the biodome with the witnesses all rendered speechless and powerless, including administrators.

The Comrade of Marganis had a Planetary Order to satisfy and a Renegade to capture.

Jimmy Greg, Cora, and Katie joined robots in the movie theater room at Marganisan Palace to watch a broadcast. The usual acronym of "HAVE" appeared on the upper right corner of the screen for the Planetary Leader's messages. Brandon Dreckhorn sat at a desk. Viewers could clearly see projected on the background wall the climate regime symbol of an ax splitting the Earth. A steady drumbeat played before trailing off into silence.

Brandon Dreckhorn adjusted the straps on his overalls. "My planetary citizens, I thank you hearing this worldwide address. My last address laid out necessary rules by which you must live. Billions of you have followed the rules. You have complied with every directive. Many ask me why poverty and starvation continue in light of such wide-scale and profound obedience to the health and safety of our Planetary Order. I have a simple answer for you. We have counterrevolutionaries continuing to threaten us at every turn. They make life difficult for you and sabotage what would ordinarily provide for affordable housing, food, and energy. We have eliminated one such woman."

Greg clenched his fists. "That's my daughter."

Brandon shared a split screen with an artificial rendering of the image of Linda Norbannick. "Look at this counterrevolutionary. Our brave soldiers protected our world from her by ensuring she would never again threaten our way of life and the struggle for continuous progress. We took out her sister Bethany before her. You can see what she looks like here. But now I'm going to show you the surviving Norbannicks and their names, including their father Greg, who leads the counterrevolutionary forces. They all support and protect the number one enemy of the Planetary Order. And here is the image of Jimmy Englewood. We must find and destroy him before he destroys our planet with his ideas about enslavement and anti-science rhetoric. He denies global warming like the traitor he is. We will capture him to teach him the realities of our global community."

Jimmy sat motionless while the theater filled with robots and three fellow humans tried to gauge his reaction.

The Planetary Leader pulled out an ax. "My citizens, we're using the power of the climate order to manage all carbon-based life forms. Regulation of carbon and the thoughts and feelings associated with humans lies in our purview. You can trust us and be free, or you can betray us and live as an outcast from society, malnourished and trapped by the rising heat levels in unprotected zones. Fear not any of the counterrevolutionaries located in Marganisan Dreamscapes or anywhere else. We will defeat them with the aid of our allies, the Lords of the Wolf Blade. They share in the desire to restrain mankind, and to protect mankind from itself. They share in the hopes of curtailing the animals that destroy the planet and eat up resources in an unsustainable way. All you need to do, my citizens, is to stay at home and avoid excessive social contact. Inform us about your neighbors' noncompliance through our many posted contacts all over your towns and cities, screens and stadiums. We can heal you as soon as you help us vanquish the counterrevolution."

Jimmy jumped from his seat to leave the live broadcast viewing. The Norbannicks followed.

The broadcast then zeroed in on Brandon Dreckhorn's face. "Help us feed, house, and clothe you. Stand with the Planetary Order and the climate experts who work to offer you a better life. The revolution lives forever. You can live forever with the movement, as long as we do it as a collective. Death to climate deniers!"

Leader Dreckhorn smiled. The screen went black.

36

MISTER PRESIDENT

The Planetary Leader did not serve as a total puppet or patsy. He exercised real power, but the Planetary Council could influence him in matters he found difficult to decipher. He also had to deal with the large class of technocrats who held tremendous influence in the climate regime. The President and his Council controlled the media. Every now and then, a journalist would step out of line and pay the price in a labor or death camp.

Brandon Dreckhorn finished his broadcast. His guards shuttled him and the Planetary Council to his modern castle, a grand estate located on thousands of acres of plush green property.

A special night of who's who leaders, managers, bureaucrats, media, and approved entertainers and athletes filed into the ballroom. The Earth's high society replaced the high society of old. Only a few of the old guard curried favor successfully. The climate regime systematically enslaved and murdered the rest, or the ones they deemed useless. President Dreckhorn led the mass slaughter of real estate developers, investors, disloyal professionals, tradesman, merchants, statesmen, religious leaders, and all artists and musicians possessing even a hint of rebellion. The Planetary Leader couldn't wait to celebrate the evening's gala, named after the movement he spearheaded, Humans Are Viruses on Earth.

Brandon went to his room first. Security ushered him into his home through a hidden entrance. He put on his finest attire, a tuxedo designed to amplify his tall, thin frame.

The President walked into the ballroom with two ladies, one on each arm. The ladies wore the most exclusive silk dresses and joined their host at the table of honor. Fresh lobsters awaited them. Cherries and cheese platters enticed their palates, as did roasted vegetables, pastas, wines, champagne, and trays of desserts. Banquet staff served the eager guests. Brandon Dreckhorn spent most of the time at his seat, greeting suck-ups and watching the crowd while his dates conversed with each other.

Speakers started off the party. Refrains about protecting the regime overtook the euphemisms about saving the climate.

Most of the one thousand guests and one hundred staff commenced a night of debauchery. Soldiers and security remained at their posts inside, outside, and above the grounds.

Brandon and the Council took no part in the indulgences. A disciplined elite, they kept up appearances and removed themselves at midnight. The President even sent away his two lady guests. The climate regime did not lend itself to the leaders engaging in any activities that would distract them from controlling the planet. With victory would come all the time in the world for licentious behavior, or so the Planetary Leader thought. He and the councilmembers had an ability to control impulses most other civilian members in the regime could not.

Soldiers modeled their demeanor and actions after the Planetary Leader, and he had their unyielding allegiance. The Planetary Forces yearned for his every command.

When the sun came up, Mike arrived at the mansion. He walked into a large meeting room, right on time. "Planetary Leader Dreckhorn, thank you for accepting my request to meet with you."

"Hello, Mike. I'm glad you're here. I put you in charge of everything that happens at Marganisan Dreamscapes. You must own this in terms of our successes and failures in the war. We're meeting in private because I want no interruptions. What do you need from me to accomplish your mission? How can I help you?"

"No help required. My men are ready. Zack is ready."

"How about the robot germs?

"We will spread the ones meant for robots first. Our robots are inoculated."

"And the robot germs for people? Tell me about those that affect both people and robots."

"It's all just robots at this point. We cannot spread the ones for people or the ones for both right now because we cannot contain the effects on people, which would put our own people at great risk. We only recently developed the ability to inoculate against and cure the germs you speak of but cannot mass produce these vaccines or remedies for another month. Neither can our enemies."

"We'll have to make the most of what we have now."

"I agree, sir. We can destroy their entire robot army within a matter of days."

"That won't be enough time to avoid sustaining heavy losses, but it's plenty of time to win the war and control every region on Earth."

"We don't know yet if we can infect every one of their robots. Some could be resistant. The enemy could be mass producing the antidote as we speak."

"It sounds like a lot of the guarantees you gave me cannot guarantee anything."

"President Dreckhorn, we have the finest fighting force the world has ever seen. From our ships to our personnel to our advanced weaponry, nobody can outmatch us. But yes, we are likely to lose millions. Hundreds of millions."

"Is the delivery method sophisticated enough to spread the robot microbes across the planet?"

"Yes."

"Good. Bring the Magician here. Bring Jimmy Englewood here. Win this war."

"There's one more problem I need to bring to your attention."

"Out with it."

"Freezing temperatures affect the spread of the robot microorganisms. From what I understand, efforts to increase the temperatures prove less reliable than the natural cycles of Earth that carry us closer to the deepest freeze possible. Leaving aside germ transmissions, it is true that our transportation, communication, warfighting, and food supplies will all suffer."

"Do I need to replace you, Mike?"

"I was afraid you'd ask that."

"It's just a question in good fun. Now grab the bag and give me the inoculations."

"Yes, yes I will. I can administer this one first before your medical staff administers the rest of them. This one's just a small shot in the upper arm. Let's sterilize the area, and here we are. This vaccine isn't even for a contagious germ. It's just a disease."

"I barely felt it. Wait, what disease? You mean it's just a vaccine to prevent a noncontagious disease."

"No, I mean I just injected you with an illness. Don't you worry. I'll deal with Marganis, Marganisan Dreamscapes, and everywhere else. I'll strengthen the climate lockdown."

Brandon Dreckhorn slumped over and fell to the floor.

Mike packed up his bag. "Goodbye, cousin. Goodbye. You are a real person after all."

The coup succeeded.

Under Mike's new rule, countless sections of the Earth continued losing vegetation. The Planetary Order collectivized the food industries all over the world. From growing food to selling it, the soldiers enforced the distribution system. Commoners had no recourse, stripped of nearly all technologies and individual thought.

Initial climate regime plans involved keeping people dependent. Plans devolved into mass starvation in areas deemed counterrevolutionary.

The memorial service for the former Planetary Leader took place immediately following his untimely death by supposed natural causes. Mike, as the new president, broadcast his affirmation of the climate regime's goals and mission. The Planetary Forces and Planetary Council supported the new leader without reservation.

Mike left the estate after his broadcast. He and a convoy of army security visited a village close by to his new castle mansion, or the deceased Brandon Dreckhorn's old castle mansion.

Mike saw the soldiers and administrators in the village. Every single one of them looked lost, dispirited, and defeated. Mike shook their hands and exchanged pleasantries. They forced smiles in the cool but still comfortable temperatures expected to drop precipitously the next day. Soldiers kept their thoughts and concerns to themselves. Administrators watched them closely and saw to it that they did stay silent. The soldiers felt loyal to the Order, the Council, and the Planetary Leader. The same soldiers felt hatred toward the day-to-day local bureaucracy that flourished in every population center. Bureaucrats felt the same level of contempt toward the soldiers.

Local residents walked up to Mike. Withered bodies and

gaunt faces pleaded for food and medicine. The village stunk of decomposing living souls and long expired dreams covered in mounds of snow.

Mike pulled aside the leading administrator of the town. "Listen to me carefully, because I don't want to hear excuses. You had enough food to keep the villagers hungry but alive. You're always granted enough provisions for that. But would you make the soldiers so uncomfortable about the ordinary civilians' plight? Some of the soldiers here are related to villagers here and elsewhere. When the soldiers witness relatives starving, this does not help soldier morale. It isn't as though you and your team of administrators would allow soldiers to feed the starving townspeople. We'd like to make the process of informing on counterrevolutionaries as simple as we can. You need to be smarter about this in your next location. You're being transferred."

The administrator nodded in agreement.

The Planetary Leader motioned for the subordinate administrators to stay back before he looked again at the main one. "You serve as the top official here. Look at all of your people's living quarters compared to theirs. We're orchestrating an infinite climate government for the world, but you get sloppy. This village is too ugly for what we're doing, for the time being. This village is lost. I'll tell your men to get rid of it and send all your soldiers and officials to new towns. They'll be well compensated for their troubles."

Mike walked away and chopped his right hand in the direction of his security officers. They promptly gunned down the lead administrator by machinegun fire. Mike flew out of town with his convoy and village bureaucrats. The soldiers stayed behind for a while to carry out their orders. Not one man, woman, or child of the 2,500 residents received the mercy of the climate regime. Mercy from the HAVE movement never existed, and it never would.

37

GOODBYE

The eve of war descended. Jimmy and the Norbannicks talked in dining room entry of Marganisan Palace. Dorian had his orders to fly the robot army into battle. Renegades and slaves from all over the planet finalized their strategies and uprisings.

Cora had no planned role in combat. Greg convinced his wife of the importance of her staying back to carry out the protection orders of Marganisan Dreamscapes.

Katie received the mission to liberate the Climate Rehab Center.

Greg would lead the recapture of the real Marganis.

Dorian finalized his blueprints for executing the war across the world.

Jimmy prepared to kill the new Planetary Leader and release billions from the hypnosis of intractable brainwashing.

The robots had already repaired the inner sanctum of the palace, but they renamed and redesigned it the Hall of Rescue.

Jimmy raised a glass of wine. "Here's to you, Norbannicks. You are my family. All my now dead old family would have enjoyed knowing you. They never got the chance. Even I really haven't gotten the chance to yet. What matters now is the fight for a planet that returns to the balance it lost. If we freeze from the Ice Age, if we die in conflict, if our enemies imprison us for decades, we will make this war worthy of everything decent the human race has ever built or shared. We will make this war worthy of the natural and manmade wonders we hold dear. We remember everything that's been destroyed, but we will return to a planet of unbridled civilizations advancing the spirits of honor and obligations we cherish. No men will lock us down for good."

Katie took a swig from her glass. "It's good wine, Englewood. I couldn't wait."

Jimmy's face beamed. "Climate orders be damned. I'll see you all when we rendezvous at the Marganis of our souls!"

They all clanged their glasses together and drank.

Cora's eyes welled up to capacity. "I'm sorry. I can't help it. The thought of not seeing you all again summons so much pain that I cannot bear to think of it a minute longer."

Katie embraced her mother. "We're with you right now, Mom."

Greg joined the embrace. "We know what's at stake, but whether we see each other again, we know for sure that the actions we're taking will never be in vain. Let's all make Bethany and Linda proud."

Cora stopped crying. "Jimmy, how come you're not over here."

"Because I'm holding off the embrace until I see the Norbannicks again. It's added motivation to return successfully from my mission."

Jimmy walked toward the arched front door of the palace.

Katie curled up a napkin and threw it at Jimmy's back. "Where are you going, big brother?"

"I have something to take care of tonight. Nothing for any of you to worry about."

Greg shook Jimmy's hand.

Jimmy opened the door and looked over the three Norbannicks for a good fifteen seconds.

A solemn Cora gave Jimmy a sealed handwritten note and waved. "Goodbye Jimmy."

"Goodbye Cora, Katie, General. Don't wait up."

Jimmy winked, turned, and closed the main door of Marganisan Palace.

Dorian met Jimmy outside the prison and accompanied him inside. A group of guards followed them to the Magician's cell and unlocked the room.

Steve remained seated, reading a book about the benefits of climate lockdowns for the planet.

Jimmy shook his head. "What's going on, Dorian? How is this stuff allowed for him."

"He has nowhere to go with his knowledge. There is nothing he can do with it, but you are correct. We need to fill this prison with books from older times. We also need to fill this prison with newer times than this."

The Magician finally looked up, sitting on his bed in a jumpsuit. He put down the book. "What are you doing here? I cannot help you trace the missing robot microbes. I don't know much about the way they work either. Mike's the one with the scientific background."

The guards kept their weapons aimed at the Magician, through the open cell.

Dorian watched Jimmy as closely as he watched the Magician. The robot shifted his yellow eyes seamlessly from one side to the other without moving his head.

Jimmy paced back and forth in the cell a few times before facing Steve. "I know you think I came here to kill you. You can't hide your expressions like you think you can. I pick up on the subtle twitches. I want to kill you, but Greg disallowed it. It's funny, you know? It's funny seeing humanoid guards work with the less humanlike robot guards. But still, androids do not work here. I guess they're just too much like people. Everyone here seems to work together. I like the harmony. I like seeing different groups work together to accomplish something. So does the Planetary Leader. He's just after something a little more nefarious than I am. Alright, a lot more. Did you know Mike very recently became the new Planetary Leader?"

"I don't believe you."

"It's the truth. Mike took the reins of power and wants to rule over the planet with complete control."

The Magician gulped. "He'll come after me and torture me for years now that he's in power. What I did in giving Zack the microbes and vaccines and cures won't make up for it."

"Greg told me they already have the vaccines and cures."

"I didn't know that."

"You know the Lords of the Wolf Blade gave me a lot of troubles over the years. It looks like the Planetary Order is now incorporating every group of Lords on the Earth."

"Not me. Definitely not me. I didn't kill Linda. I didn't even know they were going to do it."

"I believe you. It's a crazy thing that I believe you. The truth injection wore off on you a while ago. Somehow, I can tell you're telling me the truth."

"Yes, I'm glad you see that."

"I also know that you're a total fucking lunatic."

"Please, Jimmy, you don't know Mike. They want my mind. They still want my mind, probably for experiments now. I can work with you to help you defeat them and reverse the climate lockdown madness. We can all live again. I mean really live again."

"Steve, I've lost more of my soul every day for the last 20 years than I care to acknowledge. I've dealt with the murders of my unborn babies when the extinct Marganisan Council ordered a forced abortion of my twin babies. The former Marganisan Enforcers murdered my brother, and the former Marganisan

City Forces murdered Bethany. Murder upon murder committed against people I cared about. My minister and my minister's son? Murdered. And you know what? You have no clue how many people betrayed me, including my cousins."

"You can't blame me for all those things. I'm sorry. I didn't mean it. I don't want to die. I don't want to die. Not like that. Not at the hands of Mike. They'll win the war if you don't take my help. You need me. Let me help you every way I know how. You have to. I know you killed the guy on the whaling ship. This is different, though. I saved Katie's life."

"And later you tried to take her hostage. And later you shot her. You were about to squeeze my brain for your racial occultist purity bull crap. It was only a matter of time before Katie and I would've wound up dead by your hands."

"Jimmy, I can help you. I'm begging for your mercy."

"You don't have to beg me. I told you that Greg ordered me not to hurt you as long as we had you in custody. But I'm not going to use you for the war. None of us are. You're going to spend the rest of your life in this prison."

"No! What if the climate regime wins? What if Mike captures me?"

"He can't. The Planetary Order can't. Your old Lords can't. Even if the good guys lose, you're still spending the rest of your life in this prison. I didn't get a kill order. Dorian did."

The Magician furrowed his eyebrows.

Jimmy walked out of the cell and didn't look back. He stopped for a few moments. "Enjoy the Portal of Clarity."

Dorian unleashed a bullet in the Magician's skull.

Steve died instantaneously, and Jimmy walked out of the prison.

The temperatures plummeted across Marganisan Dream-scapes, freshly renamed Brimmilon by Greg.

Temperatures dropped across the whole world. In the morning, Jimmy would suit up in his climate gear and go to war.

38

WAR 360

Renegades the world over expected help from their fellow human beings. That help did not arrive in the desired numbers. In the midst of a world war, the majority of those described as common men kept to their usual concerns. Serfs and slaves tried their hardest to curry favor among climate regime nobility and enforcers. Uprisings occurred, but in frequencies and magnitudes too scarce to help Renegade actions.

Most of the marginally free people lived in cramped areas, cluttered in run-down housing complexes. People connected to regime soldiers or bureaucrats received extra food rations or the ability to work and trade. Few common men with the slightest bit of freedom dared challenge the Planetary Order. The majority did all they could to hold on to whatever livelihoods, family, and friends they had.

Countless people not in reeducation or death camps remained satisfied with their lives. Entertainment numbed them into a state of perpetual sedation. The comatose energy prevented them from acting to help free the planet. Hundreds of millions bought into the climate lockdown hysteria, yet they thought they and their descendants would see better times.

The Renegades and their backers fought with no formal alliances. Several billion people the world over did not turn out so neutral, siding silently with the Planetary Order.

Jimmy Englewood found himself inside small, abandoned living quarters just outside of the grand estate, which doubled as a base. He and his robot contingent destroyed the complex's defenses. They blew up the vessels of the climate regime's regional fleet of airships docked on the property, in addition to the ones circling above the grounds.

Mike, the new Planetary Leader, had nowhere to flee unless he and his men ceded the climate regime's capital territory to the Renegades. The Planetary Order would continue the fight at the grand estate without their ships or reinforcements. The battles across the planet delayed any possibility for sufficient resupplies of ships, weapons, and men.

Jimmy's invading force experienced little loss of robots at first, but the Renegade ships taking part in the assault suffered almost complete destruction from land-based climate regime forces. His own vessel already lay buried under a pile of snow from a blizzard. His robots entered the Planetary Order's grand estate without him, shooting up climate regime guards and soldiers with heavy firepower. Renegade androids and their Renegade robot brethren killed thousands of climate regime soldiers while Mike sat trapped in a rotunda.

Suddenly, the ventilation system sprayed a robot germ for which Jimmy's robots had no antidote. The micro-robotic viruses seeped into the Renegade androids and mechanized-looking robots alike, incapacitating all of them. The germs worked through the circulatory, respiratory, and endocrine machinery of Jimmy's fighting force. Robots dropped their weapons and crumpled to the floor. All one hundred of them in the castle mansion died after minutes of irreversible breakdowns. The robots had already drunk a liquid made to inoculate themselves. The medicine proved worthless against the Planetary Order's germ warfare.

Outside, Jimmy watched from a distance while his robots' gunfire fell silent. He would have to leave the abandoned shack and go in alone, unaware of how many enemy soldiers remained inside or on the perimeter. He had no backup in the enemy capital from his once fierce yet freshly deceased robot warriors.

Jimmy remembered the note Cora had given him. He opened the sealed envelope, finding a small medicine bottle and a letter.

"Dear Jimmy, I hope this dose spares you from animate and robotic germs. Cora."

The Renegade drank the still unfrozen liquid, even though the germs the Planetary Forces spread that day could only harm the robots. Jimmy put on his helmet and walked out the creaking door of the dark cabin into a torrential blizzard.

Brimmilon, previously called Marganisan Dreamscapes but

just renamed by Greg Norbannick, faced round after round of assault. The robot army and civilian residents suffered an onslaught impossible to repel. Tsunamis of regime vehicles from the land and air converged on Brimmilon. The Planetary Forces sustained heavy losses, using high tech weaponry to fight the Renegade robot army in the city to a standstill.

After grueling hours of fighting, the robots on the ground finally felt the effects of the micro-robotic virus unleashed by climate regime aircraft. The Renegades' liquid medicine for robots to inoculate fell short once again.

Missile after missile struck the buildings, leveling Marganisan Palace. Defenses across the city would not hold, though not much remained for the regime to complete the takeover of Brimmilon.

Cora ordered the surviving robots in the aircraft to bomb research and production facilities.

Zack surveyed the victory grounds for his forces after their final wave of attack. He walked the frigid and ice-blanketed streets of Marganis, drinking the falling crystals as the storm pelted dead robots in the fields. Zack lit up his face under his headgear. He approached the destroyed palace and spotted someone trapped under debris.

Cora reached for her broken helmet, but her strength gave way. "You barely won this battle, Comrade of Marganis."

"I'm orchestrating our war strategy all over the planet. You'll forgive me if I ignore you bragging in defeat. These were my soldiers, mostly from the Lords of the Wolf Blade. I still hate them almost as much as I hate you, Renegade."

"You will lose the war, tomorrow or five years from now."

"And to think I almost sent shock waves in here. Then I thought better of it and considered nuclear weapons. I'm glad I did neither, because now I get to watch you freeze in a pile of rubble. I shot Bethany. I shot Linda. Seeing you die slowly for your fight against the lockdowns brings me a joy beyond measure."

Cora's eyes grew heavy. "You'll die before my last daughter dies. My husband and Jimmy will make sure of it."

"Quiet down now. Let me watch you pass on in peace. I can tell you're so cold that you can't even shiver. Every particle within your body ices over. You should never have questioned us, you stupid counterrevolutionary."

Cora opened her eyes and glared at Zack.

Zack shivered for a few moments, stunned by the missiles from his enemy's blazing stare.

Cora froze in Brimmilon. A few of the robots escaped in aircraft, but tens of thousands died from the micro-robotic virus. Not a living soul or robot populated the city any longer.

Zack led the last of his invading ground and air forces out of the wreckage. He demolished Brimmilon in the assault. He spared none of the stores, cafés, offices, theaters, arenas, high-rises, or burgeoning indoor gardens. He wanted the research and production facilities, but Cora's destruction of those meant fewer rearmament and biological and anti-robot warfare capabilities for the Planetary Forces. The climate regime failed to achieve all it hoped for in Brimmilon.

The city lay in ruins, nothing more than a ghost town with a blown-up palace and another dead Norbannick.

Jimmy entered the Planetary Leader's mansion on the regime base. He slid the door open and walked in unharmed, greeted by nobody. He moved from one area to the next, witnessing one incapacitated robot, and one soldier after another with a missing pulse.

Gunshots missed Jimmy by inches. He dropped to the floor and fired his machinegun, knocking out four enemy soldiers.

The ground rattled and the walls shook. Reinforcements arrived earlier than Jimmy expected...not any Renegade reinforcements.

Jimmy sprinted outside and heard hovercraft and all-terrain vehicles in addition to aircraft. Running through the snow toward his ship, he spotted Mike and leaped to the Earth. Mike never saw Jimmy, but acting on instinct, Mike swung around 360 degrees with a rocket launcher and blew up the abandoned shack.

Planetary Forces landed on the opposite end of the grounds from Jimmy and filed into the house.

With the blizzard letting up, Jimmy made a split-second decision. He pulled out a communication device and punched in a code for activation...His vessel in the snow switched on. "Aircraft, get ready for liftoff." Instead of the aircraft rising from the snow, it stayed parked under inches of fresh powder.

Regime soldiers approached by ground on Jimmy's side of

the field.

The most hunted Renegade dropped his machinegun and used his gloves to dig out the entrance to his compact vessel. Heat from the vessel loosened the covering snow.

Light shined down on Jimmy's face from the sky while two missiles from a hovercraft landed on either side of the Renegade. The blasts hurled him through the air. Machinegun fire strafed his ship.

Resigned to losing his life, he pulled off his helmet and spotted a tiger running at him. The terror jolted him to run for the ship. Heavy winds rocked the hovercraft and led to erratic firepower.

A weaponless Jimmy grabbed the ship door and flung it open. Barely inside, and evading fire from above, he bashed the jumping tiger's wide-open mouth with his helmet. The animal reeled in the snow. Jimmy slammed the door and used his vessel's weapons to return fire to the hovercraft. Ground soldiers closed in on Jimmy just as he took off with the backdrop of the abandoned shack in flames.

Jimmy rocketed away from the estate before the Planetary Forces could set up a perimeter.

Flanked by a new set of guards, a helmetless Mike shook his fist at the sky while the Renegade escaped. "Engle-wooooooooood!"

Katie flew her vessel into battle to free the Renegades from the Climate Rehab Center. Robots from Brimmilon accompanied her in ships of their own. Kaite and the Renegade robots received no resistance until they reached the prison complex, catching the enemy by surprise and disrupting regional and global operations.

Strong defenses and the heavy worldwide blizzard prevented an excessively easy assault against the Planetary Forces. The regime soldiers guarded their prison with aircraft, anti-aircraft weaponry, and land forces reinforcing the giant territory.

Guards kept the Center on tighter lockdown than ever, ordered to stand down from the fight outside and only engage in the building complexes. The guards were soldiers, part of the Planetary Forces, and no strangers to warfare.

Snow and ice blunted the Renegades' ground vehicle attack, but overall, the land assault favored the Renegades. So did the aerial assault.

After a grueling battle outside the prison, Katie led her Renegade robots into the complex. Bullets whizzed in all directions and grenades dropped everywhere. Robots gained the upper hand from the cell blocks to the guards' living quarters to the biodome. They tracked down administrators and soldiers in all areas of the prison. They spared the lives of every cafeteria robot working for the Planetary Forces, but they left the biodome floor littered with dead guards and the newly isolated climate regime pilots, navigators, and ground forces.

Katie entered, and had her robots open, the row of cells where Mike and Zack had enabled inmates to brutalize her. "My robot fighters, it's emptier than we thought it would be. Do you know what this means? The climate regime had just released all the lunatics and Lords of the Wolf Blade."

A lone prisoner stepped out of the shadows from the back of a cell. "Katie, is that you?"

The robots turned their weapons on him.

Katie raised her hand for her robots to stand down. "I remember you, Angelo. I can't believe you're still alive."

"I can't believe you came back here. They released the Lords to fight alongside Zack in some air battle to take over a city."

Katie gulped. "What about the lunatics?"

"They're dead. The guards slaughtered them on Mike's command before he left here. It was just before Mike replaced Dreckhorn as the Planetary Leader."

"I don't believe it."

Angelo walked out of the cell a free man. "The prison stopped shaking. What happened?"

"We won the battle. We killed all enemy forces protecting this complex."

"You're fortunate."

"So are you, Angelo."

"I meant something else. The release of the micro-robotic virus did not work here. The Planetary Forces had a bad batch for some reason. They think the Magician sabotaged them."

Katie looked around at the gathering crowd of robots and freed Renegades in the grimy cell block filled with recent, lingering horrors. "The Magician is dead. If he sabotaged the regime, all the better for us. Let's hope that it was his last trick anyway."

Angelo smiled and collapsed. The freed Renegade humans

caught him and carried him out through the dark hallways to the same transport ship that brought Jimmy back and forth from Paradise Gardens.

Still daytime, the blizzard strengthened. The freed Renegades found climate suits. These human men and women accompanied the androids and all other Renegade robots who could operate without special gear for much longer periods in the elements and bitter cold than people could.

Katie took a small contingent to the biodome. "Worker robots of the Planetary Order, you're leaving with us."

One of fifty of the workers wheeled forward to Katie. "We cannot. We cannot leave. We have orders. Orders. Orders. We live to comply."

A woman moved gracefully toward the conversation while everyone else hesitated. The human freed Renegade patted Katie on the shoulder. "Miss Norbannick, we have to grab climate gear and leave."

Katie turned from the robots' somber resignation, faced the woman and nodded. Katie enjoyed seeing the snow falling on the biodome. She noticed several bears outside trekking through the powder, walking away with their heads held high. "Everybody, the prison is liberated. Take all readily available food and enemy weapons. Be grateful for the Renegade robots, alive and dead, who gave us this victory. Let's raze this place to the ground, from here to every part of the perimeter."

The Renegade land and air forces left the prison. They leveled every building, cell block, and outer wall and gate. Rumbles reverberated across the icy fields. The great biodome crumbled last, shattered by Renegade missiles.

Katie watched the hardened glass structure die a painful death. She knew the biodome crushed the working robots underneath and felt her eyes water. Katie snapped back to concentrate on the next mission at hand. She wondered if Jimmy survived his attack against the Planetary Leader's home on the heavily protected Planetary Council's base. Katie's army traveled into the setting sun. The attenuating orange rays scattered through the whiteout skies and shined on the pilot Norbannick's face.

39

NEW BATTLE FOR MARGANIS

Jimmy steered his aircraft below the clouds of Marganis. He landed just beyond a sea of Planetary Forces dressed in their bright-red climate gear. The snow-packed, frigid ground glimmered in the clear and freezing atmosphere. The Renegade exited the vessel to join the combat from house to house, leveled building to leveled building, and pavement to pavement. His friend Greg had survived the earlier aerial assault, later helped by Katie and her Renegade robots.

Greg clutched Jimmy and threw him to the ground and fell with him to avoid enemy fire. "That was close! I saw you landing! Everybody wants to control the city and the whole fucking region, so nobody's bombing it to hell!"

The racket of gunfire, battle cries, and screams of pain and confusion drowned out Greg's voice. He rearmed Jimmy with a handgun when the two ducked into an apartment.

Jimmy fired several shots through the open window, hitting two enemy soldiers and dropping them to the street. "General, how did you know it was my ship?!"

"The same way you know it's me with my helmet light off! How did you even find an empty space to lower your ship?! We're used to this!"

"I'll never get used to this!"

"Jimmy, get down!"

Bullets flew in and out of the apartment.

Renegades from the city and everyday residents tried to protect the apartment, but the Planetary Forces mowed them down and rushed inside.

Seven soldiers fired on Jimmy and Greg while the duo ran upstairs.

The soldiers chased them, but not for long. Several freed Renegade prisoners from the nearby dungeon entered the downstairs. All seven soldiers felt the sting of Renegade machinegun fire, including three who fell down the stairs and died before colliding with each other and crashing to the laminated floor.

One of the Renegades shook another. "My climate gear! They ripped it! I'm getting cold!"

"Never mind that! You've got to stay calm and—"

A ground-to-ground missile flew through the housing facade and took the lives of the Renegades in the house.

Nobody in the apartment could survive such a blast. Jimmy

and Greg had already climbed down the second-story outer staircase to the back, stumbling beyond the rubble caused by the explosion.

Jimmy got up and helped Greg to his feet. "It sounded like someone engaged the soldiers by the time we got outside. The soldiers must be trapped inside, but we have no way to hide. Let's move, General!"

"I can't move."

"You're not hurt, General. You're exhausted."

"Katie is here. She flew from the Climate Rehab Center and she's in Marganis."

"We'll find her. We've got to run!"

"I'm hurt."

"Where?"

Greg collapsed, and Jimmy rushed to his side.

The General grabbed on to Jimmy's climate suit. "There's a bullet in my chest. You've got to go, Englewood. Tell my daughter I love her. Let me die here in battle."

"General! Greg! Stay awake! You've got to stay awake."

A bullet knocked Greg's helmet clean off. In a flash, he saw an image of him and Cora taking Bethany and Linda swimming on a lake when they were kids. Greg died. Jimmy looked over and saw the shooter.

Nobody could mistake the frame of the shooter. The Comrade of Marganis slaughtered his sixth Norbannick, counting the unborn twins he stripped from Bethany's womb.

Jimmy took Greg's machinegun and fired at Zack. He missed

his nemesis and hit another enemy soldier Zack threw into Jimmy's line of fire.

The battle spilled onto the rubble, where hand-to-hand combat became more prevalent than close-range gun fights.

Once again, Zack found Jimmy in a crowd of thousands upon thousands. Once again, Zack slaughtered and got away with it.

Greg's army of robots found Jimmy and a group of Renegades. The robots were unfazed by another faulty sprayed release of a micro-robotic virus. The robots helped Jimmy and the group of freed Renegades from the Marganisan Dungeon and prisons. Jimmy commanded all robots in the vicinity to attack against the tiring army of Planetary Forces. He assumed command of Greg's robots, and he welcomed Dorian and the reinforcements when they arrived.

Jimmy glanced over to where Greg was, but the General's body was no longer there.

The old city experienced its second consecutive day of excruciating hostilities by the time Jimmy arrived.

Angelo helped Katie remove her slaughtered father from the battlefield. They lifted Greg Norbannick into Katie's aircraft while the human and robot Renegade armies continued street fighting. This Second Battle of Marganis marked one of countless battles for cities and countryside around the world against the dominant but reeling Planetary Order. The vicious warfare in Marganis reflected a personal nature found in few other places on Earth. Renegades fought for the chance to reclaim the soul of the city.

The climate regime had already demolished many homes, apartments, offices, high rises, and shops in Marganis. Recent missile attacks and prior street fighting had brought the city to ruin. The Planetary Forces had brutalized people for years and enslaved them in primitive conditions.

Hand-to-hand combat raged on in the streets, in collapsed buildings, and in the housing and abandoned commercial locations that remained standing.

Renegades fought for Marganis to serve as a message to the climate regime. They wanted to convey to the entire HAVE movement that neither the city nor the vast majority of its inhabitants would accept defeat. The Renegades denied residents the option to accept slavery.

The climate regime needed to protect their incarceration, production, and workcamp and deathcamp systems. But knowing the Renegades sought to rebuild Marganis, the Planetary Forces had a visceral hatred toward the people of the city.

Renegades reclaimed Marganis. Still, they had to rebuild and defend the city on an Earth enduring an ice age. They would not permit celebrating among their ranks for retaking territory. Renegades of the city still had to link with many similar fighters throughout the planet. They also faced an upcoming task of freeing the frightened and broken victims of Paradise Gardens.

Dorian stayed in the main part of the city to establish a base and coordinate strategies and operations in other regions. Fighting continued engulfing the lands, skies, and seas of the

Earth.

Katie and Angelo joined Jimmy and a contingent of human and robot Renegades on a short vessel flight to the outskirts of the city. They entered the grounds for Paradise Gardens.

Paradise Gardens had heavy security in the recent past, but this time, Jimmy, Katie, and Angelo found no guard presence on the perimeter.

Jimmy pressed a button on an unlocked sliding door to enter. "Angelo, wait with the ship, just in case."

The door closed behind Jimmy and Kaite. They took off their helmets and could not hear a sound near the entrance.

Back near the pool area, the residents in post-rehabilitation at Paradise Gardens enjoyed the lush setting. The artificial sunlight and warmer temperatures numbed them to anything else going on in Marganis and in the world. Some people enjoyed the pool. Others enjoyed the food, and others sat on beach chairs, talking and laughing.

The tropical surroundings, light music, and tranquil sounds of wildlife soothed the roughly two hundred people living in a bubble-wrapped Eden.

Jimmy and Katie found a couple of empty chairs and sat next to one woman drinking freshly made pineapple juice. The thin, long-haired, blond, middle-aged woman wore a brimmed hat but removed her sunglasses when the two Renegades approached her.

Katie looked around before breaking ten seconds of silence. "Do you remember anything about me?"

The woman smiled warmly and shyly at Katie. "I'm Isabel. What is your name?"

"I'm Katie, and this is Jimmy. You truly don't remember me?"

"I wish I did because you seem so nice. How do we know each other? You look like Linda. Linda Norbannick. I think so. I miss her."

"Isabel, I am her sister. Jimmy and I are here to spring you. We have humans and robots on the way to get you back to Marganis. We'll get everyone else to where they need to go."

"Is that how I know you? Do I know you from Marganis."

"Yes, Linda, you saved me one summer from drowning in the Orcasso Sea when I was a kid."

"I'm very happy I could help you, but I don't remember too much before I got to the Climate Rehab Center."

"I was there, too."

"You don't seem like they rehabbed you, Katie."

"They weren't able to rehab me, and I'm one of very few they couldn't."

"They couldn't rehab me as much as they wanted."

Jeremy tilted his head. "What are you telling us?"

"I'm telling you they never convinced me of humans or animals being viruses. I didn't believe a thing they told me. Somehow, I avoided the Planetary Order's physical experiments. They psychologically tortured me and thought they were effective. They managed to scare me and harm my memory, but they never got me to believe what I told them. I said I had sincere regret about doubting the climate regime. I agreed with them that the Earth heated up. They made Linda believe everything, or pretty much everything. She stayed warmhearted, though. There aren't any mean people here. The regime used us for propaganda movies to keep people locked down."

Jimmy got up. "Isabel, we're taking you with us. You cannot stay here. You can bring food with you, but I just got word that our backup arrived. They're waiting outside."

Isabel cried. "I can't leave."

Jimmy paused, wanting to change his voice so as to avoid scaring an easily scared Isabel. "I know the climate regime threatened and harmed you in the past, but you're safe now. You're free."

Katie hugged Isabel. "Go with us. It's the least I can do for the woman who saved me."

Isabel wiped her tears. "I can't go. I can't leave here. The lockdown is still in full effect. This is my new home. This is where I have everything I need. There's so much food and nice weather to last a lifetime and even longer. I'm too worried I'll starve and die in the cold. Look around this beautiful paradise. It's warm all the time, and everyone is my friend."

Jimmy placed his hand on his forehead. "Isabel, the Planetary Forces could send men back here anytime. They could bomb the place. They could do anything if they get the chance. Leave with us and you'll be independent again."

Isabel stared straight ahead at the pool. She got lost in the sight and sound of the waterfall.

Jimmy pulled out a communication device. "Angelo, we'll be back out in five to ten minutes. Keep everyone outside. The people in here will get frightened if more people or robots enter the tropical-type vacation zone."

Katie tapped Isabel on the hand. "Please join us. Please, Isabel. It doesn't matter if anybody else wants to go. You know the lies of the climate regime and lockdown tyranny. We've got plenty of extra climate suits. It's time for you to begin the next part of your life."

"Isabel hugged Katie, nodded to Jimmy, and walked into the pool to talk with a few women and enjoy the heated water."

Jimmy picked up his helmet. "Katie, she's gone. We took back Marganis, but the fighting isn't over. Planetary Forces really can show up anytime. Grab your headgear. Let's get back in the vessel."

"You know, Jimmy, I thought if I could save her life, I could somehow save Linda's. There's an innocence about Isabel that I want to release from this trap."

"I couldn't protect Linda at Paradise Gardens. Neither of us can help anybody here today."

Jimmy and Katie looked at Isabel one more time before walking back out through the faint mist.

Minutes later, Isabel saw a dead parrot at the base of a nearby tree. She remembered seagulls flying on a day in the past when she saved a child from drowning in the Orcasso Sea. Isabel swung her head toward the pool entrance. Her heart gave out when she saw no trace of Katie.

40

TENUOUS

Renegades won the Second Battle of Marganis. They imprisoned thousands of climate regime soldiers in the prisons the regime had made to demoralize and destroy Renegades among others.

The city thrusted Jimmy into being the leader of Marganis. He and all new leaders of the metropolis ordered the dismantling of the dungeon.

Thousands of Renegades and climate regime soldiers lay dead across the city. Burial grounds had already existed despite the incineration practices of the Planetary Forces and the eventually extinct City Forces.

Robots cobbled together two hospitals from rubble, available supplies, existing buildings, and resources from the local terrain.

The robots also helped the Renegades and everyday residents

of Marganis to produce food, make clothing, and repair and create housing.

The global and regional climates passed the point of human or robotic manipulation to enable warmth. Frigid temperature patterns had not yet reached the lowest points of the ice ages experienced on Earth.

Outside farming became almost nonexistent due to climate conditions, but the residents of Marganis regained their voices and trusted each other once again. They knew their success did not reach all parts of the planet but did spread throughout the region. The defenses of the Renegade army grew under Dorian's command across the Marganisan Valley and beyond.

After victory in the Second Battle of Marganis, the Renegade robots took over the base on Marganisan Peak and controlled the Boshquire Mountains.

Dorian reclaimed land the Planetary Forces had seized. He brought territory under Renegade control from the Marganisan Valley and beyond, and all through the highlands to the Brimmilon Sea. The Renegades constructed bases and outposts in Marganis, the Boshquires, Brimmilon (formerly Marganisan Dreamscapes), and the shores of the Brimmilon and Orcasso Seas.

Indoor food production soared, as did improvements in soil treatment for outdoor plant life. Few patches of forest survived in the Marganisan Valley, but plans took root for regrowth, using the best scientific advancements.

Medicines sprouted for preventing and curing biological and

micro-robotic germs. Much work remained, yet the research and development advanced astronomically.

Humans and robots joined forces to treat all surviving casualties on their side of the global war. To no climate regime acknowledgment, Jimmy Englewood, the regional leader for the Renegades, ensured the fair treatment of soldiers of the Planetary Forces in prisons. They did not, however, receive the same level of advanced technological appendage replacements for battlefield injuries that friends of the Renegades and Marganisan residents received.

Jimmy implemented a grand vision. The vision had already coalesced along a successful path for three months since the Second Battle of Marganis. He knew he would step aside as city manager before the vision would come to fruition. Jimmy found himself and the residents of the region building a new nation-state.

Jimmy let Angelo into his first-floor garden apartment near Marganisan Plaza. "Hey Angelo, I know it isn't like my old house. I'm waiting on a bed and appliances, but this isn't bad at all. They've already got the heat turned on. Do you want to sit?"

"I'd rather stay on my feet. It's been good to see you again."

"Likewise, my friend. I had no clue you were in that prison, thrown in the same cell as Katie. She never told me anything about anyone she knew being in that cell with her. I know about the people who brutalized her, but that was it."

"They brutalized me, too, after I tried to stop them from

assaulting her. They were absolute lunatics. I never knew people like that existed. I did to some extent, but not really. The
Climate Rehab Center encouraged them to do whatever they
wanted to us at any time. And I can't believe that prison chief,
Mike, is now the Planetary Leader."

"How the both of you survived that prison wing is something
I'll never understand. It doesn't even seem like you're scarred,
emotionally or physically. Same with Katie."

"Never mind me. What can I do to help you and Katie?"

"You can help Marganis and you can help the world. You can
lead a new country."

"You're stepping down?"

"I lead a loose coalition and I'm a city manager. You can lead
something at a larger scale."

"Why me?"

"I've known you since we were four. The people of this city
and region respect you. They know who you are. They know
your background as a soldier and enterprising individual from
an earlier time. Nobody's forgotten how hard you fought the
enemies of liberty. Nobody will ever forget your defiance of the
climate regime."

"Why not you?"

"I don't have your courage or ability for leadership. You know
that. I don't have what's needed for times like these. I survive by
miracles every day. Sure, I've got some of that warrior spirit, but
I'm not a true soldier, and I'm not a true statesman."

"What are you talking about? You've been a soldier and a

statesman. You still are."

"This is the end for me. I can't build a new civilization. I don't have the fortitude or the skill. You relate to people in ways I never can. I've got other things I need to do while you construct a new country and vanquish the Planetary Order from the world."

"Jimmy, remember when we were ten and we used to talk about going off to war?"

"I remember it like it was a minute ago."

"Who knew war would become what it did? When the regime slaughtered the McElroys, that's when I stopped thinking so much about them and the other families. I just started thinking about what I needed to do to avenge them. But when the regime threw me in prison again, I couldn't stop thinking again about memories with our old childhood friends and the families that treated us like sons."

"What are you telling me, Angelo?"

"I'm telling you not to go through with what you're planning. Run against me in a countrywide election, but whatever you do, stay in Marganis as city manager or fight alongside the Renegades as the Renegade you are."

"I'll leave all the concerns to you and other intelligent people about how to create a nation-state and run cities."

"Stay in town regardless."

"I won't."

"When they capture you, they'll punish you forever."

"They can't do that. Forever lasts a long time after death."

"Let go of your insatiable desire for vengeance."

"This isn't vengeance. I have to show the world that the climate regime cannot break me. That will bring Marganis and our new country a strength I could never achieve in battle."

"Englewood, what does all that have to do with your one-man mission to kill Zack."

"I missed my opportunity to kill Mike. I will not miss my opportunity to bring Zack to justice."

"You'll bring your life to an end! You're hunting down men instead of hunting down the HAVE movement in its totality. We need you here!"

"Angelo, my friend, you don't need me anywhere except where I'm supposed to be. And that isn't here."

The two Renegades left Jimmy's apartment to survey the latest developments in the city. They entered an abandoned hardware store.

Dorian entered the abandoned store when Angelo threw Jimmy against the wall.

Jimmy cocked his fist until he noticed Dorian.

Angelo let Jimmy go.

Dorian played a message of Mike's voice. "Knock out their minds forever."

Jimmy walked to the door and watched people and humans at work rebuilding a high-rise in the frozen rain. "How did you get that recording, Dorian?"

"It was from his first broadcast to the planet. You heard it, Jimmy? Did you hear it, Angelo?"

"Yes, they played it at the Climate Rehab Center. This is what we're up against. We've known about it for a while. They want every piece of a person's mind to obey them."

Dorian pointed to his own head. "They want the minds of robots, too. I hope you both remember all of this, because Marganis will not survive without each of your efforts. You would not be able to build a new nation-state, and you would not be able to salvage liberty anywhere in the world."

Jimmy turned around and walked from the door back to Angelo and Dorian.

Angelo stuck out his hand to Jimmy. "I think Dorian just helped us beyond measure."

Jimmy bypassed Angelo's hand to hug him.

Angelo smiled. "We're all suffering from Greg Norbannick's death. Let's set you up to get you to where you need to go. We'll help with anything we can. Dorian, you plan the effort to assist Jimmy. In the meantime, I'll do what I must to form a new country. I'll do what I have to do before the elections."

Jimmy's face lit up. "You'll have plenty of help from humans and robots. Isn't that right, Dorian."

"Yes, Jimmy. Angelo has the robots ready at his call. The humans of Marganis and the region have to determine if they want a country or not. We robots will help them."

Construction noise from outside disrupted the conversation when Katie entered from the frozen rain. She handed her helmet to Angelo. "What's going on, guys? This looks like a serious conversation. What am I interrupting?"

Angelo placed Katie's helmet on the kitchen counter. "I think the cold air and saw dust interrupt us more than anything else does."

Katie rolled her eyes. "Maybe you'll tell me, Dorian."

"Ask Jimmy."

"Well, how about it, Englewood, my brother?"

"I'm going to confront the regime again on their territory, and Angelo is going to lead the Renegades to form a new country."

"That sounds about right."

Dorian activated a small two-dimensional screen to detach from his left arm.

The screen read, "One billion erased. Seventy percent controlled."

41

BOILING POINT

The Planetary Order murdered one billion non-combatant human beings since the beginning of the war. These one billion souls did not include the millions upon millions of Renegades or anyone who suffered defeat in the midst of battle. They were victims of a mass-murder campaign across the Earth, a planet of which the Planetary Order controlled seventy percent.

Climate regime forces took merely two months and a little extra to murder people to a degree that no man could fathom. The speed and intensity at which the executions took place surprised the Renegades around the world, who had limited power to help unarmed and enslaved Earthlings.

Murder methods ranged from freezing people to dropping them off cliffs. Other people received injections of real germs or robot microbes. Some methods of slaughter struck Jimmy and his Marganisans as so horrific that they could not utter the ends or means of the barbarity. City residents would sit silently and mourn for the casualties of a sweeping butchery that overwhelmed the psyche of every man, woman, and child.

The climate regime accused hundreds of millions of breaking the lockdown orders. No show trials commenced. The regime made no effort to follow a system of just laws, and applying the lockdown laws turned into a matter of absolute ideological purity tests engineered by the Planetary Order.

The Planetary Council inflicted as much pain as it could on anyone who would not comply. Groups of Renegades, and in some areas the everyday humans, would never fall prey to propaganda. Planetary Forces also brought as much death and suffering as possible to contested areas and Renegade areas. Prisoners of war faced the wrath of the climate regime. Unrelenting propaganda, unsanitary conditions, and abuses terrorized millions of Renegade fighters.

Renegades, slaves, and everyday civilians throughout the world faced a choice when trapped on regime territory. They could turn against family and peers to live a good life. They would gain all the security, food, healthcare, medicines, games, and escapism at their disposal if granted clemency. Alternatively, they could defy the climate revolution and die mercilessly along with their families.

Mike removed the shackles. He removed the pretenses of appearances for which he initially showed concern when he became Planetary Leader. Most climate regime soldiers no longer had any misgivings about following orders to heap misery and atrocities on every living being they could. The main disappointment concerned their directives to avoid using nuclear and other debilitating weapons against their enemies. The Council had a plan, so the Planetary Forces held back from slaughtering additional billions.

Renegades had a plan as well to deliver pain to their enemies. The Renegade leader in Marganis prepared to spell it out for the planet...but not the entire plan.

An image of the mountainous Orcasso Sea spread across much of the background of the Angelo's video. He delivered a prepared speech down to the word, with no notes. He prepared the speech himself.

"Greetings my fellow humans and allied robots. My name is Angelo Cantare. As a Renegade, I am the new executive of a new country until we have the winner of the upcoming elections. and I appeal today to the sensibilities of everybody on Earth who still has any sensibilities left. This is a live broadcast, available through every major video and audio service. The Planetary Order and their minions tried to stop this message. They failed, and now that we have your attention, you can play this as a recording in the future to remind everyone that the forces of liberty cannot be denied. I am a soldier and a man of enterprise. Most recently, I also served time as a prisoner in a place called the Climate Rehab Center. We destroyed the Center. Renegades destroyed the Center, and we're fighting back all over the world."

Angelo looked to Jimmy off screen. Jimmy simply nodded.

Angelo turned his face back to the viewers. "We pray that one day the fight will end. We've already created so much in the past number of months. We are rebuilding the region, and we are building a new nation-state. The construction does not arise from the ashes of an old nation-state. It takes from the best of our old nation-state and brings back the timeless principles we had almost lost. Our ways of life never fully burned down. The physical structures did, but we're creating from a solid foundation, and the climate regime is helpless to stop us. Together with my fellow Marganisans and friends of my region, I ask that you build nation-states of your own."

An image appeared on the top right portion of the screen, showing the old Marganisan cityscape.

"One day soon, we can drop the label of Renegades, becoming citizens of new countries. My new country is the country I'm leading through war. Please welcome Orcasso as the first new nation-state on this planet. We pay tribute to all the slaughtered and endangered species that have Orcasso in their name. Never see this as a dishonor. See it as the protection of the killer whales that the climate regime targeted for wide-scale death before the regime murdered a billion people in just over two months. We do not worship wildlife, but we revere it. Orcasso stands as a symbol for defending all the best within us as people. We will protect humans and robots where we failed to protect whales, dolphins, and most importantly, where we failed to defend the humans who needed our help."

Angelo pointed at Jimmy. "Everybody, meet the Planetary Order's number one enemy. Meet Jimmy Englewood, the interim city manager of Marganis."

Angelo walked off the video.

Jimmy walked on screen and talked off the cuff. "Thank you, President Cantare. You have been through murderous punishments, much like many of you across the Earth. I'm Jimmy Englewood. While the President of Orcasso carries a message of camaraderie and peace and prosperity, he chose me to carry another message we both share."

Jimmy paused and relived the memory of kneeling down in front of his Bethany dying in the Marganisan snow. "Listen closely, Planetary Tyrant Mike, and your Planetary Order of climate regime monsters. Despite your HAVE movement's efforts to brainwash us, you will never turn us all against what we know to be true, and real, and worth defending. You've threatened and used anything from death camps to nuclear to chemical to germ warfare. We will find every single one of you and your co-opted Lords and send you packing to Hell. You have stripped billions of us Earthlings from what we hold dear. You poison countless spirits, and you do it with no remorse or regret. I promise you that the countries of the world will bring back everything you took from us and then some. The Renegades will provide your children with the kind of lives you tried to steal from us. We offer you no terms other than your complete surrender."

42

ZACK RETURNS TO BASE

Mike's security detail showed complete loyalty to Mike and the Planetary Order. His guards and every soldier on the grounds of the grand estate allowed nobody near him without his explicit approval.

Zack visited the newly repaired castle mansion, located on the expanded and strengthened headquarters of the Planetary Order. Part of Mike's security detail escorted Zack to Mike after a thorough frisking and questioning at the landing pad.

The snow-packed base teemed with aircraft, ground vehicles, missiles, and foot soldiers crossing the property during one of the region's usual howling blizzards. All the Planetary Council had moved permanently to various buildings in the enlarged zone of the climate regime headquarters. The grand estate dwarfed the other living quarters on the base in size and grandeur.

The guards left Mike alone with Zack after Mike pointed them to the door.

Mike had a giant library filled with ancient and modern texts. He sat behind a dark wooden desk in a mahogany-lined room. Zack sat in front of the desk on a wheeled swivel chair with back support up to the neck. Mike's chair rose a bit higher.

The Planetary Leader and Comrade of Marganis stared at each other. Nobody said a word for half a minute. Zack clenched his teeth for a split second, compelling Mike to grin and open the long desk drawer.

Mike slid a booklet to Zack. "Pick it up and open the front cover. Read it to me."

Zack grimaced upon reading it to himself.

Mike snapped his fingers. "Read it out loud."

Zack flared his nostrils. "The Planetary Order's strategy for continuous climate regime revolution with reduced Planetary Forces."

"Are you upset?"

"No. It's just that I have a global army at my disposal through your command. Are we supposed to achieve our ends through mass destruction instead of manpower? I'm guessing you want to rely on robots and propaganda."

"For your tall and large frame, you've always been more intelligent than anyone's given you credit for. Everyone knows you're a genius at warfare despite some costly setbacks not entirely your fault. You have an intelligence about you that sees the grand vision, even if the warrior in you doesn't want to see it."

"I'm here to ask you for something."

"You're here because I ordered you here."

"Do you want me to read the booklet?"

"I do, and I command you to accept the fact that we're scaling down the size of your global army. We cannot bring as many people to the HAVE movement as we wanted. We're not going to try to take over every city and every ounce of territory until we absolutely level a wide swath of the planet or delete the populations so we can move in at a later time. Soon we will have robots working in areas we deem too dangerous for Planetary Forces."

"What do you want me to carry out at the moment?"

"Capture Jimmy Englewood. That is your primary responsibility. Bring him to this base alive and well. Then we'll dismember Marganis and the so-called nation-state of Orcasso for good. If they won't submit to the Planetary Order, they will submit to radiation, poisons, explosions, incinerations, the rubble from the Earth's crust…you understand me?"

"How, specifically, do you want to handle that in Marganis?"

"You deal with it. I don't need to know how you capture Jimmy. Just deal with it."

"I meant how are we going to dismember Orcasso?"

"I know what you meant. You'll know when I decide."

"Should I read the booklet now or later?"

"You can read our strategy after you return with Jimmy Englewood. I don't want anything taking your mind off of your current mission. Let your subordinates handle the world in the meantime, Comrade of Marganis."

"My request becomes all the more important. Given the danger of this mission, I must ask for a position on the Planetary Council."

"Request granted. I'll find your replacement to lead the Planetary Forces."

"Thank you."

"Hold off on your appreciation until you return."

"I can taste his capture."

"I know you can, but until you capture him, you're tasting an illusion. His capture will break the defiant spirit of the counterrevolutionaries. Climate deniers will lose precious momentum when they lose him, but we're not going to spend decades on converting everybody. We'll use reeducation where we can, combined with all forms of sedation, warfare, and seduction. You'll read more about the strategy soon. We will discuss this upon your joining the Planetary Council. Good night, Zack."

Mike stood up, and his security detail from the Planetary Forces reentered the room.

Zack walked to the door of the study, followed by the guards. "What are all those books about?"

"Yes, three enormous bookcases saturated with old writings. These ideas brought us to where we are. The ideas and men like you with the courage to act on those ideas. These books hold the history and philosophy of propaganda. They contain the steps on how to shatter souls. Think about how much you already know about breaking people in pieces, psychologically and spiritually. Here, take this very short booklet in case you need it for ideas on keeping Jimmy Englewood under control when you confront him. I'll keep the strategy booklet in this room for safekeeping."

"Without windows in here, I almost forgot about blizzard outside."

"We've lost the ability to manipulate the weather beyond slight regional or local changes. Nobody can do it anymore, but we can always manipulate minds. Manipulate whatever minds you must to capture Jimmy Englewood."

"I've done that for a long time."

"Leave an impression on him this time that he'll never forget. Seize him, and if you dare, seize his defiance."

"How about Katie?"

"Well, cousin, force Jimmy to watch you erase the last of the Norbannick family."

43

VISIONS

Jimmy waited for Angelo, Katie, and Dorian at a booth in a café near Marganisan Plaza. Construction in the area halted just as he sat down to enjoy a view of the city. The snow fell while the robots did their best to clear roads and walkways as fast as possible.

***

Winter seemed for a moment to boil away in favor of Jimmy's memories. The Renegade envisioned the city filled with concert venues, theaters, beautiful landscapes lined with old oak trees, and the warmth of a spring day bringing hope for a carefree summer. He pictured families enjoying the community pool and stopping for cold drinks under shaded relief from the scorching Julys of the past. Moonlight jaunts into forests and foothills filled Jimmy's mind. Former streets and stone houses in the outskirts brought him to a Marganis he took for granted. He watched the city's formerly unrivaled high-rises transform into construction projects when the robot waiter placed a glass of water on the table.

***

The old, the young, and everyone in between watched the number one enemy of the climate regime sitting at an eatery in their shared hometown. Customers throughout the cafe observed Jimmy slip back into a trance.

***

Jimmy slid into the future, picturing a newly completed Marganis leading the way for the Orcasso nation-state. Parents cheered their children at baseball games. Festivals welcomed visitors far and wide for architecture, paintings, and the freshest foods on the planet. Wildlife populated parks and nature preserves. Jimmy felt at peace. He watched the stars rise and fall over the great lights of the greatest city on Earth. He absorbed the daylight and noticed Bethany standing close by until she walked into a wedding reception. She blended in and Jimmy searched the grand ballroom to find her. Wedding guests, dressed in the finest formal attire, watched him with awe and trepidation. He saw no sign of a bride or groom but instead spotted a bride's dress on the floor along with one baby outfit for a boy and one for a girl.

Outside, a light drizzle fell, and Jimmy walked into a growing downpour. He tried to walk back inside the wedding hall. Drenched, he pulled the locked door with all his power. Jimmy banged and yelled, "Open up!" He discovered himself trapped in a 10 x 10 x 10-foot dungeon cell with no doors or windows. The cell began to shrink, and nobody responded to his yells or pounding.

***

Suddenly, Jimmy snapped back to the present when the humanoid robot serving his booth woke him up. "Are you alright, Mr. Englewood? You must be very tired falling asleep upright in the middle of the day like that."

"Did I talk in my sleep? Everybody's staring at me."

"Can I get you anything?"

"No thank you. Not yet. I'll be alright."

Jimmy's attention turned to the cafe entrance when he heard the bells chiming from the opening door. Angelo, Katie, and Dorian arrived.

The night prior, a man in Marganis returned home from work to his wife, his 8-year-old son Julio, and his 6-year-old daughter Larissa. He hugged them all and sent his children upstairs to bed.

"Honey, the kids already ate. What's wrong? What is it,

Juan?"

"Crazy stories, Angelica."

"From your friends in the Renegades?"

"Yes. The Planetary Council eradicated everyone connected to the Lords of the Wolf Blade."

Juan's Renegade friends had told him the true story. Council members determined the Lords had completed their purpose in aerial, land, and sea warfare, not to mention in propaganda, intimidation, and mass extermination campaigns. The climate regime leaders had viewed their equal but opposite movement as hopelessly untrustworthy and deserving of a cathartic punishment. The regime had decided to rid itself of many Lords and Lords supporters who would never truly relent or submit to the Planetary Order.

"What's wrong, Juan? What is it? What did your friends tell you?"

"The Planetary Leader ordered a worldwide purification campaign. He ordered regional commanders to cleanse the Lords from all military units, administrative roles, and resident communities under the control of the climate regime."

"You look so troubled. They must have told you more. How do they know all this? How did they find out?"

"They have their ways. Here's the thing. The one-day campaign resulted in the slaughter of one hundred million Lords and their supporters. Supporters received quick deaths when they admitted guilt, but the garrison of soldiers in every locale decided guilt and sentencing based on who they deemed worthy of leniency."

For the Lords themselves, quick yet painful methods led to their demise. Mike unleashed the full fury of the HAVE movement on them, with cheering crowds basking in the dark glow of the Planetary Forces' execution spree.

Juan kept relaying the story accurately. "Renegades across the world heard about the directive. They knew the Planetary Council meant to paralyze everyone on Earth into inaction. It's just that the Renegades never completely demobilized or disarmed themselves despite having to revitalize their forces after harrowing defeats and severe suffering. The Lords of the Wolf Blade lost in battles to the climate regime and agreed to join forces in their mutual hatred of the Renegades' love of individual liberty. Lords also calculated that global defeat threatened their lives. For a while, they had spared themselves and their families by fighting ruthlessly against Renegades. And they wiped out large amounts of animals and plants adaptable to the ice age."

What Juan did not know included the hourly reports that Mike had already received during the daylight from the Planetary Council. One million dead here and another million dead there never fazed the Planetary Leader.

Mike never felt so alive yet so terrified. His dreams of complete planetary conquest drove his many moves, though these dreams paled in comparison to his ultimate goal. Mike wanted to own the minds of every Renegade and every human. He craved dominion over all living things, keeping in line with the objectives of the Planetary Order. His failure to fully control robots sent him into fits of wrath. He knew that his lack of control over the inanimate led to failures in his campaign for full dominance on Earth.

The Planetary Leader sought every which way to assuage his fears by corrupting, numbing, exciting, perplexing, and smashing the minds and souls of men. He believed erasing roughly half the Earth's population would lead him to unchallenged dominance over the individual. He lay awake in his chamber consumed by the comfort his mass exterminations brought him. He would also yearn for supremacy over a single Renegade by wiping out entire populations. In the meantime, the Lords of the Wolf Blade became extinct, consigned to the fires of history.

Juan held his wife in his arms. "Angelica, no Renegade sheds a tear knowing tyrants got taken out by other tyrants, but every Renegade knows the more powerful climate regime lives on and threatens all of us with slavery and annihilation. We already went through it before."

"I know, Juan. I can't believe you came out of that dungeon alive."

"I can't either, but there's more to the story about the Wolf Blade. Mike commanded the murder of every Lord's family."

Angelica dropped her jaw and gasped. "We can't let them take over this city. Never. They'll do even worse things to us than before. They'll do worse things to us than they did to the Lords."

"Especially to people like us they have on a registry. The

Planetary Order knows that I broke lockdown orders and served time."

"What a nightmare. A hundred million in one day."

"Angelica, the Renegades know the Lords would have wiped out families of the HAVE followers if they had the power. The Renegades are different than tyrants, though. They understand the horror unleashed by the regime eradicating the Lords' family members. The Renegades aren't animals, but they're not crying about what happened to the Lords or their supporters. Let's be grateful these guys like Jimmy Englewood defend us."

The Wolf Blade and its flaming sword of bigotry and slaughter vanished while the climate regime and its ax in the Earth persevered.

Juan looked upstairs to see Julio and Larissa listening in from the hallway. "Don't worry, kids. We've got Jimmy Englewood, the liberator of Marganis to protect us. And I'll always protect you, no matter what happens out there."

The children stared at their parents and ran back downstairs for another hug from them.

Juan looked at his wife. "What do you think, Angelica, should we chase them back upstairs?"

"I think we should!"

The children giggled and ran for their rooms. They slept peacefully, as did Angelica a short while later.

Juan just stared up at the ceiling all night next to his wife. He went to work the next day through the driving snow to open his café.

Jimmy shook off his bad vision about the shrinking dungeon cell and got up to greet Angelo, Katie, and Dorian, who all joined him at the booth. Angelo sat across from Jimmy, and Dorian sat on the aisle next to Jimmy.

The robot server walked to the booth with a tray of waters for the three additional patrons, but they declined.

Jimmy raised an eyebrow. "I'm not hungry or thirsty, but I'm going to have something before I leave Marganis."

Katie tapped her hands on the granite table. "What can we do other than join your mission?"

"Nothing, Katie. There's nothing you can do. You and your family have done more than I could have ever asked."

"It wasn't good enough."

"You've lost your entire family. You've sacrificed everything except your own life, but your mission is now to encourage life."

"You're right. It's to give birth as well. Angelo will join me in that mission after we get married."

Angelo took Katie's hand and Jimmy laughed with joy. "I don't think either of you know how much you just provided added inspiration for my mission. I fight for you, and I fight for your children, however many you have and whenever you have them. And Katie, I fight for everyone they took from me and you."

"I love your motivation to do that. It's just that when you confront Zack, don't concentrate on your unborn children, or Bethany, my sister, my parents, or your brother, or anyone else he murdered. Remember Marganis and the country we're building."

Angelo smiled at Jimmy. "Remember the liberties we used to have, Jimmy, and the liberties we need to take back."

"I hear both of you, but I'm already free. I always have been free, and so have you. So is everybody who seeks freedom in our land or anywhere else. Marganis and Orcasso are with me. I have nothing more to think about when it comes to that. I'm honored to bring justice to the one who took the lives of those closest to me."

Angelo looked diagonally across to Dorian. "Don't you have anything to say before we get you robot food?"

"I have much to say, but you're all too stubborn to listen. Oh, you find my response funny. Well, how about this? I am joining Mr. Englewood's mission, whether any of you like it or not."

Angelo shook his head. "Who's being stubborn now, Dorian? Fortunately, we have your plans in place. We have many capable people and robots to revise them and carry them out."

"Then, you allow my decision, President Cantare."

"I do."

Jimmy smiled back at Angelo. "See, you've got nothing to worry about." He looked out the window to the light snowfall, almost immersing himself in yet another vision. From the café booth, he imagined a gust of wind and cold air.

Katie waved her hand in front of Jimmy. "Englewood, let's order some food, but first I'm giving you an order."

"What's the order, sister?"

"Kill the Comrade of Marganis."

44

RENEGADE VS COMRADE

Dorian hopped on a shuttle to the Marganisan base while Jimmy walked home wearing full climate gear. After a few minutes in the gray skies and weakening sun, Jimmy reached his apartment. He grabbed his belongings for his joint mission with Dorian to track down Zack.

The light in the bathroom flickered under the closed door. Fixing it could wait until he returned from his mission, but he suddenly remembered to leave the faucet dripping. He took his helmet off, saw a shadow under the bathroom door, and switched off the living room lights.

Jimmy opened the front door to the house and closed it seconds later, but he stayed inside the house. He walked to the bathroom door and knocked it down with a front kick. The bathroom light continued flickering, and Jimmy turned around. He took a wild punch to his stomach. He fell to the floor, and the assailant picked up a wooden chair. Jimmy dodged the falling chair, which broke into fragments. He pulled a handgun that the attacker smacked out of his grip.

The attacker landed a series of jabs to Jimmy's chin. Jimmy bounced against the refrigerator when the attacker connected with an elbow and knocked out the Renegade.

Jimmy woke up on the ground with his shirt off and a needle injecting his left arm.

The assailant stuck Jimmy with a live virus and then stuck him again with a micro-robotic one. "This'll keep you docile enough for the trip to headquarters. Give me some help getting you to your vessel outside. That's what we're flying. It's going to be cold for a few minutes. Put on your shirt and climate gear. Move! Move before I ignore Mike and kill you anyway, Englewood."

"Zack, is that you?"

"Yes, and I'm going to tie you up now."

"I'm dizzy."

"It's time to knock you out again!"

"Cora Norbannick gave me medicine to inoculate myself."

"Fuck you, Englewood!"

Jimmy kicked Zack's left kneecap. He threw an uppercut to send the Comrade of Marganis into the kitchen table and his machinegun skating across the room.

The bathroom light died out. Zack hobbled along, throwing punches at thin air. Jimmy kicked Zack's right kneecap. The climate regime champion crumpled under the pain.

Jimmy grabbed Zack's machinegun and switched on the living room lights. "You hit hard, Comrade Zack. I'm really dizzy. But enough about me. How are your knees?"

Zack grinned. "My handguns are missing."

"You didn't even know I took them from you."

"Fuck you again, Englewood. Your wife is dead. Your twins are dead. The Norbannicks and your family are pretty much all dead. Marganis is next. Orcasso is next. You're next, my old enemy."

"Who's outside?"

"Can't you hear them, Jimmy. They're right outside. They're ready to bring me to headquarters and patch me up."

Jimmy picked up Zack Dreckhorn's machinegun. "Only God can patch you up. The Englewoods and Norbannicks send their regards on behalf of God's children."

Jimmy fired twenty shots into the Comrade of Marganis.

Mike Dreckhorn and the late Brandon Dreckhorn's cousin, the mass murderer and leading officer of the Planetary Forces, lay dead on Jimmy Englewood's apartment floor.

Zack's men rushed into Jimmy's place to all corners of the building. They arrived too late to save their commander, but they seized Jimmy before he could fire a shot. Turncoat humans and robots watched the perimeter for signs of Renegades. The final mission of the deceased Comrade of Marganis proceeded without the Comrade himself.

The Planetary Forces dragged Jimmy out the front door by

his arms and legs. They carried him over the mixture of glass and door fragments, taped his mouth, put on his helmet, and shut the lights.

The soldiers left Zack's corpse at the apartment. They hauled Jimmy into a Renegade robot aircraft big enough for the ten of them plus Jimmy, with empty room to spare.

Jimmy glimpsed a shot-up Dorian, fallen on the ice with a bashed-in head and missing yellow eyes.

The latest blizzard intensified during the torrent of gunfire. Zack's team of ten aimed machineguns at the twenty Renegade turncoats, killing all ten humans, five androids, and five mechanized robots. A robot Renegade vessel stayed parked in the snowfall next to the stolen Renegade vessel boarded by Zack's men with Jimmy in tow.

The door to the stolen aircraft closed, and the disc-shaped vehicle lifted off. Bullets dinged off the sides. Missiles missed their target to bring down the vehicle. Zack's men used the automatic controls to rocket past Marganis, evading the heavy fire from Marganisan Peak in the Boshquire Mountains. Renegade vessels launched themselves and projectiles into the night in hot pursuit, unable to keep pace with the hijacked aircraft's maneuvering or speed. No firepower would reach Zack and his team.

Renegade leaders continued the chase after confirming the Planetary Forces took Jimmy hostage. A hundred vessels joined in pursuit from various bases in the newly formed nation of Orcasso. The vessels trailed Zack's men for hundreds of miles until the stolen Renegade ship disappeared from sight and sound without a trace.

Ripples of gravity stampeded the sky, forcing all hundred aircraft giving chase to fall. No Renegades could move or eject to escape the crashes to the earth. The hidden weapon and its energy killed the Renegades on impact, before they burned up on the ground.

Fires scattered across the valleys in unclaimed territories. The flames eventually died off under the heavy crystals dropping from the clouds. Dead humans and robots, all from Orcasso, experienced a moment of directed gravitational power. Upon their quick deaths, they never felt the crunching or crashing of their ships or bodies in fields of silver-white powder.

In Marganis, Renegade humans and robots arrived at Jimmy's house together with ambulance hovercraft and on-the-ground medical staff. They assessed what happened when they discovered twenty slaughtered Orcassan turncoats. The Renegades concluded Zack's men had landed in the robot ship that they left behind. The Renegades also concluded that Zack had intended to escape in Jimmy's vessel, the stolen vessel that the Planetary Forces had used to escape.

The bright lights of Marganis lit up Dorian's disfigured face. An ambulance flew him toward town while others sorted through the scene of Zack and the slaughtered turncoats. Some civilians lined the streets in climate suits. Others watched from the warmth of their homes.

Suddenly, the parked Renegade robot ship flashed lights,

blinking for several moments. Renegades and medical staff looked around. One volunteer hospital worker named Juan picked up a clock from the ground next to Zack. The volunteer, a full-time café manager, closed his eyes. He thought of his wife and children for an instant. He then felt the heat of the exploding robot ship that killed him and many surrounding Renegades, medical staff, and bystanders.

The last clock of the deceased Magician marked the final strands of power of the Lords of the Wolf Blade.

And the Planetary Order had seized Renegade Jimmy Englewood.

45

THE ENEMY'S FACE

Zack's ten men flew Jimmy Englewood to climate regime headquarters. The Planetary Order established a garrison they deemed impenetrable, mainly to protect the Leader, the Council, city, and region. The Order fortified land and air defenses on the base for its reconstructed and desired new permanent capital on Earth, the recently named Alacornia.

Jimmy sat quietly, tied up in a windowless, empty vault on the grand estate. Two of Mike's security detail stood on either side of him. Pictures of Brandon Dreckhorn and the fight for climate equity filled three of the walls, with the wall straight in front of Jimmy left barren. The Renegade waited in dimmed lighting and room temperature settings. He wore a t-shirt, long pants, and nothing else.

Mike entered wearing a tuxedo. The heavy door slammed shut, blocking the small doses of sunlight caressing Jimmy's skin.

Jimmy used his right shoulder to scratch an itch on his chin. "You have anything to eat in this place?"

Mike lifted up Jimmy's chin and slapped him across the left side of his face. "I know you feel a sting, but you're going to feel the constant sting of the climate regime taking away every warm thought you've ever had. You will feel the ever-present pain of humiliation when we expose you throughout the planet and turn your Renegades against you."

"Your military commander is dead, but you know that. You arranged for his men to get there after he fought me."

"That's my cousin. Zack was my cousin. He will always be an infinite friend to the Planetary Order and the HAVE movement. He died for a great cause, as did my cousin Brandon."

"Is that right? And which cause will you die for?"

"The same as you. You will die for the climate. You will die for the carbon footprints you leave behind. I'll die much later than you, as a hero to the planet and its remaining inhabitants. You will die like an eviscerated whale, with your mind and spirit carved up beyond recognition."

Jimmy laughed, and Mike slapped him across the right side of his face.

Mike took a handheld device out of his tuxedo vest, turning up the temperature and further dimming the lights. "That's enough violence for the day. I don't intend to inflict any physical harm. I want you to see the errors of your life and how they relate to the everyday global citizens you casually endanger."

Both security guards left the room.

Mike moved out of Jimmy's line of sight. "Jimmy, we've spent some time talking together. You never appreciated just how grotesque human beings are. You've destroyed the Earth."

"You are a human being, you fucking moron."

"There's the passion I'm looking for. That rebellion against the climate helped nobody. You bring war upon a world you claim to love. All that my Planetary Order wanted didn't concern you. We could've provided everything you ever dreamed, but you didn't comply. You threw the Earth into the cosmic gutter."

"Keep yapping, you lying son of a bitch."

"Jimmy, I want to torture you with heat and cold, spears and strangulation, but I know it won't make a difference. You'll accept any physical damage to your brain, to your heart, or to anything else."

"Then go to the next stage."

"Oh, I already have. The Planetary Order already has. We wiped out almost all the Norbannicks. Katie is next. We wiped out some of your family. Well, we kept the ones that turned on you. Sure, it hurts you, but you don't show it. You're tough, right? You're made of diamonds. Let's see how stoic you really are, because we both know you aren't."

"Take me to the final stages and we'll see how tough you really are, Mike. We'll see if you're tougher and smarter than Zack."

"Yes, we will, and I'm glad you brought him up. There's only one phase to take you through. It's a never-ending phase of memories, regrets, and failed promises that haunt you. I will bring you into that world. I will shackle you to the world of constant heartbreak. When and where that fails, I will unleash things far worse than Hell on the people you crave to defend."

"You want me to beg for the lives of people on a planet you're going to ravage. You've already butchered so much of it. They'll be nothing left for you except the sad realization that you're a tinpot god who can't break down one man from Marganis."

"I promise you suffering beyond belief."

"Your word means nothing. It means less than nothing."

"But you, Jimmy. You mean something. You're special. You're a nearly fifty-year burden to the Earth. You pollute a climate that I'm trying to pull back from its heating crisis."

Jimmy shook his head. "You're fucking insane."

The Planetary Leader hissed. "Do you miss your brother Roger? What about Bethany? Greg saved your life. In the end, you couldn't save his. Let's bring you face to face with who and what you miss so dearly, my obstinate climate change denier. You, Renegade, are responsible for man's environmental carnage."

Jimmy tried to free his arms and legs from the cords wrapped around the chair. No matter how match he twisted, he could not shake or loosen the cords, but he kept trying.

A voice cried out, stopping Jimmy's futile attempts to power through the binding cords. "I miss you, brother. I'm sorry I betrayed you, but I came back. Don't let them sully my name to the world. Please, Jimmy. I love you. I love you."

Jimmy swiveled his head from one side to the next but could not turn around to see Mike.

The Planetary Leader turned up the air and floor temperature. "I have much more audio of your brother to play you."

"It isn't Roger!"

"Can you feel the manmade warming now, Renegade? It almost burns your bare feet. You're in my citadel of Alacornia forever. You're forever on climate and mental lockdown."

"Roger's been gone for years, murdered in cold blood."

The vault room went pitch black. Mike stepped further back from Jimmy and toward the door. "Enjoy the video."

"What video?"

"It's phony video footage of your life and the lives you've been so close to, combined with some real footage. Nobody can tell the difference...except us."

Jimmy watched as the footage projected on the front wall showed moments and events in his adult life that never occurred. "Is there any sound to this?"

"Why of course there is, but I'll keep it muted for the time being."

"I don't care. Broadcast it to the world if you want to pretend that I'm seditious. Try spreading any lies about me you want. See where it gets you."

"But people trusted you."

"This is all doctored or made up out of whole cloth. There's no real footage at all."

Mike paused the video at a point when footage showed Jimmy marching with a Wolf Blade uniform. "That's just part of the fun. You're an illusion for peace. That's how you'll be remembered. You'll be remembered as a warmongering rabble rouser who brough chaos and destruction to the planet."

"My feet are too hot. Any more heat and you'll scorch them."

"Your body and mind have a high threshold for such temperatures. Imagine how much I'm sweating from this black-tie outfit I'm wearing. You, on the other hand, aren't wearing shoes."

"Turn it down. It's too hot."

"I raised it slowly for a minute, but I just locked it in place."

"Please, I can't feel my nerves."

"Your wish is my command, Renegade. Such decorum from you earns my benevolence. Don't you remember using those manners when you pleaded for my help at the Climate Rehab Center? You should feel your feet cooling down now."

A perspiring Jimmy slowed his breathing. "Manmade climate change is a joke. You can't even manipulate weather anymore you fuck stick."

"The Planetary Order controls what it says it controls."

"The Planetary Order is fake! So are you!"

"Your life is a fake. It led you here. You have nobody. You have nothing. Your miscarried twins died years ago."

"Miscarried?! Miscarried?!"

"Weren't you the same man begging me for relief from the scorching heat on your skin?"

"Do your worst."

"No. I'll use my handheld remote for something else. Watch the video."

As the video continued, the fake footage showed Bethany jumping off a skyscraper, supposedly out of guilt for turning against the climate regime.

Jimmy laughed. "Nobody's going to believe this."

"Wait until you see what else you see. Wait until you hear what else you hear."

"Is that right? Wait until a missile sends you to Hell."

"Speaking of Hell, it's time to heat things up for you now, but it won't be your feet on fire. You won't be on fire at all."

"Keep threatening me."

The Planetary Leader grinned. "I'm giving you my word that my weapons and unconventional warfare will leave you speechless and compliant."

"Then we're done with the video."

"We're just getting started with the video, Englewood. We haven't even gotten to the real footage yet. I haven't forgotten your love for the Norbannicks or for people in general. I haven't forgotten your love for Marganis or the way life was for you decades ago."

"I will watch you die, Mike. I hope to be the one who kills you."

Mike talked into his handheld device. "Send the guards back in here and prepare our military for the next phase of war."

The two guards walked back in the room. One held open a medical kit while the other prepared a shot.

Mike injected Jimmy in the right arm. "I know you're inoculated against our germ warfare, but you're unprotected from the truth."

Jimmy's muscles relaxed. "Do you want the real truth? Or do you want the truth you're looking for?"

"Tell me all that there is to tell, Englewood."

"You want dead. Dead want. You want dead me."

"Shhhhh. Try not to say anything for a minute. You're not making any sense. I don't want to see you dead. I want to see you live for centuries under the grace of the Planetary Order. You need to know your rightful masters. I'm showing you your rightful place in the world."

"Marganis. Marganis."

"That's all, Jimmy. I don't need to listen to you repeating yourself. You're losing control of your faculties. I'll return them when the time demands it. Until then, I want you to watch a new video and answer my questions. Your coherence should return. All your bodily cells submit to my questions. You will answer me truthfully, and any lie will unravel before it leaves your mouth. Now, you are ready."

The guards remained in the vault and bandaged Jimmy's right arm.

New footage appeared on the screen.

Mike punched Jimmy's bandaged arm and winced at his captive's lack of reaction. "I know your senses are a bit diminished, but I wonder if this injection is too effective."

"Is that Marganis?"

"No, Englewood. That's you in real time in this room, right here in Alacornia. But I'm changing it again. This new footage is in another city. The people wear the faces of happiness, but they're miserable counterrevolutionaries bent on destroying everything we've built. Watch the people suffer for their noncompliance. We're hitting them with an old-time fission reaction."

"No, don't do it. I'll talk to you. Don't incinerate them. Don't incinerate anybody."

Mike moved up close to Jimmy and inspected his face at close range. "Englewood, a nuclear winter is just what the people need. But alright, I'll wait and see what you tell me. All I have to do is give the command to launch the missiles, drop the bombs, spread the plagues, contaminate the food, or anything I desire. It's all in the name of saving the planet. I'm going to hold you to your promise. Let's begin by discussing the moment you turned into a Renegade. You were an emergency medical technician. Why turn into a warrior?"

"I wanted to kill every tyrant in Marganis I could, but I didn't have it in me to take a life."

"You're lying. You have lived by the sword, and you will enslave yourself by the sword."

"I'm telling the truth. I didn't have it in me. Then, people assaulted me in the streets for noncompliance with the authorities. By the time the HAVE movement and climate lockdowns took hold, I couldn't turn back on the fight I joined against you tyrants."

"Did you ever think years ago that you'd defeat us?"

"No."

"How about now?"

"It doesn't matter. You've been exposed for all history and the world."

"You're not helping history or the world, Englewood."

"Neither are you."

Mike raised his handheld device up to his mouth. "Planetary Council, place the order for radioactive delivery."

Jimmy had no power to yell or lie. The injection continued weakening him, and the screen in the vault room once again turned dark, just before the atom bomb fell over a growing Renegade city.

46

DIZZY

The Planetary Leader showed another series of videos. Footage displayed biological attacks, the hunting of mammalian species to extinction, horrid conditions for prisoners at climate regime dungeons, and a chemical attack on a suburban enclave of everyday people.

Mike turned on the dimmed lights, followed by a new but muted video of people across the world enjoying parades, free housing, sporting events, and plentiful food. "Look at everything you're missing. It isn't just the things you're missing. It isn't just the festivities. You're missing out on the company of other people. These people aren't encumbered by us. No one prevents them from being free. They follow orders. They don't need constant repetition to do it. Meanwhile, you can't follow one simple directive."

Jimmy shook his head. "You're enslaving everybody you can,

but you're not the immortal you like to think you are. You're a bitch."

"I don't want to ruin anything or murder anybody. I just want to liberate you from yourself. We can play this over and over, with or without the volume. You can clearly see how much freedom you're missing. These people have humans and robots as their slaves. Why don't you want the life I'm offering you?"

Jimmy developed double vision. He closed his eyes, but when he reopened them, he felt the cold splash of reality. He had no way to break out of the Planetary Order's stronghold in Alacornia, and the double vision remained. Jimmy experienced the next stage of effects from Mike's injection of truth medicine. Hours would need to elapse for Jimmy to regain full strength and mental acuity. Tied up to a chair in the vault, Jimmy's flushed skin whitened, his double vision escalating while trapped in a room of psychological experimentation by a mass-murdering Planetary Leader. Jimmy's hands went numb, and his mind slowed from the injected poison.

Mike put his handheld remote in the pant pocket of his tuxedo. "Untie Mr. Englewood."

The guards looked at each other.

The Planetary Leader pulled a handgun out of his pocket. "If I repeat myself, you both die."

Jimmy looked at the screen, watching footage change from Bethany to his brother to himself. Untied, he walked toward the video. "That's me, isn't it? That's me at Marganisan Plaza."

The guards led Jimmy back to the seat, and the video turned

into a still image of the climate regime symbol of an ax splitting the Earth.

Mike pulled out a physical picture of Katie. "Do you recognize this woman?"

Jimmy slid off the chair, disoriented and nauseous. "I see a relative."

"Let's help you back up to your chair. Who's the relative, Englewood? Who's the relative?"

"Can you make everything stop? I want it back."

"What do you want back?"

Jimmy's double vision merged into a clear view of the photo Mike held in front of him. "That's Katie, but I don't see her sister Bethany. Bethany is my wife."

"Yes, she is. I mean, she was. I'm going to shame you and the Norbannick family in front of the world."

"I thought you could make me happy."

"The delirium hit you strongly with the dose I injected. I can bring you meaning. I can bring you fulfillment and relief from pain. Happiness died for you when you didn't comply with lockdown orders. Shame and humiliation. That's what's coming next. You will feel mortified. Or you will confide in me your hopes and fears."

"I will confide and obey you."

"Men, pull Mr. Englewood back into his seat. The poison has taken over. Let's record the world's most important Renegade revealing all he knows. Activate the audiovisual recording."

The guards activated the recording through cameras above

the screen.

Mike surveyed his nemesis. "Jimmy, are you ready to reveal everything to the Planetary Order?"

"I am."

Jimmy regained his full sight but still felt dizzy. The poison from Mike's injection kept the untied Renegade stripped of physical power and mental fortitude.

Mike took off his jacket and bowtie and handed them to the guards. "Jimmy Englewood, your time and tribulations at the Climate Rehab Center have weakened your resolve. Did you enjoy fighting the Planetary Order?"

"Never."

"Never? You didn't relish in the opportunity to fight?"

"No. I never liked fighting. I told you that."

"You were never so honest as you are now. You're afraid to fight?"

"I don't like hurting people. I don't like getting hurt."

"What else?"

"I don't like finding out what I'm capable of."

"Do you regret you killed soldiers who fought for the Planetary Forces?"

"No. I had no choice."

"You're a murderer and a thief. You murdered in cold blood and repeatedly stole our provisions."

"You left me no choice."

"You don't feel any remorse?"

"I don't."

"But you hate fighting."

"Very much."

"You champion the cause of the Renegades, yet you're a weak counterrevolutionary who doubts his cause so much that he hates fighting."

"There is no Renegade mission aside from living life free from whatever murderous dictatorship anyone tries to install or enforce."

"You don't have a cause other than being a counterrevolutionary to burn down progress!"

"I yearn for the day we're no longer called Renegades. I miss my life."

"Yes, you miss your life. Tell me everything you miss about it."

"I miss the time when the world wasn't at war. I miss the time when I lived in my home country before you erased its borders."

"Dig deeper, Jimmy. Dig Deeper."

"I miss the carefree summer days with my brother and my friends. My brother is dead, my parents are dead, and almost everyone I knew is dead."

"And Bethany?"

"I was. I was."

"You were what, Englewood?"

"I was too late to save her life. She was the best of me and more."

"You're still holding back. What about your dead children?"

"The old Marganisan Council ordered them aborted in honor of the Planetary Order."

"But you, you selfish worm, you wanted to breed. We saved you and your wife considerable pain."

"What pain?"

"The pain of raising children and being bogged down by thoughts about yourselves and your family. All allegiance goes to the climate regime. Without that allegiance, you're a nomad in a wilderness of lost counterrevolutionary souls."

"I feel the pain now."

"Which pain, Jimmy?"

"The pain of living among others but being isolated until we created the country of Orcasso."

"Stay in the recent past with me. What made you feel isolated?"

"Becoming detached from the festive and purposeful. My old Marganis, we try to recreate it, but it isn't the same. The old weddings. The old vibrancy. Food shops and music. It was all different. It was all better."

"I'm sure I can bring that meaning back to your life when we cleanse you in front of the world. We can recreate everything for you. You'll never need to worry about that again. Why are you worried? Why do we worry you?"

"You don't."

"Are you referring to me or to the Planetary Forces?"

"Both."

Mike shook his head in disgust. "How can a man so weak be a man so disobedient?"

Jimmy slid off the chair again, but this time, Mike and the guards left him on the floor.

The Planetary Leader kicked the crawling Renegade in the face, dropping him to his stomach.

Mike paced back and forth, finally crouching next to Jimmy and pulling him in with both hands by the top of Jimmy's shirt. "If I torture you, you'll delay the inevitable like before. You'll let me mutilate your body before you submit. You'll let me wipe out the planet before you give in. I can seduce you with the finest food and most alluring women. Nice homes. Nice clothing. The chance for a comfortable life. You'll always deny what we can offer to save you."

"You think yourself a lord of the universe, creator of all that creeps and crawls. You and your HAVE movement will die. You're a virus on Earth and anywhere. Your lockdown orders mean nothing."

Mike, still holding Jimmy by the shirt, shook his enemy several times. "My people have to delete the recording of our discussion. You would embarrass me in front of the world if anyone released footage showing how you mocked me. This isn't over, Englewood. I know your weakness. I know your love for your dead family and dead country. I know your love for the Norbannicks and your new country. Gentlemen, delete the audiovisual recording now. Delete it permanently."

Jimmy smiled. "You're an imbecile, Mike. Renegade weapons made with robot help are just as advanced as yours. You might own 70% of the planet or more. So what? As long as my side has any territory, we can end your lives as easily as you can end ours."

"You don't have the fight in you to ruin the Earth. You don't have the strength to obliterate our families."

"You liar. That's what you've been doing to our families. You want to control Marganis. You hate Marganis even more than you hate people and animals. That's it. You've come to hate me and my city more than you hate the planet."

"I see the injection is wearing off much earlier than expected."

"So is your power."

"What?"

"So is your lie about manmade global warming. You're a sad little deceiver, and the people of Marganis and Orcasso and Earth will recalibrate just fine without your deluded revolutions."

Mike pulled out a knife and held it to Jimmy's neck. "Let's see how brave you are."

The guards pulled their guns on the Planetary Leader.

The first guard walked closer while pointing his weapon at Mike's face. "Listen to me. The Planetary Council ordered us to keep Jimmy alive, humiliated, and enslaved. You're disobeying the climate regime."

Mike dropped the knife. "I lead the Planetary Council and the Planetary Order. I make the law, and you follow."

"Sorry, sir, but we hereby relieve you of your command over all military and civilian life."

Jimmy's disorientation finally ended while the guards relieved the Planetary Leader of his command. Weakened, bruised, and sore, Jimmy grabbed the knife Mike dropped on the floor. The Renegade held the weapon tightly, and he quietly wondered whether anybody on base could see his actions...or whether anybody had spotted the attempted coup in the vault.

47

CRUMBLING GROUND

Both guards moved in on Mike to arrest him while the ground shook. The three of them fell down.

One of the guards dropped his gun. Jimmy, already on the floor, scrambled to pick it up. He fired a shot a piece into each guard's face.

Mike pulled his own weapon on Jimmy and grabbed the second guard's weapon.

Jimmy stumbled to the floor along with Mike while the dark vault room shook once more. They lost grip of the handguns.

The antagonists rose to their feet and charged each other amid the explosions on the grand estate and base in Alacornia.

Jimmy pulled out the knife but dropped it when Mike connected with Mike's jaw.

Mike threw several additional jabs at Jimmy.

The Renegade absorbed the hits and kicked the Planetary

Leader in the chest, launching him backward.

The two of them reached for the guns on the floor when yet another blast threw them off balance and knocked them off their feet.

The restored Planetary Leader regained balance and lifted a gun from the floor to fire at Jimmy, but he could not find the Renegade.

From Mike's right side, Jimmy grabbed his enemy's weapon with his left hand and unloaded on him with his right fist. Jimmy wrested the gun away and cracked Mike across the cheek. The dazed Planetary Leader tried to track the Renegade through clouded eyes.

The explosions across the compound and city continued. Climate regime headquarters experienced heavy fighting, but the ground trembles attenuated, and Jimmy kept his footing. The vault remained locked from the inside, as did the disabled cameras.

Jimmy stood over Mike in the dimly lit vault. He pulled him up by the shirt and brought him to the chair, pressing the gun against his left cheek.

A booming voice reverberated inside the vault and through-out the estate. "The Renegade army has breached our defenses. All revolutionaries mobilize to expel the invaders. The Planetary Forces call on you to fulfill your obligations as warriors for the climate. Repeat, the Renegade army has breached our defenses. All revolutionaries mobilize to expel the invaders."

Mike sat with his back straight against the chair. He looked over at the dead guards who followed the Planetary Council's orders to depose him if he were to overstep what he imagined was his unrestrained authority. The Planetary Leader became a planetary captive to the most hunted Renegade, and man, on Earth.

Jimmy and Mike stared at each other while the battle consumed the base.

The audio returned, snapping each man into the realization that a blown-up grand estate would crush them in the vault. "The Planetary Council has abandoned headquarters for the further continuance of the HAVE revolution. Council members order you to stay and fight. Protect all our systems and capacity to launch massive warfare. Keep our weapons controls from the enemy and destroy what you must. They are encircling the base and attacking the regional army and fleet of aircraft. Let nobody enter without bringing the invader to a gruesome end. Take your climate—"

A loud foghorn sounded, and the booming voice cut out.

Jimmy and Mike heard the explosions despite all the decibels of noise blocked by the walls. The two enemies locked eyes with the vitriol of fire-breathing dragons.

The Renegade smiled. "Nobody's rescuing you, Mike. You're going to die in here."

"The climate regime hasn't thrown me overboard. Those were two corrupted guards, nothing more and nothing less."

"It doesn't matter one way or the other. The soldiers and the Planetary Council are out to save themselves. Was it worth bringing the world to the brink of permanent ruin?"

"It's been worth every moment fighting the counterrevolutionaries. You're far worse than any of those Lords of the Wolf Blade. You're a selfish group of animals, no better than the bears and whales we slaughter. You're oxygen thieves. You're carbon breathers and carbon breeders, every single one of you."

"I didn't understand how much of a true believer you were."

"Humans are viruses on Earth, but some of us have the right to live. You are not one of us. You'll never make it out of Alacornia. Never."

"All the false promises you made me. All the lies and deceptions brought you here. I can still see you killing that Wolf Blade chieftain and taking over his group."

"You don't have the will to shoot me. You want nothing to do with death or destruction. The warrior spirit left you. I sapped from you whatever drips and drops of it lingered."

"There's something you don't know about me."

"I know everything about you. I watched your every move in prison. You gave me every answer I ever asked for."

"It led you nowhere. All you have is your headspace filled with information about me that you and your regime can never use."

"You can't get out of this room without me releasing you. Your only chance for mercy is to shoot yourself in the temple."

"Make that two things you don't know about me. I'm getting out of this room, and I look to the future more than I ever get sentimental about the past."

"You miss your dead wife and fetuses. You miss your city. Nothing can ever bring back the feelings you had. Nothing will bring back the safe serenity of that greedy metropolis you call home."

"Serenity? Safety? I had nothing of either one. I had a life worth living. I miss the old Marganis and Bethany. I miss my family and my old country. Sentimentality has no bearing on it. I just remember what normal looks like, no matter how hard you try to mutilate it."

"Fuck you, Renegade."

"Not a Renegade for long. Just a man doing everything I can to keep your movement from annihilating people and life."

"I gave the HAVE movement everlasting life after Brandon created it. The Planetary Order belongs to me, no matter if I'm the formal leader."

"Regrettably you won't be around to see the full demolition of the climate regime. You starved and brutalized billions with your climate madness. You won't live to see the trial and sentencing you deserve."

The ground shook yet again. Jimmy almost lost his footing while Mike sat still, firmly pressing his back against the chair. Explosions picked up in frequency and intensity in the background.

Mike laughed. "Deactivate lights."

Before Jimmy could fire his weapon, the vault turned black, and Mike flung the seat at Jimmy. The seat flew just above the Renegade's head.

Light rushed in through the heavy door when Mike turned the wheel to open the vault.

Jimmy sprinted for the exit and grabbed hold of Mike's shirt to haul him back into the room. The door closed, the yells of vicious hostilities outside the room faded, and the vault went dark.

Mike flipped Jimmy onto one of the dead guards. He kicked the guard instead of Jimmy.

Neither man could find the other for thirty seconds. No sound or light gave away the other's location.

Suddenly, Mike found a gun. "Activate lights!"

The Planetary Leader immediately saw the man leaned against a side wall and shot him several times in the body. The previously dead guard fell to the floor for a second time.

Before Mike could turn his gun, Jimmy twisted Mike's hand and snapped his wrist. Taking the gun away, Jimmy tripped Mike to the ground and dragged him to the door.

"Open it, Mike. Open the vault. This isn't a maze. If you deactivate the lights, you'll die slowly. Open the vault."

"You said you knew how, Englewood!"

"You were my key to get out of here. Turn the wheel, planetary minstrel. You know how far to turn it. You know the directions."

Mike would not budge.

Jimmy took Mike's activation device and shot it.

"Now you can't get out of here unless you get out manually, and you don't know how. The ceiling will collapse on us. You screwed yourself, Jimmy. You screwed yourself."

Planetary Forces tried opening the door to get Mike out, but they couldn't enter. Renegades gunned them down.

Jimmy and Mike heard the gunfire followed by the bodies banging into the door and walls.

Jimmy pulled Mike closer. "If you open that door, I'll give you one of those guns on the floor and let you run."

"You mean it, don't you."

"I know you'll do anything you can to cheat death. Use that unbroken left and get us out of this chamber. Get moving, before this becomes a tomb."

Mike smiled. "I changed my mind, Englewood. Hot or cold, I command you to a permanent climate lockdown."

"That's funny hearing you command me. Look at you, you two-bit dictator. All your schemes are crumbling."

"Look at you. You're frightened of death."

"A climate regime, that's your legacy. You played an instrumental role in locking people down and driving them insane. Your waves of mood manipulation led almost all of Earth into your HAVE movement's black hole. Now you get to see all of the misery and mass slaughter fail against the Renegades you desperately want to control. Your power dies as soon as it rose."

"Renegade, you will die tonight far from your home. I will be alive to see it."

"Alive or dead, you'll never see anything. You ask me about my wife and children. Where are yours? Where are your friends? Where is your family? You have nothing. You maimed and murdered more than any mass murder from the past. Face whatever you have to face when you meet your maker, you crackpot tyrant."

"Strong statements from a man who begged me to release him from prison. I said I'll be alive to see your death."

"So what?"

"So, I'll be there to inflict it."

"You are the very definition of wicked."

"You are the very definition of weak."

"Mike, your Planetary Order crumbles right outside this door. Nobody on Earth except you power-mad lunatics wants hysteria or lockdowns."

"I'll shovel the last patch of dirt over your broken body, Englewood."

"I'll shovel the last batch of the Planetary Leaders into the underworld."

"Long live the planetary climate revolution!"

Gunfire continued outside the vault. Cries, agony, and pleas for mercy rocked Jimmy more than ongoing explosions on the base.

The Planetary Leader smirked at the Renegade. "The world blames you for its problems, just like your brother did."

"He made up for it before Zack slaughtered him, and he never blamed me more than he blamed anybody else."

"The people want comfort, not war. You bring war and invasions and decay."

"You bring lies with every word you piss from your mouth.

No person or animal that died because of you died in vain. I'm their champion. You're the failed revolutionary with a mind haunted by billions of spirits."

"Many extinct humans and animals will welcome you to the afterlife of climate deniers. You missed out on the good life I offered. I no longer offer you anything more than death in this chamber of mine. Enjoy the funeral."

"We're opening this chamber."

"Ah, now we're in this together, my prisoner. Face it. I will outlast you in this vault of damned souls."

Jimmy pressed the gun into Mike's ribs while he wrapped his left arm around Mike's neck. "Open the door. If you don't, I'll take my chances getting starved or crushed to death."

"No, you won't."

"I'll make it look like you shot yourself. How much do you want to feel an organ or two pouring out of your skin in a dishonorable death? You're supposed to be a dignified Planetary Leader and invincible. You've got five seconds before I take your life."

Gasping for breath, Mike used his unbroken hand to turn the wheel and open the vault.

48

ON THE BRINK

A burst of cold air accompanied sights and sounds of bullets and broken bones. Jimmy and Mike exited the vault into a shootout interspersed with hand-to-hand fighting. Windows and walls shattered, and the frigid night punctured the Renegade and the Planetary Leader. They had massive exposure to the elements in the expansive three-floor atrium that experienced savage combat. The bronze, domed atrium provided railing as the only protection from the bullets, knives, and fists coveting total defeat of the respective enemy.

Jimmy lost sight of Mike in the mayhem. The Renegade took down a fully equipped attacker with four shots from his only handgun. Despite wearing nothing more than a short-sleeve shirt and long pants, Jimmy charged forward to help his fellow humans and robots fighting the Planetary Forces. The Renegade returned fire from the ground after dropping to evade an enemy soldier's bullets. Two shots lodged in the headgear of the soldier, whose revolutionary fervor ended along with his pulse.

Renegade gunships attacked weapons and communication systems all around the base. One of the vessels missed its mark, hitting the atrium and igniting an inferno. Renegade hovercraft attempted to put out the blaze, but the spreading ball of heat rolled all the way through the castle mansion on the grand estate, incinerating the open vault and vast regions of the superstructure. With fighting also taking place on the second and third levels of the atrium and stairway corridors, the heat and smoke consumed many Renegades and their adversaries. The inferno collapsed the foundations and structures of the atrium and crushed men who did not already burn or suffocate.

Through the flames, Jimmy saw an armed man of the climate regime wearing a shredded tuxedo and a bright red helmet. The armed individual carried a machinegun in his left hand, letting his right hand sag by his side. Jimmy fired two shots but missed his mark. Those were his last two bullets. They sailed past the Planetary Leader's bright red helmet and fell in the distance onto the snow-drenched fields of the base. The white powder and red streaks in the sky illuminated the exploded ships, property, and weapons of the climate regime.

Mike ran outside what remained of the grand estate. He slid along a camouflaged white entrance and descended down a flight of stairs to an underground fallout shelter of the Planetary Council. He found the weather control systems destroyed. He saw activation machinery for weapons of mass destruction demolished and five members of the Planetary Council deceased. Mike searched the closets, drawers, and cabinets, finding no food or provisions. He ran back up to ground level, leaving the open fallout shelter. He looked up at a circular Renegade aircraft.

Mike swung his weapon to the left, but the arms and body of Jimmy Englewood stopped his momentum. Jimmy seized the machinegun, shoved his enemy to the wintry earth, and pulled off his headgear on the blustering field. He stared into his enemy's empty eyes while his Renegades gained control of the inferno, captured prisoners, and took over the territory. "Your climate regime is dying. This is from me, Bethany, and every human being who ever cherished liberty." Jimmy knocked out the Planetary Leader with the butt of the machinegun. He looked across the flattened base, dropped his machinegun, and marveled at the star-filled heavens.

Angelo opened his blue-lighted ship and lowered the ramp. He helped his shivering friend onto the disc-shaped vessel before setting the automatic controls for takeoff.

The ramp retracted and the Planetary Leader woke up. He grabbed the machinegun, aiming to fire at Angelo and Jimmy's aircraft. The two Renegades watched him from their slowly departing ship. A tiger with a scarred mouth leaped onto Mike, mauling him before he could fire a shot. Neither Jimmy nor Angelo could hear a sound of the dying tyrant's agony.

Jimmy covered himself with a warm, heavy blanket. "Where's Katie?"

Angelo laughed. "Hey, we needed somebody to look after Marganis."

49

ALACORNIA TO ORCASSO SKIES

The last trace of clouds and mist cleared away from the disc-shaped Renegade vessel emanating blue light. The vessel soared above scores of Renegade aircraft and ground troops approaching the base and those already on it.

Jimmy and Angelo looked over the battleground, soaking in the victory for the planet. They accelerated toward Marganis, located in their new home country of Orcasso.

Alacornia faded into the background of the vessel's vision. Angelo turned off the ship's lights, magnifying the arc of stars from the zenith to all points on the horizon. "Geometric perfection. We have the good fortune to see such a planetarium from within our own atmosphere."

"I expected to see a lot more robots at that battle. I saw some, and I still can't tell most androids apart from humans."

"They were flying half the ships, but the mission required boots on the ground, and they came through when we most needed them."

"Are we people? Are we still people, Angelo."

"You already know the answer."

"That sounded like something Greg Norbannick would say."

"If only he were here with us now."

"His soul is in a much better place than this."

"Amen, Englewood. Amen."

The armed vessel flew through the rest of the night on automatic across jagged terrain, glistening crystalline seas, and heat-famished skies.

Jimmy threw off the blanket. "I don't think I need this anymore, but you've got to get comfortable seats."

Angelo shook his head. "These are plenty comfortable. That's the last time I give you a lift from an enemy base."

"You won't ever need to again."

"Are you quitting the Renegades?"

"We turned the tide of the war, didn't we?"

"We did. Everything is crumbling for them. Fear of the climate forces will recede after news spreads of the last two days' massive victories on Earth. We're neutralizing the enemy and rolling back its overwhelming power in war and everyday life. We're already freeing dungeons and death camps."

"Then the Renegade identity passed away. The name doesn't fit us anymore. We need a new name."

"Almost. Not yet. And the people of Orcasso and new countries throughout the world can choose new names, but you'll always be a Renegade."

"Me least of all, Angelo. I need something else."

The first rays of daylight raced across the early morning. Jimmy and Angelo admired the cliffs, the forests, the deserts, and the frozen-over lakes of the ice age. They glimpsed two new countries building new cities.

Angelo walked to the front window of the 400-square foot circular aircraft. He looked back and his jaw dropped. "What happened to your feet. They're all messed up."

"Oh, that's right. They stripped my socks and boots."

"No socks. No boots. No helmet. No climate gear."

"I never thought about it. My feet just kept on going."

"How are you alive?"

Jimmy looked up and then back at Angelo.

Angelo nodded.

The two old friends crossed into Orcassan airspace, approaching their old Marganis.

50

MARGANISAN REQUIEM

Jimmy and Angelo landed in Marganis.

Human and robot residents and visitors celebrated the arrival back home. Food and festivities lined the streets, eateries, and music halls of the burgeoning city. Construction projects took a break for the day. The entire metropolis rejoiced between the snowbanks and frosted side streets. High rises, apartments, and hotels welcomed all to partake of the food and drink. Songs and games spread across Marganisan Plaza. Travelers toured the indoor gardens and aircraft put on light shows in an aerial parade. Nothing could dampen the cheer of the city refreshed with autonomy.

Katie arrived at Plaza later than planned. She walked into the lobby of a performance center that remained closed for the day.

She took off her helmet and placed it on a concession counter across from a series of royal red couches. "Sorry, guys. I wanted to be there when you landed, but I'm doing my best with the city to get all the people out of Paradise Gardens. The trauma runs deeply, but they need our help."

Jimmy closed his eyes.

Angelo shoved his old friend. "Keep your head up."

Jimmy shoved him back. "I am. That's my life now. I'm going to do everything I can to help anyone who did time in Paradise Gardens and dungeons and the Climate Rehab Center."

Angelo hugged Jimmy and then hugged Katie. "See here, Englewood. This is my wife to be. That classical music is playing for us."

"Yes, it is, Cantare. Your marriage will provide a great union for the memories of your families."

Angelo slowly broke away from the long embrace with Katie. "What is it, Jimmy?"

"Just thinking about people, mostly my family and Katie's. We all paid a heavy price to spare billions from being murdered. We're still here to remember it, but our families aren't. So, Angelo, Katie, make a new family that will have them all smiling from above."

Jimmy and Katie embraced.

Katie held back tears. "We have to hold memorials for all my family members. We've never had the chance."

Jimmy took a deep breath. "Sister, we will. I wanted to tell you that Bethany meant—"

The sliding door interrupted Jimmy. Dorian entered the performance center. "Hello all. You look dashing in your white climate gear. Mr. Englewood, it's especially nice to see you alive and in your throwback silver climate gear."

"Dorian, I thought you were dead."

"President Cantare had me back to myself in no time."

"I can see that. I've got to hand it to you, Angelo."

"Thank you, Jimmy. You never know what you can restore. Sometimes a city or a country. Sometimes a robot. And that isn't all."

"It's incredible that the HAVE movement never bombed Marganis. The Planetary Order wanted control over every mind it could capture, and it failed. It is different now, though."

Angelo put his arm around Katie. "It is different now, Jimmy, but in what way do you mean it?"

Jimmy looked intently at Angelo. "After the climate lockdown, things will never be the same. We can't relive those old moments. Not completely. Something's always off about it. At this point, it's all about what we do from here while honoring our history and brethren in liberty. I will help those tortured souls at Paradise Gardens."

Everyone's face beamed brightly except for Dorian's vertical block of a metallic head. His yellow eyes darkened.

Katie grabbed her helmet and walked up to the robot. "What's the problem."

"There's a radical group that concealed the colony it recently set up on Mars. This revived sectarian cult is growing in power by the day. They're getting help from a new group of gangsters here on Earth."

Angelo moved to the sliding door. "Dorian, do other Orcassan officials know? And our allies across the world?"

"They're learning about it as we speak."

Angelo patted Jimmy's shoulder. "I know you don't want the name Renegades anymore, but we'll keep it for now. Follow me to the base, Renegade."

"If we must. Oh, the questions I would ask you now, Greg Norbannick."

The humans put on their headgear and walked with Dorian out the clear glass door. These Renegades wore the recently unveiled jetpacks to complement their new mission. Jetpacks had just become newly but sparsely available for use on Earth to add to their traditional use outside of Earth's atmosphere.

Jimmy stopped in front of the building, looked around, and gazed up at the sky above the towering buildings. The others paused and turned back to him.

Katie shrugged her shoulders. "What are you thinking, Jimmy?"

"It's snowing. It's snowing again. It never stops as long as we're alive."

Jimmy Englewood turned on his helmet's inner light and marched into the new blizzard...

ACKNOWLEDGEMENTS

I thank God, with whom everything is possible. I am grateful to my family, friends, and readers for their outstanding support.

ALSO BY JEREMY GRAVILORE

THEY'RE AFTER YOU: DYSTOPIAN SHORT STORIES

DIMENSIONS: POEMS, VIGNETTES, AND FLASH FICTION

Get the latest on Jeremy Gravilore books and content

https://books2read.com/gravilore

https://oceannapolis.com

ABOUT THE AUTHOR

Author Jeremy Gravilore creates for audiences seeking raw stories. From speculative fiction to vignettes, the mid-Atlantic native writes evocative poetry and thought-provoking prose. Jeremy's storytelling inspiration stretches across books, radio, movies, television, live theater, and music. A Gen Xer with an ancient soul, he finds creative influences ranging from the *Bible* to *The Odyssey*, *1984* to *Lord of the Flies*, *The Twilight Zone* to *Columbo*, and *Abbott and Costello Meet Frankenstein* to *Blade Runner*. Jeremy enjoys traveling around America. He loves the natural world, but his love for captivating stories of the mind, soul, and civilization motivate him to construct old worlds and new.